DARKNESS

TAKES

US

SHARE YOUR THOUGHTS

Help make *If Darkness Takes Us* a bestselling novel by leaving an honest review on Goodreads, on your personal author website or blog, and anywhere else readers go for recommendations. It's our priority at SFK Press to publish books for readers to enjoy, and our authors appreciate and value your feedback.

OUR SOUTHERN FRIED GUARANTEE

If you wouldn't enthusiastically recommend one of our books with a 4- or 5-star rating to a friend, then the next story is on us. We believe that much in the stories we're telling. Simply email us at pr@sfkmultimedia.com.

IF
DARKNESS
TAKES
US

BRENDA MARIE SMITH

To Aaron & J.D.

Never has a mother had more inspiring sons.

"All you young, wild girls

You'll be the death of me,

The death of me...."

—From the song "Young Girls," as performed by Bruno Mars

PART I

CHAPTER 1

No matter how desperately a mother loves you, she can only put up with so much. And so, the day came when Mother Nature lashed out against us.

I understood where Nature was coming from. My family never listened to me either, which is why I didn't tell them about the guns I'd bought.

The whole thing started with the train wreck.

On a Friday in early October, the young adults in my family went to the Oklahoma-Texas game up in Dallas—a big football rivalry around here. They dragged my husband, Hank the Crank, along with them, leaving me in South Austin with my grandchildren.

At the time, I was glad to see Hank go. He'd been making me crazy since he retired: hovering like a gnat; micromanaging my coffee-making; griping at me for reading instead of waiting attentively for him to spout something terse. Lord, I needed a break from that man. The three-day trip to Dallas seemed perfect.

I wasn't a built-in-babysitter type of grandma, and I only saw my four grandkids together as a group on birthdays and holidays. For weeks I'd been excited about spending a long weekend alone with them.

A cruel trick sometimes, getting what you ask for.

After dinner as dusk turned to darkness, my seventeen-year-old grandson, Keno, started tinkering with a little robot he was building for school. Milo, who'd been playing Frisbee out back with Harry the dog, slouched inside, closing the door quickly before the whimpering dog could get in.

Harry pressed his nose against the door glass, smearing it with dog slobber, and giving me a pleading look. I shook my head at him.

"Keno," Milo said, "let's play a game on the Wii."

"Hmm?" Keno kept tweaking the robot. His real name was Joaquin, but we called him Keno because he was clever with numbers, a fact that endeared him to his gambling granddad. But science was Keno's true love.

"The Wii! Let's play the Wii!" Milo said, exasperated.

"I bought a tennis game for you guys," I said.

"Tennis? I don't wanna play tennis." Like so many twelve-year old boys, Milo would have preferred a game with explosions.

"Come on," I said. "It'll be fun."

I'd already set things up, so I switched on the TV and console and gave a quick demonstration of how to play—or more like how to flub up—the game.

"No, Nana. Not like that." Milo grabbed the controller from my hands. Keno set his unfinished robot aside and jumped up to join Milo. Soon they were bouncing around in front of the TV and laughing, swinging their arms all over the place.

"I wanna play," said six-year-old Mazie from her seat on the floor, surrounded by her dolls and their regalia. "Why can't I play?"

"You can play next, Mazie. Tasha, don't you want to play?"

"Naw," said fifteen-year-old Natasha, not looking up from where she sprawled across an easy chair, flicking the screen on her iPhone, her long legs draped over the seat's arm.

"You don't want to miss out, do you?" I said, but Tasha was too absorbed in texting to answer me. "Tasha, I'm talking to you."

"What?" She tucked her phone under her arm and grimaced at me.

"I want you to join the rest of us."

"Whatever." She went back to her phone.

"Watch your attitude," I said, but the little twerp ignored me.

The boys played virtual tennis while I flipped through the latest magazine from Greenpeace on my laptop, half enjoying the kids and half worrying about the overly warm, acidic oceans. I wanted to be in a good mood, so I put the laptop away.

I sat back to savor my grandkids, the children of my daughters. Tasha and Keno looked so much like their mother, Erin—same dusky skin and dark hair, same Roman noses and big eyes, though Keno's were green and Tasha's were brown. Milo and Mazie were light-haired and blue-eyed like their mom, Jeri, but their round faces and big features came straight from their father. My three stepsons had no kids, none that I knew of anyway.

"Y'all want a snack?" I said. "I've got some—"

A hideously loud crash-bang rang through the night. My heart took a flying leap. A brilliant light flashed across the sky and lit up the room through the rattling windows. We all shot to our feet. Milo and Mazie screamed.

"What the—" Tasha cried.

"Holy shit!" Keno shouted. I was too shaken to say a word.

An ear-smashing roar and clang rose from the direction of the train tracks, a few blocks away. I often heard loud bangs from those tracks, but this cacophonous crunch of metal on metal, coupled with an endless screech, sounded like a train wreck.

To the frantic rumble of the unrelenting noise, the kids and I ran out the front door. A fireball shooting high above the tracks was so bright it nearly blinded me. It illuminated South Austin's tree-covered sprawl like a phalanx of klieg lights at the Super Bowl.

A great gust of heat slammed into us, filling my lungs with scorched air. I coughed and slapped at my head, thinking my hair might have caught fire, while I frantically counted my grandkids, half-expecting to see them ablaze.

Blinking fast, trying to clear remnants of white flame from my vision, I shouted, "Get in the house. Now!" Keno herded them inside.

Neighbors also rushed out their doors to gape at the fire. We'd had so many fast-moving fires around Austin lately due to the drought—whole neighborhoods catching flame in mere minutes. And at the crossing, I'd watched many trains pass bearing warnings: "Hazard!" "Flammable!" "Poison!"

The head of our neighborhood watch, Jack Jeffers, jogged toward me beneath a cloud of smoke that looked green in the glare of the halogen street lamps. A shower of sparks and embers rained down a block or two behind him.

"Y'all better evacuate, Bea," he said. I looked him in the eye and swallowed.

"On my way, Mr. Jeffers. Thank you."

He ran off, yelling to others along the block, "Please evacuate now! That fire could spread fast." I squinted toward the fire. I couldn't see much with so many trees in the way, although it looked like the fire was on the tracks and not the houses that sat nearer to us. But it could spread like ... well, like wildfire.

My old, shaky heart lurched along inside me. I ordered myself to calm down. At least the rest of the family was two hundred miles away in Dallas. That helped. But my grandchildren. God. How could I be calm and get them out of here if I was on the verge of a heart attack? It had been ages since I'd managed a bevy of kids in an emergency.

"Put your shoes on," I said to the grandkids, who were staring out the window when I hurried back inside. "Grab the bags you brought with you and your jackets. Let's go for a ... for a ride."

Mazie, that wispy little blonde thing, cried out, "Ow! My eyes!"

My racing heart plummeted. I bent down to the child, my hands shaking as I pulled her to me. The skin around her eyes was bright red where she'd rubbed it raw. She blinked at me, having trouble keeping her eyes open.

"Someone, get a wet washcloth. Quick!"

Tasha darted into the bathroom. Lately she never volunteered for anything, but she adored her little cousin.

"Mazie, do your eyes hurt? Can you see?" I held my breath, dreading her response.

"There's pink spots all over," she squealed. God Almighty, did she burn her retinas?

"Does the pink go away when you close your eyes, honey?"

"Only a little," Mazie whimpered. Tasha returned with a damp washcloth.

"Close them tight, Mazie." I tilted her head back and pressed the cloth over her eyes. "Keep them closed. We'll see if resting makes them better." A lot of good this washcloth would do for a retinal burn.

"I want my mama," she whined.

"I know, sweetheart. You can call your mom after we get on the road. Tasha will help put your shoes on."

"I don't wanna go out there!" Mazie hollered.

"You don't need to be afraid," I said, though I was plenty afraid.

I ran to the kitchen and snatched up a gallon of water, my purse, my bag of medications, and a change of clothes from the dryer. I looked around for my glasses, then found them on my face. I switched off the TV and most of the lights.

"Ready, kids?" I felt I was forgetting something important, but I couldn't think what.

Keno and Milo came sliding down the banister loaded up with bags, two of which tumbled to the floor ahead of them. Tasha clomped down the stairs after the boys, lugging a wad of jackets. She picked up the Barbie doll from the floor.

"Here, Mazie. Your doll will make you feel better, right?" Tasha said.

"Maybe."

I took the washcloth from Mazie's eyes and tucked it into her hand. I wanted to cradle her, but we had to get gone.

"Better, sweetie?"

"A little."

That didn't sound good.

The kids and I gathered at the door. I took a deep breath, trying to slow my heart before it raced away without me.

"Okay, here we go. Do *not* look at the fire, whatever you do!"

The three oldest kids stared at me, wide-eyed. Mazie covered her eyes with her hand.

Though it had only been minutes since the crash, the outside air was smoky and rank. Squealing sirens filled the night, speeding from several directions and converging on the nearest train crossing. Mazie hesitated with her eyes shut tight in the doorway, so I took her quivering hand and hustled her to the car.

The wind blew from the west, which put our house right in the path of any toxic fumes that might be coming off the train. The fire seemed as bright as a gigantic welder's arc. I had to close my eyes for a moment before I could see to start the car. My fingers trembled, jangling the keys.

I backed the car out to aim us to the east just as Jack Jeffers ran past, gesturing at me to roll down my window. "I'd be surprised if our houses burn up," he said. "Should be okay to come back tomorrow."

I was hoping the same thing until I reached the intersection at Dittmar Road, the little boulevard that borders my neighborhood. A throng of squealing emergency vehicles was backing up on Dittmar in front of us, including a slew of hazmat trucks.

Hazmat trucks?

"Gotta turn around, kids." The street was jamming up with cars, so I had to jockey to and fro to get turned around. Jesus, my hands shook so much I could barely accomplish this turn.

As I drove back down our street to leave the neighborhood by another route, we passed three men in front of the Belding house, unloading an ice chest from their truck. One scraggly guy had a bottle under his arm. It looked like tequila—Jose Cuervo.

They were settling in to party? Now of all times? Dumbasses.

The Beldings' teenage daughter ran out their front door, yelling so loud that we heard her through our closed windows.

"I'm going, whether you do or not!" She ran ahead of us to jump into a car full of teenagers, who were hanging out windows, shouting and waving.

Mr. Belding stood on his door stoop in greasy coveralls, his long hair in a messy ponytail. He waved a dismissive hand at the girl and lit a smoke.

We'd just made it out of my neighborhood when Tasha said, "Where's Harry?"

My chest squeezed. Harry was still in the backyard.

"Oh no! Harry! I'll have to go back."

Why did I have to forget our dog? But Mazie's eyes! I veered into an empty parking lot and jerked the car to a stop. With kids hurling questions at me, I jumped out and rushed to Mazie's door, yanking it open.

"Mazie, how are your eyes now?"

She squeaked a nonverbal response while I cupped her little face in my hands.

"Do you still have pink blobs or pain?" I asked her. "Your eyes are better?"

"Yes, Nana." She wiped tears off her cheeks.

"Are you sure, sweetie? We can go to a doctor."

Mazie's eyes popped wide, and she gaped at me without blinking. "They don't hurt anymore. The pink's all gone."

I searched her face, half-afraid she was shining me on to avoid doctors, but she gave me a teary-eyed smile. I kissed her cheek, shut the door, and hurried back to the driver's seat. I sat for a second, worried I'd be putting the kids at risk by going back for Harry. But the fire didn't look any bigger, as far as I could tell.

"Let's get Harry," I said. The kids shouted "Yay!" and "Woohoo!" I turned across traffic and headed toward home.

"How could you forget Harry, Nana?" Keno sounded disappointed in me.

"You forgot him, too!" I shot my grandson an annoyed look.

The first street entrance to my neighborhood was blocked by police cars. I drove a quarter-mile to the next entrance, but two more squad cars blocked it as well, their lights blinking warnings, a couple of policemen milling about. I drove up beside the policemen and hopped from the car.

"We're evacuating," I said, "but I forgot our dog. I need to go get him." I was out of breath, pulling at my fingers until they hurt.

"You can't go in, ma'am," said the tallest cop.

"How could you forget your dog?" said the other.

I scowled at the squat, stern cop. "Because I'm a frantic old woman, trying to save my grandkids from a fire and God knows what all. Please let me back in for five minutes."

"We can't, ma'am. I'm sorry," the tall cop said.

"Why on Earth not?"

"Because of the fire and God knows what all." The short cop smirked at me meanly.

"I can walk in and get the dog while the others wait," Keno said, leaning out the car window. So gallant of him.

"No. No, I can't be responsible for that," the nice cop said.

"Then I'll walk in," I said, wondering if I could even do that. "You're not going to say no to a woman twice your age, are you? What about my dog?"

"Ma'am, I have to say no. I'm sorry."

I couldn't out-argue these guys. I couldn't think of a way to sneak in to get Harry. Keno might be able to manage it but, like the policeman, I could not be responsible for that. As I climbed in my SUV, I looked off toward the flames and smoke.

"Think they'll get that fire put out before it burns down the neighborhood?" I asked the nice cop.

"So far they're keeping it confined to the train."

"Thank God. You know, some of my neighbors aren't leaving."

"Oh? Who?"

"The Beldings," I muttered and gave him their address. The cop got on his radio, and I put my car in gear to drive away, defeated.

"I want Harry!" Mazie cried out.

"Me, too, but Harry will be okay." I hoped.

"But there's fire and smoke! He's locked in the yard," Mazie squealed, flapping her hands.

Watching the little girl in my rearview mirror, I wanted to hug her. I wanted to squeal and whine myself.

"Harry's real smart, honey. He knows how to get out of the yard. He'll run away from the neighborhood if he needs to."

"Well, I don't want him to run away."

"He'll come back when it's safe. He loves you too much to run away for good."

From the front seat, Tasha reached around and patted Mazie's knee. I felt like beating myself about the head for forgetting that poor dog.

"Mazie, are your eyes still okay?"

"Yeah," she said, closing those eyes and leaning back in her booster seat.

I DROVE DUE NORTH FOR A WAYS so that I could cut back west and get to the other side of the fire, upwind. Everyone had a cell phone, even Mazie. The kids tried to call their parents while I drove, but no one answered. Shoot. I was hoping the other adults in my family would calm me down.

Though we were out of immediate danger, I had a deep foreboding in my gut. Did the train derail? What crazy thing could have caused that? It was a flat, straight track with no hills or curves. Could it have been warped somehow? Did someone—like a terrorist—mess with the signal? I'd lived next to that track for thirty-plus years, and nothing like this had ever happened before.

"I bet your parents went out to eat with Grandpa," I said to the kids, "and he made them turn off their phones."

"Grandpa's mean," Milo grumbled.

"Oh, honey. He just likes people to behave a certain way."

"He bosses everybody around, even grown-ups." Milo jutted his chin, daring me to contradict what everyone knew to be true.

"He always says, 'You kids be quiet!'" Mazie imitated her grandfather's deep voice.

"Sometimes when you get old, kid noise gets on your nerves," I said.

"We can't help it if we're kids," Milo said.

"I'm glad you're kids. Kids are fun."

"Yes, we are!" Milo made a silly face, and I laughed.

But that conversation took me aback. I hadn't realized that Hank was annoying our grandkids, too. I didn't know what to do with him.

I mean, you can't stay married to a man for thirty years without having at least some affection for him, or I couldn't anyway. Hank and I were the glue that held our big family together—the family that meant the world to me. I had once believed in Hank, until complications got in the way. Though I hadn't seen much of his lovable self in years, I coached myself to trust I would uncover it again. So, I looked for reasons to stay married, tried to find things to love in my husband Hank, though they seemed to get scarcer by the day.

I FOUND A GRASSY ROADSIDE to the northwest about ten miles from home and upwind, where I pulled off and spread a tarp on the ground. We sat, Keno messing with his iPad, Tasha texting, Milo and Mazie poking at each other in true brother-sister fashion, and all of us watching the fire and eating a bag of stale popcorn we'd left in the car that afternoon. The radio said they were evacuating neighborhoods near the train wreck, but they didn't say why.

Hazmat trucks, that's why. Contaminated air.

Mazie complained that her phone wasn't working, but Keno and Milo finally reached their moms, who were out and about in Dallas with the rest of the clan, enjoying the nightlife far too much from the sound of them. Hank called me, I guess just to ask if he should come home.

"No, we can't be home now anyway. Just stay up there and enjoy the game."

"How's your heart doing with all this stress?"

"It's fine."

"Bea, you should go to bed. Get those kids straight to a hotel."

I was sick of him bossing me around. I breathed deeply, attempting to calm my aggravation. Hank, what happened to you?

"How's Harry taking it?" Hank asked, setting off a wave of panic and guilt in me.

"Harry? Oh, he's fine." I couldn't very well tell Hank that I'd forgotten the dog. My husband loved that dog more than he loved me. I said goodnight before Hank could ask me to put Harry on the phone.

It was a typical early autumn in Central Texas, so it wasn't cold. I was tempted to bed us down at the roadside, but I figured the cops would run us off. Besides, it was ragweed season—not good for me or Mazie, or especially Keno. That kid's nose ran like a faucet all day and night while the ragweed bloomed, but he refused to take a pill for it, and he seldom thought to blow his nose. Allergies in Austin plagued us year-round.

"Milo, quit spying on my texts!" Tasha hollered as we piled back in the car. "It's freaking annoying."

"She texted cuss words," Milo said. "I saw them."

"It's none of your business!" Tasha swatted at Milo, who swatted back.

"Cut it out. Both of you!" A tense silence settled over the car.

As we drove away, Keno groaned. "The internet on my iPad keeps shutting down." He sighed and stared out the window.

"Kids, if I take you to a luxury hotel, can you keep it a secret from your parents and grandpa?"

"Heck, yeah," Milo said.

"I love secrets," Mazie gushed.

Keno and Tasha grinned, seeming to like the idea.

I drove downtown, where for some reason all the traffic lights were blinking red or yellow—super-annoying when almost every corner had a stoplight. At last we arrived at the Four Seasons, and I rented us a two-bedroom suite, paying for it with the credit card I kept hidden from Hank. Very posh digs, the Four Seasons. The hushed voices, the crisp, cool air and canned music were strangely numbing.

"Oh? There was a train wreck?" said the young woman who checked us in, never losing her overly cheerful tone. "Thank you for choosing the Four Seasons."

The perfect accommodations for our luxury evacuation needs.

I'd never slept in such a place. I had always disdained them, but after our escape from danger, I wanted to spoil my grandkids—and myself, to be honest.

I texted Hank to tell him we were at a cheaper northside hotel and purposely didn't include a phone number. He could always reach me on my cell.

After the excitement of the fancy hotel suite wore off and I'd again sworn the kids to secrecy, they went to sleep. I made myself some cocktails from the mini bar. The TV news said the fire from the train was almost out. From the aerial news footage, I saw that my house and yard were intact. Thank God, Harry would not be in danger from fire.

I took a long soak in the Jacuzzi. The water jets soothed my nerves and the jasmine bath oil evoked comforting memories of my Southern grandmother. A relaxing bath could be so hard to come by.

Though I was still a bit jittery, at least now I could think.

We were kind of a mash-up of a family. Hank had three boys and I had my two girls. We got married in our late thirties when the kids ranged in age from five to nine. Since their other parents—our exes— weren't much in the picture, our kids were raised together, which was hairy but also good because they bonded like a real family, which they were, of course.

Our grown kids were now in their thirties, except Jeri, who'd just turned forty. I said they all went to Dallas for the game, but that's not completely accurate. The three of them who lived around Austin went with Hank, along with Jeri's husband and Wayne's girlfriend. Two of my stepsons lived in Phoenix. It was next to impossible to get the whole family together anymore.

Back when the kids were growing up, we used to have the greatest times going camping at Pace Bend Park on Lake Travis. Five kids were a lot to keep an eye on, but the place was so pretty and the lake so clean and clear. Not as clear as it would have been without human use and road runoff, but being there was still so lovely, so relaxing, so reinvigorating.

Hank would barbecue, and I would mix up potato salad and deviled eggs from the pre-cooked ingredients I'd bring from home, and we'd all eat our hearts out under the starry sky with our pink noses and shoulders and our bronzed chests and arms. We would tell stories and laugh and sing along to Hank's guitar, then we'd stretch out in our tents and listen to the whippoorwills and frogs and crickets and sleep more peacefully than we had in weeks. We'd wake in the mornings with our messy hair and our tents and lawn chairs covered in dew, and we'd feel the sting of yesterday's sunburn while songbirds raced about gathering scraps from the ground, and a big, giant whooping crane flew slowly, loopingly, overhead.

I would've given what remained of my life to have one more weekend like that, as long as my grandkids could be there, too. Hank would've said he'd give his left nut. I suspect he'd have given both of them.

CHAPTER 2

The next morning at the hotel, Cranky Hank called and woke me up.
"Dang, Hank, did you have to call so early?"
"Bea, it's after nine. Why are you still sleeping?"
"Well, why shouldn't we be? We were up late. We've got nothing to do anyway."
"You need to get those kids home," he said.
"Are you saying we can go home already? How do you know that?"
"It's on the internet and TV. They say you can go home later today. Aren't you paying attention?"
"No, I was sleeping. And do I have to be there the first minute they open the neighborhood?"
"You should be ready to go."
"Hank, I'm in no hurry to return to the scene of a toxic spill." My phone dropped the call, which was fine with me. I didn't feel like arguing with Hank, but I had no intention of rushing my grandchildren home.

I checked on the kids in the adjoining room. The girls lay in bed together, Mazie sprawling her tiny body across two-thirds of the bed and halfway across Tasha. They looked so pretty and sweet in their sleep, and so much like polar opposites in body type and coloring: six-year-old Mazie—thin and pale with aquamarine eyes; and fifteen-year-old Tasha—buxom, brown-eyed, and olive-skinned.

Gangly Keno had created a private space for himself on a pallet in front of the TV. Mucus rattled in his nose as he slept. Milo was sacked out in the far bed alone. He rolled over and looked at me, sandy hair in his bleary eyes, then went back to sleep.

I wished that my prim and proper daughter Jeri hadn't called me a hoarder. Before they left town, she'd walked in on Hank yelling at me for filling the linen closet with "way too much" over-the-counter medicine, and she'd taken his side. He would have busted a gut if he'd known the full extent of my stockpiling. But Jeri's comment and Hank's yelling hurt me. It felt like bad karma to be apart for days with bitter feelings in the air.

Yet the trouble between Hank and me had started long ago.

As a grandmother, I felt my purpose in life was to keep my kids and grandkids safe and healthy. So, when the climate started going to hell at an accelerating rate, scaring the crap out of me daily, I felt forced to plan for my family's long-term survival.

First, there were the long droughts and heat waves, which were a matched set around here. Then we noticed that all the frogs had disappeared from our yard. We couldn't decide how long they'd been gone, or when we'd last heard them. How did we fail to notice that the frogs had gone missing? It didn't bode well for us.

Next came the barrage of tornadoes and hurricanes, keeping me up nights tracking radar and worrying about people in their paths. Though inland in Austin, we still got storm tendrils strong enough to topple trees and cause fatal floods.

Ironically, Hurricane Katrina gave me a chance to earn extra income from my work-at-home job, where I calculated and wrote up insurance claims for commercial property. I was a whiz at building interlocking spreadsheets and arguing with tight-fisted insurance execs, forcing them to cough up more cash. The hurricane gave us so many new clients that it took me years of long hours to settle those claims.

And while I worked, I listened to progressive podcasts, particularly a guy who gave dire environmental warnings and told us, only half-jokingly, to stock up on canned goods.

Once I'd amassed all the insurance money, I wanted to install photovoltaic solar panels on our house to generate power, but Hank hated the idea.

"It'll ruin the roof. We'll have leaks," he said.

"Okay, I'll put a new, stronger roof on first—find a better roofer. And I'll pay him to check the panels to be sure they don't cause leaks."

"I don't want all that weight on my roof." Everything was his, never ours.

That evening, our TV show was interrupted by a weather alert. Hurricane Ike was bearing down on Galveston Island in the Gulf of Mexico, two hundred miles southeast of us.

"Hank, you know this crazy number of hurricanes is caused by excess carbon in the atmosphere."

"Oh, c'mon. How do you know that?"

"Because I read. We have to reduce our carbon footprint. That's why I want solar panels."

Hank looked at me sideways. "You gonna pay for this—I mean every penny?"

"Yes. Yes, I will. Can I please do it?"

He rolled his eyes and sighed. "I guess I won't stop you, as long as they don't interrupt our power in the evenings."

"Yeah, can't miss your TV shows, huh?"

"Some things are important to you." He chuckled. "Others are important to me."

"Thank you, sweetheart," I said, and I kissed him.

"But if anything goes wrong, it's on you." He just couldn't let the moment of agreement last.

Naturally, I wanted to do more than install solar panels. I wanted to stock up on food, too, but I'd already pushed Hank to his limit. Still, little by little, I slipped in other things without giving him much chance to protest. I installed gutters and a rain barrel system to collect water for the lawn. I xeriscaped the yard with drought-resistant trees, plants, and grass. I installed triple-paned windows, water-saving plumbing fixtures, energy-efficient appliances and air-conditioning.

I went tree hugger wild. Then to top it off, I built a lovely tiled patio with a rooftop for shade, I added a big storage shed out back, and I insulated our attic and garage. The more I did for the house, the crankier Hank became.

By the time my extra insurance jobs were finished, I'd spent most of the money on the house. I called it our retirement plan. But Hank and I were now at odds.

When half the State of Texas seemed to go up in flames a few summers back, and we had long-running fires to our east, west, and south, I began to implement my secret plan. I tried to talk to Hank about the plan in a hypothetical way, but I could see it was too much for him, so I shut up and took it underground.

I let a few activities remain in the open, to throw him off the scent. I collected candles and set out the decorative ones, hiding hundreds of blackout candles from Hank. I planted tomatoes, peppers, and herbs in pots around the yard. I hired someone to build a raised garden-bed along the side of our home, and I ordered beaucoup seed packets and catalogs. Hank groused about the catalogs, because he groused about everything, but I did catch him flipping through them now and then. If he saw me watching, he would slam the catalog shut and walk away, grumbling.

While much of the Austin suburb of Bastrop and the Lost Pines State Park burned to the ground, taking Hank's cousin's house, hundreds of other homes, and a million and a half pine trees along with it, by sheer coincidence I inherited a great deal of money from my maiden aunt, money Hank had speculated about for years.

"It could be millions, Bea. You'd better be sweet to her," he would say.

For that reason and so many others, I didn't tell Hank the whole truth. I put the inheritance in a secret account and used it to buy the house behind ours and fill it full of survival supplies. I did tell Hank that I inherited *some* money. I spent a couple of grand to take us on a trip to a casino, and I put fifty thousand in savings.

"I thought the old bat would be good for a whole lot more," Hank said.

"Hank Crenshaw! Shame on you for talking that way about my aunt."

I could rely on Hank not to notice much of anything around home, especially whatever I was doing. He left for work each morning before dawn, even on Saturdays, and returned after dark. He watched TV, ate dinner, and went to bed by 8:30. He felt like a drudge, and he acted like one—oblivious. Plus, he had no reason to suspect me of anything, so he didn't look for it. Easy-peasy to hide things from Hank, at least for a while.

I fought with myself over it, but in the end, I didn't tell Hank that I'd inherited nearly two million dollars after taxes. What the man didn't know wouldn't hurt him. I filed our tax return online that year and made sure Hank never saw it. I figured if he ever had the *need* to know, I could always tell him when the time came. He was already angry with me anyway. How much angrier could he get?

Still, I couldn't help but fret. I covered up my lies by bottling my emotions and putting more distance between Hank and me. What I felt guilty about was the coldness that grew between us.

HERE IN THE LAP OF Four Seasons LUXURY, I waited until ten and got the grandkids up. We ordered a sumptuous room-service breakfast: eggs, bacon, sausage, hash browns, grits, biscuits, gravy, waffles, orange juice, and for me, a half-pot of fresh coffee with the creamiest cream. Best coffee I ever had.

The TV reception was fuzzy—strange for such a fancy hotel. The news was full of reports on the train wreck and littered with solemn officials expressing sorrow over the loss of life and property—two trainmen dead, a house plowed down, although no one had been home. No houses had burned, other than the flattened one. The officials assured us that neighborhoods near the wreck were perfectly safe. The chemicals—unnamed chemicals—that the train was carrying had all burned off and should not be a source of concern.

Right.

After we ate, I let the kids swim in the hotel pool. If the other people in this family were partying up in Dallas, we could darn well party in Austin, too.

But I was worried about Harry. He was stuck outside in the rancid air. I'd meant to fill his food and water bowls after supper, but I couldn't remember if I'd done it.

"Hey, kids," I said, after they'd swam for a couple of hours. "Y'all come back to the room. I'm going to see about Harry. I'll pick us up some burgers on the way back. We'll stay here again tonight."

From the moans and groans coming out of those kids, one would have thought I'd sentenced them to the gulag.

"There's nothin' to do here!" Milo said when we got back to the room.

"I need to get on your computer," Tasha groused.

"But Nana," Keno pointed at the TV, "they said it should be safe to go home today."

"I don't believe them."

"Why not?"

"Because they never tell the truth about poisons in the environment. They've been lying about it my whole life."

The kids looked so unhappy that I sat down to think. I wanted to be home, too, so the kids could have space to be away from each other. They were getting antsy, and so was I. Plus, the luxury here was starting to feel slightly obscene.

I dialed the City's non-emergency number.

"You know," I told them, "on TV they're saying people who evacuated from the train wreck can go home today. We evacuated, and I need to know how you're so sure that it's safe. What was in that train, anyway?"

"Chemicals, ma'am."

"I know that. What *kind* of chemicals?"

"I don't have that information."

Big surprise. "So, did two trains crash into each other, or was it a derailment?"

"A derailment."

"Well, how come the train derailed?" I asked, and Keno gaped at me.

"I'm not allowed to speculate, ma'am."

"Okay, then I will," I said. "Was there a problem with the tracks?"

"Can't say for sure. It doesn't appear so."

"Alright, did something go wrong with the switching signal?"

"That's a distinct possibility, ma'am."

"So, can we go home today or not?"

"Not today. Probably tomorrow."

"But on TV, they say—"

"Our assessment has changed."

"Can I at least get my dog? He's running out of food by now."

"You didn't bring your dog with you?"

"No, I forgot him, and they wouldn't let me back in. Stupid of me, I know, but you shouldn't punish my dog for that. At least let me in to get him."

"Ma'am, the police have been instructed to keep everyone out. No exceptions."

I almost yelled at the woman, but instead I muttered, "Thank you," and hung up.

Milo and Tasha kept complaining. I fled to Dan's Hamburgers, hoping to pacify the grandkids with heaps of lip-smacking local junk food.

LOUNGING AROUND THE HOTEL gave me too much time to think. I worried about the train wreck, chemical poisons, and Harry until I couldn't take it anymore.

I needed to go home so that I could sneak into my secret house to make room for more deliveries while Hank was in Dallas. It was so rare to have him out of my hair, and now I couldn't take advantage of it. I felt fairly confident that I was ready for any catastrophe that might befall us, short of war on American soil. But I was fanatical about checking and rechecking everything, and I was forever thinking of new things to stock up on.

I had a crafty way of fixing up and stocking that house. I bought it in the name of a trust I registered in Delaware. I hired a property agency to oversee the work I had done and the deliveries of goods, and I communicated with the agency under a false name by email only. I didn't keep documentation on paper or even on my computer. I stored it on the cloud, and carefully deleted the cookies and history every time I left the website.

Under the property agency's supervision, I had a deep hole dug in the second house's backyard a few years ago, during the four weeks Hank was gone to a family reunion and camping trip out in West Texas at Big Bend. The grown kids and grandkids met Hank out there. I begged off on going with them because of my heart. It was a lonely month for me, but perfect cover.

I had the hole in the ground divided in half. In one half, they installed an enormous, cistern-style water tank to store rainwater runoff from the house's guttering system. The tank filtered and stored more than ten thousand gallons of water, which could be accessed with a hand pump inside a locked closet in the garage.

In the other half of the cavernous hole, they built a cellar. I set it up like an old-fashioned, fully-stocked fallout shelter—except it was hidden, with its ventilation going into the house's ductwork. It even had a composting toilet. Below the living space, they put a root cellar for crops, wine, and booze. Our neighbors were in a tizzy about what might be going on with all the construction, but I just acted like I didn't know any more about it than they did.

When the cellar and cistern were complete, I had the yard re-covered with rich, loamy soil. The agency paid an organic gardener to grow potatoes and other root vegetables, and to harvest the food and store it in the cellar, which you could enter only through the pantry of the house.

"What the hell happened in that backyard behind us?" Hank hollered after he'd done his post-vacation pacing across the territory of our yard.

"They built something underground, I think."

"What kind of something did they build?"

"How the hell would I know?" I was getting agitated, too.

"Bea, didn't you look?"

"No. I figured it was none of my business."

"Well, I don't like it! It'll mess up the drainage in our yard."

Such an old fuss budget, Hank Crenshaw.

If Hank didn't stop his sudden prying, he might untangle my carefully woven web of deceit. This made me exceedingly nervous. He would go ballistic unless I could keep my secrets until the day, God forbid, when we needed those supplies. Then maybe he'd be grateful. Not in his nature, I know, but I could dream—dream for Hank to be grateful, I mean, not for a cataclysmic event.

I visited the second house in the middle of the night while Hank slept. I could always count on him to sleep like the dead and to be unaware of me slipping out the back door.

I thought I was prepared to support my family off the grid on a largely vegetarian diet without power or cars for a couple of years, but of course I wasn't. I was certainly the most prepared person I knew of, but after what came next, no one was handing out prizes.

When my plans were mostly complete and I had retired from insurance work, Hurricanes Harvey, Irma, and Maria wreaked so much havoc that the costs couldn't be fully calculated. Around the same time, California caught fire—again.

Finally, politicians started talking about climate change and even made a few weak plans to try to slow it down.

It was far too little and much too late.

In our shamefully fancy hotel suite with its marble floors and pricey furniture, the kids and I settled in to munch junk food and watch movies on demand. Not a great viewing experience, since the TV kept cutting out. I thought about calling the front desk to complain, but electronics seemed to be messed up in general, so I didn't bother.

At last, I got the chance to relax with my grandchildren, laughing at the movies, cheering and booing the characters. Such fun to see the kids enjoy themselves so much.

Milo got over-excited and went to get some ice. Just when I wondered why he was taking so long, a clatter arose in the hallway, along with a loud yelp. We rushed out to find Milo rubbing his knee next to a knocked-over pedestal table and a sea of spilled ice. Other hotel guests came out and gave Milo and me dirty looks.

"Milo! What are you doing?"

"Balancing the ice bucket on my head. I didn't see the—"

"Get back in here. I'll call the desk." I kicked ice against the wall and threw a couple of towels on the spill. Such a handful, this kid.

We settled back down to watch choppy movies. Keno noodled on his iPad, and Milo played Angry Birds on his phone. While Tasha texted, I wove her thick mane of chestnut hair into an elegant French braid, then I made one for Mazie as well, although her hair was yellow and fine and straight as a board. Still, her braid looked lovely, until she messed it up when she fell asleep with her head in my lap.

I never did find out who won that football game up in Dallas.

CHAPTER 3

Sunday midday, city authorities finally gave permission for evacuees to go home. We were able to enter my neighborhood from the east on an empty but smoky Dittmar Road, heading toward the railroad crossing several blocks down. But as I drove over a rise, the wrecked train loomed in front of us. The kids gasped, and I hit the brakes.

The site swarmed with people in white hazmat suits—full suits with face-shields and respirators. Blackened trees and shrubbery outlined the scene, adding to its starkness.

Fire engines, hazmat trucks, and police cars were stacked up across Dittmar four or five deep, most with emergency lights flashing. And beyond those vehicles was a steaming pile of mangled freight cars. Huge plumes of water arced from fire engines into the wreckage, sending up frightening clouds of hissing steam.

I threw my SUV into reverse. A man in a hazmat suit trotted toward us, wielding a stubby stop sign. I rolled down my window to talk to the man, but he waved us away.

The neighborhood air burned my nose and made my eyes water, setting my pulse to pounding. Tiny black dots of ash floated in the air, almost too small to see. My lungs started to wheeze, and I felt my throat closing up. Breathing this toxic stew was extremely dangerous for me, with my asthma and bad heart, and it couldn't be good for the kids either.

"Kids, this air is bad. We can't stay. Let's get Harry and whatever else we need then go back to the hotel."

"I can't believe they told us we could come here," Keno said.

"I want to stay." Tasha scowled at me.

"Tasha, the air's making me sick. I can't stay."

The neighborhood creeped me out—so smoky and eerie. Our subdivision was almost upscale, with one- and two-story houses, three-car garages, and quarter-acre yards. Some houses looked buttoned up, with no cars in their driveways. But a few families were pulling in and unloading, and other houses seemed re-occupied—lights on inside, folks mowing lawns, coming and going every which way.

People were going to stay here with all this ash in the air? Whether or not they thought the air was poisoned from spilled chemicals, any fool should've known that breathing air full of ash was bad.

The Belding house had a slew of cars out front and country music blasting from inside. Sort of matched the rusty engine and decrepit motorcycle camouflaged by the weeds in their yard. They must have been partying all weekend. I'd known some very smart rednecks in my life, but these folks were rednecks with no sense.

I pulled into my driveway. "Kids, get my laptop from the living room, and get Grandpa's from the desk upstairs. Then come straight back to the car."

We piled out, and I unlocked the house. "I'll get Harry," I said.

"I'm coming, too." Milo ran ahead to the backyard gate, hollering, "Harry!" Mazie screamed for the dog from the front yard and scampered our way.

I expected Harry to be barking by now, but he wasn't. Milo rushed into the backyard, but no dog came to greet him.

"Harry! Where are you?"

While the kids ran around calling Harry, looking in the side yards, behind bushes, under the shed, I slipped through a slit in the waist-high hedge and into the yard behind mine—my secret house—hollering for Harry. He often escaped to this yard. Was he holed-up and hurt somewhere?

"Nana! We can't find him!" Milo called from the hedge, his face hardened with worry. Mazie flapped her hands and starting crying.

"I can't find him either," I said, panicking. "Milo, run around the block and holler for him." The boy shot to the side gate, and Mazie sobbed louder. "Come over here, Mazie. You can look under the shed and under the house."

"Okay," she said, sniffling while she came through the hedge. "Harry!"

Milo shouted from east of us, "Harry! Harry!" his voice getting harsher and more frantic. I pointed at places for Mazie to crouch down and look.

"Harry!"

Within minutes, Milo was back outside my yard, hollering louder and shriller. Then, I heard frantic barking, and Harry came streaking around the corner, almost knocking Milo over in excitement. Relief brought tears to my eyes.

"Harry!" we cried. Mazie and I rushed to the big chocolate Labrador while he licked Milo soggy.

"Good dog, Harry." I ruffled his ears. "You must be hungry and thirsty. I'm sorry I forgot you." Apparently, he'd already forgiven me. He pawed at me and made happy-dog noises, then licked Mazie to pieces while she giggled. "Harry, let's get your food and leash and get out of here."

He let out a loud cough and wagged his tail. Milo took hold of Harry's collar. No way he was letting Harry escape again.

Two more sets of neighbors pulled into driveways across the side street while we headed to my back door. And the wind was kicking up. Good. It might clear the air.

"Tasha? Keno? Are you guys ready?" I hollered as we came inside. Mazie ran up the stairs, chattering at Tasha about the hunt for Harry, who was wolfing food and water from his indoor bowls.

"I'm getting Grandpa's laptop," Keno said.

"I'm checking my Instagram," said Tasha.

"You can do that on your phone. Get on down here!"

"K, but I gotta get shampoo. Hotel shampoo is gross."

"Just hurry up."

I grabbed Harry's dry kibble, some canned dog food, and a can opener from the kitchen. I found his extra set of bowls, then rummaged through a drawer for his leash.

As I loaded Harry's stuff into the car, the Gonzales family next door pulled a van into their driveway. A flock of kids debarked, lugging bags and their brown Cocker Spaniel. I waved to Mrs. Gonzales, and she looked puzzled, probably wondering why I was loading up when they were unloading. I stepped toward her to talk, but my cell phone rang in my pocket.

"Where have you been, Bea?" Hank said, when I picked up.

"Driving home, but the air is bad. We're leaving again."

"Where the hell can you go?"

"To a hotel, I assume." Rats. We couldn't go back to the Four Seasons if Hank was on his way home. I should have thought of this already. "I'll call you when we get settled."

"We're almost to Waco. Traffic is crazy from the game," he said, "but it's moving fast, so we'll be home in a couple of hours." White-knuckle Texas driving on I-35 worried me sick. "Wait at the house, Bea, and I'll figure it out when I get there."

I wanted to tell Hank I was perfectly capable of figuring things out, but I didn't feel like explaining myself.

"Maybe I'll take the kids to Tres Amigos for lunch," I said. "If we're not home when you get here, we won't be long."

"Those kids don't need to eat out."

"You guys have been eating out all weekend. I'm taking the kids out, too."

"I don't think you should. You'll spoil them."

"I didn't ask you what you thought, Hank."

He huffed. "Bye, Bea. Love you."

"You too," I said. Stingy old bastard.

"Kids! Change of plans," I called out as I re-entered the house. "Your parents are halfway home, so we're going out to eat until they get back. Get yourselves cleaned up, please, but be quick about it."

Milo and Harry ran in from the garage.

"What are you doing?" I said to Milo. "Go wash your face and hands, comb your hair."

"I got screwdrivers for Keno's robot," Milo muttered. He held up one Phillips and one flathead.

"Grandpa will pound you if you don't put those back where you found them. Give them here." Milo reluctantly handed the screwdrivers over, and I stuck them in my bag.

ACCORDING TO MY MECHANICAL WRISTWATCH, it happened at 2:29 p.m.
The five of us were rushing about, sprucing ourselves up at around 2:15, when Harry started squealing as if he was in serious pain. We hurried to him in the living room, where he was running in tight circles and yelping. Milo looked distraught.

"What's wrong, Harry?" I crouched down near him, trying to soothe him. But he wouldn't be soothed. Then, dogs started barking all over the neighborhood. I'd never heard anything like it.

We ran out the front door, the kids clustering around me, Mazie covering her ears and screeching about loud dogs. The Cocker Spaniel in the yard next door jumped repeatedly against his fence as though trying to throw himself over it. Neighbors spilled out onto their front lawns, and we all looked at each other, like *What the hell?* No one knew what to do. People tried to calm their own dogs, but it wasn't helping one bit.

Someone had the bright idea to honk their car horn, as if that would improve the situation. Then other geniuses started honking, too. But the dogs just ran in even crazier circles as the honking trickled to a stop. The barking did not stop.

I turned to the kids. "We can't go eat now. Something's wrong."

"Just because dogs are barking, we can't go eat?" Tasha glared at me, crossing her arms.

"Honey, something is making these dogs bark. Animals often sense trouble before it arrives."

"That's true," Keno said, sniffing back a nose full. "But in that case, shouldn't we get out of here?"

"God, you're right." I took a breath. "Everyone, grab your shoes. Tasha, get my purse and phone. Keno, lock the back door. Everyone back to the car in one minute. Go!"

Within ninety seconds, the kids and Harry were climbing in the car with me right behind them. We didn't get the chance to drive away.

CHAPTER 4

A bright, greenish light rippled swiftly across the sky, accompanied by an insanely loud *WHUMP!*

Next came a barrage of short squeaks and squeals, staticky noises, the whir of motors spinning to a stop, then the complete absence of sound, yet my eardrums felt ready to burst.

An overhead power line down Pico Street snapped in two. It snaked and popped across several yards, shooting out fiery white sparks, then suddenly went limp.

Silas and Doris Barnes across the street—their car stopped dead, backed halfway onto the road. On the side street, a car engine halted. The car kept rolling slowly, its driver wrestling with the steering wheel, until the car smacked into Mr. Jeffers's front fence.

Down the block, Mr. and Mrs. Belding gawped at each other, then bolted back into their house. The dogs stopped barking for a few seconds, then started again, more frantically than ever. Out on the main road half a mile away, tires squealed, metal crunched, and seconds later, something exploded. Women, men, and children screamed on their lawns.

My grandkids and dog jumped out of the car, and Mazie took off running, hollering, "I want Mommy!" Tasha ran after Mazie. Keno turned in circles, looking toward rooftops and high wires. Milo clung to the barking dog.

"The power and cars shut down," Keno said. "Listen. No air conditioners. No humming electricity in the wires. No car engines."

"But why the cars? What was that?" I latched on to Mazie and Tasha as they returned.

"Electromagnetic pulse, maybe?" he said.

"An EMP? Jesus." I skimmed my eyes across the far horizon, hunting for mushroom clouds, but I didn't see any, even though we were on some of the highest ground around. Yet the color of the sky seemed wrong, lighter than normal. Was it glowing?

Tasha yanked out her earbuds. "My iPhone. It's dead!"

We looked at our cell phones, all dead as door nails, nary a blink or peep coming out of any of them. I searched the vault of the sky, as more green flickers flashed across it.

The cellar in my extra house—I should take the kids there, I thought. But I'd be revealing my secrets to a bunch of yappy kids, and the secrets would be secret no more.

"It could be a nuclear bomb," Keno whispered frantically in my ear.

I hesitated only for a second. Taking the kids to the cellar could mean the end of my marriage. But screw it. Their safety came first.

"Kids, come with me!" I forced the panic out of my voice.

The kids and dog and I trotted through my house, out the back door, through the slit in the backyard hedge, and into the secret house through its rear door. That glow in the sky was unmistakable now. Mother of God.

"What are we doing, Nana?" Tasha asked. "Whose house is this?"

"It's a house I have the use of," I said, thinking maybe I could hold on to some secrets a bit longer. I flipped a couple of light switches on and off—utterly useless. "Come with me, kids, to the pantry."

But the kids stopped and stared, bug-eyed, at the shelves, drums, and barrels full of food and supplies.

"What's all this stuff?" asked Milo.

"Shh! I hear a motor," Keno said.

We stood silently and listened. Even Harry fell quiet. A humming sound was coming from somewhere. Keno started tiptoeing between shelves and across the dining room when it hit me.

"It's the bees," I said. I'd had the bees installed in an exterior wall, with an outdoor flap that could be opened for honey extraction.

Mazie let out a screech, sending chills through my already frayed nerves. "Bees, bees, bees!" she howled and stamped her feet, hiding behind Tasha.

"Mazie, the bees are in a hive in the wall, and you can hear them, but they can't get in here. Everyone, get to the pantry. Hurry!"

"Why, Nana?" Milo asked.

"Just do it. C'mon!"

"Bees," Mazie whimpered.

A nuclear bomb? Glowing green skies? My heart was about to fail me.

I led the kids and dog to the pantry door, telling them to stay put while I went inside, turned a key, then rotated a wheel that opened the wall—about the only wall in the house not covered with shelves full of goods. I pulled a crank flashlight and crank radio off a ledge. I handed the light to Keno, the radio to Tasha, and told them to start winding.

"When the cranks start to resist, stop winding or they'll break."

I grabbed a regular flashlight off the ledge, inserted batteries, and shined the beam on a steep flight of cement stairs with iron handrails. The kids crowded up behind me and looked down.

"I don't wanna go in there!" Mazie scooted backwards, then plopped down on the floor.

"Why are we going in *there*?" Tasha asked, wearing the most serious expression I'd ever seen from her.

"Because we don't know what caused the power to go off and the cars to stop, and whatever caused it could be dangerous. I want us to be protected until we find out what happened."

The three oldest kids and Harry filed obediently down the stairs by the light of the wind-up flashlight Keno carried. I heard them oohing and aahing as I bent down to Mazie on the floor.

"Mazie, come with me downstairs where it's safer."

"I don't like dark places," she whined.

I had never yelled at my grandkids in their lives, but my patience was gone. Radioactive fallout could be here any minute.

"Mazie, quit arguing! Come with me now!"

She pinned me with a flash of anger in her eyes. "Where's my doll?"

"We'll get it later. Let's go!"

She made me pick her up. Although she was a wisp, she was still too heavy for me, but I carried her anyway. Holding onto her little frame comforted me, and I needed to be level-headed and strong for these kids.

When we got to the top landing on the stairs, I had to put Mazie down to shut the cellar door. I held her hand, and we descended the stairs together.

As soon as we reached bottom, Milo asked, "Nana, when will Mom and Dad be home?"

Good Lord, I hadn't even thought about how this nuke or EMP—whatever it was—might have affected the other adults in this family, who were hurtling toward Austin at seventy miles an hour on a jam-packed interstate highway. Did this "event" extend that far? For the love of Jesus!

I tried to hide my shaking hands as I said to Milo, "I'm not sure. It shouldn't be too long."

How long is too long, anyway?

CHAPTER 5

The cellar was warm and rife with the earthy smells of root vegetables and the composting toilet, but the place was roomy and comfortable. I had made sure of that.

After candles were lit and the kids had snacks to eat, I got them playing Uno while I played with the wind-up radio. It was an emergency set from the Red Cross with AM and FM, plus seven short-wave bands. Keno's attention went more to the radio than the game. The dog padded around, sniffing out this unfamiliar place.

A cramped feeling was growing in my brain, telling me my blood pressure was rising. My emotions were time bombs waiting to kill me. I had to keep a tight rein on them.

The radio was loaded with static, but no one was broadcasting. Not good. So not good. My head pounding, I systematically searched the AM then FM bands, moving the dial only a hair's breadth each time and pausing to listen. But I heard no stations cutting in and out—no music, no voices, no stupid commercials. Nothing!

I flipped to the first short-wave band and followed the same tedious procedure, but got only popping and crackling.

"Crap!" I whacked the table with my hand. I came damned close to smashing that radio to bits. With all the things I've been mistaken about in my life, why did I have to be right about impending disaster? And what kind of disaster was this? Was it earth-shattering or only temporary? Was I risking exposure of my secrets for nothing?

"What's wrong?" Tasha asked. Harry paced the floor next to her feet.

"The radio."

"I'll help you," Keno said.

I scooted over on the padded bench, and Keno sat beside me. While he examined the radio and tweaked the dials, sniffing constantly, the other kids resumed their game.

"What do you think happened?" I murmured.

"Either a nuke or the sun." Keno peeked up from the radio to be sure the other kids weren't listening. They seemed engrossed in their Uno game, with Milo gloating about his every play.

From my research of possible gloom-and-doom scenarios, I knew that nuclear weapons sent out an electromagnetic pulse, an EMP, which could take out the electric grid and even the cars. A relatively small one-megaton bomb that burst three hundred kilometers above Nebraska or Kansas could do this to the entire U.S. Since the curvature of the earth blocks magnetic waves, pulses from nukes exploding closer to the ground could only damage smaller areas.

"It almost has to be a nuke, doesn't it?" I said. "Because the cars died?"

"Well, or an EMP weapon," Keno said.

"Okay, but no one's broadcasting on the radio. That means this thing must have gone pretty far. And I thought an EMP weapon could only damage a small area. There's not even any Mexican stations on, Keno."

He gulped. "Whatever it was coulda fried those giant transformers in electric plants."

"Oh, God." Those transformers were so huge and expensive that no one kept spares. They were manufactured only in China, and even the Chinese didn't keep a backstock. "If the transformers were fried," I said, "it could take decades to replace them. That would mean no power for years."

"Are you serious?"

My hands trembled, so I hid them in my lap. I closed my eyes and counted to five.

"Nana," Keno said, "if a nuke exploded in the stratosphere, would the fallout be bad?"

"There's not supposed to be fallout because it's so high in the sky, but I find that hard to—"

"A nuke!" Tasha cried. "You mean a nuclear bomb?"

"What?" Milo shouted, slapping down his Uno cards and springing to his feet.

I cursed under my breath. I hadn't wanted the other kids to hear us.

"Tasha." I eyed Mazie and shook my head at Tasha. "Not now."

Mazie ran over and jumped into my lap, burying her face in my neck. My heart pounded so fast I thought it might explode.

What if my grandkids were exposed to radiation? How could I take care of them on my own? Milo, Keno, and Tasha were looking to me for answers, and they wanted them now.

"Mazie, honey," I pulled her forward to see her face, "I have a surprise for you."

Her eyes lit up. "What is it?"

"It's a battery-powered record player. Let's go see the record I have."

"How come a record player would work if the phones died?" Milo wanted to know.

"The batteries aren't in it, so there's no circuit to get fried. It should be fine."

I led Mazie around a corner to a space filled with bunk beds. From a drawer, I pulled out the phonograph, headphones, a pack of batteries, and a vinyl record.

"Ta-Da!" I handed the album to Mazie.

"*Frozen!* I love *Frozen!*"

I smiled to be reassuring, while I put batteries in the player, fit the headphones over her ears, and kissed her. I lifted one of her earpieces. "Lie down and close your eyes, sweetie." She grinned and willingly complied.

"Reindeers are better than people," Mazie sang as I made my way to the other kids.

"Sorry, Nana," Tasha said. "But what about the nukes?"

"I don't want Mazie to hear all this." I settled on to the bench. "So, if a nuke caused this…this thing, it probably would've been a high-altitude bomb, very far away and twice as high in the sky as the space shuttle. It would be safer than a nuclear test in the desert, and I've lived through hundreds of those."

"I think it was the sun," Keno blurted out. I took several breaths, wondering if he was only saying that to calm the other kids. He sniffled and swallowed.

"I thought the sun couldn't damage cars and cell phones," I said.

"Well, that's what they always said. But I been reading online that Earth is about to have a polarity shift. It happens every sixty-thousand years or so, and we're overdue. The scientists don't know how quick it will happen once it starts, but they said if it happens fast, then Earth's magnetic field could shrink down to five percent of normal for a while. The magnetic field protects us from the sun. So, if a CME—"

"What's a CME?" Milo interrupted.

"Coronal mass ejection—huge flames and energy shoot out from the sun. If a CME happened when our magnetic field was low, especially if the CME was extra strong and hit us dead on, why couldn't it take out the cars? They don't know any of this stuff for sure. They could have been wrong about the cars."

"But Keno," Tasha said, "you can't believe every stupid thing on the internet."

"I know that, but this was on the NASA site."

"All of it?" I asked. Mazie was still singing quietly from the bed.

"No, my idea about the polarity shift making the CME so bad is my own theory."

I wanted to believe that Keno was capable of creating a sound scientific hypothesis, although it was difficult to think of him as having adult judgment while he kept ignoring the need to blow his nose

"Okay," I said, "if it could be either the sun or a nuke, why do you think it was the sun?"

"No mushroom clouds. No heat blasts."

"Yes, honey, but those things would come from a nuke close by, not from a nuke that's three hundred kilometers over Nebraska."

"Yeah, but only the sun would make that green light."

"Oh, right. The green light, like the aurora borealis. But does the aurora make the sky glow? You saw the glow, didn't you?"

"What's the aurora bor—what's that?" Milo asked.

"Hey, I just thought of something." Keno wrinkled his brow. "The CME could have caused the train wreck."

"Seriously? How?"

"You said the wreck was caused by a problem with the switching signal, right?"

"They said it was 'a distinct possibility.'"

"Well, CMEs disrupt signals, and sometimes they happen in waves. So, when there's a lot of solar activity, flares can leave the sun at different times, and some have more power and travel faster than others. They can take several days to reach us, giving us a warning, or they can show up in less than a day. The first wave could've disrupted electronic signals before a big wave took out the grid."

Somebody, save us.

"Nature is amazing," I said.

But divine retribution was a bitch.

WE SAT PONDERING THE IMPLICATIONS, then I snapped to attention. I needed to know what was happening outside. Mazie belted out, "Let it go! Let it go!"

"I'm going up to check on things." I stood to leave. "You guys stay here. There's a Monopoly game in that cabinet over there. Watch out for the candles, and don't get burned. Don't set anything near them that could catch fire."

"I wanna go, too." Milo clenched his fists. Tasha and Keno nodded and watched me. They all wanted to go, of course.

"Not yet. Let me make sure it's safe first."

The kids frowned at me, scared faces trying to hold it together.

"If I don't come back for a while—"

"Nana! Don't say that!" Tasha cried. I sat down next to her and took her hand.

"Sugar, listen to me. We don't know yet how bad this thing is. I have to see if I can find out, so we can decide the safest course of action. But if it's bad up there, something could go wrong when I go up, and you guys will be on your own. I'm so sorry this has happened, but you have to get tough right now to deal with it."

"What if the owners of this house come home?" Keno asked. "What do we tell them?"

I shut my eyes for a moment. Did I really need to destroy my shroud of secrecy? I might be overreacting. But I'd never seen a power outage that included flashing green light, a radiant sky, and dead cars. No, this was bad. We could be in for serious trouble, and the kids needed the comfort of knowing I had a plan.

Mazie came running around the corner toward the rest of us. "The songs stopped. Can I play it again?"

"No, honey. We need to save the batteries. That was a special treat."

Tasha patted the spot beside her on the bench, and Mazie climbed up.

I leaned back and told the kids the story of the house. I told about the inheritance, about the bees I'd installed in the wall, and the books and gear to use when harvesting honey. I told them about all the food and tools. I described the gun closet upstairs and how to get into it, then I made them promise to never, ever go there except in an emergency. Someday, I thought, I'll have to teach these kids how to shoot.

My grandchildren seemed a little flabbergasted and a lot overwhelmed. I expected a barrage of questions, but instead they studied me as though I was someone they'd never seen before.

The only question came from Milo. "Are you a millionaire?"

"I guess I am." I stood to go. I wanted to hug my grandchildren, but I thought it would make my leaving seem too final. "Kids, take care of each other."

When I was halfway up the cellar stairs, Mazie lunged up after me, squealing, "No-o-o! Don't leave me here, Nana. Don't leave!" She latched on to my pant leg with a ferocity pretty unbelievable for one so small.

I scooped Mazie into my arms, letting her cry. I cried as well but kept my face against her little chest so that no one would see my tears. How were we going to cope with this? I willed my tears to stop. I motioned to Tasha, and she came and picked up Mazie and took her away, both of them sniffling.

"If I don't come back, stay here as long as you can," I said from the cellar door. "Go two at a time to get what you need from the rest of the house, but stay indoors and hurry straight back to the shelter." I dangled a ring full of identical keys in the air. "Don't any of you leave the cellar without one of these keys."

"Okay," Tasha said. The others slowly nodded. Harry scampered up the steps, ready to leave with me, but I told him to stay. He sat down on the landing and coughed.

"Nana," Keno said, "usually a CME only affects a small area—like one city or one state. But if it was strong enough to fry the cars, it could've affected a whole lot more."

"Like how much more?" I asked, and Tasha covered Mazie's ears.

"North and South America, maybe. The whole daylight side of the planet."

My heart jolted and momentarily took my breath away.

"Let's hope it was smaller then. I love you," I said, and I closed my beautiful grandchildren into the cellar.

CHAPTER 6

I crept from the pantry and into the kitchen. Its floor was covered with stacked drums of dried beans, flours, and grains, and the counters were loaded three layers high, two-deep, with five-gallon tins of vegetable oil and peanut butter. I went through the dining room, which was crammed with shelves of canned foods and supplies, like kitchen matches and soaps. I skirted past the living room with its cartons of canned goods and toilet paper, bags and barrels of beans and grains, heaped floor to ceiling. With an anxious sense that none of this was enough, I climbed the stairs.

On the second floor I passed two bedrooms, a den, and a bathroom holding more barrels, bags, and cases of food, plus another bedroom full of five-gallon water jugs. I went to a room packed with seeds, fertilizer, and gardening and canning supplies. I searched the closets, one of which was locked and filled with four bolt-action rifles, two semi-automatics, six pistols, all the requisite gear, and several shelves full of ammo.

I didn't find what I was looking for, so I descended the stairs and went to the three-car garage. There I encountered ropes, wagons, wheelbarrows, chainsaws, rototillers, and scads of tools. Behind a wood stove, kerosene stove, stacks of firewood, and jugs of various fuels, I opened another cabinet and pulled out a Geiger counter.

I wanted to check the neighborhood for radiation.

THE HUMID, SMOKY AIR OUTSIDE set my lungs to wheezing—again. This was different than the floating ash from the train wreck. This smoke was new. Scattered plumes of it rose in the near distance—beyond our neighborhood but close enough that we'd need to keep an eye out. The haze kept me from checking the condition of the sky itself.

It was late in the day, and the sun was low in the west. The glaring lack of modern-day background noise sent prickles up my spine.

I didn't want to draw attention to this house. I hunched down as low as I could manage and slinked across the garden path to the split in the hedge.

After my ears adjusted to the deafening quiet, I heard voices—first a few, then a lot. Once in the safety of my own yard, I looked over the side fence and up and down the street to see people milling about on sidewalks, sitting in yards and on porches, fanning themselves. Three guys were pushing a car from the street up into a driveway. Jack Jeffers stood with a cluster of people, hovering around the black Honda CR-V now roosting on his flattened front fence.

Ducking into the privacy of my covered patio, I switched on the Geiger counter, my heart racing as the instrument ticked and its meter steadily rose. The needle settled in the normal radiation range, thank God, though I didn't feel much better. It was chemicals of unspecified composition and consequence that worried me most. And whatever was going on with the sky.

The air out here was simply unbreathable. I was wheezing my head off. But the westerly wind was still blowing, so maybe we'd be done with this ashy air soon—unless the wind fanned the nearby flames.

I went out the gate to join the cluster of people, who were talking about where they'd been when "it" happened. Gary Matheson's car had died about a mile away, and he'd been forced to walk home. One woman had been in the shower, and since the sun was coming through her blinds, she hadn't been using the lights. She'd been out of the shower for a while before she noticed how hot her house was getting, and that none of her clocks were lit.

"It must have happened while I was toweling off my hair," she said.

People were scarily hyper-animated, their emotions glowing beneath their skin—almost like a Van Gogh painting, with faces and bodies outlined in black, making their colors more vibrant, their expressions more extreme.

"Does anyone know what happened?" I asked.

Most folks shook their heads, but our neighborhood guitarist, Silas Barnes, said, "Seems like an EMP to me." Others nodded.

"Silas," I said, "do you think it was caused by a nuke or the sun?"

"Don't know enough about it to say. Just heard about EMPs in movies is all."

"I saw an EMP on that TV show *24*," Gary Matheson said. I was surprised he watched *24*. He'd always seemed so brainy and uptight.

"I saw that," I said. "It was a non-nuclear weapon that only affected a small area."

"I saw it in *War of the Worlds*," Silas said. "Some cars still worked though."

"Yeah, but Tom Cruise had to replace parts in his car, remember?" I said. "Anyway, that was sci-fi. In real life, there's a few ways these things can happen. Nuclear bombs, non-nuclear EMP weapons, the sun. There aren't any mushroom clouds, and the radiation level is normal, so it's probably not a nearby nuke."

Everyone gave me funny looks. Jack Jeffers narrowed his eyes. Of all our neighbors, I knew him best. He and I had run our neighborhood association until we disbanded because our neighbors weren't that interested in being organized. Plus, things between us got tricky.

"How do you know the radiation's normal?" Gary asked.

"Well. . . ." I hesitated, then said, "I checked it with my Geiger counter."

"What're you doin' with a Geiger counter?" Mr. Jeffers lowered his face to my level, making me feel creepy for having such an instrument and idiotic for saying so.

"What else you got squirreled away, Bea?" Silas asked, a snarky grin on his face. They all laughed. I winced. People around here had always treated me like a quirky enviro-nut, the way most of my family did. No one but Keno took me seriously.

"I've got a dozen Greenpeace beer koozies, Silas. If you ever need one, I'm your gal. Other than that, a Geiger counter is all." I wanted to get out of here, but first I needed more information. "So, how far does this thing go? Is it just here, or the whole state, or what?"

"No one knows," Mr. Jeffers said. "There's no way to find out, far as I know, until the power comes back or someone travels through."

"Goddamn gov'ment is screwin' with us," Mel Lewis blurted out. His face was red, his eyes hard. His two stout sons stood behind him, looking equally fierce. "They're takin' our power and cars away so we're easier to control. They'll let us suffer till we're weak, then they'll herd us all into FEMA camps."

"Oh, come on," said Gary Matheson. "That's crazy talk."

"Yeah? Well, prove me wrong." Mel Lewis strapped his arms over his chest, thrusting his chin toward Gary, who gulped.

"It might be the Rapture," Doris Barnes half-whispered, cowering beside her husband, Silas.

"Doris, did you see anyone disappear?" Silas said. "Ain't no Rapture."

"Well, it could be the start."

Silas rolled his eyes.

"That glow in the sky means somethin'," she said under her breath.

Any minute, some of these neighbors would be donning tin-foil hats.

"There's no use standing around spouting theories," Jack Jeffers said. "Bea, where's Hank?"

"That's just it. He and my grown kids were on the highway, heading home from the football game in Dallas. They were almost to Waco when he called me, fifteen minutes before it happened."

"Way-co!" He shuddered and looked askance, making his voice gentler. "There's always so much traffic in Waco. Have you been out to Manchaca Road to see all the car wrecks?"

"Good God, no." Car wrecks—I couldn't bear to think about them. "What about the water—is it safe?"

"What water?" he said. "Try your faucets, but water from the main lines is gone already. You should have some in your water heater. Wait for it to cool down though."

If I had been in my house instead of the secret cellar, I would've filled water containers straight away. People were already noticing oddities in my behavior. I needed to be more careful.

"Is all this smoke coming from car wrecks?" I asked.

"Mostly, but that plane went down," Mr. Jeffers said. "Just tumbled through the sky and fell out south, toward San Marcos. Probably were other planes, too, if this EMP is as strong as people say. Some houses are burning, too."

"Good grief, and no fire trucks, I guess?"

"You got it."

"Do you think the fires will come this way?"

"Anything can happen. Anything at all. Some of us men are talkin' about beefing up the neighborhood watch into a patrol to walk the perimeter in teams."

"Good idea. Do you think anyone will come rescue us? Like maybe this is only a local problem?"

"I wouldn't count on it.... No, I sure wouldn't count on it."

"No, they'll come," Silas said. "I'm not worried. They always come."

"That's right," Gary said, nodding adamantly.

Mel Lewis huffed and stomped away with his sons.

Mr. Jeffers dropped his head and shook it. "Listen everyone. Keep your fridges and freezers shut tight. They'll stay cold overnight, but if power's not back by morning, cook up all your fresh food within a day. Put your ice in insulated containers so you can keep things cold until the ice runs out."

I sighed. "Yeah. Thanks."

As I walked away, he said, "Bea?" and I turned to him. "Waco's only a hundred miles away. Hank and your kids could walk home if they had to. It would take a few days, but they could do it."

I bit my lip. "That's true. Thanks for reminding me of that. Gives me hope."

Everything seemed surreal. None of my neighbors—except possibly Jack Jeffers or conspiracy-minded Mel Lewis—wanted to believe we'd be without power and water for more than a few hours. I feared they were sadly mistaken.

HEADING HOME, I PASSED A MAN and a sobbing woman holding each other in the intersection. I passed teenage boys hanging on a stop sign, digging their sneaker toes into the dirt. Some dads and kids were playing football in the street. It was still an hour or more until dark. How could I get my grandkids home from the secret house without being seen? How could I protect us from a neighborhood full of hungry, thirsty people if this situation continued for long?

I hadn't thought of this in my pondering of potential catastrophes. I mean, I knew I would have to protect the stuff, but in my mind, I was protecting it from faceless evil people who would wander in from some unnamed elsewhere.

With my Geiger counter back in hand, I let myself into my main house. It was on the corner of Pico Street. My other house was on the opposite corner of Mint Lane. Pico and Mint.

The first thing I did inside the Pico house was reach for light switches. Doh! I wondered how often I would do that before the power came back. I went to the dark garage and fumbled around for ice chests, which I quickly filled with food and ice from the silent refrigerator.

I couldn't leave my grandkids waiting any longer. They'd be worried sick. I slid quietly out my back door. The street football game had stopped, so at least the neighbors were a little further away. I slipped through the opening in the hedge and hunched down while I made my way to the Mint house.

Hank, I thought, are you walking home to me now? Get some rest, sweetheart. Take your time, but keep coming. Jeri, Erin, Wayne, take care of your dad and each other. I've got the grandkids, and we're alright, but get on home to us, please.

I BROUGHT THE KIDS AND DOG HOME to the Pico house after making them promise to walk in absolute silence. They did a pretty good job. Keno even held back on his sniffling.

As soon as we entered the Pico house and each kid had flipped a few light switches, they went after me with questions about their parents, wanting to know what I'd found out. I told them as much as I knew. I emphasized Mr. Jeffers' comment that their parents and grandpa could walk home from Waco within days. They seemed to be cheered up, until Milo opened his mouth.

"But they could've been in a wreck."

"Shut up, Milo," Tasha said. I glowered at him. Mazie started crying again.

"Milo," I said, "we're going to assume they're coming home to us unless we find out otherwise. Understand?"

"Yes, ma'am," he muttered. I picked Mazie up and sat in Hank's rocker with her. Hank never allowed anyone else to sit in his rocker, but too bad for him.

"Kids, there may still be water in the pipes, but don't turn on a faucet or flush a toilet. All of you hear me? We'll make a better plan tomorrow."

OUT AT THE PATIO BARBECUE, I grilled hamburger patties, and we put them on buns with pickles, cheese, lettuce, and tomatoes. Much better than fast food. I figured it might be a while before we'd have more burgers of any kind.

We ate by the light of a couple of decorative candles. I instructed the kids on candle safety. I'd heard of too many houses burning down due to candles and lanterns in my life. And with no fire department, a house fire could ignite the whole neighborhood.

The food was good, but the kids didn't eat as much as usual. Probably too worried about their parents and this strange new world we found ourselves in.

"I wish my cell phone worked," Milo said.

"I know, sugar. I wish it did, too."

Tasha poked at her iPhone obsessively, stopping now and then to sigh, and going back at it.

"Tasha, you should give up on that phone for now."

"But I need to talk to my friends," she whined.

"I'm sorry, sweetheart, but you can't. Not until we get power again."

"But they'll fix it, right?" Milo said, a little frantically.

"I imagine so. But it could take quite a while to get new parts."

"Shit!" Milo said. I didn't bother to correct him because his comment was so apt.

"This is crazy," Keno said.

"Yeah. Nutso," said Milo.

Mazie crawled back into my lap.

"I don't believe Keno's stupid theory!" Tasha cried, hopping to her feet. "It's not the sun *or* a nuke. And they'll fix it, because I need my cell phone. It's not fair!"

Self-centered teenager logic was giving me a headache.

"Tasha, fair doesn't have a thing to do with it."

PART II

CHAPTER 7

After the younger kids fell asleep, I took Tasha and Keno back to the Mint house to fill a wagon with water jugs, chamber pots, guns, ammo, and fire extinguishers. We crept home without flashlights in the eerie night that was filled with the smell of burned tires and who knew what.

Through the upstairs window, we watched a fire burning yellow along the western horizon. It didn't look like a huge conflagration, but this drought-ridden place was a tinderbox.

"Um, kids. That's more than a fire over there. There's a yellow glow behind it, all the way across, as far as I can see."

Keno and Tasha crowded up next to me at the window, making anxious sounds in their throats. We ran to the front window and saw the same glow to the north beyond the trees. Tasha gasped out loud. I gasped inwardly.

"What is that?" I asked, though my breath had left me. "It's how I always imagined the northern lights would look, except it's all around us."

"I'll google it," Keno said, then he slumped. "Uh, guess I can't."

"Damn," Tasha said.

"It could be a glow from a geomagnetic storm," Keno said, and his breathing sped up.

I whirled around to face him. "What do you mean?"

"Back in the 1800s, the sun took out all the telegraph lines once, back before electric lines."

"I think I heard of that."

"The sky all over the planet lit up with colors, like the strongest Northern Lights ever seen, except it was in Australia, too." He ran his hands along his scalp beneath his hair, like he was fixing to squeeze his head.

Tasha grabbed hold of my arm. "I'm scared."

I pulled the trembling girl close. "I know."

"Okay.... Okay," Keno said, pacing in a circle. "Our sky isn't as bright as that. That was a total geomagnetic storm. I don't think it killed anyone. This doesn't seem as strong as that. There aren't bright colors all over the sky, right?"

"Good. . . . Good," I said, releasing a breath. I hugged Tasha hard. "Don't worry." I was trying to be comforting, though I needed comfort myself.

I pulled a chair in front of the big front window and sat down to study the yellow glow that rose and fell as though it was breathing. The kids stood watching with me, all of us seeming to breathe in time with the undulations of the glowing pulses of light.

I don't know how long we watched. Could have been an hour. The lights were hypnotic, so much so that the kids started nodding off.

"Kids, you should go to bed."

Tasha went to her bedroom and closed the door. Keno lay down near me on the futon in the game room.

"I think we've been lucky," he said. "A geomagnetic storm—if it's strong enough—it can suck the atmosphere clear off the planet."

"What?" I jumped to my feet, then tried to quiet my voice. "Is that going to happen? Could it still happen?"

He sighed a stuttering sigh, taking his time. His voice shook when he said, "Well, it could always happen any time, but it's never happened yet."

"Right. In all of history, it never happened. How do you know all this, anyway?"

He shrugged under his sheet. "I like space stuff."

"I hope you're right, Keno. I really do." I leaned over to kiss his forehead and smooth his covers. "Good night, sweetheart."

"Night." He squeezed my hand with an electric strength.

I went to my bedroom and used earphones to fiddle with the wind-up radio we had at this house. I didn't find anything but static, so I gave up after a frustrating half-hour.

I didn't sleep much. How could I when the world had changed so drastically, when the sun had gone crazy, when more than half my family was far away, possibly injured or dead?

Although I was operating on the assumption that Keno's theories about our situation were correct, I hoped like hell he was wrong about the power and right that we didn't need to fear the sun.

If I had been a praying woman, I would have prayed, but I wasn't, so I didn't.

Instead, I snuck downstairs for a shot of whiskey. I confess that I drank too much at night during that first and second week. And part of the third and fourth. I tried to hide my drinking from the kids. I'm sure I didn't succeed.

THE MORNING AFTER THE DISASTER, the smoke had cleared. The glow in the sky was still there, but it had lessened some. I rousted the young ones early, sat them in a row before me, and told them they had to do their pooping in chamber pots, which grossed them out completely. Grossed me out, too.

"Why can't we go to the other house to poop?" Milo asked.

"Because we can't let neighbors see us coming and going from that house. We can't let them know how much food we have."

"Why not?" "How come?" "But, Nana...." they pleaded.

"I know this is hard. But it's extremely important that you do what I say. Don't tell anyone about the other house or the food. Do you hear me?"

Before I got answers, there was a knock on the front door, despite the early hour. I answered the door to find Silas Barnes, Gary Matheson, and several other men and teenage boys.

"Morning, Bea," Silas said, removing his ball cap.

"Morning, Silas. What's up?"

He twisted the hat in his hands. "We're, uh, we're going scavenging for food and water. We wondered if your grandson can come."

"Keno? Where are you going to scavenge?"

Silas blushed. "Stores, empty houses, you know…."

"Empty houses? But that's theft. We've only been without power for less than a day."

"But without cars and water and phones, too. This whole thing is bad. You saw that weird light in the sky. If we don't get the food first, others will beat us to it."

"Silas, really? People may still come back to their empty houses. Are you that desperate already?"

"We're trying to avoid getting that desperate," Gary said.

"I can't let Keno go."

"Why not?" Keno exclaimed from behind me. "I want to go."

"Keno, I'm responsible to keep you safe until your mother comes home. This kind of thing could get you shot."

"Excuse me," Silas said, "but don't y'all need food?"

"Not yet," I answered, then almost slammed the door to hide how appalled I was at what I'd said.

Keno stood beside me, staring down into my face. "Please, Nana."

"No, I don't think so."

He threw his hands in the air and spun away.

"Can we borrow your wheelbarrow?" Silas asked, a charming grin on his unshaven face.

Before I could say no, Keno said, "I'll get it."

"Keno?"

"What?" He glared at me as he stomped out to the garage.

I NO LONGER TRUSTED THE SUN. I kept half an eye on the sky, night and day. I told myself that the sun would not go full rogue on us and send a pulse to suck our atmosphere away, but I had a hard time believing it. The one and only consolation I had—and it was twisted—was that, if it happened, we would die fast and our worries would be gone. I tried to bury my fear of the sun and concentrate on more practical concerns, like water.

Austin sits on the dividing line between the dry Southwest and the sultry Southeast. Inside the metroplex, things are fairly lush, yet still much too dry as of late. But we had three half-full lakes, the Lower Colorado River, and a great urban tree canopy, though the drought had killed too many trees. Procuring clean water was going to be our biggest problem.

We fired up the grill and cooked all the meat from the freezer, plus pepper-tomato kabobs and ears of corn. Most neighbors did the same; the meat was fixing to go bad.

Several people—men, mostly—got in their cars and tried to start them. But the only noises that came from any of those cars were dry-clicking ignitions, slamming doors, and loud curses.

When the meat was just getting going, who should appear outside my fence but the mailman, on foot with a big bag of mail in a kid's wagon. I rushed to the side gate, which was next to the cluster mailbox for my block.

"You're actually delivering mail? What a trooper you are."

"Thank you, ma'am. We had a lot of mail at the station. Thought we might as well get it out. No telling when more will come in, but when it does, we'll deliver it best we can. Makes me wish I had a horse."

"I think we're all wishing that about now," I said. "I sure do appreciate your work. Anything for me? Bea and Hank Crenshaw, 1211 Pico Street?"

"Sure is." He handed me a box from Express Scripts. My prescriptions. Hallelujah! Three more months of survival for me, though I'd finagled quite a stash for myself already.

"Does anyone at the post office know what happened, how far this thing goes? Is it all over the state or only here or what?"

"No one knows, but we expect we'll be hearing from our bosses, soon as they figure out how to get in touch with us."

"Will you let me know if you hear anything?" I asked.

"Sure will."

"Thank you, and thanks so much for keeping your appointed rounds."

The mailman stood up straighter and made a tipping motion against the brim of his hat.

I never saw him again, or any other mail deliverer for that matter.

A GROUP OF UNFAMILIAR MEN came down my side street that afternoon. They carried ragged bags of groceries and looked half beat-up—one with a puffy lip, another with torn trousers and a limp, a third with a black eye. They stopped to talk to Mr. Jeffers, then moved on out of the neighborhood.

Mr. Jeffers saw me watching, and when the men departed, he came to my fence.

"Those guys were down at the H.E.B." That grocery store was two miles southwest of us, and Mr. Jeffers had managed it for years, until he'd recently retired. "The store opened up to hand out their food, which is what I woulda done. But hundreds of people were there and not much food. Looked like the employees already cleaned the place out. I woulda prevented that shit. Anyhow, people being people, they had a big scuffle. Not a full-blown riot, but lots of shoving and punching, trying to get the last food off the shelves."

"Heaven help us," I said.

"You got that right." He stepped back, his mustache tweaked up at one corner. "Bea, how you doin'? You got what you need for those kids?"

"We're okay, thanks for asking." Though I felt guilty about it, I refrained from telling him how okay we actually were.

AS NIGHT FELL, the glow on the horizons gradually reappeared, though perhaps less brightly. Silas and his gang of looters sneaked one or two at a time back into the neighborhood, pushing overflowing wheelbarrows. They gave us a box of Butterfingers in payment for use of our wheelbarrow. It looked like they'd mainly looted beer, sodas, and snacks from a convenience store. And cigarettes.

After we and most neighbors had stuffed ourselves with meat all day, the kids and I chatted by the fading light of the barbecue. I sat with my back to the outer edge of the patio to avoid staring at the ethereal yellow glow, which was undulating as if it were alive. I wondered if it was some kind of fire that was too far away for us to see—a town, or an industrial complex maybe. Except that I could see the glow to the south as well, and I had seen it last night to the north. Besides, it had no smoke.

I needed to distract us from our worries, so I got the kids talking about their goals in life.

"I want to be a cop," Milo said.

"Really? How come?" I asked.

"It'd be cool to catch bad guys. Being a jet pilot would be cool, too."

"Sounds exciting. Better study your science."

"Really? Then maybe I'll just be a cop."

"You still have to study, Milo."

"Not as much, though," he said with a cockeyed grin. "Or maybe I'll be a general. I like to boss people around."

"You can't boss me around," Mazie said. "Mom told you not to. I'm gonna write stories when I grow up. I already wrote some."

"Stories. That's a great thing to do, Mazie."

"I want to be an environmental scientist," Keno said. "I wish I already was one. It would come in handy about now."

"No kidding. You kids make me proud. What about you, Tasha?"

"I don't know." She stood up and shrugged. "I was gonna go to college and travel the world to figure it out."

"That's a good plan."

"Well, it was."

"Honey, it still is."

She scrutinized me, wrinkling her brow. "Maybe I'll invent a cell phone that works without electricity."

"Great idea," I said. "Could you do that tomorrow?"

As we laughed, I suddenly remembered the solar panels. They weren't working right then because they were connected to the grid.

But there was a way to disconnect them and have them generate power on their own. I'd made sure of that before I bought them.

I mentioned this to Keno, and it got us all excited, especially him. He felt certain he could disconnect the panels from the grid and get us some electricity.

"Will my iPhone work again?" Tasha asked.

"There won't be any internet or transmission of calls. Whether it will play music and games, I don't know."

"Depends on the phone," said Keno. "Pretty sure mine is burned up."

"Yes, let's not get our hopes up about the phones. In the morning we'll search the house for the solar manual. It's too dark to find anything now, plus I'm too tired from all the cooking."

I was beyond exhausted. How could I keep doing this? I looked away, choked up with worry. When I had my voice under control, I said, "Time for bed, kiddos. We're going to get up early and get ourselves some power."

"Hoo-rah!" Milo said like a Marine, and we laughed.

IT TOOK ME THREE DRINKS TO FALL ASLEEP THAT NIGHT, partly due to worry, partly due to overexcitement. Daft old broad, why hadn't I thought of the solar panels sooner?

Plus, it was too quiet around here. That and the glow outside my windows unnerved me.

I finally fell asleep when I pulled out the Geiger counter and listened to the random tick of the ever-present background radiation—the radiation that always surrounds us, that comes from the rocks and the sun, and that causes us to age and die naturally, *if* we could manage to leave it the hell alone.

CHAPTER 8

For the next two days, Keno climbed like a long-legged spider over the Pico house exterior, checking connections on solar panels. Milo helped him occasionally from the ground, usually with Harry on his heels. The girls and I planted greens galore, winter squash, and purple hull peas in the raised bed in the side yard. We also harvested tomatoes and peppers from pots, and we planted more in seedling trays that could be brought inside when the weather turned, though it was mid-October and the weather showed no signs of cooling.

I didn't have much sunscreen, so I made the kids wear long-sleeved shirts and hats. They moaned and groaned about it, but I kept after them until they gave in. The Texas sun was bad enough in normal times, but for all I knew it could be deadly now.

Harry kept getting in our way in the garden and whining, still coughing some, which worried me. I had Milo take him for walks, but I insisted he stay on sidewalks I could see from my backyard. Why was Harry still coughing? I kept kicking myself inside.

Late morning on the second day, I heard racket inside my main house.

"What the hell?" I hurried to open the back door to find a freckle-faced boy bolting out the front door with an armload of canned goods.

"Catch him, Milo. Quick!"

Milo zipped into the house and out the front door. Keno clambered down the ladder and rushed out the gate as screams and curses exploded from the front yard. With my heart jumping out of my chest, I tried to catch my breath as I hurried out the front door.

"You're a freaking thief!" Milo had the smaller boy face-down on the ground amidst scattered cans of food. Keno had just arrived to pull Milo off the kid—a damned good thing since I had no breath to even speak. I leaned against the garage door and doubled over, gasping.

"What do I do with him?" Keno asked. He had the freckled boy by the collar, lifted up so that the kid's toes barely touched ground. Mazie and Tasha ran toward us from the backyard.

"Bring him here," I said, and I sat down on the door stoop.

Keno had the squirming, squealing boy in front of me in seconds.

"Let me go!" the boy cried.

"So, Mr. Freckles, what's your name? Where do you live?"

"I ain't sayin.'" He wriggled extra hard, and Keno twisted the kid's collar tighter.

"Why would you steal food from me and my kids?"

"I dunno," he muttered.

"I'm sure that you do know." I tried to catch the boy's darting eyes. "You have to tell me before we let you go."

The kid stopped squirming, and Keno relaxed his grip, but only a bit.

"Look me in the eye and tell me," I said.

Mr. Freckles didn't say a word.

"Do you have food at your house?" I asked.

He shrugged and started coughing.

"What am I going to do with you? Do you promise not to steal from us or the neighbors again? Because, I swear, if you do, I will let these boys beat the crap out of you. I might whup you myself."

The boy gulped, wide-eyed.

"Let him go, Keno."

"Wait! What?" Tasha said. "Why are you letting that little crook go?"

"What do you want me to do? Lock him up?"

"Paddle him or something."

"He's not my kid. As much as I'd like to paddle him, I can't." A week ago, I wouldn't have considered paddling a child at all, especially someone else's. Part of me wanted to give food to this kid, but I didn't want his family thinking they could come to me for food.

"Tell his parents?" Keno asked.

"Normally, that would be the way to handle it. But how do I know his parents didn't send him over here?"

My grandkids looked perplexed and angry. Keno let go of the boy, who glanced at each of us then took off running around the corner.

"Milo," I whispered, "follow that kid and see where he goes. Don't leave the neighborhood though."

"Really?" Milo turned to rush away.

"Don't let him see you, and come home before dark."

"K," he said, and slipped around the same corner where the kid had disappeared. Harry barked like crazy from the backyard as Milo ran past.

ONCE I'D GATHERED MY WITS, I fixed us sandwiches with the last of the bread and cheese. I made the kids eat tomatoes for the Vitamin C. They resisted, but they still looked scared, and I think they knew I was doing my best to protect them. I started a low fire on the barbecue and cooked a big pot of navy beans with a ham hock in it, the only meat left in the house except what was in cans. When it was almost dark, I boiled rice and stir-fried veggies—the last in the warm fridge—or the insulated cabinet, I guess it had become.

Milo came home sporting a grin a yard wide.

"Freckles lives at that house where the old motorcycle is."

"A Belding," I said. It figured.

AFTER SUNSET, I saw no more glow on the horizon or in the sky. I kept looking for it for days.

Over those first couple of weeks, we kept to ourselves. I felt more like I was holding my family together when we stayed apart from our neighbors, most of whom I barely knew.

At this point, we were all in limbo—or more like denial—thinking the government would arrive soon or the power and running water would return. I fully expected Hank to waltz in the front door any minute and start bitching about something. He'd only taken two weeks' worth of his blood pressure meds with him to Dallas. He had to come back soon.

Fretful grandmother logic.

WHILE WE ATE DINNER THAT EVENING, I told the kids, "Our project for tomorrow, and for as long as it takes, is to go through this house from top to bottom. We're going to organize everything we have and make lists of it all. This house is jam-packed with stuff. A lot of it should be helpful to us, either to use or to trade with neighbors for things we need."

"What about the other house?" Milo asked, screwing up his face thoughtfully.

"We're going to wait to start using things in that house. I have to figure out how to do it without letting the whole neighborhood know how much food we have."

"But they need it, too, don't they?" Keno said. His big green eyes appeared sad.

I sighed and looked at my plate. "They do. But we can't take care of them all or there won't be enough for us. I have to think up a plan."

"You can't share the food," Tasha said. "We'll run out. And they don't deserve it."

"Whatever do you mean by that?"

"They didn't hoard food like you did, so they're shit out of luck."

"Tasha, where did you get the idea that I 'hoarded' food?"

"The whole family said you hoard stuff."

"They made jokes about it," Milo said.

"Did they? What kind of jokes?"

"Oh, if they couldn't find something, they said you probably hoarded it."

I wanted to run to my room and cry. "It's not hoarding if you're buying stuff for an emergency. It's stockpiling. And don't you think it's good that I did it?"

"Well, yeah," Tasha said. "But it's still weird."

I shook my head and tried to let it go. I sat there cleaning under my fingernails with an untwisted paper clip.

"So, the question is, how do we know who to trust, and how do we decide who to help and who to leave unfed? It's breaking my brain trying to figure this out." It was like playing God, and I hated the idea of it.

"Think it over," Mazie said, surprisingly. "You always say to think things over."

I gave Mazie a kiss on the cheek. "That's right, honey. We should all think it over."

I would think it over for weeks.

AS THE KIDS SETTLED IN TO BED UPSTAIRS, I let Harry in the house. He immediately started coughing so hard it made him choke. Damn it. I thought he would have coughed up all the toxic crud by now. Were the poisons still in our air?

I got my stethoscope and petted Harry while I listened to his lungs. I heard sounds like crinkling cellophane, exactly like the crackling I'd heard in my own chest when I'd had pneumonia years ago.

"Kids," I hollered up the stairs. "Come down here, please."

Milo groaned loudly.

"Why?" Tasha asked.

"Because Nana said so," Mazie replied. Smart girl.

The kids reached the bottom of the stairs and stopped in a cluster, eyeing me warily. "Come line up here in front of me."

"Oh, Nana," Milo said angrily.

"Just do it. You first, Milo. Raise up your shirt."

"Why?"

"So I can listen to your lungs."

Milo huffed and lifted his shirt over his head.

"Hold still." I laid the stethoscope on his chest. "Breathe slowly and deeply for me one time." I listened, then moved the instrument over his other lung. "Now again." I moved to his back. "Again," and, "One more time."

"You sound okay, Milo."

"I know," he said and tugged down his shirt.

I listened to each child in turn. Their lungs sounded clear to me, but I was an amateur. It was what I didn't know that worried me most.

"Why are you doing this?" Keno asked after I listened to him last of all.

"Because Harry has stuff in his chest. I wanted to see if anyone else did."

"But we didn't?" Keno said.

"You didn't."

"What does Harry have in his chest?" Mazie asked.

"Mucus, honey. He's been a little sick ever since the train wreck."

"Poison?" Tasha said.

"Yes, poison. I guess it only affected Harry because he was in the neighborhood for so long after the chemical spill."

"Poor Harry," Mazie said, running up to hug the dog. "Did Nana forget you and make you get sick?"

GUNFIRE WOKE ME IN THE NIGHT.

I'd always heard the occasional gunshot around here—it was Texas after all—but this was a series of shots, then a second series from a louder gun, probably a semi-automatic less than a mile away.

I was afraid to look outside, but I tiptoed around upstairs, peeking out windows to survey our surroundings. A couple of patrolling neighbors were walking in partial crouches down Pico Street, rifles raised as if on alert. I watched until they were out of my sight.

I sat up in bed the rest of the night, straining my ears for sounds of danger. I heard no more gunshots but didn't sleep another wink.

Gunfire already, and it had only been four days since the power went down.

CHAPTER 9

We found the solar power manual the next morning. It said the system would only work without the grid if we connected it to some type of fancy, lead-acid battery. I thought I'd set the solar up for long-term electricity generation without the grid—the salesman had assured me of it. I couldn't believe he'd lied to me like that. I could have easily afforded the $60,000 battery and several spares if I'd known we needed them.

I felt like an idiot—for trusting that guy, but mostly for thinking I'd set things up right when I hadn't. By no means the worst thing I'd been wrong about lately, but it still pissed me off.

We sorted stuff for two days upstairs, where all four bedrooms, two bathrooms, and the game room were. The kids groused and grumbled for the whole two days. I had to ride herd over Milo to keep him working, and Mazie spent most of her time playing with things we unearthed. But slowly, we progressed.

I put Tasha in charge of cooking on those days so I didn't have to climb the stairs so often and wear myself out. It had the bonus effect of giving us a break from Tasha's grumpiness. I had her warm up beans and rice, and later to heat up canned soups. Soon I would need to start baking with the solar ovens stored at the Mint house.

A good name for the place holding the family treasure: The Mint.

On the second day of sorting, Harry lay in his dog bed and watched us, droopy-eyed. Milo tried to get Harry to play, but the dog only sighed, and Milo worried. At least Harry hadn't been coughing, only chuffing now and then. I assumed he was getting better. Probably also missing Hank.

I missed Hank, too—the old Hank, the charming Hank, the one I used to talk to about so many things and who would respond like a thoughtful adult. I only hoped this time apart would bring more of the good Hank to the fore.

It's no wonder the world was running out of resources. I couldn't believe how much rubbish we had in our house—just one of millions of American homes—not things accumulated so much from my so-called hoarding as from our failure to get rid of unused or extra belongings.

For instance, we had fourteen pairs of scissors. Will someone please tell me what possible excuse there could be for us to have fourteen pairs of scissors?

And we had four outdated computers, two old laptops, and a couple of newer versions of each. Monitors, keyboards, mice, printers, DVD players, DVRs, TVs, radios, phones, iPods, stereos, game systems, satellite TV receivers, routers and modems and digital clocks.

Why in the world did we have so many electronic devices, all full of toxic heavy metals, flame retardants, and more? I'd thought I was protecting the environment, but we'd been out of our ever-lovin' minds!

HALFWAY THROUGH THE SECOND DAY OF SORTING, we heard a loud engine. We hurried to the upstairs window to see a junker half-ton truck heading our way. The kids ran outside, and I followed. Neighbors stood on their lawns with their mouths hanging open, their kids jumping up and down. Several men rushed up to flag down the driver.

"Ooh-wee! How'd you get that thing to run, man?" somebody said. I couldn't hear the driver's response, but it went on for a while since the neighborhood guys kept interrupting.

The truck sputtered a bit and drove on. We applauded. The story we heard was that truck was so old it didn't have an internal computer to burn up in the EMP. Its battery was disconnected when disaster struck, so the truck worked fine when the battery was re-installed. It had taken the driver days to find gas, but he'd finally succeeded by scrounging from neighbors. He had to promise to bring them news and as much water as he could find. His truck bed was full of empty water jugs.

Mr. Jeffers asked the man to come back soon so we could hear about his trip and whether he'd found a water source. Mr. Jeffers said he knew how to filter water through charcoal to clean it.

My neighbors looked hot, dirty, and disheveled. Most of the men had serious beard stubble. Everyone's hair was oily. I'm sure my family and I looked equally bedraggled to our neighbors.

WHEN THE UPSTAIRS WAS PRETTY WELL ORGANIZED, except for my hundreds of books, I made pancakes on a griddle I set on the grill. We smeared them with peanut butter and honey. Not bad, though I would never make pancakes as good as Hank's.

Oh, Hank....

As we finished eating, Tasha poked Keno in the ribs. He cleared his throat.

"Nana," he said, "me and Tasha—"

"Tasha and I."

Keno frowned. "Tasha and I want to go to our house tomorrow. It's only four miles away. We can walk there pretty fast, and we can get our bikes. If we can take Milo, he can ride Mom's bike, and we'll have three."

Of all the things I'd amassed for our long-term survival, bicycles hadn't been among them. I'd considered turning my exercise bike into an electricity generator, but bikes for transportation had never occurred to me.

"Yeah," Tasha said, "we can get jackets and more clothes, maybe clothes that fit Milo and Mazie."

"How come they get to go and not me?" Mazie asked.

"Nobody's going," I said. "It's too dangerous. We have clothes here that you can wear."

"Nana," Tasha pleaded, getting red in the face. "We need the bikes. It's not fair!"

"I don't care if it's fair or not. My answer is no."

THE FOLLOWING MORNING, Keno and Tasha were still after me to let them go to their house.

"You shouldn't go! I don't want you to!" Mazie hollered and ran upstairs, only to come streaking back down, trembling and spouting tears.

"Harry's sick! He's real sick! Come make him better, Nana. Hurry!"

The kids bolted up the stairs, and I plodded up behind them, short of breath.

"Harry!" Tasha squealed from up ahead of me.

"Oh no!" Milo said.

I couldn't see Harry yet, but I saw Keno rush toward the dog bed in the game room.

"Hurry, Nana!" Mazie ran back to me as I reached the top of the stairs. She gripped my arm and dragged me toward Harry, but I stopped when I caught sight of him. He lay in his bed in a pool of bloody vomit with his eyes closed and his breaths shallow, labored, and loud.

"Oh, Harry," I said softly, my heart twisting in a knot. What had I done to my dog?

"What's wrong with him?" Tasha asked, her face slick with tears. Milo gaped at Harry, then wheeled away and ran to his room. Keno bent down to pet Harry's head.

I wiped my eyes on my sleeve and went to Harry, laying my hand on his rib cage, which rattled with his every breath.

"He's burning up with fever." I couldn't quit cursing myself. It would take a lot of water to help Harry. Could we afford it? Oh, who cared? His life was at stake.

"Keno, Tasha, go get two big jugs of water. We'll put him in the bathtub to clean him up and cool him down. Mazie, get a can of dog food, a spoon, and a can opener."

Mazie ran downstairs with Keno and Tasha close behind. I sat on the floor and patted Harry. "Milo, honey, can you come help, please?"

The boy came out of his room but kept his head down, his sandy hair over his eyes—to avoid looking at Harry, I presumed, and also to hide his tears. "Kiddo, go to my room and get the bottle of Tylenol off the dresser. In the bottom of my linen closet, there's some old towels and washcloths. Bring me all those."

Milo darted into my room. "Mazie," I hollered downstairs, "bring a paper plate and a hammer, too."

"Okay!" she replied as Keno and Tasha came upstairs, Keno carrying his five-gallon water bottle while Tasha pushed hers up the stairs from behind.

Harry let out a horrendous string of coughs. How he managed to breathe after that, I don't know. He glanced at me, a pained look that sent shivers through me.

I told Keno and Tasha to take the water to the bathroom and pour five-gallons into the tub. I had Mazie open the dog food.

Harry kept coughing. When Milo returned with towels, I said, "Can you help me wipe Harry off, so we can pick him up and take him to the tub?"

"What?" Milo's eyes were as round as bottle caps.

"I know it's gross, sweetie, but Harry needs our help. Can you be brave and help me do this?"

Milo looked hard at me and set his jaw, sniffing away tears. "Okay."

I handed him a towel, and together we wiped the dog. Harry whimpered when we stuffed towels under him to clean what we could from his underside. The other kids came back just as Harry launched into a coughing fit that went on for minutes, inducing more tears from the kids and me with every sharp hack.

"Keno," I finally said. "Do you think you can carry him to the tub if we help you?"

"Yeah, I can do it."

"I'll help," Tasha said.

"Me, too," said Milo.

"Can I help?" Mazie asked.

"Honey, you're too small to carry him, but you can help wash him."

Keno bent down, slid his arms under Harry, and didn't even flinch at the slime. When Keno lifted Harry, the dog yelped, and Tasha and

Milo jumped forward to support his hind legs. Harry whined but didn't seem to have the strength to squirm loose. The kids carried the big lug into the bathroom and laid him in the tub.

Harry squealed as he sank in the water, then he licked the kids' hands. He slurped a bit of water and barely wagged his tail. Mazie started washing him off, and the other kids helped.

I put a Tylenol pill on the paper plate and smashed the pill with the hammer, then took a tiny spoonful of dog food and worked Tylenol flakes into the food. I didn't know if Tylenol would help a thing, but I couldn't sit back and watch Harry's fever kill him without trying something. I couldn't think what to give him for his cough.

"Stand aside a minute, kids. Let me give this medicine to Harry." I leaned down and held the spoon toward him. He clamped his mouth shut and turned away. Food was probably the last thing he wanted to see, but I didn't know how else to get the medicine into him.

Mazie knelt beside me. "Can I try?"

"Sure, go ahead."

She took the spoon in one hand and Harry's chin in the other. He blinked at her with doleful eyes.

"Harry, this is good for you. You have to take it so you'll feel better."

He flicked his eyes to each of us, as though asking, "Is this true?" We nodded and spouted encouraging words. He licked Mazie's hand then ate the food, wincing as he swallowed.

We drained the tub of vomity water and poured in the clean water to rinse Harry off as he shivered and wheezed. We re-drained the tub and dried him off. Keno picked Harry up and brought him to the game room couch to lay him on a quilt that Tasha quickly spread.

"Let's wash our hands really good," I said. "And Keno, take off that shirt. I don't think Harry's contagious, but just in case."

The kids and I washed up then sat around Harry and petted him. He licked our hands. Then he laid down his head, breathed several wheezy breaths, coughed once, and shuddered.

When Harry didn't breathe for a long moment, Keno, Tasha, and Milo turned to me—sad, surprised, shocked. I nodded, frowning, and

Mazie started shrieking.

"He's not breathing. Make him breathe! Nana, make him breathe!"

"Oh, honey, I can't." I reached for Mazie, but she slapped my hands away and began poking Harry's motionless rib cage.

"Breathe, Harry. You have to breathe!"

Tasha grabbed at Mazie's hands to stop her from poking the poor dead dog. But Mazie just grew more hysterical. "Make him breathe. Nana, why don't you fix him?"

"Sweetheart, I can't fix him. I'm so sorry." I couldn't fix Harry. I couldn't fix the power or the cars or any freaking thing. I could not have been more goddamned sorry.

Mazie would not let up. She continued to screech and cry and plead for help for Harry while the other kids surrounded her in a tangle of embraces. I reached into the pile of crying children and extracted Mazie.

I pulled her into my chest, saying, "Shh, sweetie, shh...." while she clung to me fiercely and her shrieks subsided to gasps for air. The room was silent except for the sobbing. At last I felt Mazie melt in my arms. She took stuttering breaths, and I continued to hold her.

"He was such a sweet and friendly dog," I said. We'd always thought of Harry as Hank's dog, because Hank brought him home as a puppy, and he loved to play with Hank. But Harry was my daily companion during those years when Hank went out to his job and I worked from home. Harry kept me from getting lonely. He followed me around and made me laugh. I already missed him mightily.

And Hank was going to kill me.

I WENT OUTSIDE TO HUNT for a place to bury our dog. Mr. Jeffers passed by, so I told him what happened.

"Aw, I'm sorry, Bea. He was a good dog."

"He had a fever. I don't know how long he had it, but I gave him some Tylenol—"

"You can't give Tylenol to a dog!"

"What? Are you kidding me?" More tears filled my eyes.

"No, I'm afraid not," he said.

"Do you think the Tylenol killed him?" I wanted to jump off a cliff, but we didn't have one around here.

"I don't know, but it didn't help."

"Oh my God. I've done everything wrong when it comes to that dog. What if I mess up that way with the kids?"

"You won't, Bea. You love them too much." He smiled at me with understanding.

"I loved Harry, too," I said.

"Yes, but you have much more experience with kids. You're not a veterinarian, but you're an awful good mother."

It was weak of me to need his reassurance so badly, but I definitely needed it.

"Thank you," I muttered, hanging my head in shame. I peeked back at Mr. Jeffers. "Keep an eye on me, will you? Don't let me screw anything else up so bad."

"I will," he said, "but you won't." I didn't know how he could be so sure about that.

I couldn't tell the kids about the Tylenol. I needed them to have confidence in me, even if I didn't have much in myself.

I LET MILO DIG HARRY'S GRAVE. The boy was devastated, and I hoped that doing something for Harry would help.

We buried our good dog in a square of dirt on the side of the house, outside the backyard. Neighbors came by to inquire what we were doing and offer condolences. Some extra kids stuck around for our little ceremony where each of us said something good about Harry and all of us cried.

A tall teenage boy with a reddish ponytail stood among the extra mourners. When Tasha's crying grew fevered, he stepped up to her.

"I'm sorry about your dog," he said.

Tasha nodded, a puzzled and embarrassed look on her teary face.

"Thank you, but who are you?" she asked.

"I'm Chas. What's your name?"

"Tasha," she muttered, her face flushing.

"I'm sorry about your dog, pretty Tasha. You look like you need a hug." He opened his arms wide, and she leaned in for a quick hug, a shy grin spreading over her face.

Isn't that nice? I thought. Tasha had found herself a friend.

LATER THAT DAY, Keno took me aside. "Nana, there's this old farm where my dad used to take us to swim in the creek."

"You're thinking of it for water? That creek's probably dried up in this drought."

"I know, but it had a well—a deep one. The pump's hidden under a falling-down barn."

"Really? So, who owns the place? Where is it?"

"Out past Manchaca. I don't know who owns it. No one was ever there."

"Do you know how to get there?" I asked.

"I can figure it out with a map."

"But how would you get a bunch of water home?"

"Silas and them could go with me. We'll take wheelbarrows and wagons and stuff."

What Keno was contemplating was extremely dangerous. Thirsty people will kill you for water in a heartbeat. But the boy was almost a man and needed to feel his worth.

"Kiddo, there's a local road atlas on the bookshelves by Grandpa's side of the bed."

Keno gave me the slightest of grins and bounded upstairs. I wondered if I should tell him about the cistern, to save him the risk of hiking miles for water and hauling it home. But the cistern only held ten thousand gallons. It sounded like a huge amount, but Hank and I alone had sometimes used two thousand gallons in a hot month. We were using a tiny fraction of that now, but with all these kids to cook for and keep clean, we needed alternative sources. And Keno needed to fight back for his family.

The risk worried me sick, but if anything was worth exposing oneself to danger over, water was it.

This is what I kept telling myself while my heart treaded water in an ocean of dread.

FOR DAYS, we couldn't stop crying over Harry. We organized the downstairs and garage while we sobbed and sniffled and sighed. I guessed Harry's death was a kind of catalyst to make us openly grieve about the entirety of our ordeal.

The only thing Milo got energetic about was bouncing a tennis ball against the garage door from the driveway, shaking the whole house and driving me mad. Ka-thunk, ka-thunk, every time I let the boy out of my sight.

On one of those afternoons, Mazie was helping make lunch when she stopped to look at me. "You said Harry wouldn't ever want to leave me, but he did."

"He didn't want to leave you. He couldn't help it."

"But you let him get sick and die, right?"

"Honey, I'm not God. I don't have any control over who gets sick and dies."

"But you're supposed to take care of everybody."

I breathed a long sigh. "I try, but I made a huge mistake. Sometimes people make mistakes. Can you forgive me, do you think?"

Mazie studied me, wrinkling her brow. "What if you forget me and leave me somewhere?"

I took hold of Mazie's arms and lowered my face near to hers. "Sweetheart, I will never forget you. Never ever."

"Do you think my mama forgot me?"

"Mazie, your mother's love for you is bigger than the sky. She couldn't possibly forget you."

"Well, when's she coming back?"

"As soon as she can, my love. As soon as she can."

CHAPTER 10

Three days after Harry died, nine days since the electromagnetic event, Keno and Tasha started bickering upstairs, but I couldn't make out their words.

Then Tasha said, "Don't tell her! Let's just go."

"I'm telling her," Keno insisted.

"Don't!" Tasha yanked Keno toward her as they reached the bottom of the stairs. Both kids were wearing backpacks and carrying empty duffle bags.

"Tell me what?" I met them in the entryway, hands on my hips.

"We're—"

"Keno, shut up!"

"No, Tasha. You hush."

"Stop arguing and tell me."

My red-faced grandson snapped his head around to lock his eyes on mine.

"We're going to our house," he said.

"What? You can't!"

"Yes, we can, and you can't stop us!" Tasha retorted.

"Tasha, shut up. Nana, we'll be home in a few hours."

I was stunned. But Tasha was right. I couldn't stop them without pulling a gun. Desperately, I made one last try.

"What will your mother say when I tell her you disobeyed me?"

Tears came to Tasha's eyes, but Keno said, rather coldly, "Our mom's not here."

Milo ran in from the kitchen, hollering, "I'm going, too!"

"Oh, hell no!"

"No, Milo. Stay here," Keno said. "Take care of Mazie and Nana."

"It's not fair!" Milo cried, jerking his hands at me in some kind of agitated plea.

"All of you need to stop this crap about things not being fair," I said. "Nothing is fair anymore."

Keno opened the front door, and Tasha rushed outside. Keno looked back.

"Sorry, but we have to," he said.

I wanted to sink through the floor or fly into a rage. "Do you have food and water?" I muttered.

"Yes. Bye," he said, and they were gone.

I COULDN'T GET MY NERVES UNDER CONTROL after this teenage revolt. Milo and Mazie slouched around all morning. I tried to get them to play ball or one of the board games we'd uncovered, but they just wanted to mope. I might have moped myself if I hadn't been so scared and pissed-off.

I fired up the grill and tried cooking biscuits in a cast-iron skillet atop the fire. I figured if I kept turning them over, it might work. The biscuits were oddly shaped, but they tasted good. We still had about a quart of melted margarine left. I hoped that the chemical preservatives would prove useful for once and keep the oleo from spoiling before we could finish it off.

For lunch we had biscuits, margarine, and a can of chili. Then I gave the kids washcloths, bars of soap, and plastic tubs full of water, and I sent them to separate rooms to clean up.

"I wanna wash my hair," Mazie said.

"That will have to wait. Get your face, your armpits, and your filthy feet. And don't forget your private parts."

"Nana, don't talk about private parts!" Mazie marched to her room with her tub of water.

I took water to my own room, cleaned up, and tried to read a novel by the sunlight streaming through the window. But it was hard to see the words with my weak eyes, and my warring emotions had exhausted me.

"NANA!"

I woke to Mazie's cry and a loud bang on my bedroom door. I leapt to my feet.

"What?" I barked.

"I'm hungry," Mazie shouted through the door.

"Hungry?" Good lord, it was almost dark outside. My wind-up wristwatch read 6:45. "Mazie, are Keno and Tasha home?"

"No. Where are they?"

Oh my God. They should have been home hours ago.

"I don't know, honey." I rushed out of my bedroom and down the stairs. "Mazie, come help me light candles and make some food."

Why did I fall asleep, and why for so long? How could I feed Mazie and Milo when I needed to go find Keno and Tasha? And how could I even go find them?

"Where's Milo?" I asked, out of breath.

"He went outside a long time ago," Mazie said.

I opened the back door and yelled, "Milo? Milo, come home!" No response. I rushed to the side fence and shouted louder, "Milo Raintree, where are you?" A bunch of kids laughed down the street. I went through the gate to the front yard with Mazie tagging along.

"Milo!" she shrieked in a pitch shrill enough to wake the dead.

"What?" he hollered.

"Come home!" Mazie ordered.

"Who says?"

"I say, Milo," I cried. "Get over here."

"Yes, ma'am."

I watched him approach in the quickly fading light, and when he reached our corner, I headed for the backyard. "Come with me, kids. I need your help. Milo, have you seen Tasha and Keno?"

"Hey, no. Why aren't they home?"

"I wish I knew." I lit two kerosene lanterns. "Milo, you cannot leave this house without permission."

"But you were asleep."

"Then you should've stayed home. You left Mazie all alone. Here, take these lanterns very carefully and set them on the sidewalk that leads to our front door. Not the big sidewalk, the little one."

"Why?" he whined.

"So Keno and Tasha can see."

Milo headed slowly for the front yard, carrying the lanterns. I sent Mazie to light candles in the front room. I went to the kitchen, where I lit more candles and scrounged for food. Way up high in the pantry was an old box of graham crackers out of my reach. Why did I have to be short at a time like this? I swatted at the crackers with a long-handled spatula until I knocked them off the shelf and caught them before they hit the floor.

I grabbed a paper plate, a jar of peanut butter, and a plastic bear with a few ounces of honey left inside. I frantically smeared peanut butter and honey on several graham crackers.

"Mazie, come eat." I poured her a cup of water.

"This is my dinner?" She sneered at the messy plate in the candlelight.

"It's a special treat dinner, since you had to stay home today." I slapped together another "special treat dinner" for Milo.

I can't raise these kids, I thought. I'm too old. I need Hank to help me. Before he'd grown so cranky, he'd been good help with the grandkids. Keno and Tasha wouldn't have dared defy their grandfather.

"Come with me, Mazie. Bring your food and water." I took Milo's plate and cup and headed for the front door with Mazie in tow.

"Here's your dinner," I said to my grandson, who was bouncing that danged tennis ball against the garage door by lantern light.

"That's dinner?" He caught the ball, wrinkling his nose.

"It's a special treat dinner," Mazie said with her mouth full.

"Take this plate and cup, Milo. Hurry up."

"Okay. Geez Louise."

"That's what Daddy says, 'Geez Louise.'" Graham cracker crumbs flew out of Mazie's mouth.

"Is that so?" I stepped to the middle of the street and strode back and forth. It was black as a dungeon out here. Where was the glowing horizon when I needed it?

Keno. Tasha. I kept repeating their names in my head like a magic chant, in between calling myself an idiot for letting them get away.

"Kids, stay here and be on the lookout for Keno and Tasha. I'm going to see if Mr. Jeffers can help us find them." But as soon as I stepped farther from the lanterns, I couldn't see anything except blurry candlelight in a few spots across the street.

"Milo, run and get me a flashlight!"

"I'm eating!"

"Well, stop eating and go get a flashlight."

"Geez, Louise," Mazie said. "Nana's mad." In the lantern light, I saw Milo shoot me an angry look before he ran inside.

"I'm not mad. I'm worried."

"I told you not to let them go," she said.

"I didn't let them go. They just went."

As Milo came running outside with the bobbing flashlight, a rifle shot zinged through the air. Crap, it was close.

"What was that?" Milo shouted.

"In the house, kids. Now!"

"Why?" Mazie said.

"Gunshot. Go!" Though I barely had the strength, I yanked Mazie across the threshold with me.

Once inside, the panic-stricken kids went straight to the front window.

"Get away from that window!" I was nearly hysterical.

They got away, but after I paced the room, freaking out, I went to that window myself, straining my eyes for sight of my grandkids or a gunman, my ears about to pop from listening so hard. No more shots. Not yet. I stepped away to start pacing again.

"Is that a bell?" Milo asked. He and Mazie rushed to the window with me.

"I don't hear a—"

A dinging bell rang through the dark—a bicycle bell.

"There they are!" Mazie said. Sure enough, two flickering lights were approaching. Two bells sounded, and two sets of tires whooshed against the asphalt.

"We're here!" Keno hollered.

I rushed outside to meet Tasha and Keno, practically shoving them into the house, bicycles, backpacks, and all.

Tasha said, "What are you—"

"Get inside. Quick!"

I grabbed the lanterns and dashed inside behind the kids and bikes.

"Did you guys hear that gunshot?" I asked, completely out of breath. I set the lanterns on the coffee table and plopped down in the rocking chair. I'd like to see Hank try to get this chair away from me now.

"What gunshot?" Keno said.

Tasha let her bike clatter to the tile floor and ran over to smother me with a hug. "I was so scared. It's so dark."

"What happened?" was all I could manage to say.

"The wheel popped loose on my bike. I fell and scraped up my hands." She reached her hands into the lantern light. Her palms were covered in red abrasions, and her cheeks were stained with dust and crisscrossed by tear tracks.

"Ouch," I said. "Thank God you didn't break a bone."

Keno stood his bike with the kickstand. "I had to fix Tasha's bike," he said. "Good thing I got some tools from home."

"If you had listened to me, you wouldn't have needed tools. What if something had happened to you? How would I have known it? I have to ground you, you know."

"Yeah, I figured," Keno muttered with his eyes fixed on the floor. He looked up but past me. "Milo, come help me unload stuff."

"I'm eating." Milo took a defiant bite out of a graham cracker.

"I'll help." Mazie ran to Keno's bike and pulled off a bag so heavy it almost knocked her to the floor.

"What are you eating?" Tasha asked with a laugh.

"A special treat supper," Mazie said.

I tried to smile, but that gunshot. Why was it so damned close?

Tasha and Keno unloaded bags full of hoodies and other clothes, plus a little food and a six-pack of good old Coca-Cola. I told them they had to go to bed at dark for a week. I couldn't exactly take away their TV or driving privileges. They didn't complain much. I think their rebel excursion had spooked them.

"Mazie, look what I found from when I was little," Tasha said. She pulled a pink, ruffled skirt from her backpack.

"A Disney princess skirt?" Mazie said, in an excited state of awe. "I love it!"

Mazie put on the flouncy tulle skirt over her clothes, and was seldom seen without it for months.

"Tasha, that was sweet of you," I said, and she blushed.

We had another special treat supper of Ritz crackers and spray cheese with olives and smoked oysters that the mutineers brought home. Then we drank warm Cokes and listened to the tale of Keno and Tasha's trip while I tried to settle my still-fluttering heart.

It had taken them hours to get to their house because they'd passed so many things they stopped to look at: burned-out houses, some of them still smoldering; godawful piles of wrecked cars; dirty kids running in little mobs; a convenience store with its windows smashed out and nothing left inside; scads of people camped in the post office parking lot; a creek where folks had set up a hoist and were filling water jugs. I hoped those people knew how to filter that water.

Keno and Tasha said their house was weird without their mom and with no lights or TV. And they were upset because their mother's bike was missing.

"I don't get it," Keno said. "Everything was locked up. It didn't look like anyone broke in. How could the bike be gone?"

"Does someone else have a key to your house? Like a neighbor or a friend? Or the landlord probably has one."

"The landlord," said Tasha, in a worried way.

"Maybe he just borrowed the bike," I said. "Was anything else missing?"

"I don't know. I was scared, and I wanted to get out of there," Tasha said.

They'd started home fast without stopping to check their surroundings because they were nervous about being away from here so long. But then, Tasha's wheel came loose.

"There's tons of stuff in that house," Tasha said. "Blankets, clothes, candles, plus a bunch of food. And Mom has some big bottles of water in the garage."

"Well, that's good to know. I don't know how to get it over here though. If you kids keep going in, someone will notice and break into the house after you leave. Anyway, now that you've scared me to death, I don't want you to go back."

"But Nana," Keno insisted, "I can get the bikes in better shape before we go. And I can bring tools."

"But what about the gunshot? It's not safe out there."

"The gunshot was here, not out there," Keno said.

"Nana, we need all that stuff," said Tasha.

"I'm sorry, but it's not safe. We have lots of stuff here."

"But Mom's pictures and jewelry are there. And her wedding dress that she gave me!" Tasha was so adamant, the veins in her temples were throbbing.

"Nana, don't you want the wine from their cellar?" Mazie asked.

"What cellar?" Keno and Tasha said together. Mazie's mom and dad, Jeri and Tom, were much wealthier than Erin. Leaps and bounds wealthier. Poor privileged Mazie thought everyone had a wine cellar.

"They don't have a wine cellar, dummy," Milo said.

"I'm not a dummy!"

"If we all go and take wagons, we can get more stuff." Milo changed the subject before I could reprimand him.

"I can't walk that far," I said.

"Why not?" Milo asked.

"Because I'm almost seventy years old, and I have a bad heart."

"That's really old." Mazie looked somewhat amazed.

"I could pump you on my bike," Keno said.

"Ha. Can't you just see me, balancing on your handlebars?"

We all started laughing and couldn't stop. The kids flailed their arms and made horrified faces, doing funny imitations of me freaking out on Keno's handlebars.

When we settled down, I said, "Sooner or later, we'll have to team up with some of our neighbors. Once we do, maybe a contingent of neighbors could go to your house and bring back things to share."

"Yes!" said Tasha. Keno didn't seem so sure. For no discernible reason, Milo did a cartwheel across the living room.

"What's a con-tinge-it?" Mazie asked.

MUTINOUS TEENS LEFT ME FEELING TERRIBLY LONELY, but it was only late at night that I allowed despair to show its face.

Back when I'd tried to convince my family we were headed for cataclysm, I hadn't pinpointed it to either a nuclear EMP or a solar pulse. In fact, I'd fully expected us to die from drought, famine, plague, a poisoned environment, or increasingly devastating storms.

But I knew we were ripe for traumatic trouble and were in poor condition to survive it. Openly discussing such things marked me as an outlier, a kook, a nut to ignore—even in my own family. "You're paranoid," they said. "Don't be a downer," they said.

I tried to explain that it wasn't paranoia if the threats were real, but my family tuned me out. They had shopping sprees to plan, lovers to romance, Netflix shows to binge-watch.

They made me furious, but more than that, I was hurt to the core. I could not understand why they didn't love me enough to hear me out.

Finally, I thought, "I'll get ready anyway. I'll show them!" But, alas, I hadn't shown them a thing since the adults weren't even here.

Oh, Hank, if I had done a better job of explaining things, would you have heard me?

Are you trying to get home to us now? How soon can you get here? I can't find where you've stashed your screwdrivers. I can't sleep without your loud breathing in the bed. I don't have another adult to talk to, even one who doesn't listen.

There's a Hank-shaped hole in my life without you.

CHAPTER 11

Bang! Bang! Ka-Bang!
Loud knocking at the back door made me fly out of bed. Was it Hank? Or trouble?

Keno beat me to the door, but I was right behind him, pulling on my robe and holding a pistol.

"Sorry to wake you," Mr. Jeffers said, his mustache askew. "You're usually up making breakfast by now. I've got something for you all." He had a bundle tucked under his arm.

"I didn't fall asleep until dawn," I said. "Did you hear that rifle shot? I've heard a lot of guns lately, but this was close."

Mr. Jeffers turned red in the face. "Sorry. That was me."

"You? Why would you shoot a gun? Did someone attack you?"

"No, I—"

"You scared us to death. What were you thinking?"

"I shot a deer in the field behind my house. Brought you some meat." He thrust out his hand, which held a bloody towel, apparently covering a deer haunch. But I couldn't accept such a gift from this particular man. It would open a door that I'd tried to keep closed.

"That's kind of you, Mr. Jeffers, but do you think it might be poisoned? That deer could've been grazing by the train tracks."

"I've never seen deer around here before. Have you? I think this one came in from the country, since there aren't cars and other noises to scare her away."

"I'm afraid to eat it."

"Really? More for me then." Grinning wryly, he retracted the meat. This was an offering of fresh meat, the main food we didn't have.

"It's very generous of you," I said, "I guess I could boil it and pour off the water. I'd lose the vitamins, but we'd still have the protein."

"There ya go. You need the meat for your kids."

"Keno, please take this meat and set it in a roasting pan, then wipe your hands with a bleach wipe."

Keno looked nonplussed, but he took the meat. I followed Mr. Jeffers out the back door, though it was hard to keep up with his long, lanky strides.

"What are our neighbors doing for water?" I asked. "How will they survive?"

"Interesting that you're worried about neighbors but not yourself." He looked me hard in the eye.

I grimaced. "I've got my rain barrels and some bottled water."

"I'll tell you a secret," he said, "but you can't tell anyone. There's a drainage pond surrounded by trees, so it's pretty well hidden over by the train tracks."

"There's poison down there."

"No, this is almost a mile upstream from the wreck. Only my patrollers know about it. There's not enough water for the whole neighborhood."

"Okay, but what are the patrollers doing for food? Seems like all Silas and his crew have found are snacks and beer."

"And they're lucky to have it. We found a bunch of food in that train."

"But the chemicals!"

He sucked in his lower lip. "Relax, Bea. It's canned goods. Lots of big cans of beans, vegetables, tuna, cooking oil, beef stew. It should last us a couple more weeks."

"And then what?"

He sighed deeply. "Don't know."

"Are your patrollers sick from climbing in that train?"

"Two of them have coughs, so yeah."

"That's awfully grim."

"Grim ain't the half of it," he said.

"You should have told me. I have gas masks."

"Do you?" Mr. Jeffers narrowed his eyes to scrutinize me while I struggled to meet his gaze, struck by a wave of emotion I had forbidden myself to feel.

As he turned to leave, I said, "It's awfully sweet of you to bring us the meat."

"Yeah?" He grinned, erasing the tiny age lines around his wide mouth. "I was hoping you'd like it."

"I do," I said, smiling back.

A GROUP OF NEIGHBORS WALKED many miles around the city and came back to report seeing no open businesses of any kind and no signs of a repair effort. Mostly they saw evidence of looting and people toting water in various ways.

Why wasn't anyone trying to fix the electricity? Was it because they knew it was hopeless?

I guessed folks were too absorbed in saving themselves and their families to think about saving others. But what happened to the people who trained for emergency interventions, who dedicated their lives to this sort of thing? Was our entire society going to descend into chaos for want of power and cars?

Something wasn't right about this. Maybe the government was helping, but hadn't made it to our area yet. There was nothing we could do except to keep waiting—for our loved ones and for any relief.

OUR INDOOR PLANTS WERE EITHER HALF-DEAD OR WORSE. I watered them a couple of times because I didn't want anything else to die. But I soon gave up and took the plants outside to fend for themselves.

And the candlelight, which I'd always found so magical in the past, now cast a gloom over everything.

The boys and Mazie seemed to be in better moods. I was relieved about finishing the house organization, but I was in a worse mood than ever about Hank and the grown kids. It had now been ten days and we hadn't heard a word. Even if they'd walked only ten miles per day, they should have been home by now.

The man with the truck came through again and said other neighborhoods in town were in about the same shape as ours. He'd seen a few other old vehicles making their way between dead cars on the roads, and cops in wrinkled uniforms hanging around outside the police station downtown.

"People are getting restless," the man said. "Got to get them water and food soon."

"I think we better figure on getting those things for ourselves," said Mr. Jeffers. "Did you find a place to get water?"

"Me and hundreds of other folks were downtown taking it out of Town Lake. Don't know how long that will work out, but we've got that for now."

"Don't forget to filter it," Mr. Jeffers said as the man drove away.

Lady Bird Lake—that had been the name of Town Lake for years. Evidently, I wasn't the only old coot who kept forgetting that.

Tasha seemed very unhappy. I often heard her crying at night, missing her mother I'm sure, but also missing her familiar life and her cadre of friends, who, without telephones or internet, might as well have been in Bangkok. I wondered if she longed for a particular boyfriend, but she refused to discuss such things with me.

And I kept catching Milo wasting water, pouring a quart or two over his hands to wash them, dumping drinking water in the toilet to flush it, being careless and busting a gallon jug of fresh water when he slammed it on the counter.

"Milo, please! You have to treat water like it's life and death. We can't live without it, so it *is* life and death."

"But we have all that water at the other house," he said, brushing me off with a cocky grin.

"Milo Raintree, you have no idea how fast that water will disappear."

I gathered the kids and watched them roll their eyes and tap their feet, slouching this way and that, while I went through the mathematics of our water usage versus our limited supply. I didn't mention the cistern, hoping they'd be thriftier with water if they remained unaware of the reserve.

By the end of the lecture, the four kids looked gloomy. I hated making them gloomy, but I wanted them to survive.

CHAPTER 12

Twelve days since catastrophe struck, and still no cavalry, no electricity, no Hank.

Certain neighborhood kids were becoming a problem—kids between about eight and fourteen, mostly but not all boys. They ran in a pack like dirty, snot-nosed little animals. Their parents seemed to lack the gumption to deal with them. Folks were losing heart. I almost wished the adults would act crazy and show some fight, rather than sitting back resigned to the end, like the proverbial frog in the water as it rose to a boil.

I forbade my grandchildren from going near the misbehaving kids, but my grandkids had outdoor chores to do, and the unruly kids were running wild everywhere.

Worse though, in our neighborhood with no power and little water, people were getting sick. We heard them upchucking in their yards—first a couple of Gonzales kids next door, then someone across Pico Street, then others at the end of the block. Mr. Jeffers thought they must be drinking bad water. My kids and I put four five-gallon water jugs in two wagons, along with a kitchen funnel. Keno stayed home to chop firewood while the rest of us went to houses where I'd heard or seen sick people.

Milo and Mazie knocked on doors then hightailed it back to the sidewalk with Tasha and me. When people answered their doors, I told them we didn't want to get too close in case they were contagious, but if they'd set out containers, up to three gallons per house, we'd give them water.

Mrs. Gonzales was so grateful that she cried.

An irritable old man said, "Are you crazy? I'm not taking water from kids." An admirable sentiment, but he could have been nicer about it.

"We have enough water for a while, sir," I said. "I wouldn't be giving it away if we didn't."

He scowled, but he set out a jug and glowered at us while we filled it.

I asked people if their water had made them ill. Some folks didn't seem to know, others said probably. But the teenage girl at the Belding house said she was sure it was the water, because she'd refused to drink it, and she was the only one in her family who wasn't sick. The girl was rumpled and dirty, her reddish-blonde hair hanging in uncombed tangles down her back and over half her pale face.

"Why did you refuse?" I asked her.

"Because they got it out of the creek." She curled her upper lip in disgust.

"Did they filter it?"

"Yeah, but it was gross."

"Well, creek water would taste bad, honey, but you have to stay hydrated or your kidneys will shut down. Which creek did they go to?"

"The one by the train tracks."

"The train tracks? Didn't they remember the wreck and the chemical spill?"

"That's what I told 'em. But they said the news told us everything was safe."

Good grief. Didn't people know that the news only repeated whatever lies the chemical companies told them?

The girl hung her head, wiping her eyes. "What's your name, sweetie," I asked.

"Darla. Darla Belding."

A loud groan arose from inside the house—the sound of a man in pain? Mazie took a big step backward. Darla cringed and turned to hurry inside, then she shot me a look of sheer panic.

"You need help?" I asked. She nodded yes.

Sweet Jesus, I did not want to go in that house. But this dirty, wan girl with her pleading blue eyes had a grip on me.

"Wait here," I said to my brood. "Don't leave, but don't come inside either." They gaped at me solemnly, scared I thought.

I followed Darla into the filthy house that smelled like vomit and diarrhea and something rotten and sharp. Mr. Belding—thinner than I'd ever seen him—sprawled across the couch moaning, his breaths loud and raspy, like Harry's. This family had stayed in the neighborhood after the train wreck, too.

Mr. Belding didn't look up, and Darla led me deeper into the house. The stench took my breath away and made my eyes water. Once this family had gotten sick from the poison, opportunistic germs must have been having a field day in here.

We passed a room containing a teenage boy, lying on his bed, wheezing and staring at a poster of a bare-breasted woman on his ceiling.

At the end of the hall, Darla tapped on a door. Bedclothes rustled, followed by a string of harsh coughs. A raspy voice said, "Darla?"

Darla slowly opened the door. When Mrs. Belding saw me, she gasped and pulled the sheet to her chin. Her face was gaunt, her arms shockingly thin.

"Hello, I'm your neighbor, Bea Crenshaw. Darla says y'all are sick. I thought I'd see if I could help." Based on my experience with Harry, I doubted I could keep the Beldings alive. I'd never much cared for them, but I certainly didn't want them to die.

"I don't got no way to pay you." She made it sound like a curse.

"You don't have to pay me. We're neighbors. I'm glad to help."

The woman sighed and let her head fall into the pillow, choking back a cough.

"Do you mind if I check your pulse and temperature, Mrs. Belding?" I stepped toward her. She nodded feebly. Her pulse felt rapid and thready; her skin was plenty hot to the touch. The bruised-looking circles around her eyes frightened me.

"I can send you some Tylenol and Pepto-Bismol, some clean water, potatoes, and cans of soup. Will you be so kind as to accept these things from me?"

"Yes," she said and closed her eyes. She shivered as I backed away. I shivered, too.

Just as Darla and I re-entered the hall, that freckled boy who'd tried to steal our food came out of the bathroom. The kid was so thin that his ribs protruded. His chin and chest were splotched with what had to be dried vomit. He coughed loudly without covering his mouth. I didn't want to go near him. He was like a lawn-sprinkler, throwing out germs far and wide.

The boy registered shock at seeing me and stepped back into the bathroom. The reek coming out of that bathroom was horrendous. I almost wretched.

"I guess your little brother is sick, too, Darla?"

She nodded and wiped tears and snot across her face.

"Okay, I'll send this stuff in a few minutes. You'll need to wash your brother then wash your hands very thoroughly. Don't touch your face until you've washed your hands. And you need to open some windows in—"

"I opened the windows, but they were too cold."

"They have fevers, so they have chills. Give them blankets and open the windows. We have to get this germy air out of here. Plus, all of you have to stay out of that bathroom. Use buckets or pots. Dig a very deep hole and bury it."

Darla looked horrified, and I felt the same way. But I couldn't stay here any longer and risk getting sick myself, or risk carrying germs to my family. I had an urge to invite Darla to our house for supper, but I didn't dare. She mumbled her thanks.

"Imagine that—drinking polluted creek water," I said to my kiddos as we made our way home. "That poor girl's whole family is very sick. If you drink something with lots of germs in it, you can often get over that. But if you drink chemical poisons, it could kill you."

"Nana, don't say 'kill'!" Mazie hollered and ran off ahead of us toward home.

What I didn't say to Mazie—or any other child—was how worried I was about poisons in our surroundings. I'd been assuming that those who got sick didn't evacuate or drank bad water, but I didn't know this for sure. We might be a bunch of dead people walking, already doomed to early graves.

I checked my kids' chests with the stethoscope again as soon as we got home.

I had Keno take Darla the food and other things I'd promised.

"Stay outside, honey," I told him, "and try not to touch her."

Keno was gone for a couple of hours. When he came home, I raised my eyebrows at him.

"She was lonely. She needed someone to talk to."

"That's nice of you. But you stayed outside, right?"

"Yeah, we sat on her back porch."

"Bless her heart." I smiled at him, pausing for a beat. "She's pretty, isn't she?"

Keno ducked his eyes and turned a bright shade of pink. "Yeah," he muttered.

THE NEXT DAY I FOUND KENO SCANNING MY BOOKSHELVES.

"Whatcha lookin' for, kiddo?"

"You got any books of poetry?"

"Yeah. What kind of poetry?"

"Something real nice," he said.

"Because … ?"

"Darla likes pretty poems."

"Ah. I've got just the thing. Come to my room." It took me a minute, but I found my own favorite on the shelves. "Here's *The Complete Poems of Emily Dickinson*. They're some of the most beautiful poems ever written. You can loan the book to Darla, but I want it back."

"I'm going to read them to her. She likes the way poems sound," Keno said. "She can't read too good."

"Too well, honey. She can't read too well." I don't know why I cared about his grammar, given our circumstances. Grasping at threads of civility, I supposed. "That's a sweet gesture, Keno. I'm proud of you."

After supper for a few evenings straight, Keno washed up, combed his hair, and scampered down the street with the poetry book in hand.

He always took Darla some dinner and water as well. So cute....

IN THE DEEP DARK, late on the second night that Keno visited Darla, it rained and rained. I woke the kids up, and we ran in and out of the house, setting up every pail, pan, and bowl we could find to collect rain. I didn't care if the containers were dirty. I could use that water to flush toilets or mop floors.

Through the lantern light in my window and a few dim lights around the neighborhood, I saw other folks setting out pails and buckets as well. One guy used a long-handled cooking pot to scoop up water along the curb and dump it into a trash can he dragged behind him. Ingenious, really. I didn't see any of the Beldings out there. Too sick, I guess.

We came inside, laughing and soaking wet, changed into dry clothes, and went back to sleep.

Our rain barrels were almost full come morning. Two hundred fifty gallons of clean water, and several more pots and bowls of it. The ten-thousand-gallon secret cistern should have been topped off as well.

Mazie and I came down with colds that afternoon. Did we catch them from the Beldings? From the rain? Who knew?

CHAPTER 13

Over and over since the disaster, I woke before dawn in a stew of sweat and worry. It always took me a while to catch my breath. Then I listed possible scenarios in my head of what might have happened to the other adults in my family and why they hadn't come home to us. Without question, they could have died, but it seemed so unlikely for all six of them to die in one car crash.

They could have had horrible injuries, and without medical care, languished in terrible pain and discomfort until they died from complications or neglect. Perhaps they got split up in the chaos of the event and spent days trying to find each other. If they'd started walking home, they could have been beaten or killed along the way.

In more hopeful moments, I thought the family must be camped out somewhere, or that aid workers were taking care of them. Or maybe some were injured and others not, and the uninjured ones had refused to leave the hurt ones behind. If Wayne's girlfriend, Pam, was the only one in good shape, she might have gone home to her family and couldn't reach us. She was Wayne's fourth girlfriend in recent years. I'm not proud of it, but I hadn't put much effort into getting to know her. I'd had my heart broken too many times by my kids and their erratic romances.

But the parents of my grandkids—Erin, Jeri, her husband Tom—they would have moved heaven and earth to get home to their children, and Hank would have wanted them to. He would've insisted they leave him behind so they could get back to his grandkids and check up on me.

I hoped if Hank ever did make it back that—once the initial euphoria wore off—we wouldn't have problems getting along. I was a different person after being independent and in charge these past weeks. I might have a short fuse for his micromanagement of me, or I could be so happy to see him that I'd let him boss me around for the remainder of our lives.

None of this brainstorming helped me get back to sleep. Instead it fueled my paranoia.

SINCE I HAD A COLD, I didn't do much the following two days except tinker with the wind-up radio and play board games with bored kids. Well, I did get the toilets flushed with rain water we'd collected in dirty containers, and I supervised the kids while they mopped floors, did dishes, and scrubbed counters. I told them we'd wash our hair after we were better from our colds.

And we each laundered our own shirts, socks, underwear, and towels. We didn't wash jeans and shorts, because it was less important that those clothes be clean.

The pollen around here was so noxious that I didn't want to hang our clothes outside to dry. We would always be sick with allergies. Pollen could give us sinus infections and bronchitis, which could kill us without the right meds. So, Keno put up a laundry line with pulleys in the game room upstairs. We hung our dripping clothes on the line and raised it to the high ceiling. We didn't use much water to rinse the clothes, so they were plenty stiff later when they dried.

The first night after we came down with colds, Keno and I had to sneak over to the Mint to get food that didn't need to be cooked, since I didn't have energy to fire up the grill three times a day. I was running out of firewood at the Pico house anyway. My charcoal needed to be saved for water filtration.

We had to wait until two a.m. to do our sneaking because so many men were out on patrol, plus the wild kids were roaming around. The men didn't have anything to occupy their time, so they paraded around feeling useful at all hours of the night. My guess was that the honest patrollers were keeping the kids from busting in to the Mint. But any minute, Silas and his friends might decide to break in, and who would stop them?

While Keno and I waited, one fellow passed by with an old-fashioned torch on a big stick. Freaked me out, it seemed so medieval.

But I guess that's what we were now, medieval. Only we didn't even have a feudal system to grow and distribute food. What a bunch of spoiled idiots we were.

Keno and I languished on the patio until the patrolling thinned out. One of the few good things about the lack of electric light was the panoply of newly visible stars. Truly amazing how many had been blocked by urban light pollution. Now we could see the Milky Way, which I hadn't seen since I went to the desert fifty years ago.

But I was plenty nervous about sitting outside at night, what with all the gunshots. Hardly a night passed that I didn't hear some kind of gunfire, sometimes in the far distance, sometimes too close to home. Mr. Jeffers told me that his patrollers had chased off distressed men and women many times. I felt sorry for those people, but their desperation scared me to death.

On this night, several men had congregated in Mr. Jeffers' front yard. I suspected they were burning his wrecked cedar fence in his *chimenea* because so many sparks were flying through the air. Those guys needed to save that fence for firewood or garden stakes, but instead they were using it as a focal point in some sort of male bonding ritual. It wasn't even chilly outside.

When the men seemed to be deep into loud conversation, probably tippling some of the last of their booze, Keno and I sneaked through the hedge into the Mint yard. Luckily, I had tight blinds in the Mint so that we could use a flashlight inside without alerting the patrol.

If my neighbors ever found out that the Mint was mine and decided to question my ownership, I would never be able to prove it. I'd hidden all my documentation online. Brilliant, Bea. Simply brilliant.

The internet. Was all that data forever lost?

KENO AND I CAME BACK WITH FIREWOOD, cold medicines, cans of tuna, beans, chili, and two boxes of Vanilla Wafers. I gave Keno a whole box of wafers; he looked awfully skinny.

"I don't know what to do about the neighbors," I said. "They need food, and I have what they need. But I'm afraid if I share it, we won't have enough for our family, especially when the rest of them come home."

"Yeah, but you can't let people starve."

"That's why it's such a tough problem. We can help a limited number of people, but as soon as we do, everyone else will know what we have in the Mint. We'll have to keep it under armed guard."

"Desperate people can overrun guards," Keno said.

"I know, and that'll be a bigger risk once the word spreads to more and more people."

"It's a risk we have to take though," he said, rather adamantly.

"Yes, but it scares me. What if we run out? On the other hand, if anyone catches us hoarding food, they might take it away from us."

Keno blinked at me, sniffing his nose.

I wondered if it might be better to die together than to live while we watched our neighbors die. Some of them were terribly thin already. From my yard, I often saw neighbors sitting listlessly, as though they had no energy at all.

But my first responsibility was to my grandkids, and I was loath to put them at risk. God knows what the future might hold for them or how long they could survive on my stockpiles, if they could even hold on to the food in the event of an attack.

"Nana," Keno said, "Me and Tasha—Tasha and I—we're going after the water tomorrow night."

"What? There's all that gunfire at night. You can't." I could not cope with this. "And you have to realize that Tasha is a beautiful girl in a lawless world. You can't take her away from home anymore."

"That's not fair to Tasha."

"Yes, but neither is rape or kidnapping."

Keno swallowed hard and sat down next to me. "If I go during the day, people will see me. They'll follow me there or attack me for water on the way back."

"Have you thought this through and planned it? Why don't you and someone else ride your bikes out there during daylight? You can find the place, for one, and be sure the water's still there. You can look for paths that will conceal you. Be like an advance scout, the way the military does."

"Can Milo go?"

"No. Don't you know anyone else you could bring?"

"No one that I trust," he said.

I exhaled loudly. "How far is it?"

"Seven miles, unless I find a shortcut."

I closed my eyes. I hated this whole idea, but if I could keep Keno talking to me about it, maybe I could make the trip safer.

"Milo's only twelve," I said, opening my eyes.

"He'll be thirteen any day," Keno said, as if that made it easier for me to let Milo go. But it was only a bike ride in the daytime, I told myself.

"I guess you can take Milo for the bike ride, but never at night."

"Thank you," Keno said. "Thank you."

But the next morning as Keno and Milo were leaving, Tasha pitched a fit about wanting to go.

"Why does Keno get to do all the cool stuff? You just want me to clean and cook and garden and babysit!"

"Tasha," I said, with as much patience as I could muster, "this is not a safe world for pretty young women to be away from home."

"What about pretty young boys? How am I supposed to grow up if you won't let me leave home?" She had me there.

"Honey, maybe things will get better soon."

"Yeah, right." She flopped onto the couch, burying her face in a pillow. I left her there. I didn't know what else to do.

The boys returned in late afternoon, overexcited and exhausted. They'd found the farm and the water pump. They'd even found a shortcut that reduced the trip to six miles, plus an abundance of tree lines to hide amongst. The water they brought back tasted clean and sweet. I should have felt happy, but fear knotted in my stomach.

I told Keno about Mr. Jeffers' secret pond. "You can't go back to the well until the pond water runs out," I said.

"But everyone doesn't get the pond water. It's a secret. What about the Beldings?"

"I'll give them water for now. No more arguing," I said.

Keno blew a frustrated buzz through his sputtering lips.

Mr. Jeffers spotted me on the patio a day later, cooking biscuits and scrambling powdered eggs on the grill. I invited him into the yard and offered him food and coffee. He didn't turn me down.

Unlike most of my neighbors, Mr. Jeffers looked better to me than he had prior to the EMP. He had some spring in his step, and his hair had more body—a little mussed on top, similar to the deliberate messiness so popular with the young ones. His scruffy whiskers balanced out his mustache, which had struck me as too militaristic before.

"Where did you get these eggs?" he asked. "You didn't cook old eggs, did you?"

"No. They're powdered."

"Powdered? I haven't seen powdered eggs since I was in Nam. How come you had powdered eggs? Don't you like real ones?"

"No, I love real eggs. I love real food in general. I had the eggs for—you know—camping."

"Well, that's damn fortunate," he said.

My face felt hot. "So, have the patrollers caught any more intruders?"

"Caught some two nights ago," he said.

"Really? I was outside and didn't hear anything."

"It was down at the other end of the neighborhood. But you shouldn't be outside after dark. Not anymore."

"You're right, Mr. Jeffers."

"You can call me Jack," he said, frowning.

"It's been a long time since I called you Jack. I don't know if I can do that or not." I liked having him around to talk to, but I didn't want him getting the wrong idea. Why didn't I call him Jack? To keep him at a distance, that's why.

"Suit yourself." He dug into the biscuits and eggs. I let him eat while

I dished up plates for the kids and called them to the patio table. I gave them bigger helpings than I gave Mr. Jeffers and myself.

When he finished, he leaned back and rubbed his slight belly. I picked at my food. Those rubbery eggs were congealing in my gullet.

"Did you see that young couple who drove the red VW—they moved away yesterday?" he said.

"Did they say where they were going? How did they go?"

"They walked out wearing backpacks and pushing bicycles loaded with camping gear. Said they were heading to the Hill Country to find a place to live off the land."

"Sounds rough, but at least they're young. I hope it works out for them." I gathered my hair and twisted it around to tie it in a knot. For years, I'd kept my graying hair in a neat little bob, a little too short to tie back.

"The Slaughters are leaving, too," Mr. Jeffers said.

"Really? But they have all those kids. How will they do it?"

"She's got family on a farm out near Smithville somewhere." He pulled a toothpick from his shirt pocket and chewed on it. "They're going to walk and ride bikes, push a wheelbarrow."

"Good Lord, that's sixty miles," I said.

"My friend who drives the old truck, Sam? He says lots of neighborhoods are emptying out fast. Ours seems to be running behind."

"Do you think ours will empty out, too?"

"It might, Bea. It just might."

"What about you, Mr. Jeffers? Are you leaving or staying?"

"I'm staying for now."

"I have to stay because I can't walk very far," I said.

"Makes sense. You seem to be doing pretty well, though. You look kinda rosy-cheeked." He leaned toward me with a glint in his eye. I drew back, thinking how old I looked with my arms and hands covered in liver spots, and so many wrinkles in my neck.

"Well, I'm losing weight, which is good for me. What worries me is the kids looking so thin."

"You got plenty of food, Bea, for these kids?" He surveyed the kids as they scarfed their breakfast.

"We have enough for now, Mr. Jeffers. We have enough for now."

I now had an answer to my dilemma. I would wait until more people moved away, and I'd feed those who stayed behind.

"Shouldn't we do something about our neighbors not having food?" I said.

"Like what? Don't even think about giving them your food. You need it for these kids." Thankfully, the kids kept their heads down and their voices quiet.

"What about hunting?" I said. "Are there more deer nearby, do you think?"

"I've been looking, but I haven't found any. There's lots of deer west of town, but they won't last long next to a city full of starving people. Thousands of people live out there anyway. The squirrels are disappearing. Did you notice?"

I gasped. "No, I didn't."

"I trapped a possum and ate it the other day."

"Really? I've seen raccoons around here, but they won't last long either, I guess."

"No. Neither will the doves." He gazed at me intently.

Tasha jumped up and hurried to the fence to talk to that kid Chas as he passed by.

"I'm surprised we haven't been attacked for the food we have," I said.

"Me, too, but we've got our patrollers keeping us safe so far."

"Yeah, that probably scares folks away for now, but they'll get bolder as time goes on, and if they ever band together, we're screwed."

"I reckon you're right," he said. He ran his eyes over me as though he was sizing me up.

Jack, I thought, surely you know not to go there.

CHAPTER 14

The next afternoon, as I cooked pots of rice and beans on the barbecue, two policemen in dirty uniforms rolled down the street on bicycles. The pack of wild kids and the increasingly scraggly dogs chased the cops down the street and around the corner.

The following morning a troop of people came into the neighborhood, carrying clipboards and shoulder bags full of leaflets. They fanned out, going up and down blocks, knocking on doors, lingering on doorsteps. They looked hot and ragged, and when they came to my house, they identified themselves as workers for the City of Austin. They were trying to ascertain who was still in town and what kind of shape people were in, what we needed most, that sort of thing.

The leaflets—which were actually mimeographed and appeared to have been typed on a manual typewriter—gave information on how to filter water and said medical care would be free now.

The flyer confirmed that the disaster was caused by a coronal mass ejection from the sun. As Keno had thought, the solar pulse had affected the whole of the Americas. They didn't know whether other continents were affected. The feds couldn't contact ships at sea or their overseas bases, but they'd sent a courier to our mayor's office. Who knew we still had a mayor?

We shouldn't count on being rescued, but we already knew that. We should do what we could to take care of ourselves, our families, and our neighbors. Different levels of government would work on making water more available, distributing food, and trying to get medicines under production and vehicles on the roads. Due to the lack of fuel, they would concentrate on solar-powered electric vehicles.

Finally, they think of that. To be fair, they'd thought of it before. But maybe now they would actually do it, necessity being a mother and all.

One day later, we heard rumbling in the distance, like semi-tractors or heavy equipment, out on the main road then slowing and growing closer.

Soon the noise was so loud that everyone in the neighborhood stood in their yards staring south. At last, a tractor-trailer came around the corner and stopped near the Mint. Another big truck drove past the semi, then stopped in the middle of the road, both trucks killing their engines.

"Attention! Attention! We are the Texas National Guard," came a voice from a set of speakers atop the second truck. "We have relief supplies, but we will not hand them out unless everyone—everyone!—behaves in an orderly fashion. We are well-armed, and we won't put up with any pushing, shoving, or arguing. Gather your families and line up behind the semi. Distribution will begin in three minutes."

"Woohoo! Told ya they'd come," Silas Barnes hollered from behind me, amplified by other exclamations around us. Folks grabbed their spouses and kids and headed for the trucks.

"Keno, get a wagon or two," I said. "I'll get in line." I trudged in that direction but was overtaken and left in the dust by that kid Chas who'd hugged Tasha. He wore a baseball cap obscuring his eyes, and his ponytail had disappeared beneath his hat. He shot to the front of the line as it formed and bounced in place.

"Hey!" said a man Chas had jumped in front of. "I was here first!"

"Snooze, you lose, man," Chas said, turning up his hands in an exaggerated shrug.

"We're not kidding about no arguing. We'll just drive away," said a skinny guardsman with his hand on the rifle strapped to his shoulder.

"Sorry." With a shit-eating grin, Chas stepped behind the other guy, then paced back and forth, licking his lips, a few pounds lighter than he'd been last time I'd seen him up close. All the neighbors had lost weight; some seemed shaky and frail.

A pair of guardsmen strutted up the lengthening ration line from the rear. When they reached Chas, the kid said, "Y'all got any booze? I could make a real fair trade."

"You ain't old enough for booze, kid," said one guard.

"What you got to trade?" the other asked.

"Somethin' good and harder than hell to find," Chas said.

"Get your food and come around to the front of the truck," muttered the second guard. He leaned into Chas's face. "And keep your mouth shut."

"Yes, sir," said Chas, snapping off a salute.

"Stop that shit, smart ass," the guard growled under his breath.

"Yes, sir," Chas mumbled. He returned to his pacing, swinging his arms and smacking his fist against his palm.

Two guards opened the back doors of the semi, revealing a trailer crammed floor to ceiling with half-boxes of canned food and packs of twelve-ounce water bottles.

"Okay," shouted a guard with officer bars on his collar. "We've got two cases of mixed canned goods per person and two six-packs of water."

"What? That's not enough!" Harvey Zizzo shouted from behind me. "There's a lot more than that in this trailer."

"Yeah, and there's a lot more neighborhoods in Austin," said the officer. "Take it or leave it, folks. It's all we've got."

"We'll take it," I said.

Guardsmen climbed into the trailer and handed down canned goods and water to guards on the ground, one of whom gave Chas his share.

"That's a case?" Chas snapped. "There's only twelve little cans in there."

"Yeah, it's a case. Now shut up and move on! Next!"

Chas glared at the guard. "I need two more, uh, sets for my mom and dad," he said.

"Your mom and dad can get their own, kid. Now move!"

Chas took his rations and walked away toward the front of the truck. Soon the guard he'd talked to earlier stuck a wrapped bottle into Chas's backpack. The teen slapped the guard on the shoulder and shook his hand. I didn't see what, if anything, Chas gave the guard in exchange. I supposed a little booze wouldn't hurt the kid. He needed to calm down.

At least he couldn't drink and drive in this world.

"Excuse me, sir. Can I talk to you a minute?" Jack Jeffers said as he made his way toward the officer in charge.

"Step to the side," the officer said, and he followed Mr. Jeffers around the corner of the trailer. "What I can do for you?"

"This food is supposed to last how long?" Mr. Jeffers asked. "You'll be back in a few days, won't you?"

"I doubt it. Don't know when or if we'll be back."

"What? Why?"

"We don't have more food to distribute."

Mr. Jeffers's jaw dropped. "But what about our emergency stockpiles? Where are they?"

"You mean the twenty million meals-ready-to-eat that got taken to Dallas-Fort Worth, where more than seven million people live? Or maybe you mean the fifteen million MREs that went to Houston, where six million people live?" The officer clearly saw the irony, but he was a tough old bird.

"Are you telling me that's all they had?" Mr. Jeffers lifted his hat and wiped his brow.

"Yes, sir, I am."

I let the Zizzos and Barneses go ahead of me for rations so I could keep listening to this conversation that no one else seemed to be noticing.

"What about Austin and San Antonio and all the other cities? And rural people?" Mr. Jeffers asked. "Don't we have a food reserve?"

"Only enough to last the police, National Guard, and essential city officials for a couple of months."

"What essential city officials? Why do they get food and not us?"

"That's a decision above my paygrade, sir," said the officer.

"Okay, what about food warehouses? I used to manage an H.E.B. We had warehouses all over the state."

"Yeah, and we went to every one of them we could find. Someone already cleaned them out. We think the Guard up in Waco did it. They had trucks running quicker than the rest of us did, and they always were a bunch of assholes."

"That hardly seems fair," said Mr. Jeffers.

"No one much cares about fair anymore," said the officer.

"Jesus H. Christ!" Jack Jeffers stomped away. My turn came in the line as he passed me, shaking his head. "Don't expect more," he said and kept moving.

I had to argue, politely, with the guards to get five sets of rations for me and my grandkids plus another five sets for the Beldings.

"They can get their own rations," said one guard.

"No, they can't. They're gravely ill."

"If they're too sick to get their rations, maybe they don't need any," he said.

I glowered at the man. "Seriously? We're going to turn into animals just because we don't have electricity? Survival of only the fittest?" The guard just shrugged.

Keno showed up with an empty wagon at this point, and Milo was right behind him with another.

"What's wrong, Nana?" Keno asked.

I looked at the guardsman, he skimmed his eyes over my scrawny boys, and his mouth slid sideways. "Okay, five sets of rations in one wagon and five in the other, then?"

"Yes, thank you," I said. "And bless you."

"You too, ma'am. Next!"

Milo headed home with one full wagon while Keno pulled his toward the Belding house.

As I turned to go home, I looked around for the girls. Mazie was on our patio, but Tasha was talking to that boy, Chas. He was stroking her chin with his thumb.

"Tasha, time to cook dinner," I hollered.

"Coming!" She giggled at Chas, kissed his cheek, and ran home. Yikes.

CHAPTER 15

23 days since the EMP and counting.

That evening I sneaked vodka and water on the patio while twisting dials on the wind-up radio. Suddenly I heard a man's voice on one of the short-wave bands. He said his name was Rick, and he was broadcasting from Clifton, Texas, "afta the disasta."

"Kids, kids, come out here," I hollered into the house, where the kids were playing their umpteenth game of Uno.

"What, Nana?" "Why?" "What's going on?" they said on top of one another as they hurried outside.

"The radio!"

"Oh, my God!" Tasha said, throwing her hands to her mouth.

Mazie jumped up and down, giggling, while Milo and Keno slapped each other in an elaborate pattern of high-fives.

"Shh, listen to the radio," I said.

"Here in Clifton, we been havin' quite a time since this thing happened, but at least we're in the country, and we got some things we need. A fella came through here, said he'd walked from Fort Worth. Said it was hell up there. It took him four days to—"

The radio stopped, and Mazie squealed.

"It's the wind-up thing. It ran down." I began cranking. "Milo, go to my car and get the roadmaps out of the glove box. I need to know where Clifton, Texas is."

Milo was back in a minute with a handful of maps.

". . . . That Ft. Worth guy—his neighbor was some sort of scientist. He says this here EMP came from a thing called a CME. They had one once, he said, that lit up the sky like a light show for days. Called it the Carrington Event. The scientists tried to warn us that this thing could happen again because of all the solar activity going on. Damn gov'ment people wouldn't listen to 'em, though. It figures.

"*This CME is magnetic, see, so it distorts the magnetic fields around the Earth. The guy said somethin' about the planet's polarity shifting. I don't know if it can knock us out of orbit, I surely don't, but the solar pulse sends out godawful amounts of electricity. Our old power grids couldn't handle the extra load. The power might be working somewhere, but most of the U.S. probably went down. Don't we pay enough for our power bills and taxes that they coulda fixed that doggone grid?*

"*Let's talk about something besides that durned old sun. I don't know about y'all, but I keep worrying it's gonna happen again, only worse.*"

No kidding, Rick, I thought.

"*I'll give you a rundown of how my neighbors are doing. Mrs. Ebberly's been havin' a hard time. She needs oxygen, and she had one of those electric concentrators. If anyone knows where to find mechanical oxygen tanks, please get the word to me. . . .*"

While Rick kept talking about his neighbors, I sorted through maps and opened the best-looking one for the State of Texas. I finally found Clifton in the list of towns, right as the radio needed to be wound up again.

"*This is Rick, and I'm gettin' skinny as a stick. Just got this radio working again after the EMP. Been working on it day and night. Had to scrounge parts from all over creation, since some circuits were fried. Wish I had a better ham setup so I could find other people out there. It's pretty lonely broadcastin' when there's no one else to listen to.*"

"Here's Clifton, about twenty, thirty miles west of Waco." The thought of Waco made my heart cramp. I was hoping Rick would say something about people who were on I-35 during the solar pulse.

Keno ducked inside and came back several minutes later with a very old *Encyclopedia Britannica, Volume C.* "The Carrington Event is in here," he said. "This says that there was a white glow in the sky, brighter than the full moon. People could read newspapers outside at night."

"Holy sh—, um, holy macaroni!" Milo said. Tasha giggled at him.

"Blows my mind," said Keno.

"When it was over, did their cell phones work again?" Tasha asked.

"No, Tasha." Keno gave his sister a withering look. "It was in 1859.

They didn't have cell phones."

Milo burst out laughing.

"I didn't know in it was 1859!" Tasha said.

We kept listening, but the kids soon grew bored with the radio and went back to playing Uno inside. Keno left the encyclopedia volume on his chair. I scooted close to the lantern and read all about the Carrington Event. The information was scarily tantalizing, but frustratingly sparse.

I sipped vodka and listened to Rick until he quit broadcasting around two a.m. He never said a word about Waco or I-35. I guessed twenty or thirty miles was pretty far from him now that cars and telecommunications were out of the equation.

On my way to bed, I saw Chas tramping down the street past my front window, so I stepped quietly onto my front stoop. Chas was pacing in front of the Belding house, 'round and 'round, back and forth. What the hell was he doing?

His shoulders were hunched and his head hung low, though his eyes were darting around. Perhaps he sensed that he was being watched. He certainly was an agitated kid, but he also seemed sad and forlorn.

CHAPTER 16

Many mornings when I woke before dawn, from my upstairs window I surveyed the sky, wary of the sun and what random impulse might come over it next. Often, I watched a column of neighbors trudging out of the field behind Jack Jeffers's house, lugging buckets and jugs of water. I assumed they were coming from the secret pond, but they ought to have been more careful if they wanted to keep it secret. They could have been seen from upstairs in a dozen houses nearby.

On most of these mornings I saw my neighbor Sonja Carrera carrying water, accompanied by her small son. At first, I didn't think much about it, but when she came alone with her son day after day, struggling with her heavy bucket, I got a little outraged. Why wasn't her husband helping her?

This morning, as I watched the sky begin to lighten, a string of gunshots pealed out. I ducked at my window but peeked back up to see people scurrying for cover, water slopping from their buckets. Then Sonja tripped and spilled her entire bucket. She froze, staring at the lost water, until Jack Jeffers came and dragged her and her son into his house.

"What was that?" Tasha said from behind me, sending my heart through the roof.

"Gunshots. Get down," I said. She was trembling when I reached her, and another set of shots rang out. She squealed.

"Shh, honey. Shh." I enfolded her in my arms, and we crouched lower.

Outside, everything fell quiet. I was about to hurry back to the window when someone shouted, "We got him. It's all clear."

Got who? I sprang to the window to see a thin figure sprawled in the street. Other people stood over him, but it was too dark to see more.

"Stay here, Tasha, away from the windows. Keep an eye out for Mazie in case she wakes up."

"Don't go out there, Nana!" Tasha grabbed my arm as I passed her.

"Honey, we need to know what happened in case more trouble's coming. And I'm *not* sending you out there."

She wiped her eyes with a quivering hand.

"Someone tried to shoot us for our water," Sonja Carrera said when I rushed outside full of questions.

"Was he alone? Is he dead?"

"Yes, and yes, but I lost my water." I guessed our priorities had become rather stark.

"Come with me," I whispered to Sonja. "I'll give you some water, but don't tell anyone."

Quickly before the sun rose, while other neighbors gabbled about the dead man, Sonja, her son, and I slipped into my house. I gave her two gallons of water and some leftover biscuits.

Sonja was shaky and extremely thin. She was a lovely, tall Latina, but she wasn't exuding the confidence I'd seen in her before. I'd never known her well, but I'd had a couple of stimulating conversations with her. Today she seemed at a loss for words.

Sonja's young son wheezed as he ate a biscuit. Tasha came downstairs, still shaky herself, so I poured us some sun mint tea to settle our nerves. We sat quietly sipping it, each of us staring in different directions, me worried witless about encroaching doom, until Sonja muttered a thank you and went home.

How many people without water were out there surrounding us, anyway? And how long until they banded together to plunder us into oblivion?

ONE MORNING, KENO APPROACHED ME.

"Nana, we're going tonight." He cringed away as though he expected me to slap him.

"Who's going where?" I asked, as if I didn't know. It was one of countless things I continually shoved out of my mind when I couldn't cope with the emotions that came with them. Too much feeling could kill a person, and I often felt on the verge.

"We're going to that old well to get the water."

I sank into a chair, trying to maintain my equilibrium. "Do you have to? Why now? Who's going?"

Keno stooped before me, sensing my distress. "Because the pond water's almost gone, the Beldings don't have water, and we need to do something. Silas is going, Mr. Jeffers, some other guys I don't know too well."

I sat back in the chair. Was this how women felt who had to send their sons to war? I darted my eyes around the room but found no answers.

"I wish you didn't have to go at night," I said weakly. "It's so scary out there."

He nodded and smiled a bit. Very adult of him to humor me so.

I took Keno's hand. He looked into the distance as though mulling things over.

"We need the water. We have to try."

"But, Keno, I can take care of *you* for water. *You* don't have to go." I was prepared to tell him about the cistern. I was that desperate to keep him home.

He furrowed his forehead for an uncomfortable moment. "Didn't you teach us to take care of everyone? Aren't we supposed to think of other people besides ourselves?"

"But you're just a boy," I said.

Keno gazed at me. "I'll always be your boy, Nana, but I'm a man now." By his comportment, I knew he was right. I had to let him go.

"How long do you think you'll be gone?"

Keno stood up. "We're gonna try to do it in one night, but if takes too long and morning's too close, we'll stay at the well until the next night. We figure the walk there should take two or three hours. The walk back will be more like four or five. We'll be slower with loaded wheelbarrows, and we'll have to rest more."

"Darkness lasts for how long this time of year? Twelve hours?"

"Your almanac says thirteen and a half."

"That gives you five hours to fill the water jugs, to eat, to rest...." I wanted to say to deal with anything that goes wrong, but I held back. I narrowed my eyes at Keno. "Do I need to speak to Mr. Jeffers about this?"

"What? No!" He seemed stunned by the very idea.

"I need to be sure you're safe," I said.

"And I need you to trust me."

To Keno, it was a matter of trust, of proving his mettle as a man. A million things could go wrong that would be beyond his control. How could I trust anyone's ability to deal with that? I'd have been just as worried if Keno were forty years old.

When mid-afternoon rolled around, the water volunteers began amassing wheelbarrows, empty jugs, and packs of food and water in our backyard. I gave them some canned tuna and biscuits to take, to keep their energy up.

The number of water jugs they could fit in their wheelbarrows looked paltry to me, given the risk they were taking. I took Keno aside.

"How many men are going? And how much water can each of them get home with?"

He counted on his fingers. "Eight men and a couple of teenagers. I'm thinking each guy can push about ten gallons home in a wheelbarrow. That's all that will fit. It's about a hundred pounds per guy."

"Would wagons be easier than wheelbarrows? I have six of them." I called them wagons, but they were fold-up garden carts. Each had room for three five-gallon bottles with a little space for food or supplies. They had beefed-up wheels and were supposed to carry up to four-hundred pounds each. "I also have a bunch of empty five-gallon jugs," I added.

"Yeah, wagons probably would be easier. Maybe we could go faster."

"You can only go as fast as your slowest person," I said. "Maybe you should see if any neighbors have carts or wagons."

"I'm on it." He rushed out the gate into the neighborhood.

Before long, Keno returned pulling two wagons. One was only a kid's wagon, the other more of a utility cart, each big enough for two five-gallon jugs. That made eight carrying vehicles other than wheelbarrows. I had an idea.

"I have a couple of personal shopping carts. They should hold one bottle apiece. It might be better to use those instead of wheelbarrows. You'd get less water, but you'll move faster."

I retrieved the grocery carts from the garage and inserted empty bottles inside. They fit snugly, but they fit. "I wish you'd told me yesterday that you'd be going today. Most of the carts and water bottles are at the Mint. How will we get them without being seen?"

"I'll get Milo on it," Keno said. "That kid can be pretty sneaky."

"Can he?" I was completely unaware of this talent of Milo's. No telling what he'd sneaked past me as a result.

Soon it was six p.m., and daylight was fading. Milo had pulled the carts into our yard—each with three empty water jugs inside—by hunkering low in the Mint yard and moving fast. Luckily, the wagons were new and didn't squeak much.

One hundred twenty gallons of water—so little for so many people. The folks with no water had no choice, but we did. It was crazy for Keno to take so much risk. But I had taught him to care about others, and now I had to live with the consequences.

As the men and boys lined up to leave, Tasha strutted out of the house wearing her grandfather's camouflage shirt and a hat with her hair tucked inside. She'd done something to flatten her ample bosom—an overly tight sports bra perhaps.

I started to stop her, but she gave me such a self-satisfied look that I backed off. I was a little proud of her, frankly. I had to admire her guts.

"Kids, come here," I said to Keno and Tasha. I hugged them and looked them each in the eye. I reached into my pocket and pulled out a Glock. "Do you know how to use this?"

"Yeah, our dad taught us," Tasha said.

Of course he did. I showed them the safety and reminded them not to touch the trigger unless they intended to fire the gun. They hugged me again, then they and the others pulled their carts out of the yard and rolled them down the street, heading south. My heart sank through my feet.

I was pretty sure Milo was planning to sneak out and catch up to the rest of them, so I kept him busy in the house until well past bedtime.

I didn't even try to sleep. I looked at family photos until I was too sad to continue, then I darned socks by candlelight through the long autumn night. I hummed songs and recited poetry to distract myself. I tried to remember the entire Gettysburg Address, but I'm sure I got it wrong.

Around five a.m. when worry had the best of me and my hands were so cramped that I could barely unclench them, I went outside to cook breakfast and started a fire on the grill. Just as the oatmeal was ready, I heard wagons rolling on the pavement, and a line of heads appeared outside my fence. The side gate banged open, and Jack Jeffers came through, jerking his hat off and holding the gate open.

"Bring it in here, y'all," he said. "We'll divvy it up later."

A slew of wagons and carts bumped up the curb and through the gate, pulled by men and boys who looked exhausted. Last came Keno and Tasha, helping each other through the gate.

"Man," Tasha said as she made her way to me. "It was so freaking dark out there."

"I'm sorry, honey." I hugged her. "I made breakfast. You must be starving."

"Too tired to eat. Goin' to bed."

"Well, sleep tight," I said. She went inside as Keno reached me. "How'd it go?"

"Okay," he said. "A lot of work for only a little water though."

"Did you have any trouble?"

"We saw some guys hiding in bushes and watching us on the way back. I'm worried they'll attack us if we pass them with water again."

"Is there another way back?"

"I don't know. I'll figure it out later. I'm taking Darla her water." He loped over to Tasha's cart, adding, "When I get back, I'm goin' to bed."

"Shoot. I made too much breakfast," I said.
"I'll eat it later."
Cold oatmeal. Yum.

CHAPTER 17

Nights later, frantic pounding on our front door woke us in the depth of night. Keno ran down to answer while I threw on my glasses and robe, grabbed my pistol, and made my heart-thrumming way down the stairs.

As Keno opened the door, Darla screamed, "Help! Please help! It's Bucky."

She stepped off the stoop to the sidewalk, where in the moonlight I saw a mop of snarled red hair and a pile of dirty clothes on a tarp. Then I saw small hands. Darla's little brother?

"It's Bucky!" she cried, tears and spittle flying. "Help me!"

I latched the safety on my gun and stuck it in my pocket. As I crossed the threshold, I said, "Darla, did you pull Bucky down here by yourself on that tarp?"

"Yes. Somethin's wrong with him!" She covered her mouth with her hands, suppressing another shriek.

With a gasp, Keno pulled Darla to him, stroking her wild hair while he stared unblinkingly at Bucky. My other grandkids rushed out to the stoop and stopped still.

I bent down to the little pile on the tarp. I touched the clothing and felt a bony shoulder blade, which I pulled gently toward me. As the small body rotated, the ashen face of Darla's little brother revealed itself beneath his red hair. His eyes were glassy and empty. He was not breathing.

I let out a breath and put my fingertips to his neck, feeling around the cooling flesh for a pulse, but there was no pulse to be found. His freckled face was clean, though. Darla had tried. I closed the little boy's eyes.

Darla let out a soul-curdling scream, and I stood to hold the convulsing girl with all my strength. Tasha pulled Mazie and Milo back inside.

"I'm so sorry, honey," I said, latching onto Darla tighter until she slid from my arms to the ground. Keno crouched beside her, and she collapsed against him.

I almost slid to the ground myself. This could have been one of my kids. How did our world get so horrid so fast? I wasn't sure I had the strength to face it.

THE NEIGHBORS SEEMED FROZEN IN DISBELIEF. Though no one actually said it, I felt sure that they, like me, were asking themselves which one of us would be next.

"We should have done more to help those poor people," Doris Barnes said. I didn't point out that we'd been helping the Beldings and it hadn't done a lick of good.

Doris, who'd volunteered at a hospice in her past, assisted Darla in taking care of her family for the next few days, and Keno visited constantly. Since I was sure he was going inside now, I doused him with hand sanitizer every time he returned.

But one night well past dark, when he should have been home long ago, Keno came huffing into the house, slamming the door and pounding his fist against the wall.

"Don't hurt your hand! What's wrong?"

"Nothin'," he said, tramping into the living room.

"Keno, what is it?"

"Stupid Chas Matheson."

"Uh-oh. What did he do?"

"I keep seeing him outside Darla's. Walking back and forth on the sidewalk, all hyped up. Pacing in the street. So, I finally asked him, 'What's going on?'"

"What did he say?"

"'None of your business, Simms.' So I say, 'You should leave Darla alone. Her parents are real sick.' 'What?' he said. 'Are you sweet on that little hillbilly?' I wanted to punch him, but his friends came running up, yelling."

"I wonder what he's up to. So mean, calling that sad girl names."

"I told Darla he was out there pacing around. She said she knew. I asked her if she liked him. She said she hates him. 'Well, why's he out there?' I said, but she just shrugged."

"Let's make sure someone's always with her, so he can't bother her. Is Doris there now?"

"Yeah, but I want to go back." He looked at me despairingly.

"Honey, it's not a good idea. Chas and his friends are there."

"I can handle his ass."

"Keno, Darla's family is suffering. The last thing they need is a fight."

Keno slumped, ran his hand through his dark hair, and headed upstairs.

OVERNIGHT, THE REST OF DARLA'S FAMILY DIED—one right after another, as though their psychic wiring had been sequentially linked.

Doris tapped on our door around dawn to tell us the horrible news. She needed to sleep, and wondered if one of us could stay with Darla.

"I'll go," Keno said. He threw on his clothes and shoes and ran down the street.

"Such a sweet boy," Doris said.

"Get some sleep, honey. We'll take over."

I cooked a quick oatmeal breakfast so I could go on down to the Beldings' house. Such unfortunate people, and such an alarming portent for the rest of us.

DARLA CAME TO LIVE WITH US. We fixed her up with a bed and small dresser in a corner of the living room and put them behind a Japanese screen.

For the most part, the soil in our subdivision wasn't deep enough to bury anyone, and the few areas of deep soil needed to be planted with food. Jack Jeffers and several other men used my wheelbarrow, along with their own, to take the Beldings down by the train tracks to bury them in soil that was too poisoned for farming.

Before they left, I explained the shallow soil dilemma to Darla, then asked her, "Is it okay with you if they bury your family by the tracks? You won't be able to visit their graves down there."

"I ain't gonna visit 'em anyway." she mumbled.

I almost asked her why. I felt like trying to convince her to visit the gravesite for her peace of mind, but I caught myself. Not in this world, Bea. No such niceties around here.

I loaned gas masks to the men in the burial detail, to help not only with the toxins but also with the serious germs that surely infested those corpses. And I gave the men latex gloves to wear.

Mr. Jeffers got sick anyway. He went around coughing for days. Jesus, he had me worried. It took some work, but I finally convinced him to let me listen to his chest. He had a few crackles, so I gave him some of my limited supply of antibiotics.

Then I redoubled my germ-killing efforts, bleaching down the kitchen sink and counters every day, constantly harping on the kids to wash their hands. Listening to their chests each evening became part of our family routine. It also reassured me, because their lungs always sounded clear and strong.

FOR THE FIRST DAYS SHE WAS WITH US, Darla seldom came out from behind her screen. She even ate, or picked at, her meals back there. I knew she was grieving something awful, so I left her alone. Even Keno steered clear of her, seeming at a loss about how to help her. But after a few days, I decided to draw her out.

"Darla, we're going to play Monopoly. Would you like to play?"

"Um ... okay." Darla's bed squeaked and, via her silhouette, I saw her sit up.

She came out fairly quickly, but she kept her face down and stood to the side of the table. I smiled at her and patted an empty chair beside me.

"Why don't you sit here?"

She shrugged and sat down, fiddling with a strand of hair that hung across her face.

"I want to play Scrabble," Tasha said.

"No, let's play something everyone can play."

Tasha shot a suspicious look at Darla.

Mazie said, "I can play Scrabble. I'm not too little!"

"No, I mean play a game that six people can play at the same time."

Milo pulled out the Monopoly game and began to set it up. "I'm the banker," he announced, and no one opposed him.

"Does she know how to play?" Tasha said, nodding toward Darla but looking at me.

"Tasha!" I couldn't believe she was being so rude.

"I know how," Darla muttered, crinkling her eyes at Tasha.

The game went along, with Darla playing tentatively, Tasha eyeing Darla's every move, and me giving Tasha stern looks. At last all the properties had been purchased, and Milo and Keno were buying houses and building empires.

Darla only had a few low-rent properties. The high rent she was forced to pay on her trips around the board had depleted nearly all her cash. Then she got sent to jail, where she languished in increasing discomfort, trying unsuccessfully to roll doubles. She couldn't afford to bail herself out. It was depressing to watch her play out this sad metaphor for her actual life.

"Darla, why don't you mortgage a property to get yourself out of jail?"

"I ain't never done that before," she said. "What is it?"

"Ain't? You said ain't," Mazie said. "We're not supposed to say that."

Darla looked mortified. So did Keno. Tasha smirked.

"Hush, Mazie. Here, Darla, I'll help you." I could barely get Darla's attention. She had retreated into her head. But I explained how to mortgage New York Avenue, and we turned over her deed, got Milo to fork up cash from the bank, and bailed Darla out of jail.

"Don't I get a house now?" Darla asked.

"No, honey. Did you think you'd get one?"

"Well, yeah. When my grandpa got a mortgage, he got a house."

Tasha spat water straight out of her mouth. Milo started cackling. And Darla, shaking all over, pushed back her chair and rushed out the back door, with Keno right behind her.

"I'm ashamed of you kids for treating Darla that way!" I grabbed a tea towel and started wiping the Monopoly board, then I flicked the towel to Tasha. "You clean it up. You laughed at Darla after everything she's been through."

"I don't care. She's stupid," Tasha said, rising to her feet.

"She is not stupid. She hasn't been educated, and it isn't her fault."

Tasha started to rush away.

"Don't you dare leave this room. Clean this mess up!" I stayed on Tasha's case until everything was cleaned and put in its place. "Now, go to your room. Candles out!"

"Fine," she said and sashayed away.

Milo and Mazie were lolling around in the living room.

"I'm not happy with you guys, either. Cackling at Darla like loony birds. And, Mazie, you've got to leave her alone about how she talks. She hasn't been taught, and it doesn't matter anyway."

"My mama told me people who say 'ain't' are white trash," Mazie said.

"White trash? That is an offensive, very mean thing to call someone, and you are not allowed to say it as long as I'm responsible for you."

"What's wrong with it?" Milo asked.

"It's making fun of someone for being poor or uneducated, and when you're privileged like we are, it's just wrong."

"But you said the Beldings are rednecks."

Did I say that? I had certainly thought it, but I didn't realize I'd uttered it aloud. "Well, if I said it, I shouldn't have. It was bad of me, and I'm sorry."

"I think my mama's right," Mazie said.

"Go to bed, kids." I couldn't take another minute of them.

Mazie and Milo took their sweet time slouching their way up the stairs. I blew out the downstairs candles, except for one by the back door. Then I sat in Hank's rocker in the near-dark, fuming at the boorish behavior of my grandkids.

Soon Keno and Darla crept inside through the back door. "Good night." Keno patted Darla's shoulder.

"Night," she said, flinching at his touch.

Keno locked the door and went upstairs. I waited until Darla was breathing like a sleeper, then I blew out the candle and headed to bed.

I gave Darla a few more days to grieve, but I ultimately had to put her to work due to our circumstances. Yet, understandably, she didn't have any initiative. If I asked her to do something, she did it without argument, then she sat and stared out the window. I didn't know how to comfort her. She wouldn't let me get close enough.

EVERY NIGHT I LISTENED to the short wave and worried about my missing family.

Rick said lots of his neighbors around Clifton had water wells, but the electric pumps weren't working. Hand pumps had fallen to rust, so only a few good pumps remained.

Still, they owned chickens and goats, horses and cattle, hogs and milk cows. And they had gardens and fields full of crops. A lot of them owned old farm equipment—plows and reapers and such—that could be pulled by horses, but they were short on the kinds of horses they needed for such heavy work. And the people weren't used to that sort of hard labor either. They, same as city folks, were accustomed to comforts—like milking machines, or tractors and harvesters with air-conditioned cabs. Yet, some had old tractors that still ran, as long as they could find diesel fuel. And they had water in creeks and ponds, even stocked ponds full of catfish.

God, catfish.

I tried to listen to everything Rick said. I didn't want to miss a thing. But whenever I stopped bustling about, I welled up with grief and pictured Hank's face. Or I envisioned my two daughters as tiny girls running down the street, carrying helium balloons and laughing. I saw my three stepsons lined up for a photo, making devil horns behind each other's heads.

It was about to break me, this grief.

Finally, after I'd listened for several nights straight, Rick talked about Waco.

"Like I told y'all the first time I broadcast, there was an awful bad wreck over on I-35 in Waco when this thing happened. A tanker truck exploded. We saw the fireball all the way over here in Clifton, thirty miles away. They had to carry hurt people to hospitals, and it wasn't easy, believe you me. The hospitals didn't have power, and they ran out of water and medicine real fast.

"I don't know what happened to all those hurt people. I figure a bunch of 'em probably died. Damn cryin' shame. We think my Uncle Dave was one of 'em, because he went to Waco that day, and none of us have heard from him since."

I didn't realize how much I was crying, listening to this, until I put my hand to my chest and discovered that my shirt was wet.

I did not tell my grandchildren about the wreck on the highway near Waco.

CHAPTER 18

Day 43, and still no sign of my missing family. God All Freaking Mighty!

Things were getting vandalized. Somebody spray-painted dirty words on my back fence where it faced the side street. The next night, they dumped out my trays of tomato and pepper seedlings, though I was able to save a few of them. Worst of all, someone rode a bike through the potatoes and other root vegetables in the Mint garden.

I talked to Jack Jeffers about those kids. I found him in his front yard. He said he and his patrollers would see what they could do. Then he glanced around the neighborhood. No one else was nearby.

"What's going on with you and that house, Bea?" he asked, almost in a whisper.

"What do you mean by that?" A gush of bile clogged my throat.

He stood in front of me, towering over me. "Come on. I've been watching you go in and out of that house since before the EMP."

"What? You were spying on me?" I said, preparing to lie to him, then realizing I'd already blown it.

"It's not exactly spying to look across the street and see you sneaking around. Is that where you store all your food? In that house?"

"What makes you think I have food?" This nosy bastard. What could I say?

"Come on. You've been dropping hints left and right." He pushed his sunglasses tighter against the bridge of his nose.

"I'm sure this is none of your business, Jack." I wanted to scream at him, but I tried not to.

"So now you call me Jack when you're pissed off? I think it's damned insulting that you won't call me Jack." He lowered his head to my level and glared through his dark, oval sunglasses, reminding me of an annoyed traffic cop.

"I find it insulting that you're so freaking nosy. What do you care about me and my house, anyway?"

"It is your house! I knew it!" He flicked his hands at me backwards.

"Yes, it's mine. So, what are gonna do? Go tell the whole neighborhood? Isn't that what you do—spread the news like a gossipy old fool?" I tucked my hands under my arms to keep from wagging my finger.

"You know better than that." He snatched his hat off his head and scowled at me, lowering his voice. "You damn well know better than that."

"So, you won't tell?"

"Not if you don't want me to."

"I don't."

"Well, okay then." He dropped his arms to his sides.

"Well, okay." I glowered at him, boiling inside.

"I guess you'll keep those potatoes for you and your kids then?"

"I don't know what I'm gonna do." I spun around and started home, incensed with a head full of curse words for Jack Jeffers and for myself. But I did believe he wouldn't tell. Then I made a snap decision. I whirled back abruptly, catching him still staring at me.

"Why don't you organize the neighbors to dig up some of that food and share it? The half that's closest to the street should be ready to harvest. The rest will have to wait. Tell the neighbors you checked the plants or something."

He swallowed. "You want to call all that attention to your house?"

I hadn't thought of that. I needed more adult conversation to keep my head straight.

"We have to do something, don't we? Just don't tell them I own that house."

"Are you sure about that? The neighbors are already suspicious of you. It might be a good idea to make peace with them."

"What in God's name are you talking about?"

"They've been wondering why you don't go scavenging—"

"I don't have the health for that."

"They know, but they think you should send your grandkids. They wonder how come you're always cooking when they don't have much to cook. They're convinced you're hiding food."

"Are they?" Their suspicions were well-founded. I sank into an internal pit of gloom.

"Bea," Jack said, taking my arm. "What do you want me to do?"

I snapped my head to shake myself alive. "Harvest the food, but don't tell them."

"I won't." As I hurried away, I peeked back to see him shaking his head.

THE HARVESTING BEGAN THAT VERY AFTERNOON. Jack Jeffers brought us a pillowcase full of potatoes, a grocery bag of sweet potatoes, and another of carrots, garlic, and onions.

I let Tasha answer the door. I didn't feel like facing Jack Jeffers.

"Nana," Tasha said after he left, a puzzled look on her face. "It's weird. They're over there digging up *our* food, and he brought some of it to *us*."

"He certainly did, my love."

LATER WHEN THE MINT HARVESTING CREW was breaking up to go home, Tasha was puttering in the Pico garden, supposedly digging holes for tomato plants. But she wasn't putting her back, or her heart, into the work. She was merely using the tip of the shovel to toss aside bits of already loose soil.

From my perch at the barbecue, I saw Chas, bare-chested, in the Mint garden, wiping his face on a T-shirt in his hand. As he lifted his head, he turned to see Tasha. Man, did his face light up.

"Hey, Tasha, need some help?"

Tasha startled and looked toward Chas, her face turning red.

"Uh.... Yeah, sure," she said.

Chas jumped over the big hedge—not an easy feat—and landed smack in our yard, loping toward Tasha with a grin wide enough to split his face in two. Tasha gave him a more restrained smile but began digging enthusiastically.

"Whatcha doin'?" he asked as he reached her.

"Digging holes for those tomato plants." She pointed at the dozen or so plants lined up beside the garden.

"How about I dig and you plant?"

"Okay, cool." She handed him the shovel, smiling as she backed away. I watched her like a mother bear.

For the next little while, they conferred about their planting endeavor, worked briskly, and made eyes at one another until the plants were ensconced in the garden, standing tall and ready to bear fruit.

And now I knew the secret of getting Tasha to enjoy gardening. Stock the garden with a strapping, handsome boy whose bare chest and arm muscles would bulge, slick with sweat. Why hadn't I thought of this sooner? But why did it have to be this questionable boy? The kid smelled of trouble, and I didn't trust him one bit.

I turned away to see Keno scowling at Chas.

CHAPTER 19

I still couldn't sleep worth a flip.

My most recent cause of sleeplessness was my mind-breaking worry about nukes. There was a noticeable uptick in the Geiger counter readings for gamma rays. The increased readings were slight, but increases were serious bad news. Radiation was leaking into the environment from somewhere. Something had exploded or melted down. We had no way to know what happened or where, or how much danger we were in. Distressing beyond belief.

On this particular night, I was so agitated that I went downstairs, lit a candle on the dining table, and drank a shot of vodka. In spite of the dangers, I stepped out to the patio, thinking the magnificent Milky Way might calm me down—put things in a more cosmic perspective, perhaps. I brought the near-full bottle of vodka with me, and I sat there, brooding and sipping, sipping and brooding, relieved that nothing was glowing out here.

Footsteps on the sidewalk jolted me alert. A human silhouette. A dim flashlight. Shit. I held my breath and tried to blend in to the house. But when I leaned back an inch, the chair made a loud creak.

The footsteps halted. "Who's there?" a man shouted. Was it Jack Jeffers? "Identify yourself! I've got my pistol drawn!"

"Jack, it's just me!"

"Shit, Bea. You scared the crap out of me. What are you doin' outside?"

"Couldn't sleep. Looking at the Milky Way settles my nerves. Why are you out?"

"Goin' home from patrol."

"Wanna have a drink with me? I've got vodka." A peace offering after our quarrel, I thought. I needed an adult friend, and he was the closest thing I had to one.

"At two in the morning?" He took a loud breath. "Well, I can't turn down a rarity like that. Sure you want to share it?"

"If you get here before it's gone." As he approached the patio, I asked him, "Did you ever think we'd find ourselves in a situation like this?"

"Can't say that I did." He sat in a padded chair next to me, and I handed him the vodka. "Takin' it straight, are ya?" He examined the bottle in the candlelight through my window, then knocked back a swig. He shuddered a bit, and held the bottle toward me.

"No, take more," I said. "I'd invite you in and pour you a glass, but Darla's asleep in the living room."

He swigged again and wiped his mouth with the back of his hand. "Why can't you sleep, Miss Bea?"

I fixed my eyes on the stars beyond the patio roof. "Oh, about a thousand reasons. I could keep a dozen psychiatrists employed for years. Did you know, for instance, that the gamma ray levels are rising?"

"Shit. Are they? How bad?"

"Not horrible, but any increase is bad. More cancer. I'm trying to figure out what caused the uptick and whether it'll get worse. What if we had a nuclear EMP after all, instead of a solar pulse?" I pushed my hair off my face. "The feds told our mayor it was solar, but maybe they're trying to avoid a panic. Maybe that glow in the sky was from bombs. Maybe they're covering up some stupid accident."

"Take a breath, Bea."

"If I was calm enough to take a breath, I'd be calm enough to sleep." But I did take a breath—a few of them—wondering what my grandkids would think if they found me out here in my nightgown, getting sloshed with Mr. Jeffers. "Anyway, we've been told that if a nuke bursts at a high enough altitude to black out the whole U.S., there won't be fallout, but that could be another lie."

"Jesus. Have another swig."

I took the bottle and slugged down a mouthful, cringing as it burned its way down.

"I don't know if fallout's the source of this uptick or something else. I hope to God a nuclear missile didn't launch." I closed my eyes and pinched myself between them.

"No shit."

"Right? But nuclear reactors … they're another matter."

"Well, there's nothin' you can do about it, so why worry so much?"

"Because," I turned to face him, "because I have a houseful of developing kids. Radiation can damage their genes and their children. It's a nightmare, is what it is."

"Christ Almighty." He ran his hand through his thinning hair, making it spike like a halo in the hazy candlelight. "Now I'm wide awake, too."

I leaned in closer and lowered my voice. "No one tells us the truth about any of this. They just lie, they lie, they lie."

Jack stared, slack-jawed. I gulped more vodka, which hit my stomach and threatened to come back up. I wished he would stop gaping at me.

"So, Mr. Jack Jeffers, I think … I think, if a Texas nuke melted down, the radiation here would be higher. But a far-away nuclear 'accident'—if you can call such a—"

"Bea." Jack laid his hand on my arm. "Is there anything I can do to comfort you? Something to make the kids safer?" He looked sweet and sincerely concerned. I dropped my eyes to gaze at his hand on my arm.

Tears filled my eyes. "I can't protect them from this, Jack. How can I protect them from this?"

Jack frowned, his eyes glistening. "Maybe you can't," he said, and I let out a moan. He stroked my arm, smoothly taking the vodka from my hand. "I believe you've had enough of this."

"And then there's that god-damned wreck." I stood up and immediately sat back down, wracked with a loud sob.

"What wreck is that?"

My whole body shook with involuntary sobs. "You know. The tanker truck—it exploded. Jesus, it exploded!"

Jack stooped before me, searching my face, his forehead wrinkled with concern. "What tanker truck? What explosion?"

"It just—Ka-boom!—a big ball of flame. No one had a chance."

"Bea?" He put his arm around me. "What do you mean?"

"Huh?" The weight of his arm on my shoulder. His earnest face in front of me. Everything was a jumble. "I gotta get up." I mopped my wet cheeks with my fingertips. Jack grasped my arm to steady me and helped me to the door.

When I opened it, he said, "Why don't I walk you up the stairs?"

"Thank you, but I'm gonna sleep in that recliner over there." I nodded toward the recliner, and my world started spinning. "Whew!"

Jack gripped my arm tighter. "Let me help you."

"No, no, I got it." I tried to shirk his hand away, but he guided me over the threshold, sliding his fingers down my arm to squeeze my hand, light and fast.

"I got it," I said and wove my way to the recliner. As I flopped down into it, Jack whispered good night and reached in to lock the knob-lock as he closed the door. His boots clicked on the patio tile as he clomped away.

"You okay down there, Nana?" Keno asked from upstairs.

"I'm fine. Sorry." I was as dizzy as a spinning top. I planted my foot on the floor as the room movement slowed and I passed out.

That was the night I had my last drink for a while. I couldn't allow myself to get plastered like that, blabbering like a maniac in the middle of the night. Plus, I was getting far too morose, and I was almost out of booze at the Pico house anyway.

A killer hangover awaited me come morning. I felt like my head had been nuked.

CHAPTER 20

Mel Lewis's nephew biked into our neighborhood to check on his family and invited them to move to Bastrop, where all the pine trees had burned up. The fires had created lots of newly cleared land, and people were using it to plant food.

The Lower Colorado River was there for water and fishing. Because so many people were camped out and the wildlife had thinned from loss of habitat, hunting had been forbidden. Park rangers were trying to enforce it, though I couldn't imagine how.

Mel convinced two other families to move east with him and his grown sons. "The gov'ment can't fuck with us so easy out there," he said, whatever exactly that meant.

I was ashamed to admit it, but I was glad to see our neighborhood empty out. It wouldn't be long until I could open my stockpiles for some sort of systematic distribution.

Keno and his water team went on another mission. Naturally, Tasha went along. Darla joined in too this time. In fact, the crew added wheelbarrows and more teens, including Chas. A recipe for trouble. I would have to trust that Silas and Jack could keep the kids in line.

This time I didn't try to stay awake. Whether this meant I was getting more sensible or more jaded on the dangers we lived with, I didn't know—probably I was just worn out.

Again, I went to the patio at dawn to make breakfast, but I heard no squeaking wagons on the street, saw no heads above my fence. Damn it. Breakfast was ready. Mazie and Milo woke up, but still no returning water questers.

I fed the kids and fixed myself a plate, but I froze in my chair, not eating. I tried to remember prayers but was too distracted, straining my ears in the silence. Even the birds seemed quiet.

Finally, when the sun had been up more than an hour, I heard wagons rolling, wheelbarrows rumbling, and feet slapping fast against the concrete. After the preternatural silence, this manic activity sounded as loud as the train wreck. I jumped up and rushed to the gate with Milo beating me there and Mazie squeaking questions.

Keno led the pack, balancing a wheelbarrow full of gallon jugs. When he saw Milo peek through the gate, he hollered, "Open it, Milo!" and the whole crowd clambered through, huffing and puffing, pulling and tugging, until the vehicles and people were inside.

"What the hell happened?" I asked, trying to count moving heads.

"Ask Chas," Keno said, clenching his fists and glowering at the pony-tailed kid.

"Shut up, Simms!" Chas shoved Keno two feet backward.

Silas and Jack grabbed Chas and pulled him to the back hedge. "Everyone, take five gallons of water and go home," Jack shouted.

What in the name of God? I rushed to Keno. "Are you alright?"

My red-faced grandson muttered, "I'm fine."

The yard was full of men and teens talking loudly. "That was some fucked-up shit," someone said.

"All my kids, come in the house!" I cried. "The rest of you, please go home."

"Sorry, Bea," Silas said as he herded the others through the gate, taking Chas by the arm and tugging him down the street. My kids and Jack followed me to the patio.

"Fuck this shit," Jack said as he collapsed into a chair. "We'd have to do this every other night to keep enough water for the neighborhood. Too damned dangerous and too much work."

"We woulda been fine if Chas wasn't there." Keno lowered himself to the patio tile.

"Leave Chas alone. It wasn't his fault!" Tasha said.

"Was too," Keno said.

"Quit arguing and tell me what happened."

"On the way there," Keno said, "we saw those same guys watching us, and Chas hollered, 'What are you looking at?'"

"Idiot," Jack said.

"Sounds like it."

"We had to run to get away from them," Keno said.

"I lagged behind so I could blow my air horn if those guys tried to follow us," Jack added. He probably couldn't run too far either, I thought.

"It's not Chas's fault those guys were there," Tasha said.

"He didn't have to antagonize them."

"Whatever." Tasha tromped into the house and up the stairs. Darla followed her inside but stopped and sat down at the table.

"Then," Keno said, "when we came back those guys were waiting. They had a bunch more guys."

"Silas was our scout," Jack said. "He saw them, but they didn't see him. He came back and told us, and we had to wait them out."

"No wonder you were late."

"They left just before daylight. We hustled the rest of the way," Jack said.

"Practically ran with all that water, two or three miles," said Keno.

"There's got to be a better way to do this." Jack popped his gimme cap against his knee and slapped it back on his head. "We need to leave people at the well to guard it if we expect to keep it for ourselves."

"We could take turns living in that barn," Keno said. "Part of it has a decent roof."

"Maybe," Jack said, "but we need a truck. I should ask my friend Sam to help us with his GMC."

"You could." I started pacing. "But you'd have to share water with him. You'd probably have to come up with the gas."

"Yeah, but we could put eighty or a hundred five-gallon bottles on that truck. Even if we give Sam half, that's still forty, fifty bottles for us. Two hundred gallons should last several days. I've got gas in my shed. I'm sure others do, too. It'd probably only take a gallon per trip. We've all got gas in our cars. Keno, I can teach you how to siphon gas."

"What's that?" Keno asked, and Jack guffawed.

"Do y'all want to eat?" I asked.

"Naw. See ya later." Jack moseyed away.

"Milo and Mazie, go inside," Keno said.

Milo snapped his head toward Keno, ready to argue, but he saw Keno's stern expression and stopped.

"I need to talk to Nana," Keno said. "Go on."

"What is it?" I asked as Mazie and Milo slinked inside. Keno watched the door until the kids were clear of it. I sat down.

"There's another reason we were late." Now he sat up straight. "Out at the well, we were filling water bottles, and Chas and Tasha disappeared."

"What? How'd you let that happen?"

"They waited until I was busy, and they snuck into the woods. Didn't come back for two hours. Some of us went looking for them, but it was so dark. And we couldn't shout their names, only whisper."

"Well, what were they doing?"

Keno looked away. "What do you think?"

My heart kicked me in the chest. "How…how do you know what they were doing?"

Keno swung his head around and studied me for a minute. "Tasha's clothes were all messed up. She had leaves and sticks in her hair."

"Shit." I shot up and whacked the table. "Shit!" Mazie and Milo appeared in the window then ducked away when I glared at them.

Of all the people for Tasha to fall for.

I marched up the stairs to Tasha's room and banged on her door, shouting her name.

"What?"

"You are banned from going on water trips!"

"Leave me alone!" she yelled. I was happy to oblige.

"THIS IS RICK THE STICK, broadcastin' from Clifton, Texas. I know city folks have it bad, but we got it bad out here in the country, too. We don't have medicine anymore. Colds, diabetes, back pain, rheumatism—we got no treatment for any of this stuff. We always kept going with medicine before. Blood

pressures are out of control, and that can't be good. The old and sickly folks are suffering. Bell Jones had her appendix burst and now she's gone. She was only thirty. Hard to take, watching people die too young. . . .

"The Gardners have that big ranch out south of town. They'd just finished harvestin' their hay when the sun went crazy. They had that hay stored in their barn. Well, o' course, they didn't have lights in that barn no more. Old Joe took his lantern out there to check on his cows. I don't know where he set that lantern, but his old stud horse kicked that lantern into a hay bale, and Poof! The whole barn and all that hay burned fast. Old Joe barely got his horses and cows outa there. That stud horse died, and Joe ain't doin' so great after breathin' all that smoke."

CHAPTER 21

48 days, and no more National Guard, no returning family, no nothin'. How much longer could this go on?

It was getting easy to tell who had water, food, and medicine and who didn't, simply by looking at them. I noticed people glaring at my healthy kids, turning away if they saw me watching.

The water excursions didn't bring us nearly enough water. The National Guard rations and the veggies I'd let people harvest wouldn't last much longer. A few more neighbors, including the Gonzales family next door and their passel of kids, walked or rode bicycles off into the unknown.

We were the only family with barely sufficient water. It was obvious because we'd washed our hair a couple of times. We kept our house reasonably clean. Other houses smelled bad. You could tell if you passed by when their windows were open, which they usually were.

Though it was mid-November, it was still abnormally warm. I wondered if climate-change deniers would finally see the truth, but I figured some birdbrains would never face the facts.

The fall garden in the Pico yard was thriving, especially the squashes I'd planted before the CME. The kids and I carefully dripped water over the greens, squash, tomatoes, and peas in the raised bed. Tomatoes and peppers were flourishing in pots and would be producing before long.

But it was harvest time for the rest of the Mint garden. Thanksgiving loomed next week. It was time to let my secrets out of the bag.

Yet, I was hesitating, and I wasn't sure why. My hesitation was hard on the health of my neighbors. They didn't know this, of course, but I did. I also knew that once you open Pandora's Box, you cannot unopen it.

What finally made up my mind was catching the gang of kids digging up potatoes from the Mint garden in the middle of the night. I chased them away by brandishing a broom at them. But I couldn't get the skinny ribs of that dead child Bucky out of my head. And I was worried senseless that some intruder—or a trusted neighbor, or those wild kids—would break into the Mint and leave us to starve. My grandkids and I couldn't properly guard the Mint on our own, not in a world like this.

The next morning after breakfast, I went to see Jack Jeffers to discuss the wild kids. But he met me with his arms crossed in an intimidating stance.

"Bea," he said, "tell me what you've got in that other house."

My lips started to quiver, so I looked away. "I'm terrified to tell anyone."

"You don't need to be afraid of me," he said.

"It's not you I'm scared of . . . It's life—this new life." I exhaled slowly, resigning myself to the inevitable. "Let's go to my patio and get comfortable. This could take a while."

Once I'd related the story of the Mint and the full extent of my stockpiles—except the cistern and cellar—Jack said, "My God, Bea. I'm flabbergasted! What does Hank think of this?"

"Hank doesn't know a thing about it."

Jack gaped at me, speechless.

We spent the rest of the day going over my inventory lists—thank God I had printouts—estimating how much food people needed, calculating how long it might last. I didn't have enough bottled water to share, and there was no way I would disclose the cistern. We'd be forced to continue the water trips and to collect rain. For food, we had fifteen to eighteen months before we'd be dependent on whatever we could produce.

Overnight, Darla, the grandkids, and I sneaked into the Mint and moved food and water into the cellar as our private hedge against starvation.

Before we headed over there, Tasha cornered me. "Why are you telling Darla about the cellar? She'll steal stuff."

"Stop it! She lives with us. She'll find out anyway, and we need her help."

WE HELD A NEIGHBORHOOD MEETING late the following afternoon, when the worst of the glare from the sun was gone. People brought chairs and set them in the intersection next to the Pico house.

Jack called the meeting to order to the jeers of a bunch of young ones. Likely the taunts were attempts at humor, although Texans don't much care for anyone who acts like he's in charge of anything. Jack was either undaunted or oblivious. He said I had important news and would they please give me their attention.

"I know y'all have been hungry," I said. "So, if it's okay, we brought supper."

The five kiddos passed out tuna and pickle relish sandwiches on big biscuits, along with plastic cups of water. People eyed me anxiously.

"Whatcha tryin' to do, Bea? Bribe us?" said Silas Barnes—not as heavy as he used to be, but still stocky and round.

"What's the matter, Silas? Don't you like food?" said Kathy Zizzo.

"Love me some tuna fish." Silas took a gigantic bite. "Got any more, Bea?"

Everyone laughed. I smiled nervously. Tasha gave him another sandwich and handed out more to those who wanted seconds, which was nearly everyone.

I sat in a chair facing the others. "I'm sorry," I said. "I can't stand up too long, but I have important things to tell you."

People nodded and shuffled in their seats, jiggling their legs, wringing their hands. There were twenty-five or more adults, and almost as many kids.

Jack said, "We'd like to hear it, Bea."

"Is it bad?" asked Harvey Zizzo.

"No, I imagine you'll think it's good."

I scanned the faces of the gaunt, dingy people before me. They were stone-faced for the most part. The old man who'd almost refused my water weeks before seemed downright angry.

"It's hard to know where to start. Most of you only know me in a neighborly, social way, so you don't know much about me. Some of you know me better, and I may have told you in the past how worried I was about the environment, that we might find ourselves in a catastrophe before long."

"How's that solar power working for you now?" Silas said. People laughed awkwardly.

"Hilarious." I smirked at him.

"Folks, let Bea talk," said Jack.

I sat up straighter and raised my voice. "Okay, so even though most of you thought I was a kook—and, apparently, some of you still think so—because I was worried about an ecological calamity, I prepared for one. I inherited a great deal of money, and instead of living high on the hog—"

"How'd you do all that fancy work on your house?" said some guy I didn't recognize.

"Not that it's any of your business, whoever you are—"

"That's Gary Matheson," Jack said. Good Lord, had he ever changed. He looked ten years older than he had a few weeks ago.

"Anyhow, not that it's your business, Gary, but I worked sixty-hour weeks for three years to renovate my house. Anything else not your business you want to know?" I glared at Matheson until he hung his head.

"So, as I was saying, I bought another house with my inheritance and filled it with food and survival gear and seeds. Lots of all these things." Faces in the crowd began to light up.

Then Chas said, "Where's this house?"

"I'll get to that. First, I need to talk about how I want this stuff handled."

Murmurs burbled through the crowd.

"I'm willing to share with you, but I have conditions—"

"What do you mean, 'conditions'?" said the angry old man. "You've been hoarding food while some of us are starving, and you have 'conditions'? We oughta take the food away from you out of principle."

"Yeah!" Chas shouted, with some back-up hoots from his friends. "Rich bitch, you think you can boss us around just because you have food?"

Tasha winced and turned away from me. Chas was showing his colors, the little shit.

"Chas, be quiet!" Lyla Matheson yelled from across the crowd. I guessed this kid was her son. Chas and two other boys booed.

"That's enough!" Jack stood tall and straight-shouldered, pointing at the Matheson boy. "You better shut up, buster, or—"

"Or what?" Chas jumped to his feet and took a threatening step toward Jack. A couple of guys rose to block the kid's path.

Sonja Carrera stood up, making emphatic hand gestures. "People! What is wrong with you? Mrs. Crenshaw is trying to help us. These arguments are unacceptable!"

"Yeah!" someone yelled, then silence descended for a moment.

I caught my breath and tried to compose myself. I don't know why, but I hadn't expected this kind of reaction. Silly me, I'd thought they might be grateful.

"Look," I said loudly, "I'm not going to be a tyrant, but I'm not letting anyone else be one either. And I'm sorry I didn't share sooner. I had to wait for people to move away or there wouldn't have been enough for everyone.

"But you all know about the intruders and the gunfire. It's probably going to get worse. Any day we could be invaded by a horde of desperate people. If we don't band together, we could be dead soon. You need my food and seeds. I need all of you to help protect it and put it to use. Don't you think we can make some sort of deal?"

The looks of astonishment on my neighbors were hard to describe. For one thing, none of them had heard me talk so forcefully before. To them, I'd always been mousy Bea Crenshaw, wife of that pillar of the community known as Hank.

I'd made my appeal, and now I started shaking. I was scared of these people, whose changing expressions ran from pissed to hopeful, many of them unreadable. Some whispered amongst themselves, others stared ahead. I wished I'd never told them about my stores. Now I had no choice but to share, damn it. I had put the lives of my grandchildren at risk to feed a bunch of ingrates.

"I've told Bea I'll defend her and her treasury of goods," Jack said, still on his feet. Thank God I had him for an ally. "Anyone who's not willing to defend her—as far as I'm concerned, you don't deserve to share in this bounty. Bea's doing a good and generous thing. She's got four grandchildren to care for, and she took in Darla Belding when her family passed. I wouldn't be nearly as willing to share if I'd been smart enough to be prepared. So, I'm not going to hear more bitchin' and moanin'. Do you want to work for shares of food, or don't you?"

"We do!" "We do!" shouted Harvey and Kathy Zizzo.

"I do, too!" said Lyla Matheson.

"I'm in," Silas said, with his wife nodding beside him. Others, including Sonja Carrera, said yes as well.

"Go on, Bea," Jack said, comforting me with the look of respect he gave me.

"Alright." I held up my hand to buy time. "What I have in mind is for us to work together to grow food in the neighborhood, and to trap as much rainfall as we can. I have what we need to plant and fertilize every spot of deep soil in these four square-blocks, plus the field behind Mr. Jeffers's house. I have enough food to feed us for a year, possibly longer, if we're careful how we manage the food."

Silas raised his hand, and I nodded at him. "What happens when people in surrounding neighborhoods get wind of this?" he asked. "They'll attack us for the food."

"That's right," said Jack, "so we'll have to keep it under armed guard night and day, and we'll have to be careful not to flaunt our good fortune. People are moving away from town. Maybe if it keeps thinning out, the people who're left won't pose much threat."

"Or maybe there'll only be a few of them, and we can feed them, like good Christians would do," said Doris Barnes. I never expected *her* to speak up in a meeting. Even her husband appeared surprised to hear her voice.

"Okay," I continued, "my conditions are that you must, first, sign an agreement for every able person in your family to work at least thirty hours per week on this project, and, second, you must share what you have that will help make it a success. So, if you have tools or seeds, or maybe you know about machines and can keep the rototillers running. . . . Whatever you have, whatever you know how to do, you will share it."

"How are we going to write this agreement?" Gary asked.

"It's already written. I typed it on my grandfather's old typewriter."

"Ain't she somethin', folks?" Jack Jeffers said, lifting my heart. Some people applauded. The openly angry people—Chas, the old man, a few others—stared hollowly, sinking my heart once again. The group of wild kids hooted and hollered, happy for an excuse to be loud.

"The agreement also says that you will not disclose to anyone outside this group where the goods are stored. You won't try to enter that house without me or Mr. Jeffers or one of my teenage kids. Anyone caught breaking this agreement can be kicked out of the co-op by me or Mr. Jeffers, and our decisions are final. Everyone okay with that?"

They weren't okay with it, but they were desperate people, thirsty and hungry and worried sick about their kids and their futures. I'd given them a reason for hope that they hadn't expected to get. So, under the direction of Jack Jeffers, everyone lined up and signed the agreement. Surprisingly, no one refused or seemed to hesitate.

I'd been around enough communes, collectives, and co-ops in my life to know that they needed a dedicated membership to succeed. The odds of this working out well, of these folks from disparate backgrounds being able to avoid internal wars over dwindling resources, weren't great. This, along with my concern for my grandkids and the rest of my family, should they return, had kept me holding back all these weeks, and worried me now more than ever, given people's scary reactions to what should have been good news.

But I stood by my decision that—for the sake of my soul and to set an example of grace for my grandkids—I had to feed my neighbors. I could not stand by and watch them die, simple as that. If helping them ended up causing my own death, then so be it and praise the Lord.

Not that I blamed God for this freak show. I didn't believe God laid traps for us to teach us things, although he—or she—evidently smote us with a bolt from the heavens. Perhaps I was employing magical thinking, yet I couldn't help but wonder if the fact that the CME didn't kill us outright but merely kept us from further destroying the planet wasn't a merciful disciplinary act. That it was so hard on us was no one's fault but our own.

CHAPTER 22

As the meeting disbanded, I handed out rice, beans, flour, and salt. People thanked me, but they were reserved about it. I guess they were waiting to see if I would turn into some sort of dictator. I told them we'd hold an organizing meeting tomorrow afternoon, and I took my kiddos in to bed.

All the next day while Tasha did the cooking, Keno and Milo hauled home wagons full of firewood from the park, Mazie and Darla half-heartedly weeded the garden, and I made lists for the upcoming meeting of things that needed to be done in the neighborhood. It was one of those never-ending lists I could have added to for weeks. Instead, I put tasks into categories, the main ones being collecting water and firewood, growing food, providing for sanitation and medical care, and getting the kids under control and educated. We were forty-eight souls in all, including me and mine.

Luckily, we were a bit protected from surrounding neighborhoods. Our four elongated blocks were bordered on the east by a park, on the north by Dittmar Road, and on the west and south by two vacant lots, a cluster of empty houses, and one open field. Austin had grown around our property, which had once been pastureland that was scraped down to the limestone bedrock and re-sodded when the subdivision was built more than thirty years ago.

For growing food, we needed garden plots to be built, fertilized, and planted, and we would have to beef up the shallow soil. We needed chickens and goats, maybe even hogs. Then there was weeding, composting, harvesting, drying, canning, the care of seeds and seedlings. We needed to educate ourselves about all of these things.

In the realm of sanitation, I wanted to show people my composting toilet—the one inside the Mint, not the one in its cellar, which I intended to keep secret for now. I had a couple of books about composting toilets

I planned to share. How we would get components of these toilets I would leave to the committee. I did have a good deal of lime though.

Garbage was piling up randomly around the neighborhood, probably breeding rats. It definitely attracted flies and stray, potentially violent dogs. We needed to create a specific area for the garbage. We couldn't recycle exactly, but we could reuse as much as possible, and we could compost organic matter and use paper and cardboard for fire-starter.

For medical care, the City's mimeograph had said they would try to provide it, but we couldn't rely on that, especially given the lack of transportation. I had several books on folk medicine. Maybe someone in the neighborhood would know more about it. If not, a couple of someones would have to learn. Most of these people were tech workers though—not too skilled when it came to bare survival.

God, how I hoped that throwing our lot in with these neighbors wouldn't backfire and leave my grandkids to starve. It was going to take all of us, working our hardest on our best behavior, to be sure that most of us survived.

THE ORGANIZATIONAL MEETING WENT BETTER THAN I'D EXPECTED. The angry teens weren't in attendance, and the crabby old man, Mr. Bellows, held his tongue. Most people seemed animated about having important work to do, something to keep their minds off everything they'd lost.

At the meeting we broke into committees: one to harvest and replant the Mint garden; a big one to build and plant other gardens; still another to work on toilets and garbage. It turned out that there were three families who owned a few chickens, and they conferred on how to breed more birds and to build coops.

We had an electrician, Phil Hendrix, whom Keno befriended since they had a common love of science. A couple of guys offered to build rain barrel or water-collection systems. One of them was a welder, and he had enough acetylene on hand to build several systems.

In his committee meeting, Keno got into a heated debate with Silas and Gary about the cause of the EMP—nuclear or solar—and whether or not the power would come back soon. When Keno calmed down and thoroughly explained his hypothesis, especially the probability of blown giant transformers, the men gaped at him and quit arguing. A depressing theory: no power for years.

Jack was concerned about security, as we all were. We decided that adults who knew how to use guns and were reasonably strong would take turns guarding the Mint in teams of two at night and solo during the day. The patrollers would organize themselves so that people would get enough sleep to do all the work.

I decided to wait on letting neighbors come inside the Mint to see what I had there. I was full of misgivings about allowing these people to know too much about my business. I didn't trust them not to gang up on me, especially the angry ones who might win more people to their side.

What we did was carry food out to the neighbors. I cringed at how little most of them knew about basic sanitation and nutrition. Before we handed out food, I gave a quick speech on killing germs and matching beans with grains to make whole proteins. I asked people to empty their flower beds and pots so that others could come through and plant them with greens and herbs. Someday we would set up communal baking with my woodstove, but for now we'd make do with biscuits, tortillas, and pancakes that we could cook on our grills.

We brought out twelve gallons each of peanut butter, rice, cornmeal, oatmeal, vegetable oil, and several types of dried beans and peas. That amounted to one quart of each item per person. For whole-wheat and unbleached flour, we gave them triple rations; for sugar we gave half. We also passed out salt, pepper, canned meats, leavenings, soaps, toilet paper, kitchen matches, and powdered milk and eggs.

Then we distributed food from the root cellar, from last spring's harvest: russet and sweet potatoes, onions, garlic, cabbage, beets, and carrots. From my growing pots, I gave out tomatoes, bell peppers, jalapenos, basil, and oregano.

I told each person as I gave them their shares, "Don't use clean water for flushing toilets or washing floors. Use gray water for that—water leftover from bathing or dishwashing, or rainwater that you've collected in dirty containers. You can use gray water—if it's not too soapy or bleachy—for gardens, too."

I didn't mention that I had a sizable stash of bleach. I figured they'd want to use it up, and I wanted to keep it for purifying water if things got more desperate in that realm, or for saving us from bacterial outbreaks, which were very likely to be in our future.

My neighbors didn't say much except to thank me for their food. They seemed overwhelmed. Doris gave me a hug, and she cried.

The next morning, I found a dozen fresh eggs and a dead and dressed chicken in a box on the patio when I went out to cook breakfast. That made *me* cry.

CHAPTER 23

November neared its end, and our workloads only increased. My grandkids were doing almost everything physical at the family enclave. I spent all my time organizing and supervising not only my kids but the whole neighborhood—facilitating decisions on how much of what food to plant where, which roofs were best for rain collection, where to build outhouses, composting toilets, garbage dumps, *ad infinitum*.

My patio turned into a neighborhood office. Gary drew up a big map on butcher paper, showing yards, houses, garden plots, outhouses, compost piles, and everything else. I added labels to various spots as we made decisions about their use. I had to explain in great detail how to plant, grow, harvest, and preserve food, and I was forced to help settle the disagreements that cropped up as soon as the work began.

"The Carlisles don't work," said some woman, whose greasy hair was plastered to her skull and whose name I could never remember. I tried, but I seemed to have lost my ability to learn new names.

"Don't the Carlisles have twin toddlers?" I said. "And isn't she pregnant again?"

"Not my problem," the woman said. What exactly *was* her problem then?

I kept my voice even. "I saw Bobby Carlisle building a new garden yesterday."

"It's in his own yard. It doesn't count."

"It counts if he grows food for all of us. He's planning to grow lima beans this spring."

"I hate lima beans," she said.

I was tempted to say, "Not my problem," but instead I folded my arms on the table before me. "Bobby's growing food to share. If you get hungry enough, you will love lima beans. His work counts. Anything else?"

She walked away, muttering. Half the people here seemed to think that they and their families did more work than anyone else.

My episodes of breathlessness were growing more frequent. I had plenty of my normal meds—enough to last another year, I thought—and I had the basic food groups in my diet. I'd given up the late-night drinking, but I didn't have any gumption. I couldn't sustain physical effort. I was getting pretty old, but there were people older than I was who seemed to be doing better, Jack being the prime example.

I'd lost quite a bit of weight. My old clothes hung on me. But I'd been running forty pounds over my ideal weight for a decade, so shedding pounds should have been good for me. I just hoped I would perk back up after I got more accustomed to the new diet and new routine.

But the kids were the true heroes.

They were all thinner, naturally. Their skin was more tanned, except for Mazie, whose fair skin was pinker. Their hair was usually filthy, but I insisted they brush it every morning and keep it tied back or trimmed short, whichever they preferred. I told them what my own grandmother had taught me: that a person has to have dignity even in the face of disaster. Dignity could sometimes keep you alive when you had little else.

The kids also seemed taller. This was partly due to their thinness, but Milo in particular, who'd turned thirteen earlier in November, must have grown four inches already. His voice was breaking, too. Such an awkward time of life, when young men sound like their mothers on the telephone—or they used to sound like their mothers, back when we had telephones.

Milo seemed generally fine, working in gardens and riding a bike around to deliver messages, water, lunches, and tools to the work crews. He'd made a niche for himself that gave him independence, kept him outdoors, and allowed him to learn new things. He'd found a pair of Aviator sunglasses that were too big for him, making him look like a nerdy young outlaw.

Always adorned in her evermore tattered princess skirt, with its scraps of pink ruffles trailing behind her, Mazie liked to tend the home garden, wash laundry, and feed Harry's dry food to neighborhood dogs. But she spent most of her time helping Tasha in the kitchen and at the grill, where Tasha let Mazie chatter all day about whatever came in her head. I wished I could get them to talk about grammar or math or history.

Often Mazie spoke about her parents as if they were merely out for the afternoon, asking regularly when they would be home. "I'm sure they'll be here as soon as they can get here," I would say, wondering whether it was bad of me to let Mazie harbor too many delusions. But she was a trooper and didn't complain nearly as much as Tasha and Milo did. I didn't want to break her spirits by telling her I had my doubts that her parents would ever come home. It was a fear I couldn't give voice to.

When Keno wasn't splitting wood, building gardens, or toting water or bags of food and fertilizer, he stayed busy looking through my books for information about alternative ways to generate power, often while sitting with Darla. Keno didn't complain about our situation, but he looked increasingly worried and worn out.

Naturally I thought Keno was handsome, but the handful of teenage girls in the neighborhood seemed to think so, too. They blushed when talking to him; they watched him walk down the street; they sometimes sat and listened while he and Phil talked about solar and wind power. Even Darla, who seldom showed more emotion than a stone, lit up around Keno. What he thought of this, I wasn't sure.

Darla left the house every weekday morning. "Goin' to work in the garden," she would say, if she said anything at all.

The first time she did this, I asked, "What garden are you working on?"

"The one down the road."

"Which one?" I had to drag everything out of this girl. "The one on Palace Parkway?"

She thought for a minute. "No, the one by the park." The garden by the park *was* on Palace Parkway. Darla was going as far from us as she could get without leaving the neighborhood. No way I could watch over her down there.

I noticed that Darla always came home fairly clean, so I asked her how she managed to build a garden without getting dirty.

"Just good, I guess," she said. Good at something, I thought.

Then one day Harvey Zizzo said, "Darla's supposed to help in that garden we're building, but she never shows up."

"She leaves the house every morning. What's she doing?"

"I've seen her around her house a couple of times," Harvey said.

"She's not going inside with all the germs and poison, is she?"

"I wouldn't know."

Shoot. Now I would have to confront Darla.

Tasha asked often if she and Keno could ride to their old neighborhood to "see friends." I didn't want to tell her that many of those friends would have moved away, that some might be ill or even dead. So, I gave excuses, like, "Not today. We need to weed the veggies," or bake squash in the solar ovens, or shuffle and organize goods at the Mint to prepare to hand out rations.

She still cried at night. All the indignities of our new life seemed to upset her more than they did the rest of us, and her complaints were never-ending.

"Why can't I wash my hair? It's gross." "I can't use this stinky toilet anymore. It's full of pee." "I'm sick of smelling like wood smoke." "I can't just cook and garden all the time."

But Tasha's most valid complaint was this: "Why can't I do something important? You always talk to Keno about stuff, but not me. I'm gonna go crazy, I'm so freaking bored!"

My eldest granddaughter was still pissed at me for keeping her from the water excursions, which continued to happen twice per week while Jack tried to convince his friend to let us use his truck. I kept Tasha home to separate her from Chas, but I was stifling her, even I could see that, and I needed to fix it. So, when she again bitched about boredom, I offered her some ways out.

"You could teach school to the little kids," I suggested.

"That's babysitting. Still boring."

"Okay, do you want to build something, or repair things?"

She thought for a moment. "What could I build?"

"Outhouses?"

"Oh, puke," she said, and she looked like she might.

"Silly. They're not full of poop when you build them. How about trellises for gardens? Maybe we could grow grapes and you could be in charge of them."

Twisting her mouth sideways, she said, "Maybe."

"You could learn about folk medicine. I have gobs of books about it."

"Another girlie job, being a nurse."

"Tasha, if you really studied it and learned a lot, you'd be more like the neighborhood doctor. You could find medicinal plants and grow them, study anatomy and the way the body works. That is super important work."

"It sounds hard," she said.

"Almost everything worth doing is hard. Will you at least think about it?"

"I guess," she said.

I gathered all the standard and folk medicine books in the Pico house and dragged them in a box to Tasha's room.

"Do I have to read all those?"

"If you want to be good at this, you do. I have more books over at the Mint."

"Great," she said, and left the room without opening a book.

ONE EVENING AFTER SUPPER, Tasha yelled at me when I asked her to help with the dishes.

"I'm tired, Nana! Can't you do it yourself?"

"Tasha, don't yell." I stared at her, astounded, as she grimaced back. Then she twisted away, took off up the stairs, and slammed her bedroom door.

How much longer could I put up with this shit? I was supposed to be retired now, the wise and adored matron of a large, loving family, taking long afternoon naps, going on sea cruises, making quilts. I wasn't meant to be raising yet another set of stubborn children. God, did I ever miss Hank at a time like this. He had a real talent for managing recalcitrant teens.

The other grandkids were stonily silent. "Kids, I'm sorry you have to work so hard and aren't getting to have the lives that you wanted."

"Nana," Keno said, "Tasha had a fight with Chas today. He thinks he's such hot shit."

"Don't say 'shit,'" Mazie said, covering her ears.

"Hush, Mazie. . . . And Keno, please refrain from using that word in front of the little kids."

"There's only one little kid here," Milo said. "Not two."

"Yes, Milo, it's true you're not little anymore, but you're littler than Keno and Tasha, and you shouldn't be using those words."

"'Shit' isn't that bad of a word."

"Milo, hush. Keno, please finish the story."

"There's not much to tell. I saw them arguing on the corner. Chas grabbed Tasha's arm, and I started to go save her, but she jerked loose from him and ran home."

"Maybe that's why she's upset," I said. "She doesn't need to see that boy."

"I know," Keno said, "but Tasha thinks he's cool."

Bad-boy infatuation. I hated it.

"And," Keno added, "she says you make her do everything."

"I don't do that, do I? I make all of you do more than you want, because that's what it takes for us to survive."

"But you don't do nothin', Nana," Mazie said.

"What?"

"Mazie, be quiet," Keno said.

I looked from one grandchild to the next, trying to read their thoughts, to get clues from their steely faces.

"You guys think I don't work? You know I'm old and have health problems, don't you?"

"We know," Keno said. "The little kids don't always understand it, though."

"I am *not* little!" Milo insisted, and he stomped off up the stairs as well.

"Milo, wait! Keno just means that you're younger than he is. He's always teased you about being littler. Why are you upset about it now?"

"I don't think it's funny anymore!" He slammed the door to his room.

Not much of anything was funny anymore.

DARLA HAD BEEN UPSTAIRS in the game room, doing God knows what, while this bickering went on. Now she came downstairs, looking troubled.

"Sorry for the arguing," I said.

"It's okay," she muttered. She went to the kitchen and washed the dishes in cold, soapy water. No one had asked her to help.

"I'll get you some hot water to rinse with." Keno went to the grill to retrieve the water pot we always set to heat as soon as supper was cooked. Maybe when Tasha complained about her workload, she meant that I should make Darla do more.

But Darla was too depressed. Trying to make her work was depressing for me. She'd get such pained expressions, as though my words caused her physical distress. I needed to have a private conversation with Darla about this.

But first, I had to talk to Tasha. I trudged upstairs to knock on her door. She didn't answer until my third try. She let me in, and I sat beside her on the edge of her bed. We collapsed against one another, sighing and apologizing.

"Nana," Tasha said, "you don't make Darla work. Can't she live somewhere else?"

"You still don't like her?"

"No. She's weird. She's lazy, and she eats scraps off our plates."

"Tasha, she's different than you. Try to be more tolerant. And it's good she eats scraps so they don't go to waste."

"Well, I don't like her." Tasha tried to be cute by pouting her lips, but I didn't buy it.

"Think about how lonely she is. Maybe that will help."

"You like Darla more than you like me. You baby her."

"Honey, you're my granddaughter. I absolutely love you more. But Darla's lost her whole family."

"I lost my family, too," Tasha said, tears brimming.

I exhaled a loud breath. "I'm sorry if you don't know how sad I feel for you, how much I worry. I think about it all day, every day."

"You do?" Tasha half-smiled. She took a stuttering breath. "Darla uses my makeup."

Lord, it just kept coming. "Then put the makeup in your room."

"She came in here once. I saw her."

"Tasha, what do you want me to do? Kick her out? She'll starve."

"I don't care."

"What's wrong with you? You can't let this disaster make you hard-hearted. All you have is your soul, my love, but lately you don't seem to care about that. You're still seeing that boy you snuck into the woods with, the one who called me a bitch. I don't want you near him."

She leaned away from me. "He didn't mean it. He was hungry and mad about it."

"If you fall in love with a boy you have to make excuses for, he'll do you wrong every time."

"You make excuses for Grandpa."

"Tasha!" My blood pressure spiked. I felt it in my head. Tasha had me pegged on that one. I tried to calm down and think.

"Grandpa Hank is my husband and your grandfather. It's complicated. You're right that I make excuses for him. But you should listen to me about Chas because I'm the only adult around who has your best interests at heart."

"But Chas won't treat me bad. He loves me."

"Tasha, people can say anything. It's what they do that matters."

"I know that."

"Then bring him inside tomorrow night so I can get to know him." Maybe I could influence him to behave better, since I couldn't seem to make him disappear.

"He's busy."

"At night? Doing what?"

"I don't know. Stuff."

"Busy avoiding me is more like it."

"He's not avoiding you. He's just—"

"What do you see in him? He's hyper, and he's mean."

"No, he's cool. He's not afraid of anything. You just don't know him."

I scrutinized my granddaughter, who was growing into a stunningly beautiful woman. But she was much more troubled than she would admit, and she was cruisin' for an emotional bruisin' with Chas. It wouldn't have done any good for me to harangue Tasha about her attitude. Curing it was a long-term project.

Though I would later come to regret it, I patted her hand and left the room.

When I slipped down the stairs, Mazie and Milo were playing Yahtzee by candlelight, and Keno and Darla were sitting close together on the dark patio. Geez, was everyone falling in love around here?

I hadn't even thought to stock up on condoms. I could be such an old woman sometimes.

CHAPTER 24

About the time our kids started leaving home, the biggest problem between Hank and me involved those two world-class marriage wreckers: fairness in the treatment of stepchildren, and the equitable distribution of a finite supply of money.

Lord knows Hank and I worked hard and made reasonable salaries, but he brought home more money than I did. We set up a college savings account, and Hank had a 401(k), but we had little in other savings. It took all our income to maintain a home and two cars, and to feed, clothe, and educate five kids.

As the kids started finishing high school, it became clear that only Jeri and Wayne wanted to go to college. We divvied the college savings equally between them. The other three, Peter, Eddie, and Erin, wanted money for cars, for deposits on apartments, for furniture, and so much more. We told them if they weren't going to college, we could only loan them the money. They whined, yet they had little choice but to accept our terms.

This was years before I got my inheritance, which I'd had no inkling was coming. Hank and I had debt coming out our ears. Our house needed tons of work. We couldn't afford to give away so much money, no matter how much we loved our children.

Once they were out of the house though, Peter and Eddie kept coming up with more things they needed money for: tires and car repairs; tools, boots, and clothing for jobs they expected to get. They seldom—if ever—made payments on their loans. Erin didn't start out paying either, but I taught her how to budget, and I stayed after her until she whittled her debt away. But when I tried to do the same for Hank's boys, Hank freaked out.

"Leave them alone! They're my kids. I'll work it out."

"But you're not working it out. You keep giving them more money.

This isn't what we agreed on. How is it fair to Erin to make her pay and not them? And how is it fair to us? We need a new roof."

"I said, 'Leave them alone!'"

"But it's not right!"

We had this same argument over and over, until Peter and Eddie owed us ten thousand dollars between them. Finally, Hank let the true reason behind his intransigence out of the bag.

"Bea, I make more money than you do, and I can give it to my boys if I want to."

Whoa! What had Hank just said? That he loved his own kids more than he loved mine?

I'd thought they were all "our" kids, that we'd agreed to treat them as equally as possible. I was too stunned to keep arguing.

So, I fixed Hank, and I fixed him good. I drained our savings and gave five thousand dollars to Erin. Plus, since Wayne always needed more help with college expenses than Jeri did, I gave two thousand to her. I told my daughters we were giving money to all the kids—which was effectively true—but they were not to mention it to Hank or their siblings. I didn't want them to be hurt by Hank, though I was furious with him.

Because I managed the family money, it took Hank months to learn what I'd done. But one day, he called the bank to check our savings balance when he needed another car. He came home from work red-faced and raging, screaming at me for taking "his money." In the midst of our argument, he slammed his fist on the table and stormed out the door. He didn't speak to me for a solid week, and when he started speaking, it was terse and business-like.

Soon he was working even on weekends and not coming home until bedtime. With the kids out of the house, I was left lonely and miserable. Then I discovered that Hank had opened his own savings account. I was so pissed that I couldn't confront him about it. I sat home during the evenings and stewed for months.

At last I thought, "Screw him!" and I got involved in nonprofit work, helping Habitat for Humanity raise funds and serving on the board of the Wheatsville Food Co-op, often coming home at midnight.

After nearly two years of this, Hank asked me to be at home more in the evenings.

"Why? You're never here. The kids aren't here."

"Because," he said, "I miss you."

I missed Hank, too. I missed our sense of a close family. I missed Hank's touch so much that I was having an affair. With a great deal of pain, I ended the affair and tried to rededicate myself to my husband.

HANK USED TO TAKE ME DANCING, especially when he was wooing me, but also for the early years of our marriage. It was during those slow dances that I first let him into my heart. He towered over me and wrapped his arms around me tenderly, tightly. He sighed when he drew me close. The particular song that reeled me in was Marcia Ball's, "The Power of Love."

> *"I feel the power when we touch*
> *And I love you, I love you so much*
> *I just can't get over . . . the power of love."*

Intoxicated with his muscles and aftershave, I let Hank kiss me during our first dance to that song. Thereafter, I initiated the slow-dancing kisses. Hank was a little embarrassed to kiss in public, but I wasn't. Once I planted my lips on his, he didn't shirk me away.

At least he didn't for many years. Lately, he never even touched me in public. I thought he still loved me, though. I certainly hoped he did.

God, what if Hank was alive but hadn't come home because he didn't love me anymore? I wished I'd never thought of that.

But I did think about it as yet another thing to lose sleep over. And when I seriously delved into the question of love between Hank and me, I came to understand that Hank had fallen out of love with me years ago. And as a consequence, I'd lost most of my regard for him as well.

Tasha had been right. I did make excuses for Hank, especially to myself. I'd made so many, I'd failed to grasp that my husband didn't love me at all.

What a hateful thing to realize—just the kind of revelation I did not need in the midst of so much loss.

CHAPTER 25

At last the weather turned cold for a few days at the onset of December, and this brought us a new set of problems. Our homes weren't built for cold weather—they were designed to keep us cooler in summer, which was an especially good thing for most of the year, now that we had no air conditioners. But during late fall and winter in Austin, the weather vacillated between warm and cold, and we needed ways to keep warm.

Most of the time extra layers of clothing were enough, and sitting near the grill while meals were cooking. Extra blankets had to suffice for sleeping. But a few days in early December were real bears, the kind of cold we hadn't seen in a decade. We even had light freezing rain, which was as it should be, but we weren't prepared.

"We can't go get water tonight," Keno said. "It's not safe to light fires out there."

I should have been worried about the people with no water, but I was infinitely relieved that Keno wasn't going out.

The Pico house was an awfully big place to heat with its one fireplace. The open floor plan meant no doors between upstairs and down, so that any heat went straight to the second-floor ceiling.

I taught the kids how to build fires and keep them going, how to use the damper to keep out smoke. I told Mazie and Milo they could only work with fire under supervision—another thing that made Milo bristle.

Since the kids were stuck inside, I tried to get them interested in reading, as I had a big library of books for all ages. But if the kids, other than Keno, picked up a book, they wouldn't stay with it long. They said they couldn't see, but they wouldn't use lanterns either.

"Listen, kids, it's time you started doing some school work. You don't want to grow up uneducated, do you?"

"What difference does it make?" Tasha said.

"Oh, honey, I know things seem bad, but to think education isn't important is a very cynical view of the world. It means you don't have hope for the future."

"I don't have any hope," she said.

IN ALL THE POST-APOCALYPTIC STORIES I'd ever read or watched, the thing they never showed was the grief of it all—the persistent, soul-crushing misery from the loss of people you loved and relied on. Then there was the loss of your way of life, the pointed fear of what else you might lose, the dangers you had to watch out for, the hard work you had to do day in and day out simply to stay alive.

I used to think these flat characterizations of fictional denizens of after-the-catastrophe worlds were poorly rendered, were unrealistic and too cold. Now I realized that when your grief is too great, you grow numb. It's the only way you can protect yourself and keep moving. It was a kind of gift from God, this numbness, but if you spent time considering it, the emptiness inside you could strip you of any will to carry on.

Maybe I wasn't physically ill; maybe I was sick at heart.

ON A FEW COLD DAYS, I TAUGHT THE KIDS HOW TO SEW.

"Being a boy doesn't get you out of it," I told Milo, who put up a stink about having to "sew like a girl." "We're not sexist here. Everyone has to learn to do as many things for themselves as possible."

We sewed buttons on clothing that needed buttons. Milo tried to be inept, refusing to pay enough attention to keep his thread from tangling and knotting. Threading a needle was hard for me to teach. My hands shook too much, my eyesight was too poor for the dim light, but I finally managed to get each of them to thread a needle.

Once everyone had buttons down, we moved on to reconnecting seams and making hems.

"Mazie, take that princess skirt off. The ruffles are coming loose.

Let me sew them back on." She watched me warily while I stitched up the skirt, afraid I wouldn't return it.

Finally, Milo got into sewing and managed to hem his pants faster than the rest of us. Then he pranced around, showing off his mini-muscles and making us laugh.

WE LISTENED TO RICK THE STICK from "Afta-the-Disasta Radio," as he was now calling it. I pretty much hated listening to Rick at this point, on account of the emotions he set off in me. In my mind, he was forever associated with the horrid wreck in Waco and my lost family.

Rick had connected with neighbors who owned ham radios, and they'd scrounged up abandoned generators so they could contact other hams around the country. Someone in Clifton had died and left behind a stash of gasoline they were using for the generators.

So, Rick had news from around the United States, if you could call it that anymore. The federal government still existed but had gone "underground"—not necessarily in the literal sense, more like the clandestine sense.

The government still had a lot of power, firepower mainly, but also running vehicles and a few planes they'd slapped back together by replacing parts. But the feds weren't doing relief work—the need was too great and widespread. Instead those in charge had grown more militaristic than ever, guarding the borders against intruders and marching around population centers to keep people in line.

There were food and water riots and a lot of death in the biggest cities where people had no way to get to the country or to forage for themselves.

It was sheer luck we hadn't had riots around here. Every time Keno and his crew went to collect water, I waited for a band of armed marauders to follow them home and kill us all.

BEFORE IT HAD GROWN SO COLD, the gardening had been going pretty well, so now we had a lot of planted territory to protect against a freeze. A few of us owned outdoor thermometers, so we knew when it came close to freezing. But we had no way to guess what the weather would do next—truly maddening when our crops were on the line. Sure, people had lived this way for millennia, but we weren't accustomed to using our senses and reading signs from nature to predict what was coming. We covered our gardens with blankets and tarps and uncovered them when the sun came out, hoping for the best. Most crops survived the freezing rain this way, but it wouldn't be enough for a hard freeze if it came.

We had a kind of dump now, populated with rats and feral cats, on a scrubby vacant lot around the corner from our four-block perimeter. Compost piles were growing under trees in several yards—on land that couldn't be gardened due to tree roots. And we had a few rain barrel systems welded together out of scrap metal, much of it taken from enamel-coated major appliances. A couple of above-ground outhouses had been built, and two community composting toilets were under construction. We were making progress.

Keno and Phil had managed to get a low-water washing machine to turn 'round and 'round as long as someone rode the exercise bike they attached. They hadn't figured out the water flow yet, but they had ideas related to gravity feeds off of rooftops.

I should have felt better about the progress, but instead I felt breathless.

ONE EVENING NEAR DUSK, I went to the side yard to cover the garden for the night. I'd only been out there a minute or two when I heard kids come out to the patio.

"Come here," Keno whispered, and Darla giggled. This was followed by a long, quiet interval, with smooching the only sound coming from the patio.

Shoot. I needed to go inside but didn't want to interrupt. Too embarrassing for all of us. I sat on a bench and rubbed my hands together to keep warm. The breaths coming from the patio grew faster and heavier. Damn it. It was cold out here.

"Don't!" Darla said, giggling.

"Why not?" Keno said.

She giggled more. "'Cause your Nana will see."

"She won't see. All kinds of shit goes on around here that she doesn't see."

Like what? I thought, alarmed, and feeling a little betrayed by my grandson.

"Well, okay," Darla said. The smooching and breathing got louder.

"I love you," Keno said.

Are you kidding me? Did someone put aphrodisiacs in our water? Darla didn't reply that I could hear, and Keno let out a loud sigh.

"Don't you love me?" he said.

"Umm.... Maybe."

"But, Darla, I need you," Keno pleaded.

"No one never needed me before," she said.

"Well, I do. Don't you like it?"

"Maybe." The kissing and loud breathing resumed.

Crap. I was freezing, and now I was freaked out about Keno being crazy in love with this troubled girl—also at the thought of what I might be missing. I stood, picked up a hoe, and thwacked it at the ground, making sure to scrape the railroad tie bordering the garden.

"Shit," Keno said, trying to be quiet, but clearly surprised.

"I told ya. That old lady sees everything," Darla whispered. The back door opened and closed, followed by silence.

I went through the house and called Keno and Tasha to the garage. They weren't happy about being there.

"You kids cannot have sex. Do you understand me? We don't have condoms, or any other birth control."

A guilty look came over Keno, but Tasha huffed with exasperation.

"Mom said you let her have sex when she was a teenager," Tasha said.

"She said you bought her condoms and birth-control pills," Keno muttered. "She said she'd buy them for us."

I threw up my hands, staring back and forth between these kids, who were watching me with earnestness and more than a little anger.

"I didn't 'let' your mom have sex. I bought birth control for my kids because they were going to have sex whether I wanted them to or not." I sighed and sat down on a storage bin.

"Alright. I'm not making myself clear." I ran my hand through my hair and chose my words carefully. "I'm not judging you. It's understandable for you to want sex. But for the first time in my life, we can't control the consequences. We don't have birth control, or medicine for venereal diseases. We have no doctors. There are diseases that can kill you without meds. And then, there's pregnancy."

Keno gulped, but Tasha half-grinned, dismissively.

"My mom says it's not a disease to get pregnant. It's natural."

"Tasha, there is so much you don't know." I took a deep breath. "Before we had modern medicine, women often died during child-birth. We're almost back in the Dark Ages now, as far as medicine goes.

"Back in the seventies, natural childbirth was all the rage. Some of us had trained midwives, and everything went fine. But I heard of a couple of deaths and some really close calls—babies and mothers in distress who almost didn't get to the hospital in time. My friend nearly died from gangrene rotting her uterus."

"Nana, that's gross!" Tasha said.

"Real life without doctors is gross. You have to face up to that. . . . Those women were saved by fast transportation and modern hospitals, but we don't have that anymore. No matter how old you are, it's a terrible idea to get pregnant right now. I'm telling you possible consequences, hoping they'll make you think."

"But what if I'm in love?" Tasha said. "My mom told me to save sex for my true love."

"You might think he's your true love, but you don't know that." Tasha gaped at me with tears in her eyes. "Honey, these are not normal times. No matter how much you love him, sex is a bad idea. Understand?" She looked away from me.

Keno said, "We can have sex without, you know … going all the way, right?"

"Well, yes, but no penises anywhere near vaginas. Men leak semen without even knowing it, and it only takes one drop."

"Gaw!" Tasha said. Keno looked worried.

I was glad he asked his question, but how did sex education end up being *my* job?

LATER, I WAS STRAIGHTENING the living room and picked up a book from the floor near Darla's screened space. It was my book, *The Complete Poems of Emily Dickinson*, with lots of dog-eared pages. Darla had messed up my book, but at least she was reading, which was more than I could say for most of these kids.

A slip of paper was poking out from between pages. I shouldn't have done it, but I looked at the paper and was stunned. "Poem by Darla Belding," it said.

"My daddy could not stop for Death
He tried to speed right past it
So Death whacked Daddy on the head
'Cause Daddy was a bastard

"Death took my momma too
Even Juan and Bucky
But Death left me behind alone
No Eternity for me"

It broke my heart. I would never think of Darla as an ignorant girl again.

CHAPTER 26

One warm afternoon, when the grandkids and Darla were out in the neighborhood, working on gardening and whatnot, Jack came to join me on the patio and helped me shell peas. We didn't say much for a while, then Jack leaned forward and cleared his throat.

"Bea?"

"Yes?" I ran my thumbnail up the seam of a peapod to open it, dropping peas into one pot and the hull into another.

"Whaddya think happened to Hank?"

I hadn't expected that question.

"God only knows. I guess he's either hurt really bad or dead. Otherwise he'd have come home by now."

"So . . . y'all were gettin' along alright? Do you think he wants to come home?"

"What?" I stopped working to stare at Jack while my heart pounded heavily under my ribcage. I narrowed my eyes at the old man before me. "Why would you ask that? He's got my kids. He has to come home with my kids."

"Of course, your kids want to come home. I'm wondering what you think about Hank."

My thoughts screamed at Jack to run him off, but I guessed there was no point in doing that. I put down my peapods and straightened up in the chair.

"Hank hasn't loved me for years. I guess that's been obvious to anyone paying attention. But he does love his family, and we have a kind of partnership in that regard. I think he would come back for the family if he could. It's all he's got, especially now."

"He never had another lover?"

"Not that I know of, and not that I much care."

"So, you don't love him either?"

I fixed my attention in the distance and thought a minute. "I care about him. There are things I love about him. But, no, I haven't been in love with Hank for a very long time."

"For about fifteen years?"

I sighed. "Yes, for about fifteen years.... And you? Have you been in love since your divorce?"

"I have been, but you know that."

"I guess I do, don't I?" My hands quivered, so I clasped them in my lap.

"So," Jack said, "how long are you gonna keep waiting for Hank?"

"I guess forever. I don't have much choice. I can't leave the man when he's down."

"I believe you do have a choice." He locked his eyes onto mine.

"Not yet, I don't."

He set his lips into a straight line, brushing his hands on his thighs. "Okay then," he said, and went home.

THAT AFFAIR I HAD FIFTEEN YEARS AGO——it was with Jack. I'm pretty sure Hank never knew about Jack, but he may have suspected the affair. Now Jack was trying to reignite it. I can't say that I minded, though I was scared shitless to release my grip on the invisible Hank.

CHAPTER 27

Day 66, and I was still holding my breath, waiting for a break from this misery.

This boyfriend of Tasha's, Chas Matheson, was turning out to be more trouble than I'd realized. He was sixteen and too old for this behavior, but he was a ringleader in the band of roving kids. He sent them on missions of vandalism and theft, and they brought the spoils back to Chas. After our patrollers caught the thieving kids, they stopped robbing us and branched out into new territory.

As far as we could tell, our neighborhood was the only one getting organized for miles around. Abandoned homes were scattered all over town, and the ones near to us were getting defaced and robbed with some frequency. I understood taking useful stuff from empty homes, but what was the point of defacing them?

I found out this news about Chas not from Tasha or Keno, but from Darla when we finally had our talk, days later than I'd intended. Time escaped me more than ever lately. It seemed like time would have dragged by without television or internet to suck it away, but the opposite was true, at least for me.

I asked Darla how she was doing, and she shrugged. Her light hair looked cleaner than usual, her face a little plumper than before. I wanted to tell her how good her poem was, how well she'd evoked emotion. But since I saw the poem by snooping, I had to leave this unsaid.

"Honey, I know you're going through an awful lot, but you haven't been doing your gardening work. Why not?"

"I had other stuff to do," she said. She still wouldn't look at me.

"Darla, I need you to try harder to keep busy. I don't like nagging you about it, and I'm sure you don't want to be nagged. But there's a whole lot of work to be done if we're going to survive, and you need to do your share. You don't want other people doing your work for you, do you?"

"No," she said, as tears pooled atop her creamy cheeks.

"Well, will you please do your garden work? And I mean all the hours, every day."

"Okay," she muttered.

"Good. Is there anything you'd like to talk about?"

Darla didn't hesitate. "Chas steals," she said.

"Chas? What does he steal?"

Darla finally looked up to tell me about Chas strong-arming the smaller kids into doing his dirty work. Shrewd of Darla to change the subject from her negligence—and bad on me, because it worked.

Alarm bells went off in my head—about my granddaughter's boyfriend being a thief, yes, but also about Darla. Was she lying? Why would she betray a teenage code of silence to an old woman like me?

"How do you know all this, Darla?"

"Chas told me."

"And why are you telling me?" I narrowed my eyes at her.

Darla looked confused. "Well, because he's Tasha's boyfriend, and she's so young."

Darla was eighteen. Was she really concerned about Tasha, or was she trying to get Tasha in trouble?

"And why did Chas tell you about stealing? Was he flirting with you? Trying to impress you?"

Darla stuttered out her next words. "N-no. He j-just—he talks a lot."

She sat watching me with her mouth hanging open, so I said, "Thank you for telling me. You can go now."

She jumped up and lurched toward the stairs.

"Wait, Darla. Are you and Keno having sex?"

"What? No!" Flames flared in her cheeks. She stopped at the landing and peered at me sideways. "But Tasha—"

"Tasha what?" I bolted to my feet.

"Nothing. Never mind." She took a step downward.

"Darla, I asked you 'What about Tasha?'"

"Nothing! Forget it!"

Darla ran down the stairs. I hollered, "Wait!" but in seconds she was out the back door. I would have chased after her, but I didn't have the breath.

Soon I heard her using the push lawn mower below my window. That lawn didn't need to be mowed, but at least she was working.

Apparently, Darla didn't want to rat about Tasha having sex. I had not done enough to prevent this. Now I needed to confine Tasha to my house and yard, which I had no idea how to accomplish.

SOON I CAUGHT TASHA ALONE UPSTAIRS. "I need to ask you something."

"K," she said, gulping.

I took a breath, trying to stay calm. "Do you know that Chas is the ringleader of the stealing kids?"

I didn't have to tell her how I knew. She screamed, "Darla, you bitch!" and turned to rush away, but I grabbed Tasha's arm and spun her around to face me.

"Stop it! This is not about anyone but you, and keeping you safe. You're only fifteen. You're too young to be in love with any young man, especially one who gets little kids to steal. He's not an honest boy. Don't you know that?"

"What's wrong with taking stuff that nobody's using? It's stuff people need."

"Like what kind of stuff?"

"I don't know. Food mostly. Blankets."

"Jewelry? Alcohol? Does he steal alcohol?"

"I don't know. Maybe," she said.

"Maybe," I muttered. "Does Chas let those little kids drink?"

"I don't know, Nana. God!" I did not believe her.

"Those kids are tearing up houses. They're breaking windows and ripping down siding. That is a huge waste, especially now. They might be starting fires inside those houses, and that is crazy dangerous."

"But those kids do that. Not Chas."

"How do you know?"

"He told me."

"And you believe him?" I shook my head at her.

This girl—just like her mother Erin, always with the boyfriends she had to bail out of jail, who didn't help pay rent. And Tasha's father, Jimmy, hadn't been a good role model either.

"Tasha, are you and Chas having sex?"

"What? No!" She glanced into my eyes for a second, then looked past me. Not exactly reassuring.

I aimed my gaze straight into hers. "Are you telling me the truth?"

"Yes, Nana. Yes!" she said, incredulous.

Tasha stared at me, tears washing down her cheeks, snot dripping from her nose. I took a handkerchief from my pocket and reached to wipe her face, but she jerked back. So I passed her the hankie and watched while she wiped her eyes and blew her nose.

"Tasha, I know how it is to fall in love. And I know those bad boys can seem so cute and exciting. They're hard to resist. I had a couple of bad boyfriends in my day."

"Not you, Nana. You're so—"

"So old? So uncool? When I was a kid, we called it 'square.' We thought our parents and grandparents were squares and didn't know anything. I know it's hard for you to believe I was ever a cool person. But Chas isn't cool. He's a thief, and I need you to stop seeing him unless and until he starts behaving himself."

"Nana!" she squealed and threw herself face-down on the couch.

I patted Tasha on her back until her weeping slowed down, then I kept patting her because I somehow couldn't stop.

"I want my mom," Tasha said.

"I know. But she would keep you from seeing Chas, too."

"No, she wouldn't." Tasha might have been right about that.

A SHORT WHILE LATER, a screaming fight erupted in the backyard. By the time I got there, Keno had ahold of Darla, Milo had ahold of Tasha, and Mazie was whirling in circles, screeching, "Stop!"

"What the hell's going on?" I shouted on my way out the door.

"Slimy bitch, leave my brother alone!" Tasha yelled at Darla, straining to get away from Milo and almost succeeding.

Keno tucked Darla behind him. "Tasha, I like Darla, and it's none of your business."

"I don't want you kissing that slut."

"Who's the slut?" Darla said under her breath.

"What did you say, you whore?" Tasha shrieked.

"I'm not a whore. You are!" Darla shoved Keno aside, tears bursting from her eyes as she lunged for Tasha, grabbing a fistful of Tasha's hair. But when Keno yanked Darla back to him, Tasha's hair came with. Then both girls were kicking boys out of their way, slapping and slugging.

"Stop it! Both of you, stop it!" No one listened to me, and blood flew out of Darla's nose. I needed to startle them. I picked up a shovel, hollering, "I said stop it!" and I slammed the shovel blade against the brick of the house.

The shovel handle busted to pieces, sparks flew from the blade, and all the shovel pieces except a short stick in my grasp flew through the air. Stick parts rebounded off the girls. The blade bounced off Keno's forehead, leaving a thin line of blood.

"Damn, Nana!" he cried, reaching for his forehead then examining his wet, red hand.

The fighting instantly stopped as I raced to Keno. A fringed curtain of blood streamed down his forehead toward his eyes, which he shielded with his hand.

"Keno. I'm so sorry. I didn't think the shovel would break. Mazie, get me a jug of water and some washcloths."

Mazie stood there in shock, shaking all over.

"Go, Mazie! Now!"

She went.

"Keno, lie down on your back." He lay down, and I plopped down next to him, dabbing up blood with the hem of my shirt. "Tasha, go to your room! Now!"

"You always pick on me!"

"Stop acting like a child. You think you're so grown up, then do what I say. Go!"

"Darla started it!" Tasha hollered as she slammed her way into and through the house.

"Darla, go sit on that bench by the side garden. Now!"

"I wanna go with her," Keno said.

"No. You have to lie down. And Darla," I raised my voice so she'd hear me as she sped away, "I can't have you girls fighting. Understand?"

"Yes, ma'am." She was swiftly out of my sight, sobbing loudly as she went.

I sent Milo to Darla with a wet washcloth for her bloody nose. It needed ice, but what could I do?

I doctored Keno as best I could. In our previous world, he would've had stitches on that forehead. And head wounds bleed like crazy, so it took a while for the bleeding to stop.

To get him bandaged up, I had Keno come inside to the dining table. Every so often, he asked if he could go to Darla, but I kept saying no. I told him I was waiting for everyone to calm down, but if I'm honest about it, I was waiting to calm down myself. When I couldn't stop my hands from shaking and my breaths from coming too shallow, I let Keno go, and I went to take some meds.

But Keno was back in half a minute, carrying Darla's blood-spattered washcloth.

"She's gone! Where did she go?"

"I don't know. Maybe she went for a walk to cool off."

"What if she ran away?" He held back a sob.

"Give her a few minutes and see if she comes back." I'd had my fill of teenage girls and was in no hurry to see one.

"But if she ran away, she could've gone pretty far already. I need to find her."

"Honey, come here." I took his hand and looked into his deep green eyes below his forehead bandage. "You really think Darla would run away? How would she survive?"

"Nana, please!"

I had never seen Keno so distressed.

"Okay. Go. But take your bike and come back in one hour if you don't find her. She might come back a different way from the route you take."

"Thank you," he said and squeezed my shoulders. Then he was in the garage, on his bike, and down the road.

He'd been gone about twenty minutes when we heard the explosion.

CHAPTER 28

"Oh, no!" I yelled and rushed out the front door, almost falling over Mazie and Milo. Tasha hightailed it down the stairs behind us.

Down the block, a fireball and huge plumes of black smoke shot into the air above a house. I ran into the road to see that it was the Belding house. Oh, my Christ!

"Keno!" I wailed.

My family and I and several others ran toward the burning house as thick smoke filled the air along the street.

"Keno!" I screamed again. Jack caught up to us just as I stumbled. He grabbed me as I collapsed in gasps, and he guided me down to sit on the pavement.

"Keno! He might be in there!" My heart beat like a kick drum, stealing all my breath.

"Keno!" Mazie screeched. "Where are you?"

Tasha put one hand to her mouth, the other to her stomach, squealing out a sob.

The fire made several loud pops. Streaming flames shot toward us on the street.

"Keno!" Mazie yelled. Tasha scooped the girl up and away from the fire.

"Get back everyone!" Jack shouted. "More stuff could blow!"

"Keno!" I cried with what felt like my last breath.

"Nana!" A charred-looking boy rushed toward me through the smoke. Keno! "Darla's in there! Someone, help me get her out!" Keno whirled in a circle, flapping his arms. He lunged back toward the burning house.

Jack and Silas caught hold of Keno, but he was screeching and jerking himself around so much that he almost got away. Gary and Tasha also latched on to the boy, and together they pulled him back from the fire and down to the pavement. Keno continued to cry and moan.

"She's in there! Nana, make them help me get her out!"

If Darla was in that fiery house, there was no earthly way to save her, God rest her soul.

"Keno, your arm is burned," Tasha said, and I pulled myself up from the street.

"Bring him home, y'all!" I shouted. "Please bring him home so I can take care of him."

"No! I won't go! We have to get Darla out of there!" The boy fell forward over his extended legs. "Darla! Why?"

Men from the neighborhood stood clustered around Keno. Jack reached down and patted his shoulder, but Keno didn't seem to notice. My boy was not going anywhere. I would have to doctor him here.

"Tasha, go get the first-aid kit, some scissors, and in my bathroom linen closet there's ointment in a blue jar called Silvadene. Mazie, you get towels, washcloths, and a pillowcase. Milo, get my rolling office chair and bring it to me so I can sit down before I fall down. And get a gallon of water."

The kids ran toward home. The fire in the burning house was dying down enough for us to see that the garage was what had exploded. It had taken the front half of the house and part of the kitchen along with it.

Blackened garage rafters burned themselves out atop a charred and gutted minivan. All the window glass from the van was gone. The van was full of busted metal drums, leaking fluid that quickly turned to smoke. One van door had been driven halfway through the collapsing garage wall.

Good God, did Darla blow herself up in the van? I looked closer and saw what could have been a blackened hand.

I stationed myself behind Keno and gently turned him away from the fire to look at me. The hair on the left side of his head was singed. He had black scorch marks on his clothes. He'd lost the bandage off his forehead, and his cut there had bled, leaving crusted blood down one side of his face.

"Honey, I love you. I am so sorry this happened. So very sorry." I reached to hug him while we trembled and shook. "Are you burned anywhere else?"

"No," he said flatly, huffing for breath.

Milo arrived and rolled my chair up behind me, forcing me to sit down so fast that I almost tipped over backwards. Luckily, other people steadied me because Milo was already gone, running home for water.

"Bring liquid soap and a wash bowl, too, Milo!"

"Why did this happen?" Keno cried. His stark expression sent shivers through me.

"Honey, I don't know."

Soon, Mazie and Tasha arrived, with Milo running along behind, pulling a wagon full of supplies.

I had Tasha help wash and bandage Keno's arm. Neighbors started speculating about how Darla might have caused the explosion. I asked Jack to have them move away until I could get Keno cared for and take him home.

But Jack whispered in my ear, "He's the only one who knows what happened. We have to talk to him about it."

"Why? What purpose would it serve other than to satisfy some kind of morbid curiosity?"

"If you're talking about what I think you're talking about," Keno said despairingly, "I'll tell them. People have a right to know."

"Do they?" I said. "Really?"

"I'd like to know," Tasha said, and she started crying and shaking as much as Keno.

I pulled Tasha to me. Of course, she wanted to know. She probably felt partly responsible, after the fight and all. There was too much to protect these kids from in this world. Far, far too much.

"Keno can tell the story after I get him bandaged up," I said.

Keno's burn wasn't too horrible—about six inches long, on the inner side of his left forearm. Thankfully, he was right-handed. The burn went through a couple of layers of skin in a few spots. Good thing I had the Silvadene. I probably wasn't supposed to bandage the burn, but I couldn't see how Keno would keep from rubbing it against his body without a bandage. So, I wrapped the burn loosely with gauze, and I cut up the pillowcase to make a sling.

"Doesn't it hurt?" Tasha asked.

"No," Keno said, and I wondered why. Were his nerves damaged? Was Keno in shock? How could I tell?

"Doesn't anyone have medical training around here?" I asked, though I knew that no one did. I would have to keep my eyes on Keno.

Most of our neighbors went home and returned wearing jackets, as a north wind was blowing in. Fortunately, the house fire was pretty much dead by now, though there was a chance it could flare back up. The smoke blew away with the cold wind, but an acrid chemical stench permeated the air.

"Should I start telling it or what?" Keno asked me.

"Let me gather them up. Come on, everyone. It's cold out here. Let him tell the story so we can go home."

The neighbors from our co-op group gathered around, as did three men who looked like extra-grimy bikers—two wearing leather and chains, one with a huge skull earring. Maybe they'd come from another neighborhood to investigate the explosion? Or maybe they were related to someone in our group?

Chas paced behind the crowd, trying to catch Tasha's eye. She seemed to be purposely ignoring him. The man with the skull earring nodded to Chas, and the kid nodded back but quickly looked away. Something was up here, something not good.

Keno stood up, and several people sat down on the pavement or the curb. I stayed where I was, hoping Keno would look toward me and not at the garage and what had to be Darla's burned-up, disembodied arm.

"She ran away from our house because she was upset," Keno began.

"About what?" Silas asked.

"That's not important," I said. "She had a disagreement, and it upset her. She was a very sad girl. We don't need details."

Silas looked annoyed, but he stayed quiet. Keno took a breath and went on.

"I'm not sure how long she was gone before we noticed. Maybe half an hour? I got on my bike and went looking for her. First place I came was her house. She didn't have anywhere else to go. I thought she'd be afraid to leave the neighborhood."

Keno kept stopping every few words to catch his breath. That burn was clearly affecting him. I couldn't quit shaking with worry.

"I knocked on her door. No one answered. Then I saw her through the curtain. She was—oh God!" Keno bent forward, crying. I started to get up to take him home, but Jack held my shoulder. Tasha ran up to hug Keno, then she stood with him, holding his hand.

"Darla," he said, "she had a glass pipe. I begged her to let me in. But she wouldn't. She was acting funny. Kind of crazy. Laughing a lot but not in a happy way. I guess she was stoned. I don't know what on."

"Meth," said Tasha.

Keno spun toward his sister. "How do you know?"

"I heard her parents sold meth."

"Seriously?" I said. "You could have told me that."

"Sorry, Nana. I didn't think to tell you." Surely Tasha didn't think I'd believe that.

"You could have told *me!*" Keno said.

"I'm sorry!" Tasha cried.

My heart beat erratically, and I felt like I had so much grief inside that I might drop dead of it then and there. I made a conscious effort to breathe slowly to settle my heart, but breathing this acrid air suddenly seemed a very bad idea.

"Let's go to my house for the rest of this," I said. "This air might be full of methamphetamines."

"Darla wouldn't let me in," Keno continued. "She was acting weird. I told her. . . . I told her I loved her. She said I shouldn't love her because she was a bad girl."

He paused to breathe, his hand over his heart.

"I told her I wouldn't fall in love with a bad girl. Then she started screaming. Saying I didn't know about her family or all the boys she's been with. She said she didn't love me. And I should go home to my Nana because I was a big baby.

"I didn't believe her. . . . I kept trying. But she went away from the window. Then I heard her in the garage. I banged on the garage door, and she yelled at me to go away. Then I heard her get in the van and slam the door. I figured she couldn't hear me anymore.

"I was gonna get help to get her out of there, with the germs and poison and dope and stuff. But just when I got to the street, the house exploded."

Keno stopped speaking. He was breathless and shaking, and his face was covered with ashes and tears.

"I don't know why she did it." His eyes were empty and lost. "Maybe she just. . . . I don't know, lit her pipe and the whole place blew up?" Keno's voice trailed away. "I don't know. I don't know. I dunno." His legs gave way beneath him, and he sat down hard on the pavement, holding his stomach, rocking and moaning.

"Please help me get him home!" I cried out. Jack called over Phil and Gary. Phil, being the most well-acquainted with Keno, bent down and murmured something to him, then Phil and Gary pulled the boy up by his armpits and walked him home.

Milo grabbed Keno's bicycle and ran ahead to open the door. Tasha was right behind Milo, pulling the wagon. She ran inside to get blankets and pillows so they could lay Keno on the living room couch.

I pushed my rolling chair home with Mazie at my side. She wanted to push the chair, but I wouldn't let her. I needed it to hold myself up.

CHAPTER 29

The family sank into a deep, dark funk. Keno stayed glued to the couch for two and a half days. He was so distraught, not to mention injured, that he seriously needed rest.

When I checked on him before bed that night, he said, "Why did she do it, Nana?"

"You think she blew the house up on purpose?" I said, startled at the very idea.

"Yeah. But why?"

"She was very sad, Keno, and lonely without her family."

"But I was there. I was trying to help her."

"I know, honey. Sometimes people can't be helped, though. Sometimes they're just too sad." Did Darla commit suicide? What a horrid thought.

"I shouldn't've kissed her in front of Tasha. I didn't know it would start that fight."

"Sugar, she'll have your sweet kiss to keep her company for all of eternity. Think of that."

"She will? Is there an eternity, Nana, do you think?"

"Oh, Keno.... No one knows. But don't you find it comforting to think of your loved ones still being out there, even though we can't see them?"

"Like Mom and Grandpa?" he said.

"I don't know. I like thinking they're still alive, and that they'll come back to us someday. It makes me too sad to think otherwise."

He sighed and stared past me, lost in despair.

I debated whether to show him Darla's poem, but I decided to wait until he was less raw. I sincerely hoped that Darla had found the eternity she longed for.

THE NEXT MORNING, Jack brought over a chicken and some eggs. I made omelets, then chicken soup with rice. Tasha set up a solar oven and baked three different kinds of winter squash, which she shared with our neighbors.

Milo and Mazie were thrilled to have Keno inside with them, a captive audience. They played games with him, moving his game pieces for him. Milo read him comic books. Mazie read him *Winnie the Pooh*, and he helped her with the words. I had to practically force them to give Keno time alone to rest.

When Keno's burn had to be cleaned and his dressing changed, I got Tasha to help me until she learned to do it herself. I was proud of her and made sure she knew it. She'd been scared sober, I thought, and was trying to quit whining and grow up. Not all the way up though, unfortunately.

Four times in two days I saw Chas lean over our back fence to talk to Tasha, but she didn't say much to him. She turned away and worked on the garden or cooking. If he persisted, she came inside.

But once, I stepped out to the patio to see Tasha talking to Chas at the fence.

"How'd you get so pretty?" Chas asked. "No one else in your family is pretty."

Rude.

Tasha started giggling. She was buying this bull crap? She threw her shoulders back and swayed her hips. She knew she was alluring. When Chas eyed her up and down, she grinned. Damn it. What could I do with her? Dress her in a nun's habit?

On the third day, Keno got up, but I made him promise to only work half a day, and that included time spent doing household chores. He had more color in his cheeks, and his burn looked better, but he was still weepy, too skinny, and weak. That day I served him several meals. I told him he couldn't resume his regular schedule until he put on some weight. He didn't want to eat so much, but he didn't have the heart to argue with me.

JACK CAME BY to tell me that a group of men had buried Darla by the train tracks with her family. I was relieved.

"This thing has cast a pall over the whole neighborhood," I said.

"Lots of things casting a pall around here. People are still gossiping about Darla and the explosion. Some of them think Keno's more at fault than he's letting on."

This pissed me off. I felt like punishing the gossipers by cutting off their rations. But, besides being a massive overreaction, it would have invited mutiny. I asked what the basis was for this ridiculous speculation.

"Well, they say Darla looked pregnant, if you really want to know."

"Pregnant? She didn't look pregnant!"

"She'd gained weight since she moved in with you."

"Because I was feeding her. If her parents were into meth, maybe they didn't cook much."

"Silas saw Darla sneak off behind her house with Chas several times."

"Are you serious? I thought Chas liked Tasha."

"I think he likes it however he can get it," Jack said. "Look, besides the exploded barrels of chemicals, there were all kinds of vials and flasks and tubes in that house. It had to be a meth lab."

"How did I not smell a meth lab in the middle of our neighborhood?"

"Everyone missed it, Bea. Not just you. Chas must be using meth or some kind of drug. He's always so hyper. Maybe he was wooing Darla so she'd give him dope."

"I know people don't have TVs or internet to entertain themselves, but are they really going to turn into a bunch of small-minded gossips?"

"Don't shoot the messenger. I just thought you should know this was going on."

"I don't want Chas anywhere near my kids, but what can I do about him? Run him off with a gun? Turn his parents against me, when they're some of my best allies? If I make an enemy of that kid, it will start a war."

"I don't know, but I'll think on it. Maybe you can find a way to befriend him."

"I have no intention of befriending that boy. Why don't you talk to him about the meth? Ask him about Darla, too."

Jack winced, his eyes glued to my face.

"Maybe the meth's gone now," I muttered. "Maybe he'll be done with it and settle down."

"Maybe." Jack continued to watch me, as though he had something else to say, until I told him I had to make dinner and shooed him out the door.

AFTER SUPPER, I asked Tasha to sit down and look at me. She did so with reluctance.

"I've been told that Chas was seen several times sneaking behind Darla's house with her. Did you know about this?"

"What?" Tasha looked shocked.

"I've been told—"

"I heard you, but.... Oh, that explains everything. That's why Darla told you about the stuff with Chas. She wanted him for herself. She thought you'd keep me away from him.... I know she's dead, but I still hate her."

"There's no point in hating her. She was a very sad girl, so sad that it killed her. The person you should be mad at is Chas."

"I am mad at him. But it's hard to stay mad when he says all these cute, funny things. I love him, Nana." Tasha fell against me and sighed.

"Then you're being brave to resist him. We don't know if Chas was cheating on you with Darla, but he was sneaking around, and he couldn't have been up to anything good. You can't trust a man like that, and you deserve so much better."

"But there's not anyone better around here," she whined.

"Honey, you're better off with no man than with the wrong man. And, it won't be long before people figure out more ways to get around town. We have empty houses in our neighborhood. If we're successful with our farming, other folks will want to move here to join us, or they'll want us to teach them how to do the same thing. There'll be lots of opportunities to meet young men. There's no hurry. Hurrying gets you into trouble. We've had enough trouble to last us a while, don't you think?"

"Yeah," Tasha said, "but it sucks."

"I know. It sucks big fat ones."

"Nana!" Tasha started laughing, smiling for the first time in days. "Please don't tell Keno about Darla and Chas sneaking around. Someone ought to keep a good memory of her. Besides, he's been traumatized enough. The only reason I told you is so you'd see that Chas can't be trusted."

Tasha's smile disappeared. I had given it to her then snatched it away, or so I thought. Much later, I came to understand that Tasha was mad at me for shielding Keno's feelings but not hers.

WHEN KENO GOT BACK TO FULL CAPACITY, he found a set of weights and started pumping them every morning and night, except when he went on water missions. He was working off his grief, but I worried he was obsessed. He should've been eating more if he wanted to build muscle, but if anything, he was eating less.

I needed to do something to cheer these kids up. The weather was warmer. Maybe we could collect pecans at a secret spot Jack had mentioned. The big obstacle to this idea would be getting me there. No way I could walk or ride a bike very far. I got winded going halfway down the block.

"Keno," I said one day at lunch, "do you think you could rig me up a way to get around, you know, to leave the neighborhood either under my own power or with you guys pushing or pulling me?"

"What about those wheelchairs at the Mint? I haven't checked the one with the battery to see if it still works, though."

"Well, will you check? Although... those electrical chairs are heavy and clunky. If the battery dies, they're very hard to push. But the other chair might be too flimsy to go over rough terrain."

"Where are you trying to go?" Tasha asked.

"I don't know. I just think we should take an excursion. Get out of here, and away from our troubles for a day."

"Yes!" said Milo, thrusting his arm in the air.

"Can I go? I wanna go!" Mazie jumped up from the table to dance around the room. It was so nice to see her happy.

"If we can figure it out, we'll all go. The hard thing will be to keep those pesky neighborhood dogs from following us." They weren't bad dogs, but they might cause trouble in another neighborhood.

"We'll scare them away," Milo said.

"Okay, Milo, you work on a way to scare off the dogs, and Keno, can you fix me up with a ride? Maybe you could put the heavy wheels from the electric wheelchair on the other chair, or maybe you can think of something else, like a cart to pull me behind a bicycle."

"Yeah, a cart. That's a great idea. I know I can figure it out."

Now the kids were excited to have something new to focus on. I didn't expect it to cure their despair, but I hoped it would ease it. Even if we never got to go anywhere, the effort alone should cheer us up.

CHAPTER 30

Mid-December, two and a half months since the EMP, and still no miraculous arrival from Waco.

That morning, while Keno worked in the garage on the bicycle cart, his new ropy muscles starting to show, Jack came to the door with a box of chirping baby chicks.

"Aww," we all said.

"Please Nana, can I hold one?" Mazie cooed, bouncing on her tiptoes in her tattered tutu.

Jack cautioned Mazie against holding the chicks, saying it would make them sick. He gave us an impromptu lesson on them: what to feed them and how often, how long it should take them to grow up, and when we could expect to get eggs. He came back later to build a coop complete with a chicken run covered with wire netting, to keep away hawks.

Mazie was over the moon. She watched the chicks for hours on end, and I'm sure when no one was looking, she picked them up. She told me she had names for each of them.

"How can you tell them apart? They look the same yellow and fluffy to me."

"I can tell, Nana. Believe me, I can tell." I wanted to believe her, but I didn't really.

THAT SAME AFTERNOON, the Zizzos brought us a dressed rabbit. They'd been keeping their rabbits a secret, but now they had enough bred to set up more hutches, and to start feeding rabbits to neighbors once in a while.

Kathy Zizzo took my hand. "I want you to know how much we

appreciate what you're doing for us. We might've died by now if not for you. Very generous and very brave, raising all these kids by yourself and still sharing."

"Why, thank you, Kathy." No one else had complimented me so. "You have any special tips for cooking this rabbit?"

She spent another quarter-hour telling me different ways to cook rabbit. I thought this first time I would keep things simple, so I roasted it on a spit over the barbecue flame.

AT OUR YUMMY RABBIT DINNER, Keno told us he was ready for a test run of the bike cart. He wanted to give the kids rides in it tomorrow so he could get it running smoothly before giving me a ride.

"Nana, you're gonna like it. I put a car seat in it, and I made a step and handrail so you can get in and out real easy."

"Did you?" I said, a little choked up. "That was considerate of you." Keno blushed beneath his oily hair.

"I wanna ride. Nana, can I ride?" Mazie asked.

"If Keno says you can. But you ought to wear a helmet and pads in case something goes wrong."

"I don't need a helmet or pads," Milo said.

"Yes, you do. What if the whole thing falls over? You would land on the concrete."

"I hate helmets and pads," Milo said, poking out his plump lower lip.

"Well, I hate head injuries. You either wear the helmet and pads, or you don't ride in the cart. Got it?"

"Got it," he muttered. Darned little daredevil kid.

AROUND SEVEN P.M., I answered a knock at the door to find Sonja Carrera with her little son hanging on her, wiggling around.

"Hi, Sonja. Is everything alright?"

"Yes. Well, no. Can I talk to you?"

"Uh … sure. Come on in."

The little boy wore blue pajamas with feet in them. He clutched a toy, a robot I think, and his black-brown hair hung in front of his big brown eyes. Sonja was so thin that she looked like she might snap in two from the weight of her dangling child.

They followed me to the living room. "Can I get you some water?" I asked.

Sonja looked at her son, who nodded. "Cesar would like some, please."

"Don't you want some?"

"No thank you, Mrs. Crenshaw."

"You can call me Bea. Have a seat."

She sat tentatively on the edge of the couch, with her back erect and her hands folded in her lap. Cesar stood next to her legs, rubbing his face into the couch cushion. I poured him some water in the dining room, where my grandkids were playing Monopoly. For some reason I couldn't pinpoint, I had an ominous feeling about whatever Sonja was going to say.

"Kids, please take your game upstairs and take Cesar with you. Let him play, too, or if he doesn't want to play, find him some toys."

The grumbling kids carried their Monopoly game upstairs. Cesar didn't say anything, but he followed willingly. Upstairs, Tasha yelled at Milo, accusing him of moving a Mediterranean hotel to Boardwalk. Keno, with a lowered voice, seemed to settle the dispute, and soon all was reasonably calm with the kids. Cesar kept peeking downstairs, probably to be sure that his mother hadn't left.

"So, what can I do for you?" I asked.

Sonja closed her eyes and fanned at her face. Tears gathered in her long, dark eyelashes.

"I cannot stay here. I cannot," she said.

"Well, where would you go, and how would you get there?"

"I must go to Mexico. Cesar's father is there. I—We need him. He will take care of us." So that's why her husband never helped carry water.

He wasn't even here, and I hadn't noticed.

"Don't you think it would be better for your husband to make his way to you? A man can travel more quickly and safely than a woman with a small child."

"I have waited and waited, and he is not here. I must go to him."

"Oh, Sonja. I don't know what part of Mexico Cesar's father is in, but it could take him months to get here. And if he's on his way here, you could pass each other without knowing it. How would you find him then?"

Sonja's erect bearing collapsed, and her face dissolved into a grimace of pain. Then she sat back up and gave me a dry, hard look.

"My parents are doctors. We will be safer with them."

"But I don't see how you can't get down there."

"This is why I have come to you," she said. "I would like to buy one of your wagons. I will pull Cesar to Mexico."

"Sonja, you can't pull Cesar all the way to Mexico. You're so thin. Would you have the strength for that? And you can't go this time of year. It could snow and sleet on you. You could die of exposure."

"I'm going. I have decided."

"Can't I convince you to wait?"

She didn't respond. She merely looked at me with a steely resolve. I sat back, my mind rushing through possible ways of stopping her from going on this suicide mission and taking her son with her. But the desperation in her eyes wrenched my heart.

"Tell you what, Sonja. I can't sell you a wagon. What would I do with money? And we need all the wagons we have. But maybe I could find another way to help you, if you'll help me in return."

Sonja sat forward. "I'm listening."

"Okay." I leaned toward her. "I need help around here. I'm wearing Tasha out doing so much cooking, cleaning, and gardening. As you can see, I'm old and in poor health. My grandson Keno is building a bicycle cart for me to ride in so that we can go to other parts of town. That's the kind of vehicle you need for a trip to Mexico.

"I won't sell you the cart that Keno's making for me. But if you'll help me here while he works, he can finish my cart, then he can build one for you. In the meantime, we'll put some meat on your bones to build up your strength." I leaned back and added, "What do you think of that?"

"Will it take very long?" Sonja asked.

I hoped that building a cart for Sonja would give me time to convince her to change her mind. Maybe her husband would show up soon, and the problem would be solved.

"Shouldn't be too long," I said.

AFTER SONJA LEFT, I couldn't reconcile my conscience to helping her do something so dangerous. I kept picturing her lying dead in the desert, Cesar crying beside her, buzzards circling overhead.

When I talked to Keno about building her bike-cart, something came over me, and I said, "Take your time building it—at least a couple of months until the weather warms up."

"Sure," he said.

"Don't tell anyone that you're going slow, okay?"

He nodded and went to pump weights.

SONJA ARRIVED SHORTLY AFTER DAWN the next morning, as soon as smoke started rising from my barbecue. I showed her how to make the grill-top biscuits and the cowboy coffee.

I made sure that Sonja ate a lot of breakfast, the same way I did with the kiddos. I even persuaded her to drink the awful powdered milk that I exempted myself from drinking. Of course, we fed Cesar as well. I told Sonja I would love to see her eat here *and* at home to get extra calories.

We showed Sonja what we were doing with our home garden. I said that this week we'd fire up the wood cookstove and bake some bread. If it went well, we might set up a neighborhood co-op for canning and baking.

"Sonja, Keno can show you my bike cart and the parts he needs for yours. Maybe today you and some kids could go around the neighborhood to look for parts. Then you can come back and help with dinner. Tomorrow, you can cook and do a little cleaning. We can work out a weekly schedule for all this. How does that sound?"

Sonja seemed a bit overwhelmed, but she said, "It's fine." She headed off to find Keno but turned around, wearing a shy smile. "Thank you for helping us. You are a hero to me."

"Why, thank you." My face grew hot. I couldn't help but like Sonja. I realized that I was deceiving her, but I felt that I had no choice.

Because we spent so much time getting Sonja oriented, the kids didn't get to have their rides in Keno's bicycle cart until the next afternoon. It was a cold and blustery day, and all the dogs kept getting in the way. Milo got Sonja's permission, then led the dogs into her backyard and locked them in. Our neighbors didn't seem to care that their dogs were locked in someone else's yard. They'd been running in packs and were working everyone's nerves. I thought we should lock the dogs up more often, but from all the yowling and jumping and whining, I knew the dogs didn't agree.

The kids took turns riding in the cart, and I made sure they wore helmets. I gave up on insisting they wear pads; they were mysteriously missing and Milo had a suspicious gleam in his eye. Even Sonja took a ride. The whole set-up looked wobbly and very bumpy to me. Keno agreed that he needed to make the cart more stable. The best thing was that the kids enjoyed themselves so much, laughing and shrieking with delight.

Milo put in a heavy lobbying effort that he should be allowed to pull people in the cart, but I was afraid he'd spill children left and right, and no one would be laughing anymore. I told Milo he'd have to wait until Keno got things adjusted. Milo walked away pouting, but soon he was laughing again, chasing the bike down the street, his sunglasses askew, while Mazie and Cesar rode in the cart together.

CHAPTER 31

Within days, Sonja was well-integrated into the household, and I wondered how we'd survived without her. Now I wanted more than ever to stop her from going to Mexico, but I kept this to myself, searching for some way to change her mind.

She already looked healthier, with rosier cheeks and more roundness to her face. And Cesar was a godsend for Mazie. He would hang out with her all day as she washed laundry or supervised the growing chicks.

Tasha didn't appear to be seeing Chas for the time being. I saw her flipping through a medical anatomy book—I was ecstatic about that. And Jack had finally convinced Sam to use his truck for the water runs out south of town.

Keno went on all these runs as an armed guard. I couldn't bear to think of him in a shoot-out over water, but he wouldn't discuss staying behind. The water quests were his brainchild, and he was determined to see them through. He wanted to take weeklong shifts at the farm to guard the well, but I begged him to stay home to protect us. I sincerely needed his help. This was the only thing related to water quests that I won his concession on.

GETTING THE WOOD COOKSTOVE GOING was harder than I'd anticipated. At first a couple of pieces were missing. After a lot of cussing and shoving things around in the Mint garage, Phil and Jack found the misplaced parts. Then the stove had to be leveled, which meant the best place to set it was on the Mint patio.

But I was afraid the smoke would chase away my bees, which I still hadn't revealed to anyone. I hadn't done a thing to take care of those bees or to harvest the honey either. I said I didn't want the stove on the

Mint patio because it would smoke up the house. We settled on my front yard as a temporary place, until we could set up vent holes and smoke stacks in someone's garage.

By the time we got the stove put together and leveled with a short smoke stack attached to its backside, it was too late in the day to fire it up for more than a simple test. We built a small fire in the firebox and cooked split pea soup and rice on the stovetop. There was more smoke than with the barbecue, but the stove seemed to cook well. The tricky part would be controlling the temperature for baking and stewing.

The next morning, I was up early, starting a yeast and sugar-water mixture to rise, rousting Keno to fetch flour and oil from the Mint, and getting Tasha to help knead bread dough. By the time Sonja arrived, we had eight loaves rising in pans, and Keno was damping down the oven to regulate the temperature.

One nice thing about the woodstove was that the top heated up while the oven was going, so we cooked breakfast on the stovetop—oatmeal and hot cocoa made from powdered milk. So much starch in this diet of ours. Ugh. I made myself drink lumpy cocoa because it had protein in it. I hoped my kids weren't getting their growth stunted from the lack of whole protein. I would have given a fortune for some goats.

While the kids and I ate breakfast, Sonja put the bread loaves in to bake, and with some instruction from me, she started another batch, this time of twelve loaves. I'd already scammed bread pans from the neighbors, so I had about thirty pans. Everyone was happy to provide them. Just the thought of fresh bread made some of us get teary-eyed.

By mid-morning, the air above our yard was loaded with the warm and yeasty smell of baked bread. As we pulled the first loaves from the oven, neighbors started strolling past the yard, eyeing what we were up to.

"Oh, come on and get some," I said. Soon almost every neighbor was in our yard, munching on hot, fresh, whole-wheat bread. I saw smiles on faces that I hadn't thought capable of smiling. Since we didn't have honey yet, I set out my stash of maple syrup.

"Merry Christmas," someone said. Was it Christmas already? I'd quit paying close attention to the calendar because it made me too sad to think about how long my family had been missing. Going on three months now. I mean, I knew Christmas was coming, but I had tried to ignore it and apparently succeeded.

Later when I came inside, Mazie and Tasha were draping the mantle with Christmas chains made from construction paper and glitter, and Milo was belting out, "Si-i-ilent night, ho-o-oly night," in his crackling contralto voice.

They put me to shame, these hopeful kids. I sat down with a full heart and proceeded to pine for the rest of my family the remainder of the day.

AT LAST, Keno pronounced the bicycle cart ready for me. I got instantly nervous, I couldn't say why. If this thing worked, it might suddenly expand our horizons.

I pulled Milo aside and insisted he produce the missing knee and elbow pads. He was evasive at first, but he finally coughed up the goods when I explained what a bad thing it would be for an old woman to break her elbow in a world without medical care.

We'd already had a broken arm in the neighborhood, and Silas had been forced to pull his wife's abscessed tooth with a set of pliers, using whiskey and ibuprofen for anesthetic. What were we going to do when the pain relievers and liquor ran out?

I strapped on the pads, donned the helmet, and let Milo help me into the cab-cart behind Keno's bike. The whole contraption looked a bit like a chariot. Keno grinned from ear to handsome ear. The kids giggled, and Sonja smiled. Jack watched us from his driveway.

"Ready, Nana?" Keno said.

"I guess, but go slow, okay?"

"I can't go too slow or we'll fall over." Keno laughed, and so did I.

"Does this thing have a seatbelt?"

"No, but I'll put one in later. Can we go now?"

I crossed myself and held on to the sides. "Ready. Set. Go!"

Keno took off. Our speed as we raced past the scenery, plus the wind in my face, scared the wits out of me. It had been twelve weeks since I'd ridden in a car or any sort of vehicle. We took a left turn and went over a bump, sending me several inches into the air, and I squealed. My heart sped up, which always worried me, but I hung in for a trip around two long blocks and a victory lap in front of our house.

Neighbors cheered for us, and we had a good laugh.

"Someone help me out of here," I said. Tasha rushed forward with Mazie, who almost knocked me down trying to hug me, she was so excited.

"Keno," I said, "that was a lot better than riding on your handlebars." We cracked up at that.

Jack came over to join in the fun. While I had him here, I asked where to find the pecans. He swore me to secrecy, then followed me inside to draw me a map. It was a place about a mile and a half away, a vacant lot surrounded by storage lockers.

"There's two big pecan trees, and they always bear, even when other trees don't," he told me. "And the nuts are big with those good paper shells. I haven't had a chance to go back, with all the gardening. But you better be careful over there. Hungry people are mean, and some folks must be mighty hungry by now. If someone found that place and staked it out, they won't be happy if you intrude."

"Okay, I'll take a gun. I guess it's too close inside town to do shooting practice. I was hoping it'd be a place where I could teach the kids to shoot."

"It would be better to do that in the neighborhood. It's less likely to draw unwanted attention. Maybe I'll build a little shooting range."

"Thank you for watching out for us."

"It's my pleasure to watch out for you, Bea." His eyes twinkled in the fading daylight. For the first time in a long time, I noticed how blue they were.

"See ya, Jack," I said, and he grinned.

Sonja offered to bring a bike for Mazie to use—a bike she'd bought for Cesar to learn to ride someday. Now that Sonja was getting into being resourceful, maybe she wouldn't feel so helpless anymore. Maybe I could persuade her not to go to Mexico. I crossed my fingers and zipped my lips.

RICK THE STICK, reporting from the radio that night when I was alone, dropped this bomb on us listeners:

"There's a rumor goin' around the ham community that some nukes went bad back east. Some folks don't believe this rumor, but others swear by it.

"One guy claims he knows for sure. Says that two nuclear reactors in Virginia—up by D.C.—they exploded and poisoned the whole area and all those people. God above, I can't imagine how bad that must be. Guess that's why the gov'ment ain't helpin' us.

"Someone else said the Indian Point nuke up by New York City melted down. I don't think it exploded, but it leaked radiation. No one knows if it's killin' people or what.

"Sorry to have to tell y'all somethin' so bad, folks, but maybe it explains a few things."

Oh, it explained some things, alright. Without power, cooling water couldn't be cycled through nuclear reactor coils, and they would've run out of gasoline for backup generators pretty fast. Nukes were bound to melt down. Damn them for putting us in this peril. But my blood pressure wouldn't allow me so much anger, so I lived in a state of anxious resignation.

I could not live without hope. I had to constantly make room for it.

I checked the Geiger counter, and the reading was a touch higher than last week. I shoved my thoughts of nuclear devastation to the bottom of my mind, as I'd done repeatedly throughout the course of my life.

CHAPTER 32

84 days. 84 Godforsaken days.

On a balmy late December day, we went pecan hunting. By the time we'd finished our morning chores, it was near noon—already too warm for jackets, although I insisted that everyone bring one. This was the time of year when the weather could turn quickly, and we would have no warning.

The kids herded the dogs into Sonja's backyard. Sonja offered to pull the garden cart we'd filled with jackets, water, and bags for pecans.

"That's sweet of you," I said. "How about if you and the kids take turns?"

"Okay." Sonja's eyes were puffy, her expression hollow.

"Are you feeling up to this, Sonja? You don't have to go."

"Today is my husband's birthday." She turned her back to me, wiping her eyes. I patted her shoulder. I couldn't think what to say. Hank's birthday had come and gone in November, and I had deliberately ignored it. What kind of hard-hearted person this made me, I didn't know, but I wasn't fond of this icy aspect of my new self.

I told Milo to pull the wagon with Cesar riding inside. Milo was peeved, but soon we were rolling down the street, with Tasha and Mazie riding bikes, Sonja walking fast, and Keno pulling me in the bike cart. The Zizzos waved as we passed. The kids got downright giddy, even Milo. I felt a bit giddy myself.

When we reached the storage lockers and the lot with pecan trees, the place looked deserted. Keno hoisted Milo to the top of the chain-link fence, and Milo climbed over to scout around. He came running back.

"There's a billion pecans. Two billion maybe!"

"Great," I said. "But how will we get in?"

"I can lift kids over, then climb over myself," said Keno. He looked askance. "You might want to wait over here though."

Shoot. I'd been looking forward to gathering pecans. But the main thing, other than adding to our food supply, was for the kids to have fun.

"Okay, everyone up and over. Alley-oop!" I stood back to watch the kids make fast work of breaking into someone else's property.

"I'll wait with you, Bea," Sonja said.

"Sure, but you can gather pecans if you want to. I'll be fine."

She looked uncertain. "I'll go for a while, but I'll be back." I nodded, and she was up and over the fence, nimble as a cat.

I LAY ON A BLANKET, thinking about my missing family, which was more torturous than restful. Tasha came to the fence after about an hour.

"You okay, Nana?"

"I'm fine. Thank you for checking on me," I said, and she grinned. The girl was having fun, for once.

A good while later, Sonja climbed the fence and sat down beside me, sighing. We chatted a bit about the crazy-good overabundance of plump pecans. She was obviously hurting, so I kept making conversation, hoping to cheer her up.

I gave Sonja's arm a light squeeze. "Want to tell me about your husband? It's his birthday, right? How old is he?"

"He's thirty," she said quietly. "His name is also Cesar, the second. He's a computer engineer. So am I, but I haven't worked since Cesar the third was born."

"Such a devoted mother. Why did your husband go to Mexico? For his job?"

Sonja's face went ghastly pale. She shot me a horrified look, then jumped up and ran around the far corner of the storage lockers. Shit, Bea, what have you done now?

From out of my sight, Sonja let out a guttural sob. Cesar snapped his face toward the sound then looked around fast for his mother.

Not seeing her, he dropped his bag, spilling his pecans and tripping over them, scrambling to the fence and plastering himself against it, screaming, "Mama!"

Mazie went into action, squealing her little head off. "Keno! Come help Cesar over the fence! Hurry!"

Keno rushed to Cesar, whispered something to him, then lifted the boy to the top of the fence.

"Be careful getting down, Cesar!" Mazie shouted, stealing the words right out of my mouth. "Don't worry about your pecans. I'll get them!"

"You're a good helper, Mazie." I almost cried at Mazie's sweetness, but I couldn't cry. I'd already set a woman to weeping just to satisfy my curiosity.

I stood by while Sonja returned to embrace Cesar, but when her tears didn't stop and Cesar started wheezing, I stroked her arm.

"I'm so sorry. I didn't mean to upset you. I know you need to cry, but Cesar's getting wheezy. We should pack up and take him home."

I wanted to hug Sonja, but she was so reserved that I doubted she'd want to be hugged. I took hold of her hand and used a clean hankie from my pocket to wipe her face.

"Sweetie, it will get better, I promise you that. And if you ever want to talk, I'm here."

"Thank you," she muttered, averting her eyes.

I hollered for the kids to grab their bags of pecans. "Time to go home!"

The kids made a big production out of getting each other and their pecans, plus Cesar's, over the fence.

"Nana," Milo said, "I got more pecans than Keno! See!" He showed me his bag, then grabbed Keno's so I could compare the two. They looked about the same to me.

"Milo," I winked at Keno, "I believe you beat his socks off."

Milo danced around pointing at Keno and rejoicing, while Keno feigned a scowl.

We put the pecan bags into the wagon. "It looks too heavy to pull home," I said.

"I'll pull it," Sonja said. Before I could protest, she added, "I want to."

"If you're sure," I said. "Thank you."

Tasha winced and held her stomach. She looked a little green.

"Did you eat too many pecans, honey?" I asked her.

"Not that many," she said.

"We'll fix you some mint tea when we get home."

Cesar was still breathing raggedly, so I put him in the bike cart with me. Sonja lagged behind, lugging the wagonload in fast spurts, stopping often to pinch the top of her nose.

What in the world could have happened to cause Cesar II to go to Mexico and leave Sonja alone with a child and a well of grief? I wanted to know, but no one would catch me asking about it again.

Midway home, a half-naked old man leapt from the overgrown bushes along the roadside, slashing a stick through the air—a filthy white man with matted hair and beard. I'd never seen more insane-looking eyes. We halted as the man ran straight toward Sonja and the wagon, parrying his stick at invisible demons.

Sonja dropped the wagon handle and dashed backward. I grabbed hold of the pistol in my pocket and hopped from the cart to the ground.

"Give me some!" the man cried, slicing the air and spinning around the wagon.

"Take a bag!" I shouted.

"I want two!" He lowered his stick, darting his eyes. "What is it?"

"Pecans," I said with no breath.

"I'm taking two!" But he picked up one bag, clutching it to his chest as pecans spilled out the top.

Then the sky abruptly lit up with ribbons of blue, yellow, and green light. We all screamed, though my scream was a croak. There was no *whump* sound this time—nothing electric was running to make the sound. A spectacular technicolor lightshow swirled across the sky above us, and the hairs on my arms stood up.

The crazy man dropped his pecans and cried, "I knew it would come back!" lifting his stick to the sky like Gandalf in *Lord of the Rings*, proclaiming, "It came for the Mayans. It came for the Egyptians. It came here in 1859, and now it has returned!"

I stood in a three-point stance and aimed my pistol at the man's head. "Run, kids!" I shrieked. "Run home, now!"

The kids and Sonja gaped at me. Green and yellow light continued to stream across the heavens. Tasha scooped up Mazie, mounted a bike with her, and took off toward home.

"Cesar's bike!" Mazie hollered as they hurtled down the road.

"I've got it!" Milo yelled. He hopped on the little bike and pedaled like a speed demon.

Keno stood still, balancing the bike and whipping his eyes between me, Sonja, and the crazy man, whose jubilations had gone incoherent.

"I'm not leaving you here, Nana."

Tears shot into my eyes. "Go, Keno. I've got this!"

"Bea, you must come," Sonja said.

"I'm not letting this man follow us home. Go on. Both of you!"

Sonja trotted toward us with the wagonload. Keno grabbed Cesar from the bike cart and stuck him on top of the pecans in the wagon as Sonja passed. She broke into a sprint.

"I'll wait down the block," Keno said. "You can't get home without this cart."

I inhaled sharply, and the pistol began to shake.

"Okay, just go!"

Keno ran, dragging the bike and cart down the block.

The half-naked man shot his gaze into my eyes with a terrifying intensity.

"Unbeliever! The Sun God is king! The dancing rainbows are his children. Disbelieve and you will die the death of civilizations who turned their backs on the King of the Heavens!"

"Go back where you came from. Now!" I cocked the pistol.

"Unbeliever!" he screeched, but he scrambled into the tunnel of bushes from whence he'd come. I stood frozen with the pistol aimed into the tunnel, then I pointed it into the air and fired. Branches fractured and leaves crackled as the man crashed deeper into the woods.

I collapsed to sit on the curb, keeping the pistol up, until Keno whooshed up on the bike, helped me into the cart, and sped home so fast I had to cover my eyes.

The colors in the sky receded, but a white glow filled the firmament. King of the Heavens, spare us please.

AT HOME, I checked everyone over to be sure they were okay. We ate cold leftovers on the patio and stared at the sky, which glowed whiter than ever as the sun began to set. I stepped into the house, grabbed a book, and brought it back outside. The skylight was like a soft reading lamp. The words were easy to see. I closed the book, cringing.

"Sonja, why don't you and Cesar spend the night with us," I said.

"Thank you, Bea. We will."

"Do you think ancient Mayans and Egyptians had solar storms?" Keno asked.

"It's possible," I said, "but that guy was making shit up. We used to have healthcare for the mentally ill, though never enough. That poor man needs it."

"Yeah," Keno said, "but half the neighbors have their own crazy theories. Not sure his was any crazier than others I've heard."

"That's true," I said, sighing. "It's tragic. Seems like he was a literate man. He got the date right for the Carrington thing. Maybe he knows something we don't know."

"Maybe he *is* in touch with the Sun God," Keno said, snickering.

"I'd like to give the Sun God a good talking-to."

As Sonja and most of the kids started heading to bed, I gave Tasha a hug. "Thank you, honey, for thinking so fast today and getting Mazie away from that guy. You're always been so good with Mazie. I really appreciate it."

"Thanks." Tasha blushed, seeming a little thrown by the compliment. I hadn't been giving her enough of them.

Keno stayed outside, sprawled on a lounge chair next to me.

"Honey, thank you for saving me today."

He looked at his hands and mumbled, "You're welcome."

I leaned close to him. He peered at me, and I held his face. "Keno, the day may come when you'll have to make a choice between saving me or saving yourself. And you will have to save yourself and let me do my job of protecting you so that you can live on to take care of these kids."

He blinked at me, emitting a soft whimper.

"It's scary, I know, but it will be your job. Understand?"

"Yes," he said, and jerked his face away to cover it with his hands.

The white glow in the sky lasted another day and night, then disappeared.

CHAPTER 33

Three days after the second solar event, two days before New Year's, we took our excursion to Tasha and Keno's house—well, their mother Erin's house. I had to force myself not to let my two daughters and three stepsons wash into history like so much water down the drain. I had to work at keeping them alive in my mind and heart. But if I thought about them too long, I would break down like Sonja, and I couldn't afford that.

All but a few people in the neighborhood went on the trip to add to our food and supplies. Sandra something-or-other stayed behind with her nursing baby. She, pregnant Melba Carlisle, and a preteen girl volunteered to keep the smaller kids. Mazie flipped when we wouldn't let her and Cesar come with us, but after our encounter with the madman, I wanted our most vulnerable to have more protection.

Three men stayed to patrol the neighborhood and keep guard. I didn't know the names of these men, although I felt I'd once known them. Now I wasn't only having trouble learning new names, I was forgetting old ones.

Most of the men who came along were discreetly armed. They didn't want to brandish weapons for fear of inviting trouble, but I saw pistols bulging under clothing and rifles in the bottoms of wheelbarrows.

We were quite a sight making our way down the street: bicycles ridden by teenagers; men and women with wagons and wheelbarrows; a gaggle of tween kids running amongst us; and me, perched at the end of the procession in the bicycle cart propelled by Keno.

Though we'd left our own dogs behind, a dozen other dogs followed us much of the way. I'm sure we were the most exciting thing they'd had to chase lately.

People in the first neighborhood we passed through came outside to watch us, some saying hello, others hollering out silly comments like:

"Y'all going to rob someone?" or, "Moving to a better neighborhood?" These people looked thin, same as we did, but mostly okay. They must've had food reserves, too.

But the hard thing, the sad thing, was the next neighborhood we came to and the ones that followed: rail thin people with hollow eyes, cracked lips, open sores. They looked like famine victims pleading for relief. This was only three miles from my home. I hadn't imagined things getting this dreadful so quickly.

And the kids—we ran into three or four groups of out-of-control kids, who must not have bathed for months. These kids begged us for food or threatened to steal our bikes and wagons. One group blocked the road, wielding lawn tools and homemade cudgels, insisting we'd have to give them something before we could pass.

"Listen here, you brats," Silas said, looming threateningly over the leader. Silas wasn't taller than that kid, but he was certainly heftier and made himself seem huge. "I paid for this road with my taxes. You didn't pay for shit. Now, get out of our way before I beat you bloody." Silas stuck his hard-bitten face in the dirt-smeared face of the leader, and the menace drained from that kid before our eyes. He didn't apologize, but he moved aside, and his friends went with him. Sometimes it's good to have a hot-headed friend.

When we'd left home, we'd been fairly jubilant about going on a quest. But our jubilance quickly left us. We passed a cell-tower that was fried black. We passed a lot of burned houses, and their numbers increased as we got closer to Erin's neighborhood. A corner liquor store had been ransacked. We saw some hideously wrecked cars and many more dead ones, most with trunks and hoods pried open and vandalized. At the post office, a couple dozen people were camped out, hoping for government aid I supposed, but not looking as though they'd found it.

Tasha slowed her bicycle and drifted back until she was riding beside Keno and me.

"I don't remember so many houses being burned when we came here before."

"Me neither," said Keno.

"What could have happened?" I asked.

"I don't know, but I don't like it," Keno said. We rode silently the rest of the way.

By the time we reached Erin's, I'd worked myself into such a tizzy that I could hardly believe her house was still there. Why hadn't it been burned or looted, given the state of her neighborhood?

When we gathered at the door, our antsy teenagers were jiggling around, the way teens so often do. Some had greedy little gleams in their eyes, especially Chas. That kid seemed to have a permanent sneer.

"Listen, everyone," Keno said. "This is our mom's house. There's stuff we need to keep for Mom when she gets back, some of her clothes and stuff. And me and Tasha—Tasha and I—we want the pictures and Mom's jewelry. Everything else we can share."

"Please be respectful," I said. "That's all we ask."

"Okay, let's go." Keno unlocked the door.

His talk must have done the trick, because people were pretty darned nice about tearing Erin's house apart. They went through like an organized whirlwind, divvying up linens, kitchenware, clothes, books, toys, and more. Doris took charge of the food and made sure everyone got something good, including those who stayed behind.

Tasha was teary-eyed the entire time we were in the house. I felt horribly sad myself but managed to stifle my tears while packing clothes and shoes for Erin and the kids. Tasha crammed framed photos and picture albums into her duffle bag. She tried to stuff in more but got upset when she couldn't zip the bag.

"Honey, let's take some pictures out of their frames to make more room."

"Didn't think of that," she said. "What about Mom's trombone?"

"Her trombone? She hasn't played that thing in years. I didn't know she still had it."

"She played it for me and Keno. I can't leave it here."

"It's okay to leave things behind. You'll always have your memories, my love."

"And my mom. I'll always have my mom. I'm taking the trombone."

"You'll have to carry it and let someone else ride your bike."

"Fine," she said. I merely sighed. Together we took photos out of their frames, then Tasha asked, "Can I go see if my friends are around?"

I had kept her from looking for her friends long enough. "Go ahead," I said, "but take someone with you and make it quick. We'll need to head home soon."

"Thanks." Tasha ran through the house and out the front door, grabbing Milo on the way.

Other people ate their lunches and sifted through remaining things in the house. I felt frantic, aching for my daughters, looking for something to do to keep from crying, when a red-faced man with a bald head and white beard showed up at the open front door.

"What the hell's going on?" he snarled. "This is my property. Get off it!"

"Who says it's your property?" Silas snapped.

"The items in this house belong to my daughter, sir," I said.

"No, ma'am, they do not. She ain't paid rent for months. These items are mine."

"Paid rent? How could anyone pay rent in this world? What good is money anymore, Mr.—what is your name?"

Keno made his way to the door through a cluster of folks staring at the visitor. "Mr. Gillespie, we came to get Mom's stuff."

"Where's your mom, boy?"

"She was out of town when the thing happened, and she hasn't made it back yet."

"Great. So, she's dead and won't be paying her back rent, then."

"Mr. Gillespie, watch your mouth!" I wagged my finger at the man.

"Well, dead or not dead, she ain't payin' rent, so this stuff is mine, and y'all are trespassin'! Put everything back and get out!"

"How much money do you think my daughter owes you?" I asked.

"Five thousand dollars."

"That's ridiculous!"

"Our rent was only eight fifty a month!" Keno said.

"Yeah, well, there's penalties and interest, and she ain't paid in four months. Plus, I've been guarding this house night and day, else all this stuff would be gone. I saw you kids sneaking around, but I let you do it. All that's worth somethin' right there."

"Will you take a check, Mr. Gillespie?" For some inexplicable reason, I'd never bothered to take my checkbook out of the bag I'd brought with me.

"No way!" Gillespie shouted. "What good would a check do me?"

"Same good as cash money will do you. When the banks open back up, you can cash the check."

"Think so?"

"I know so. I can't get cash, so it's a check or nothing. But we'll be taking these things with us either way."

Gillespie appeared to be weighing his options. He wasn't happy with any of them. "I'll have to have six thousand, for the trouble of taking a check."

"Fine. Who do I make the check out to?"

"Dan Gillespie will do."

I dug in my bag for the checkbook, and I'll be damned if I didn't find Hank's screwdrivers that I'd been hunting for everywhere.

"If we pay him all this money," Keno murmured, "he needs to give back Mom's bike."

"Right. I forgot about the bike. Mr. Gillespie, I will hand you this check when you return with my daughter's bicycle and all her jewelry that you took."

Gillespie turned redder, sputtering sounds of protest, lusting after the check I waved before his eyes.

"You're not going to tell me you didn't take any jewelry, are you?" I fanned my face with the check. "You will also bring back anything else you took."

Gillespie glared, clenching his jaw, then he pivoted and hurried away. I couldn't believe he was letting things of real value get away from him in exchange for a useless check. But these items belonged to Erin, and I felt no compunction about taking advantage of the man's stupidity.

"How did you know he took Mom's jewelry?" Keno asked me.

"I just figured. He's obviously been snooping around, he took the bike, and he's nutty enough to think Erin owes him money. A guy like that would take anything he thought was valuable. I'm surprised he didn't take the food."

"I bet he took the meat from the freezer. Mom always had lots of meat in there, and the freezer was empty when we came before."

"Didn't waste any time, did he?" I said.

"He gives Mom the creeps."

"He's creepy, alright. But we won't have to deal with him anymore."

Mr. Gillespie again appeared at the front door, holding onto the bicycle with a pressure cooker balanced on its seat. Keno took possession of the bike and the cooker. I reached out my hand, and Gillespie unapologetically dropped two gold necklaces, four pairs of earrings, and a silver money clip into my palm.

"What happened to the money in the clip, Mr. Gillespie?"

"Wasn't no money in that clip, I swear to God."

"Alright, thank you. We'll leave the key on the kitchen counter, and you can consider my daughter's lease terminated as soon as we're finished here."

"Yeah, and you better not come back. When the Good Lord returns any day now, he's gonna leave you people behind."

Keno and I and our neighbors laughed at the old fool landlord as he walked away, more red-faced than ever.

Hadn't God already left us behind?

TASHA AND MILO CAME RUNNING INSIDE, and Tasha grabbed my hand. "I need to talk to you." She dragged me to her bedroom and shut us in. "All my friends are gone. Their houses are empty, except one. My friend Alma's there with her little brothers. She doesn't know where her parents are. They were shopping in San Antonio when it happened, and they never came back."

"Good Lord. How are they eating?"

Tasha looked away, her eyes tearing up. "A man gives them food and water when she … when she … you know."

"When she gives him sex?"

"Yes."

"For God's sake!" Some people lost their decency when they lost their electricity. "Go get Alma. Tell her to pack as many clothes, shoes, and jackets as she and her brothers can carry. We'll take them home with us."

Tasha jumped at me and hugged me so hard that I fell against the bed and had to sit down on it.

"I knew you would say that. I knew you would!"

"They'll have to work hard at our place. And someone else might have to take them in. But they can stay with us for now."

"Thank you, Nana. You're the best Nana ever!"

"Thanks for saying that, but hurry. We need to leave soon to get home by dark."

Tasha scurried away, leaving me fuming about predatory men.

Alma was seventeen and exotically pretty, with a punk hairdo that had a splotch of fresh pink dye in it. Despite what she'd been through, she didn't seem shy and troubled like Darla. This was a girl who'd known parental love.

The minute he saw Alma, Chas gave her the once-over, eating her up with his ogling. I shot him the evil eye. He smirked and turned away.

Alma was worried about how her parents would find them if they moved, so we tacked our address to her refrigerator with a magnet. Nothing was permanent in this world, but it was all I could think to do.

Alma's brothers—Pedro, ten, and Chris, twelve—were quieter than their sister, but they smiled shyly when I met them, and they seemed relieved to have adult help. The three kids, whose last name was Ibanez, worked quickly to close up their house, the boys doing what Alma told them without argument.

When we gathered to go home, some neighbors grumbled about me bringing along extra kids.

"I'll feed them my family's food," I said. "I won't reduce rations. Plus, they're young and strong and can help us." This was somewhat disingenuous of me, because if I didn't reduce rations to feed more people, the food would run out sooner, but no one said a word in rebuttal. I figured I'd hear more bitching soon enough.

All of us were worried we'd get robbed on the way home, or that crazed, starving people would follow us home and rob us later. The men fanned out with weapons drawn to surround us. Two men with rifles lagged far behind to deter anyone from furtively following. The trip home was nerve-racking, to say the least.

Two gaunt women ran up to us, pleading for help. "Where'd you get food?" "Why aren't y'all skinny like we are?" Christ, it was heart-wrenching. I had no answers for them, but I gave them some cans of soup, and Sonja gave them canned beans.

Halfway home, we passed the mean kids who'd blocked our way, leaning against a house and glowering.

"Stop a minute," Silas said. He rummaged through his wheelbarrow and pulled out a bag of rice and another of dried beans.

"Come here, kid," he shouted to the leader.

"Why?" The kid looked half-scared, half-pissed.

"Just come. I got something for you."

The kid shuffled over with a bowed head. His friends followed, cudgels at the ready.

"Here's some food," Silas said. "Your folks will know how to cook it."

"Don't have enough water to cook it with," muttered the kid.

"Yeah?" Silas pulled two gallons of water from Doris's wagon. "Take these. And you can have my lunch. I didn't eat it." Silas handed the kids a crumpled paper bag. A few other people forked over lunch remnants, too. "See," Silas said, "if you ask nicely, people might help you if they can."

"Thanks," one boy mumbled.

"God bless you," Doris said.

By the time we reached home, it was almost dark. The neighbors milled about in our yard, sorting out goods and dispersing toward their homes. Chas stationed himself between Alma and our house. He kept stepping in front of her as she tried to get past him. Alma moved more widely beyond him and saw me watching before Chas, who had his back to me, stepped in front of her again.

"Young man," I said. He ignored me. "Mr. Chas Matheson!" He turned to face me. "What do you think you're doing?"

"I'm not doin' anything," he said.

"Too late. I saw you." I set my hands on my hips. "Leave Alma alone. In fact, I forbid you from talking to Alma or Tasha anymore. You've caused enough trouble in this neighborhood, and I'll not have any more of it!"

"Hey, it's a free country," he said, a stupid expression on his face.

"Not anymore it isn't. Not in regard to young women in my care, it isn't. Now go home."

Chas whipped his face back and forth between Alma and me. He looked like he wanted to argue but was too taken off his game.

"Jerk," Alma said.

"Bitch," Chas shot back.

"Get out now!" I shouted. People turned to look at me.

From directly across the street, Gary said, "What's going on?"

"Chas is being obnoxious. I'm sending him home."

Gary's wife, Lyla, stood behind her husband, shaking her head at her son, then leering at the back of Gary's head with something close to hatred in her eyes.

Gary seemed bewildered. "Chas, leave those people alone."

Chas made a huffing noise and stomped away, in the opposite direction of his parents. Tasha watched him as he moved down the street, then she took off running after him.

"Wait, Chas. Wait!"

"What?" He spun toward her from halfway down the block.

I guess Tasha was too upset to care that we were listening. She wasn't all the way to Chas when she hollered out, "Why are you flirting with Alma?"

"Tasha! Come back here!" I cried.

A sly grin spread across Chas's face. "I thought you didn't like me anymore."

"Well, I do, but I'm confused." Her face puckered as she tried not to cry.

Chas wrapped Tasha in his long arms. She all but disappeared, and after that, I couldn't hear what they said.

"Tasha, come inside! Now!"

She backed slowly away from Chas and shambled home, studying the pavement beneath her.

"My stomach feels bad again, Nana," Tasha said as she came inside.

"Probably stress. You don't need that boy, you just think you do. You have to stop worrying about him so much or he'll give you an ulcer."

"What's an ulcer?" she asked.

CHAPTER 34

New Year's Eve.

The Ibanez kids left the house early to get a tour of our farming operation from Silas and Doris. I think Doris was working on her husband, trying to convince him to let her take in those kids. No one told me this; it was something I picked up from the animated way she acted around the children and the looks she gave her husband, her whispers in his ear.

To top off the year from hell, Tasha threw up her breakfast.

Oblivious to the implications, Milo and Mazie laughed at Tasha for barfing under the kitchen table. Keno shot me a worried look, as did Sonja. Tasha groaned until she stopped puking, then she ran upstairs to her room.

"This is gross!" Milo hollered, laughing so hard that he snarked oatmeal up his nose.

"Milo, settle down!" I knew his laughter was innocent, but I was not in the mood.

I got a bucket of gray water and some rags and knelt down to start wiping, but Sonja took the rags from my hand and helped me to my feet.

"I'll do this," she said. "Go see about your girl. I'll make her some mint tea."

I shut my eyes and whispered, "Thank you," then I plodded up the stairs, feeling so breathless that I wondered if I would make it to the top. No one noticed me, though. Sonja was occupied with the mess, and Keno was busy hustling Milo, Mazie, and Cesar out the back door to do chores.

As I reached the top of the stairs, there was a knock on the front door. Jack peeked through the window.

"Jack, we're busy. We have a little problem," I said as loudly as I could, given my lack of breath.

"Is everyone okay?" he asked through the window.

"I think so," I answered, knowing full well that everyone was not okay.

"Guess I'll come back later."

"Do that." I continued to Tasha's room. But as I reached it, Tasha burst out the door, knocking me sideways as she stumbled into the bathroom to vomit. I sat down and waited for her to come out, but she was in there moaning, and she seemed to be settling in. I went to the open bathroom door, but I couldn't see Tasha at the toilet, which sat behind a half-wall.

"Tasha, are you alright?"

"I don't know," she whined, spitting and sputtering. "I think those eggs were bad."

"The eggs? But they were powdered. What makes you think they were bad?" I almost wished they *were* bad, even if it meant we'd all get sick and barf our brains out.

"They smelled bad," she said.

"If you thought they smelled bad, why did you eat them?"

"I didn't want to waste food."

"Honey, can I come in? I'll help you clean up, and we'll get you to bed. Sonja's making some mint tea."

"Okay," she said weakly.

I stepped into the bathroom to see a pale and disheveled Tasha, looking like a twelve-year old, kneeling in front of the toilet with her forehead resting on the seat. I needed to get her away from that filthy toilet before she got sicker.

I wet a washcloth from a jug of water, and wiped Tasha's face. I wet another cloth and folded it over to press against her forehead.

"Do you feel like you're done throwing up for now?"

"I think. I don't know."

"Let me get the plastic tub from under the sink. We'll take it to your room. It'll be easier to clean the tub than it's going to be to clean that toilet."

"Sorry," Tasha said and slowly rose from the floor.

Once in her room, I had Tasha change into pajamas so we could wash her clothes. Sonja brought the mint tea, and we thanked her. I waited until Tasha drank tea and lay down before I started The Talk.

"Tasha, honey, you realize that if the eggs were bad, you probably wouldn't have thrown up so quickly and other people would be getting sick by now?"

She wrinkled her eyes. "Then what's wrong with me?"

"Sweetheart, have you been getting your period on time?"

She opened her mouth in horror. "I don't know," she whispered, her brown eyes bugging out of her head. "I can't be … you know … can I?"

"Did you have sex with Chas?" I crossed my fingers, hoping for a no.

"Yes," she said, under her breath.

"And did Chas use a condom?"

"No." Her lips quivered; her eyes blinked too fast.

Deluged with rage and remorse, I reared back my hand to slap her, but I grabbed hold of my hair. Count to ten, Bea. Breathe.

"Tasha … tell me this. How do your breasts feel?"

"My breasts?" She sat up, peering down at her buxom chest. "Why?"

"A lot of times when women get pregnant—"

"Don't say that word!"

"It's not a magic word. We can't make it go away by not saying the word." We were both trembling. "Usually when women get … get that way, their breasts get fuller and feel extra tender."

The sharp intake of breath coming out of Tasha told me all I needed to know about her breasts. "I thought I hurt them working in the garden or something."

I wanted to scream and cry and pitch a fit. I wanted to beam away to a world where teenage girls didn't get pregnant when there was no medical care, no parents around, no father of the baby worth a flip. I wanted Tasha to have her innocence back.

Erin and my whole family were going to line up and shoot me. And I would deserve it. How did I let this happen?

I had to take my time to avoid upsetting Tasha more. I needed to be helpful and supportive and not a source of additional concern for her. It was all I could do to speak in an even voice. I'm sure I sounded robotic.

"What we need is a test, but the only way we'd have one is if your mom or Aunt Jeri left it here. I don't remember seeing one when we were sorting stuff in the house. Do you?"

"No, but I don't know what they look like." She collapsed backward on the bed.

"Different brands have different designs, but they come in little boxes with cheerful names on them."

I almost told Tasha I'd ask around the neighborhood for a test, but she would've been mortified. I wasn't sure about asking neighbors anyhow.

Why, oh why—with everything I'd stockpiled—hadn't I bought condoms by the case, by the freaking truckload?

I was thinking: mortality. I was thinking: complicated deliveries and fussy babies and spit-up and poopy diapers in the midst of a severe water shortage and a probable shortage of food. I was thinking: abortion.

I WAITED IN TASHA'S ROOM until her overwhelmed emotions put her to sleep. Then I went to my room to cry. How was Tasha going to deal with this? How would we all?

Melba Carlisle was pregnant. My first instinct was to pick her brains about her plans. I wondered whether I could pull that off without seeming suspicious. I was a pretty good liar. I'd fooled Hank for years, and I had once considered him my soulmate.

At last, I decided to go downstairs. Keno would be worried, and so would Sonja. Even Milo, Mazie, and Cesar might be concerned. They were old enough to understand that getting sick was a much bigger deal than it used to be. I had impressed this idea on them repeatedly. I hoped I hadn't scared them too much, but I wanted them to be wary and prepared.

By the time I got downstairs, Sonja was making lunch. I asked her if we had anything that someone with a queasy stomach could eat. Sonja looked me in the eye, nodding as though she understood everything.

"I have a noodle-making device. I could get it and make her some noodles."

"Nice. Back when I was … you know," I still couldn't say the word even though Tasha and the other kids were out of earshot, "I lived on saltine crackers."

"I saw a case of whole wheat crackers at the Mint," Sonja said.

"You did? I don't remember buying them."

Sonja took my hand. "You have a lot of stress. It can make one forgetful." Stress hardly covered the shit shower of emotion crashing over me.

"Thank God we have crackers and noodles," I said. "If we can get her through this first part with those, then we can try to get some soup into her, and some milk."

"I have prenatal vitamins."

"You do? What we really need is a pregnancy test."

"I have one of those as well," Sonja said.

"Do you mind if we use it? And the vitamins—do you think they're alright? They might be too old."

"They're not old. I got them a few months ago."

I wanted to ask why, but I was afraid of setting Sonja off again. I needed her to be level-headed since I was nowhere near level myself.

Sonja had a defeated expression, but she seemed determined to hold it together.

"Sonja, are you getting what you need from us? I hope you don't feel like we take you for granted. To me, you're an angel from heaven."

"I am fine, Bea. You all are not. I'm honored to help you." A lump formed in my throat made up of gratitude and guilt. Sonja smiled at me thinly and blushed, then she hurried out the door.

Keno came in to the kitchen from the garage. He peered out the bay windows to see where the other kids were, then he spun around. "Nana?" I wondered if I should tell him such a private thing about his sister, but I knew we would need his help.

"Honey, I'm afraid your sister is in trouble, as we used to say."

"Trouble? You're not mad at her, are you?"

"I'm furious with her for being so bone-headed and lying about it. But I'm mostly sad and worried sick. By trouble I mean that she's in for enormous changes in her life, and the timing couldn't be worse."

Keno's face fell to a look of bereavement. He lowered himself into a chair, as if he felt unsteady on his feet. "God, Nana," he said. "What will she do?"

I sat beside him and put my arm around his newly muscled shoulders. "I don't know, honey, but I'm going to figure it out." He nodded and wiped at his eyes, then he stood, shook his face, and headed back to the garage.

What kind of God would torture my grandkids this way?

CHAPTER 35

After Tasha ate a handful of crackers and I picked at lunch, I coached her about how to take the pregnancy test until she was thoroughly annoyed with me. Her hands shook when she showed me the test stick with the pink plus sign on it.

She was pregnant alright, pregnant as could be. This confirmation seemed to stun Tasha. I'd expected a round of weeping, but she stared into the distance.

I was so angry I could have kicked the girl around the block. I could have shot that boy Chas and his whole damned family. I went to my room and unloaded my gun to keep from going on a shooting spree. Shooting Chas wouldn't help. It was God I was maddest at for doing this to my girl.

But I repressed my anger and tried to comfort my granddaughter, who wouldn't even be sixteen until March. I wouldn't bring up her options, because in this world I didn't know what options she had. I would comfort Tasha and do my research.

I changed the sheets on her bed. I couldn't remember when we'd last changed anyone's sheets. I helped Tasha wash her hair while she bathed in a few inches of warm water that Sonja poured for her. I sat Tasha in front of me in her room, and I made her a pretty French braid. She was still my little girl, no matter what.

"Tasha, the first minute you feel a teensy twinge of hunger, you have to eat some crackers. If you wait even a few minutes, that's when you'll get sick. They call it morning sickness, though it doesn't always happen in the morning. It usually goes away within a few weeks, but not always."

"I can't be sick all the time," she whined, still the same fifteen-year-old she'd been yesterday.

If you had listened to me, I thought, you wouldn't be sick now.

"We'll do everything we can to keep you from being sick, but chances are good you'll be sick sometimes, and you'll have to be brave. Almost every mother on Earth has gone through it, and you can do it, too."

She sighed so deeply that I dropped the pieces of her hair I was braiding and had to undo part of my work to get back on track.

"Nana, do I have to tell Chas?"

"We have time to think about that. But when your belly starts to grow, people will notice."

Tasha whipped around to face me, yanking her hair right out of my hands. "Do I have to do this? Can't I have one of those, you know, abortions?"

I took Tasha's chin, studying her dewy brown eyes.

"First of all, I would much rather you end your pregnancy than become a mother at your age. But abortion can have complications. Then, whether or not you have physical problems, you could grieve over the loss of your baby even if you're certain you did the right thing. And in your case, if you *want* an abortion, it would be the right thing."

"If it's the right thing, why would I grieve?"

I brushed Tasha's bangs from her eyes.

"Every woman is different. Maybe you won't grieve so much. Your mother and Aunt Jeri and Grandpa don't know this, but I had an abortion once, when your mom and aunt were little, before I met Hank."

Tasha looked astonished. "Why?"

"I couldn't raise more kids by myself. It wouldn't have been fair to that baby or to the daughters I already had. So, I had the abortion, and I knew it was the right thing. That didn't keep me from grieving though."

Tasha nodded, her bright eyes riveted to my myopic ones.

"Here's the thing, honey. It was difficult enough to get a safe abortion in Texas before the EMP. I don't know if it's possible at all now. In the old days before abortion was legal, some women tried to give themselves abortions, often with horrible results. I don't want you to think for one minute about doing such a thing to yourself or letting anyone do it to you. Understand?"

I could tell by the fright on her face that she would never consider such a thing.

"Some people will try to convince you to drink this tea or eat that plant and you'll have a miscarriage. There may be herbs or plants that could give you a safe miscarriage, but I don't know what they are, and I don't trust anyone to tell us, so I don't want you to do that either."

Tasha gulped, wincing.

"But I will try to find out if it's possible to get a safe abortion in or near Austin these days, and if it is, we'll take you in and see what the doctor says."

"Thank you." Tasha hugged me so tightly it took my breath away, but then everything took my breath away lately. She shivered like a frightened baby chick in my arms. How could she be so fragile and scared on the one hand, and so strong as to squeeze me to death on the other?

I finished Tasha's braid and tucked her into bed. I was exhausted in every way and didn't feel like going downstairs. I called down to Sonja to ask if she'd send dinner for Tasha and me whenever it was ready, and to have Keno come see me.

Keno came up soon after. I told him to get his bicycle in good shape and to pack water, sandwiches, and bike tools, because tomorrow I'd be sending him on a mission for his sister.

"What kinda mission?"

"I'll explain in the morning. Please ask Alma to sleep in Mazie's room tonight."

He hesitated, seeming puzzled.

There was a loud knock at the front door. Keno ran down to answer it. I heard heated talking, but the words were indistinguishable. I went to the top of the stairs where I could see the entryway.

"Keno, who is it?"

"It's me, Miss Bea." Chas leaned his head over Keno's shoulder. "I came to see Tasha."

"She's sick, Chas," I said. "And I want you to leave her alone."

"I told you that!" Keno barked at Chas.

"How sick is she? What's wrong?"

Keno slammed the door in Chas's face.

CHAPTER 36

At dawn I wrote down directions for Keno to the South Austin hospital and the big hospital downtown. I also gave him addresses for two of my friends who were nurses. They lived close to each other, or they had before the EMP.

"Keno, you need to ask my friends if they know where to get an abortion or a midwife or a doctor. At the hospitals, ask about getting medical care for your sister who's a pregnant teenager."

He gulped, his eyes wide. "God. An abortion? Really?"

"Well, she wants one, and she asked for it herself. I didn't bring it up, even though I think it's the best thing. But I'm only letting her have one if we can be sure it'll be safe. I don't know if that's possible anymore."

"But, what will Mom say? What would Mom want Tasha to do?"

"Honey, I know Erin doesn't want her fifteen-year-old daughter to have a baby. And since she isn't here, it's up to Tasha and me to figure out, and we're doing our best." I studied Keno's downcast eyes until he looked back at me.

"Don't I have anything to say about this? Tasha's my little sister, and without our parents, I'm kinda like her dad."

"Not exactly like her dad, honey." I squeezed his hand. "This is a big issue, Keno. Right now, we don't know what kind of medical care is available. Your mission for today is to find out. Once we know the options, she'll decide what to pursue. You can talk to Tasha about it then, and if she wants to listen, she can. But the decision is hers. No one should be able to tell a woman that she has to give birth to a child. Not me, not your mom or dad, not you or Chas or the government. No one."

"I didn't think of it that way," he mumbled.

"I understand. Head home well before dark, whether you're finished or not."

THAT DAY, Tasha had three episodes of incessant vomiting after every single thing she put in her mouth, even water or mint tea. I worried she was getting dehydrated.

Sonja was downstairs cooking and making noodles, running up and down to help Tasha and me, and corralling the kids, including the three new ones. I wanted to go talk to Doris and Silas about taking in the Ibanez kids, but I couldn't leave Tasha alone.

In early afternoon while Tasha rested, Jack knocked on the door. He'd knocked yesterday, too. I hoped he didn't have bad news. When Sonja let him in and called me, I came down and sat on the bench in the entryway.

"What's going on?"

"I've got an update about our friend Chas," he said.

"I can't think about Chas."

"Don't you want to know that he was on meth like we thought, and he's kicked it now that it's not available?"

"Good for him." I smirked sadly.

"Bea, what's wrong? Yesterday you said you had a problem. Are things working out with these new kids around?"

"I haven't paid a bit of attention to those new kids or most of my own for that matter." I sagged down to lean against the wall.

"That's not like you. Aren't you feeling well?"

"No, Jack, I'm not feeling well at all. I'm sick to death if you want to know. Sick to fucking death!"

"Bea! I've never heard you use that word. What in hell's going on?"

I sat breathing hard, trying to decide if I should tell him.

Jack placed his hand on my forehead very tenderly. I closed my eyes. It felt so good to have someone touch me in such a caring way.

"You don't seem to have a fever," he said. "Are you ill?"

"Not any more ill than usual." I opened my eyes and peered at the tall, rangy Jack Jeffers, who was tending to me more sweetly than Hank had ever done.

"So," he said softly, "do you want to tell me about it?"

"Oh, Jack, please don't ask me to tell you."

"I'll give you a break since you called me Jack," he said. "I'll come check on you tomorrow."

As Jack opened the door to leave, Tasha rushed out of her bedroom above us to vomit loudly in the bathroom. Jack looked up the stairs then back at me. I froze, attempting to contain my tears.

"That Tasha?" he said.

"Yes."

"Is she alright?"

"Why don't you ask your friend Chas?"

"Chas?" Jack looked perplexed, but then he got it. "Oh no. Is she—?" He held his breath, and I held mine.

"I'm sorry," he said. "I really am."

"Don't you tell a soul!"

"I wouldn't tell, and you know it. I've never told your secrets for all these years."

As far as I knew, he was right about that. He closed the door quietly behind him as he left my house.

"Nana!" Tasha hollered.

"Coming, honey. I'm coming."

AFTER I GOT TASHA CLEANED UP and settled down, I laid her head in my lap on the game room couch so we could be closer to the bathroom. I hoped she'd feel less miserable being out of her bedroom for a while. I heard Sonja telling the kids downstairs that they couldn't go up.

"Does everyone know?" Tasha asked me, wincing.

"No. Only Sonja and Keno."

"Keno must be so mad at me," she muttered.

"Honey, your brother loves you. He wants to help." I paused for Tasha's response, but all she did was sigh. "Do you want to see Milo and Mazie? It might be good to let them see that you're okay so they won't worry. They might cheer you up."

"If you think so." She was giving herself up to me, wanting me to be responsible for her. I let her do it for now. She would have plenty of responsibility soon enough.

WHEN KENO CAME HOME AT DUSK, I left Tasha in the care of Mazie and Milo, and I went downstairs to talk with Keno. As I reached the ground floor, Jack knocked again.

He had a big bouquet of flowers, tied together with a silky, purple ribbon—blue asters and yellow mums.

"For you, Bea." He tipped his hat and backed away.

"Why, thank you," I said to the old fool. "Where did you get flowers in January?"

"My little hothouse. I never watered them, but I guess they got enough when I set them in the rain."

"I didn't know you had a hothouse."

"Well, you oughta come visit sometime, and you'd know these things." He grinned wryly and headed home.

We had lost so much, but we still had flowers, and we had neighbors who cared.

And, God help me, I felt a deep surge of tenderness toward Jack.

CHAPTER 37

Keno hadn't found a place for Tasha to get an abortion. A few obstetricians were working out of the main hospital downtown, but they were only handling complicated deliveries, not prenatal care or terminations. The hospital was a scary place—almost no one to get information from, dark and filthy waiting rooms crammed with desperate people, some of them near death. Keno seemed traumatized by his experience there.

I wondered what people were doing who were seriously ill, in need of respirators, kidney dialysis, heart surgeries, that kind of thing. Suffering miserably or dying, I supposed.

Keno did find my nurse friends, Charlotte and June, who'd moved in together and were growing a garden in their backyard. They were elated to see Keno and kept him there, chatting and serving him tea. Their neighbors had moved away, so my friends were lonely. They were thin and a little shaky. They hadn't felt their health would allow them to walk to Bastrop or anywhere else.

"I think they need help," Keno said.

"Well, honey, do you have any ideas for how we could help them?" I felt weary of the growing need surrounding us and the limits of our ability to do anything about it.

"We could bring them over here to live in an empty house."

"You're a good man to want to help. If we brought them here, do you think they could work much, like help with gardening and cooking and canning?"

Keno looked stunned. "Nana, they're your friends."

"I know that. And I love them, but that doesn't mean I can help them. The horrible, hard truth, my love, is that old people like me and my friends are not a priority to keep alive in this terrible world. Young people are the priority, and the strong adults who can take care of the young."

If my grandkids hadn't needed me so much, I might have lain down and died right there.

Keno regarded me with shock in his eyes. I looked away into the ultra-dark sky.

Later after everyone had gone to bed, I went to the Mint, found a bottle of Merlot, and drank the whole damned thing.

I SENT KENO ON TWO MORE EXCURSIONS THAT WEEK, looking for pregnancy help for Tasha. I also had him take food to Charlotte and June and ask them about healthcare options. But they'd been cloistered at home and were unaware of what options might still exist. Keno promised to return soon to check on them, bless his heart.

The only medical care for Tasha that Keno found was a general clinic not far from his mother's house, about five miles from mine. If I could get Tasha's stomach to settle, we would take her there.

EVEN THOUGH OUR SKIES SEEMED CLEARER these days without automotive and industrial pollution, the weather and seasons were all screwed up. When the cedar pollen season came weeks later than usual, I thought it might kill us all. Pollen permeated the air outside and in. I saw a cedar tree down the street surrounded by a thick gray cloud of pollen. It looked like smoke.

Keno's nose went back to running like a faucet with a never-ending drip—at least he was blowing it now. Mazie sneezed all day and night. And my asthma made me wheeze like a set of bagpipes, sapping every last ounce of my already limited energy.

The pollen was hardest on Cesar, who seemed to be developing allergy-related asthma. He came over with his mother every morning and sat on the couch with books and puzzles, laboring for his breath. Several times per day Sonja brought Cesar a pot of steaming water. She draped a towel over his head and shoulders, then around the pot of water. Cesar breathed in the steam and coughed until the water cooled. Mazie and I sat with Cesar through these rituals, patting his back and offering encouragement. But the sweet little fella was getting worse.

Then one day a strong cold wind blew in, and a rainstorm crashed down upon us. We ran outside with our buckets and bowls, but we had to leave them and hurry back inside because the rain was so hard and the wind so cold.

By morning, the air was clear, and Cesar could breathe again. He recovered within days.

ALL OF US EXCEPT TASHA were eating lunch one day, when Sonja said, "Keno, how soon will you be finished with my bike cart?"

He looked at me, goggle-eyed, almost choking on his food, acting completely flummoxed. I tried to look natural.

"Excuse me," Keno said, and he gulped some water. Sonja stared at him, flicking her eyes toward me then back to him.

"It's taking a lot of time," he said. "I don't get to work on it enough with all the other work."

Sonja flipped her gaze toward me. "Bea? Why is Keno acting this way?"

I shrugged slowly. "Maybe he's embarrassed that he hasn't got more work done?"

She narrowed her eyes at me for a long moment, while I tried to keep my face blank.

"I see," she said. She stood, marched to the kitchen, and madly scrubbed at a counter. Then she threw down her dishrag and tossed a pan into the sink, making a loud clatter.

"Sonja?" I said.

She turned her back to us and let out a moan, then she whirled back around.

"I thought you were my friend! You are telling me lies!"

Oh shit.

"Do you think I'm some stupid woman you can get work out of by lying to me?"

The kids gaped at us. Cesar dropped his spoon on the table, and it bounced to the floor.

I jumped to my feet, almost knocking my chair over. "God, I'm an idiot! A stupid, controlling idiot!"

She huffed at me incredulously. Tasha yelled from the top of the stairs, "What's wrong down there?"

"Don't worry, honey!" I called to Tasha, trying to rein in my runaway emotions. "Sonja, can we talk about this on the patio, please?"

Sonja's shoulders slumped, but she followed me outside, then stood staring at me while I sat down to face her.

"I'm so sorry." A wad of guilt clogged my throat. "I didn't mean for it to turn into a big lie. I was worried about you and Cesar taking off to Mexico on your own in the cold weather."

"What did you do?"

"I, um...." My face contorted as tears fought their way out of me. "I told Keno to take a month or two to get your bike cart built."

Sonja's eyes shone with disappointment. "So, you thought it was fine to have me work for you under false pretenses? I never knew you were so mean."

"I'm sorry! I couldn't be sorrier. I didn't think of it that way, but of course you're right." I was a blubbering mess.

"*Why* are you crying?" Sonja asked, eyeing me suspiciously.

"I can't stop right now. I'm sorry." I wiped my face with my shirt. "I hate to ask you this, but would you please sit down and give me a minute, so I can apologize properly?"

"Maybe I should go home."

My heart sank deeper. "Please don't go. At least until—"

"Until you can get out of this by justifying what you did?"

"I'd like your forgiveness, but it's probably too much to ask." I tried not to cry more, but tears kept squirting out of me. I covered my face for a minute.

Sonja sighed very deeply and sat down with her arms crossed. I shuddered with more sobs.

"Don't you think I know how dangerous this trip is, Bea? But my son needs his father. I need him, too, and Cesar needs my mother—she's a lung specialist—to help him with this asthma he is having. Once we get there, we will be safer than anywhere else we could be."

At last my crying slowed down, and I took a breath.

"It was your decision to make, Sonja, about whether and when you would go to Mexico. Not mine. I guess I got full of myself, thinking I was some kind of protector of everyone. I kept imagining you dying out there. That's not an excuse, but it's what happened."

"What does this mean, 'full of yourself?'"

"You know how I am. I think I'm right about everything. But I took it too far with you. I probably take it too far with everyone. I'm so ashamed, I just want to give up and crawl in a hole."

"Well, you can't. We have too much to do to take care of these children."

"I know it. But maybe we could leave Keno and Tasha in charge, and you and I could crawl in a hole for a little rest. You probably wouldn't want to be in the same hole with me, though."

"Bea." Her face softened a bit.

"What can I do to make this up to you? I'd go build your cart right now if I knew how."

Sonja leaned forward and touched my hand. "Don't ever lie to me again. Start there."

"I won't. Believe me, please, that I won't." I tried to smile at Sonja, but I'm sure the effort looked pathetic. "I can get Milo to do some of Keno's chores so he'll have more time for your cart. You can stop helping us if you want. You've more than earned your cart already."

"This may surprise you," Sonja said, "but I like it here."

"Thank you for saying that."

"I'm going to watch out for you, though, and this . . . this thing of yours to always think you're right."

"Good. Somebody needs to. I'm not good at keeping myself under control."

Sonja laughed, a short mirthless laugh. "None of us are," she said. "I'm going home now, but I'll be back in the morning."

"Thank you, Sonja. . . . Thank you."

AFTER SONJA TOOK CESAR HOME, Keno came outside. Mazie and Milo watched us through the bay windows.

"I screwed up." I was too ashamed to look at him squarely. "Would you please fix that bike cart as fast as you can? I'll get Milo to do some of your work to give you more time."

Keno sat down in front of me, studying my face. "You were protecting Sonja, like you protect all of us."

"Yes, but maybe I need to let people make their own decisions and their own mistakes."

"Yeah, probably," he said. "We end up making them anyway."

"So true." I sighed. "Maybe I should quit caring."

"Don't do that. We need you to care."

I puckered up again. Keno squeezed my shoulder and left me wondering where this need of mine to control things came from.

CHAPTER 38

On a cold but sunny morning in mid-January, I answered a knock at our front door. Two filthy, bony, reeking men stood on my stoop, wrapped in clothes that I could only call rags—blackened, dirt-caked rags. They wore tattered backpacks with rifles protruding from the tops.

I almost slammed the door on these men, but one of them said, "Mama Bea? You're so skinny I didn't recognize you!" That voice. Whose was it?

"I—"

"Pete, she doesn't recognize us, either. Mama Bea, it's us, Eddie and Pete."

"Eddie and Pete?" I couldn't find a context for that pair of names. I looked at these men with my mouth hanging open until I saw a familiar crooked smile. Tears flew from my eyes. "Oh my god, Eddie and Pete!" My stepsons. My stepsons who lived in Arizona.

I threw myself into Pete's arms, and Eddie hugged me from behind, their backpacks and rifles slamming noisily to the entryway floor. I was smooshed between them like a piece of bologna. Their odor brought more tears to my eyes, but I didn't care.

"You must be hungry. You must be thirsty! Kids! We have a big surprise!"

Mazie was inside in seconds, but she stopped still and stared. She wasn't quite four when she'd last seen her uncles, and that was nearly three years ago. They didn't look the same. They looked horrible, really, except for the grins on their grimy faces.

"Mazie, remember Uncle Eddie and Uncle Pete? Where's Milo?"

"Down at the garden on the corner." She twirled a strand of hair around her finger, rocking back on her heels in her dingy pink skirt.

Eddie stooped down to Mazie. "I know I look scary, but I'm your Uncle Eddie. I used to spin you around in circles, remember? When I get cleaned up, maybe you'll let me give you a hug?"

"Maybe," she said, and he laughed.

Keno came in the back door, wiping his hands on a rag.

"Uncle Eddie?" he said. "Is that Uncle Pete, too?"

"Keno!" the travelers cried. But as soon as they grabbed hold of Keno to hug him, tears flooded his eyes.

"Aw, kid. I'm glad to see you, too," Peter said.

"Where's Dad? Where's everyone else?" Eddie asked. Keno stepped back and looked at the floor. Eddie's smile faded to a frown.

"There's a lot to tell you guys," I said, a quiver in my voice. "A whole lot."

"What is this smell in here?" Sonja said as she came into the kitchen from the garage, still out of our sight. She stopped as she rounded the corner, her breath catching.

"Oh, pardon me," she said.

"Guys, this is my neighbor, Sonja. Sonja, these are my sons, Eddie and Pete. They just got here from—how *did* you guys get here? Do you have a car?"

"We walked," Eddie said.

"Sweet Jesus. All the way from Phoenix? But that's twelve hundred miles! How long did that take?"

"Two months and fourteen days," Eddie said.

"My God!" I clasped my hands and smiled forcedly. "Tell you what. You guys are a little ripe, I have to say. Why don't you go upstairs and get cleaned up? I think we can spare the water to wash your hair since it rained last week."

"Mom," Peter said. "What's going on?"

"Get upstairs and get clean, or I might throw up." I grinned big with my less-than-truthful mouth and held my nose.

Eddie and Peter hesitated, looking first to Keno, who stared at the floor, then to Mazie, still speechless, then to Sonja, who went into motion, heading for the stairs.

"This way, gentleman," she said in a tone that called for obedience. "Mazie, come help me find clothes for your uncles. Keno, please bring two big buckets of water then go back for two more. You gentlemen can bathe in cold water, can't you?"

"Hell, yeah!" Peter said. "Just having water is so...so...." He stopped speaking to eye Sonja up and down. "Your name's Sonja, did you say?"

"Yes." She proceeded up the stairs. All business, this woman was, but sly. Peter bounded the stairs, obviously wanting more. Eddie grinned at me and followed Peter. Keno went to get water from the rain barrels, and Mazie scooted up the stairs with the others.

Good. Now I could think of what to say to my boys.

MY CLEAN SONS JOINED ME in the dining room half an hour later. How handsome they were. Eddie had even shaved. They had nicks and scrapes on their faces and arms, and they were determined to get answers out of me.

"Mom, where's Dad and the rest of them? Where's Tasha?" Eddie asked, his arms strapped over his chest.

"Tasha's not feeling well. She's asleep."

"No, I'm not!" Tasha said from halfway down the stairs. She had color in her cheeks and a huge grin on her face as she and her uncles hurried toward one another. They laughed in a hugging cluster in the living room.

I refrained from telling Eddie and Pete about Tasha's condition, and instead watched concern grow on their faces as I explained what we knew and didn't know about their father and siblings. I told them about the radio broadcasts from Clifton, although I avoided the tanker explosion that I didn't want the grandkids to hear about.

Milo, Cesar, and the Ibanez kids came in, and, after more excited greetings and hugs, Sonja called us for lunch. When she saw Pete cleaned up, she did a quick double-take and blushed.

Lunch was tasty beans and rice. Eddie and Pete had seconds; Pete even had thirds.

"Don't make yourself sick, honey," I said. "There will be more when you want some."

"God, really? How come you have so much food? Everyone we knew in Arizona was out of food within a week or two."

"Well, remember when you guys used to give me a hard time and call me a hoarder?"

"Um, yeah," he said warily.

So, I told my stepsons about my secret inheritance, about the Mint and our stashes of goods, plus the neighborhood farming operation.

"Man, Dad will be surprised about this," Eddie said.

"I expect he will be, though he'll be furious with me for not telling him."

"Oh, he'll be mad alright," Pete said. "I mean, shit, Mom. Hiding two million dollars? That's fucked up."

I didn't mean to, but I smirked at Pete. He had a point, but what did he know about how hard it had been to coexist with Hank after the kids left home?

"I, for one, am proud of you, Mom," Eddie said, "for being so smart and taking care of all these kids." Such a sweet son, Eddie, and so unlike his two brothers.

"They're good kids. They take care of themselves and me, too."

"Hey, look at these guns!" Milo called from the entryway. He had hold of a rifle, pointing it at the rest of us. I gasped.

Eddie and Peter jumped up.

"Put it down, Milo, very slowly," Eddie said.

"Point it at the floor!" Pete insisted.

"It's so cool," Milo said, waving the gun randomly.

Eddie and Pete rushed forward. Milo saw them and pointed the rifle toward the floor.

"Hand it to them *now*, Milo," I said, breathing for the first time since Milo picked up the gun.

"Man, you can't handle guns like that! You coulda killed someone!" Peter said, looming over Milo. Eddie took the gun and ejected the magazine plus a round from the chamber, then did the same with the other rifle.

"Sorry." Milo hung his head.

"Someone needs to teach these kids about guns," I said.

"We can do it, Mom," Eddie said.

Can you call it dodging a bullet when no bullets were fired? Damn, that was scary.

I TOOK EDDIE AND PETE TO THE MINT, along with the whole gang of kids, related and unrelated. Tasha came, too, though I watched her closely. When we reached the Mint's patio, Eddie said, "Mama Bea, are you alright? You're all out of breath."

Finally, someone noticed.

"I think I'm okay, but you know, I have that heart thing."

"Don't you have a wheelchair or something to get around with?"

"We have one over here somewhere."

"I know where it is," said Keno.

"Well, will you please get it?" Pete said to Keno. "Your Nana needs to sit down. You kids need to look out for her."

"Pete, the kids have tons of responsibility these days," I said. "Don't put more burdens on them."

"Sorry, kid," Pete said, tousling Keno's thick, oily hair. "I'm just worried about her."

"I'm worried, too," Keno said quietly.

"Me, too," Mazie said. Milo, Tasha, and even Cesar nodded.

"What? You guys are worried about me? Why didn't you say something?"

They stared at me, then Keno said, "I guess we didn't know what to say."

"Pretty grown-up kids, if you ask me," said Eddie.

"I'm very proud of them." I wiped at a wetness beneath my eyes.

KENO FOUND THE WHEELCHAIR, and Eddie dusted it off, then guided me into it. For the next several days, I was not allowed to leave the Pico yard without one of my stepsons pushing me in the chair.

That day, I waited while the kids took Eddie and Peter upstairs in the Mint, where food, seeds, guns, and the remaining bottles of water were stored. Then we all went to the living room, dining room, kitchen, and garage to marvel at the food and equipment I'd amassed.

This house was so much like my own—two stories with four bedrooms, a den, and two bathrooms up top, and a living area, dining room, kitchen, bathroom, and three-car garage below.

When I showed the secret beehive cabinet to Eddie and Pete, they got plum silly with excitement.

"Hot damn!" said Pete.

"Mom, you thought of everything!" Eddie said.

"Well, not everything."

"Practically everything! I haven't had honey for years. When can we eat some?"

"I guess as soon as someone can figure out how to harvest it."

"We can harvest it, can't we, Pete?" Eddie said. "How do we do it?"

I told Eddie where to find the bee books and equipment, then we went for a stroll—or they strolled, and I rolled—around the neighborhood.

Chas seemed to be following us around, though he tried not to act like it. He passed by us several times, gazing at Tasha, tipping his hat once to me. Smart ass.

"Who's that smug little shit?" Pete asked under his breath.

"His name is Chas."

"Prep school kid?"

"No, why?"

"Prep school name," Pete said. "Should I run him off?"

"I wish, but he lives here."

Most of the neighbors didn't know Eddie and Pete. Plus, although they looked better now that they'd cleaned up, they were awfully gaunt, with dark circles under their eyes. Pete had a catch in his step. He said it was from his shoes, which did look a mess.

Some neighbors gave my sons wary looks. "Who's gonna feed those guys?" the woman with plastered oily hair asked me.

"They're my sons. I'm absolutely feeding them." Why was I feeding her? is what I wondered. The woman glared at me while Eddie and Pete looked half-embarrassed.

"Hey, they're gonna help us," Silas said. "Right, guys?"

"Definitely," Pete said.

"Of course," said Eddie, and we moved on.

I introduced my sons about a dozen times. Jack recognized them, thank goodness, and he greeted them warmly, leading them to his backyard to see his chicken coop that doubled as a hothouse. I waited out front to talk to Tasha about how she was feeling.

"I'm better." She did have the happiest grin I'd seen from her lately. Nothing like good uncles to cheer a kid up.

I heard a loud squawk, almost like a honking goose. To our west, above the railroad tracks, two very large birds were circling and calling to one another—white, elegant birds with black wingtips.

"Look, Tasha," I said quietly. "It's two whooping cranes! I've never seen one around here before. Maybe they feel safer now, since it's so much quieter."

"Wow, those birds are huge."

"They're amazing. When I was a kid, whooping cranes were almost extinct. People worked really hard to save them, and they're slowly coming back. But they live around water. There's no water out here."

"There's the pond," Tasha said.

"Yeah, but I didn't think it would be big enough. Maybe they're scouting."

"So cool."

We sat watching the cranes, then Tasha's face crumpled. "Nana, did you tell Uncle Eddie and Uncle Pete about me?"

"Not yet, honey. I figured you wouldn't want me to."

"They'll be so disappointed in me!"

"Tasha, they love you. They'll be concerned, but they will understand."

"Please don't tell them ... at least not yet."

"Okay ... but if you have much more morning sickness, I'm sure they'll notice."

"Yeah, but I didn't throw up yet today," she said.

"Well, that's good. I guess we can wait for now, but we'll have to tell them eventually."

"Maybe I'll tell them myself ... eventually," Tasha said.

I CAN'T DESCRIBE HOW RELIEVED I WAS to have Eddie and Pete with us: more family around, strong men to help manage farming and rain-collection projects, to keep a handle on these kids. I felt like it gave me permission to be the sickly old woman I actually was, to let my guard down, if only a bit.

But it also reminded me that Hank and the others had been missing for three and a half months. The increasingly likely explanation for this was that my husband, other stepson, and the parents of my grandchildren were dead.

CHAPTER 39

At supper, Pete and Eddie told us more about their monumental trek from Phoenix to Austin. They tried to act upbeat, but their eyes were haunted. Pete had an undercurrent of anger running through everything he said. He'd always been a little hot-headed, but this was noticeably more pronounced.

"Why did y'all come in the winter?" I asked. "Wasn't it awfully cold?"

"Yeah, pretty damn cold sometimes," Eddie said. "But we thought you guys would need our help. And it seemed better to be cold than to die of heat stroke in the summer. Plus, there's no water out there in the desert."

"No water." I tried to imagine how dreadful that would be.

"We saw snow when we passed through the Guadalupe Mountains around Las Cruces," Pete added.

"You climbed mountains to get here?" Milo cried, his big eyes aghast.

"Sort of," Eddie said, chuckling. "We followed Interstate Ten, so it was more like walking up and down a bunch of super steep hills."

"Man!" Milo said. "So cool!"

"How did you stay warm?" I asked. "How did you eat?"

Eddie and Peter told us about abandoned cars they'd sheltered in, fires and lean-tos they'd built by the roadside, layers of blankets and clothing they'd worn. For food, they'd packed pita bread and canned beans. Then they'd shot jackrabbits and coyotes.

"You ate coyotes?" Mazie squealed. "That's gross!"

"They were bad, alright," Pete said, "but we didn't have anything else to eat. We only ate them twice. We found some canned food along the way, and we shot a deer one night."

"I think it was an antelope," Eddie said.

"Maybe, but we couldn't preserve it, so we stayed put for a day to rest and eat as much as we could. We packed some for the next day and left the rest for the buzzards."

"We did a little work at a couple of ranches along the way," Eddie said, "and they fed us."

"One guy gave us steak and potatoes and let us sleep in his barn," Pete added.

"That was nice of him," I said. "Good to know there are still decent people out there. Did you run into any trouble?"

Their faces clouded over. Eddie's mouth opened wordlessly, while Pete cleared his throat and looked away. I flicked my eyes between them. They glanced at each other quickly, until Pete again averted his eyes.

"Lots of hungry, desperate people out there." Eddie sighed and closed his eyes. "A whole lot of them."

"I can imagine," I said, waiting for them to tell us whatever they wanted to tell.

Pete swallowed. "Someone stole one of our blankets while we were skinny-dipping in a stream."

"That sucks," Keno said.

I had a sick feeling this was not the worst thing that had happened to Eddie and Pete. It was what they chose to tell in front of the kids.

"Yeah, but we shouldn't have left it unattended," Eddie said. "At least they didn't rob us blind, and they could have. They probably needed the blanket pretty bad." Eddie's eyes teared up, and he breathed loudly for a moment. He struggled to get out his next words. "People kept asking us for food, Mom, but we didn't have enough for ourselves."

I patted his shoulder. "You couldn't help it, honey."

"I know." He shuddered. "I hated it, though."

I hugged Eddie hard. "Of course you did, because you're so good."

Eddie sighed. "I can't stand to think of kids with no food."

The big-eyed grandkids watched Eddie and pushed away their empty plates.

"I'm glad you're here now," Tasha said.

AFTER THE KIDS WERE ASLEEP, Pete, Eddie, and I drank Merlot on the back patio, bundled up but glowing with the warmth of being together.

"Man, this wine is good," Eddie said. "I can't believe I'm drinking it." He ran his hand through his thick brown hair. He was still muscular, despite his thinness.

"I know, right?" Pete said. "It's great." He sniffed at his glass, then took another sip of the full-bodied wine. His dark hair was cropped in a raggedy way. He'd always been tall and lean, but now he looked taller and leaner—wiry, like Keno.

"It's my post-apocalyptic treat for you," I said, and we laughed, a little grimly.

I told them about the tanker wreck in Waco. They were very upset, of course, but I felt they had to know.

"Eddie," Pete said, "we should go up to Waco and look for them."

"But it's so far!" I said.

"We already walked twelve hundred miles, Mom," Eddie said. "It's only a couple hundred more round-trip."

"I guess you're right. But you just got here. I can't bear the thought of you leaving again."

"But we gotta find Dad and the rest of them, Mom." Pete scowled at me. "Why didn't you try to find him?"

"Find him? What was I supposed to do? Walk to Waco with a bunch of kids? Think what you're saying."

"You coulda sent Keno to Waco."

"Pete! You guys just told me it's crazy out there. I can't send a seventeen-year-old boy on a solo trip to Waco. It would be a suicide mission."

I knew Pete was grieving over his missing father and brother, but he was completely irrational—a normal response to grief, but still. And he was triggering all the guilt I felt about surviving without the rest of them. Blood pounded in my head.

Pete looked off into the night sky, dark shadows dancing on his face. "I'm sorry," he said. "It just doesn't seem like you care much about Dad. You told him those huge lies. You're just going on like everything is great."

"Pete, I care so much that I am numb from caring. I'm just putting one foot in front of the other and trying to survive, trying to stay hopeful for the kids. I can't think too much about the rest of them or it will ruin me, and we won't live through this."

Pete dropped his head.

"We gotta go look for him, Mom," Eddie said, with an extra dose of kindness. "You understand that, right?"

"Yes, but will you please stay a couple of weeks before you go—to regain your strength, re-equip yourselves, fix up road food, all that?"

"Of course." Eddie glared at Pete until Pete nodded his reluctant assent.

"I'm going to bed," Pete said. He patted me on the head and went inside to crash on the couch.

"Eddie," I said, "what happened to John?"

"John didn't want to come with me—with us." Eddie watched the wine swirl in his glass. "Said he had to stay in Arizona for his folks."

"That's understandable. His parents are pretty old. It's a shame, though."

"Yeah, but we weren't getting along anyway. I think he's in love with someone else—someone he couldn't leave behind. So . . . he made his choice." Eddie looked at me with a firmly set jaw and rueful eyes.

"Well, it's his loss."

"Then how come I feel like it's mine?"

"Aww, honey. . . ."

I gave Eddie some time, then got up to pour the last of the Merlot. "When you passed all those wind farms in West Texas, were the turbines running?"

"A few were. Most were dead still—like they were locked down. But a couple of clusters were turning pretty fast. We saw a guy on top of one, then another guy on a second one a ways off. Guess they were trying to fix them."

"You didn't talk to them?"

"Naw. When we got into a walking rhythm, we didn't want to stop."

"I see."

Eddie came over to sit next to me. He took my hand.

"We had to steal sometimes to eat," he said.

"That doesn't surprise me."

"Yeah, but we broke into a barn and stole some home-canned food, a chicken, and some eggs."

"Well, honey, you had to eat."

"But what about our souls, Mom?" Eddie smoothed his shaggy hair then re-gripped my hand. "Do you think God will forgive us for stealing someone's only food?" This was the sort of question only Eddie would ask. He'd always searched for moral truths, unlike Pete, who ran on instinct.

I blew out a gust of air. "I don't know, honey. This is all pretty soul-crushing. I'm hoping things will get better once people get used to our circumstances. They'll grow more food, find more ways to take care of themselves. But I do know that the best way to forgive yourself is to help others, so you can repay the universe for the gifts you've been given."

"Or stolen?"

"Yes, or stolen."

"Mama Bea." Eddie took a deep breath, searching my eyes by the light of the kerosene lantern. "Pete shot a man near El Paso."

"My God! Why?"

"The guy snuck up on us in our sleep and pulled a knife on me. Held it to my throat. I froze. Nearly shit my pants. Next thing, I hear a loud click, then, ka-boom!"

"Shit. What did you do? Was he dead?"

"Probably. We took his knife, scooped up our stuff, and took off running. We ran as much as we could for the next two days."

"Jesus."

"I know," Eddie said. "Pete's been kind of an asshole ever since. I've been trying to cut him some slack."

"Of course." I wrapped Eddie in a hug while he shook with silent sobs. We sat together until he started nodding off.

What about our souls? It was getting harder and harder to remember that we had them.

LATER, I WAS HEADING INDOORS WHEN CHAS STOPPED ALONGSIDE OUR FENCE.

"Miss Bea?" he called, stepping from one foot to the other. Agitated, but not necessarily jerking like a speed freak.

"What is it, Chas?"

"Is Tasha feeling better? I saw her outside today."

"She's a little better, but she's still sick. Anyway, I told you to leave her alone."

"Can't I even ask about her?" he whined.

"She'll be fine," I said. "But *you* have to stay away."

Chas shook his head and slinked off down the road, probably calling me a bitch in his head.

CHAPTER 40

Pete and Eddie spent the following day outdoors, so they didn't seem to hear Tasha vomiting upstairs. They cleaned their rifles, then sorted their belongings, cutting up most of their clothes for rags and washing the rest. They found a couple of pairs of shoes apiece in our stashes of clothes, then took their hole-filled, broken-soled sneakers around the corner to the dump.

Milo and Mazie watched their uncles with fascination, hammering them with questions all day. Eddie and Pete seemed to enjoy the kids' company, so I didn't interfere.

I sat inside making calculations about our food stores. The rice wasn't going to last longer than two or three more months, especially if we didn't harvest some other high-carb foods soon.

Through the bay windows, I watched Pete and Eddie in my peripheral vision. It was so comforting to lay eyes on them. Whenever Sonja came near the back windows, Pete watched her pass. I thought about telling Pete that Sonja was married, but she hadn't mentioned her husband lately. So, I didn't interfere with Pete's admiration of Sonja either. I figured she could handle him herself.

Jack came in the backyard mid-afternoon and chatted with my sons. Before long, Pete stuck his head inside.

"Mom, is it okay if we take these kids to do some target practice with Mr. Jeffers?"

"Can I go?" Cesar quietly asked his mother. I'd lost track of Cesar and didn't realize he was reading a book in the living room.

"Mr. Peter," Sonja said, "can Cesar come along?"

"Sure. But you can call me Pete."

"Okay, Pete. Thank you."

Eddie, Jack, and my grandkids waved goodbye to me. Pete and Cesar waved to Sonja.

OVER THE NEXT FEW DAYS, my stepsons helped with heavy work at the Mint and in neighborhood gardens. Then Pete started noticing things that needed repair, and he set about fixing them.

One warm day, Pete and Eddie took Keno to the roof to patch a few loose shingles. I dug some boxes out of my closet and called Tasha to my room.

"Yeah, Nana?" My tall, leggy granddaughter appeared at my doorway in her cut-offs and skimpy T-shirt, looking exceptionally beautiful and particularly young.

"My, you're pretty," I said, and she blushed. "Wanna come look through these old baby clothes with me?"

Her face froze.

I patted the bed beside me. "Come see, honey."

Tasha swallowed and sat on the edge of the bed.

"These clothes belonged to your mama and your aunt when they were babies. They're old, but some of them should still be good."

I pulled out a pile of baby T-shirts and onesies. I loved the feel of cotton baby clothes. I loved babies. As I unfolded each onesie and smoothed it on the bed top, Tasha grew more and more solemn.

When I pulled out a stack of tiny blouses and dresses, Tasha said, "My mom used to wear those?" and she began to cry.

"Oh, honey." I squeezed Tasha's shoulders, but that only made her cry harder. "Sweetheart?"

"How can I have a baby when I don't have my mom? Can't I have an abortion?"

"We haven't found a place to get one. If we don't find one soon—in the next month—it will be too late."

"I can't do this, Nana. I can't!"

"Can't do what?" Eddie was standing atop the patio roof, leaning toward my open window. "Everything okay in there?"

Tasha covered her face with her hands. I held still, flicking my eyes between Eddie and Tasha.

"What are y'all doin'?" Eddie asked.

"Oh, going through some old things." I turned my face away from Eddie and touched Tasha's knee so she'd look at me. "Do you want to tell him?" I mouthed.

"I guess," she said, and kept crying.

"You guess what?" Eddie said. "What's up, you guys?"

"Eddie, can you and Pete take a break and come to my room for a bit?"

"Uh, yeah, sure." He turned away and shouted toward the second-story roof. "Pete, Mom needs us inside."

I rearranged myself so I could give Tasha a better hug. "You don't need to be afraid or ashamed. Your uncles love you."

She tried to stop crying. I stuffed baby clothes back in the box. Pete and Eddie came in, sweaty and smelly, and looking uneasy.

"Is this gonna take long?" Pete asked. "We're kinda busy."

"Tasha has something important to talk to you about. Tasha, should I leave the room?"

She flashed me a look of panic. "No! Stay!"

"What's up, doodlebug?" Eddie asked, giving Tasha a big smile.

Tasha glanced at her uncles, taking ragged breaths, then closed her eyes.

"I'm, uh… I'm pregnant."

The beat of silence that followed was as pregnant as Tasha, and just as loaded with emotion.

"Oh, Tasha," Eddie stepped forward to grab her in a mighty hug. Tears ran down his face.

"But you're only—what—sixteen?" Pete said.

"Calm down, Pete," Eddie said.

"I'm fifteen," Tasha said, sobbing.

"Fifteen? Jesus!" Pete plopped down on the loveseat along the wall.

"Pete," I said, doing my best not to yell at him. "Your niece loves her uncles, and she needs your love and support, please."

Tears welled in his eyes. "Sorry, Tasha." He stood to hug her while Eddie gripped her hand. "That was a shock," Pete said, laughing awkwardly.

"Yes, well, we don't judge Tasha because we were all young and impulsive ourselves once, and we're going to take care of her."

"Of course," Eddie said. "So, what's the plan?"

"Who's the father?" Pete asked, too loudly.

"Pete, settle down. We'll get to that."

Tasha and I explained our search for options. Pete was fairly outraged at the idea of an abortion, but I shut him down quickly on that count. He had no business upsetting Tasha, and I made sure he knew it.

We didn't tell them that Chas was the father. I was afraid Pete would kill him.

FOR THE REST OF THE TIME PETE AND EDDIE WERE HERE, Tasha sat with her Uncle Eddie on the couch every evening. I heard him talking to her about men and being sure they treated her right. Mazie often cuddled up on Eddie's opposite side, and he gave her some good attention, too. He even took care of Tasha through a couple of bouts of morning sickness, cleaning up vomit without complaint.

Though he seemed uncomfortable about it, Pete helped in his own way, bringing Tasha bowls of noodles, even washing and hanging her laundry. Helping with Tasha's noodles also gave Pete an excuse to spend time with Sonja.

Keno and another teen called Max took the opportunity to guard the water well out south for a few days, while his uncles were here to guard the family. My excuse to keep Keno home was gone.

Over the next week or so, Tasha's cheeks grew rosier, and her morning sickness slowly abated. Little by little, she took up her kitchen and gardening chores, and she didn't complain. We carved out time to sort through baby clothes, and Tasha enjoyed it.

"I can't believe babies are so tiny," she said. "So cute! I can't wait to see my baby."

Wow.

But Pete found me alone one night on the patio and lit into me.

"Mom, how come you let Tasha get pregnant?"

"*Let her?* You think I gave her permission?" My heart did a flip-flop inside my chest.

"You let it happen. Why didn't you supervise her?" Pete's face reddened, and spit flew from his mouth.

"Pete, honest to God! What was I supposed to do? Lock her up? And quit yelling!"

He sighed, lowering his voice. "It just doesn't seem like you care about anything. You didn't hunt for Dad—"

"Yeah, why didn't I send him a tweet?"

Pete's face got grimmer. "You don't reprimand Tasha or punish her—"

"Punish her?" I sat down fast. "Don't you think she's being punished enough by reaping the consequences of her actions? She's been vomiting a blue streak. She doesn't have her mother here. She is scared to death. She needs care and comfort, not scorn and shame. This isn't the Middle Ages, son."

Pete looked away and shook his head.

"Pete, when did you get so judgmental? Didn't you have lots of sex as a teenager?"

He jerked back. "You knew?"

"I know the signs, Pete. I've had sex before.... Look, I didn't tell your dad because I was afraid he'd beat you bloody. I'm different than your dad. I think if teenagers want to have sex badly enough, they'll have it if they get the chance. The best a parent can do is to limit the chances, and teach your kids how to protect themselves. If I hadn't made your dad lecture you guys about condoms—if I hadn't bought condoms for him to give you—no telling how many girls you would have knocked up."

I wiped tears from my face and shifted in my seat while Pete continued to stare.

"I'm seventy years old. I have a heart condition. I had four kids to take care of with no electricity or running water or another adult to help until Sonja came along. I had a neighborhood full of hungry, thirsty people who didn't know how to survive. But I knew how, Pete. I knew!

So, I had to help. I had way too many things to pay attention to, and I screwed up with Tasha. I screwed up bad. But don't you ever—don't you dare accuse me of not caring. I care so much it's about to kill me!"

Pete stepped toward me. "I'm sorry, Mom. I'm sorry." He leaned over to hug me. I let him do it, but I didn't hug him back.

"You hurt me, Pete. Being a stepmother is hard. Being a stepson is hard. But I thought we worked all that out years ago."

"God, Mom. I'm an ass. It's just this whole—this situation—it's freaking me out."

"Well, obviously," I said. "We're all freaked out. I'm so angry, I could kill people if I only knew who to kill to make it stop. But you have got to quit taking your anger out on the rest of us, because I can't take any more of it."

"I'm sorry." He squatted before me and squeezed my hand, his brow creased in distress. I took his scruffy-whiskered face in my hands. His green eyes glistened in the moonlight.

"Pete, maybe if you weren't so hard on yourself, you could be easier on the rest of us. You should forgive yourself, my love."

"Forgive myself?" He looked mystified, then his eyes widened. "Eddie told you?"

"He was trying to explain your hot temper. He said I should cut you some slack. And I have, honey. I'm cutting you slack now." I paused, watching Pete subtly nod his head.

"So please cut the rest of us some slack. And please work on forgiving yourself. You saved your brother from that man, sweetheart. You did the right thing."

My tall, grown-up stepson, Peter Crenshaw, tough-talking libertarian carpenter, grabbed me in a constricting hug and sobbed like a broken man.

CHAPTER 41

The Saturday after our argument, I overheard Pete talking to Sonja in the kitchen. They were alone in there for a rare moment.

"Would you like to go to the park for a picnic?" Pete asked. Chances were good he was asking Sonja for a post-apocalyptic date, but she threw in some complications.

"Yes! We should all have a picnic at the park. We can play ball, and Frisbee."

At the word picnic, kids began to appear out of nowhere.

"Picnic?" Milo rushed into the kitchen from the living room. "I love picnics!"

"I wanna go! Can I go?" Mazie twirled on her toes across the dining room, the ruffles that remained on her ragged skirt swirling around her.

Pete sighed loudly. "Everyone can go."

"Go where?" Eddie said, coming in through the back door with Keno.

"A picnic!" Mazie squealed.

"Hey, yeah," Eddie said. "Mom, do you still have Dad's guitar? Pete had to leave his in Arizona. Pete, will you play the guitar?"

"Hank's guitar is up in the game room. So, when is this picnic? It's just us, right? No neighbors?"

"Right—just us." Pete grimaced a bit—at the thought of neighbors, I'm sure, and also because "just us" included so many people.

"We'll do this tomorrow," Sonja said, "if people will help prepare food today."

"I'll help," said Pete, naturally.

"We'll all help," I said.

Sonja made two kinds of refried beans, a coffee cake, and a delicious tomato-less salsa concoction out of jalapenos, garlic, onions, and finely minced cabbage.

She taught Pete how to roll whole wheat tortillas. I think he played dumb to get more of her attention, but he must have rolled about sixty of those suckers. I made potato salad, Eddie made kale salad, and Keno roasted small sweet potatoes—which we'd taken to munching like candy bars lately.

To get our ingredients, we had to dip secretively into the common food supply. I hadn't taken rations for the Ibanez kids, or for Eddie and Pete, so I felt justified. All I was doing was catching up, but I didn't want neighbors to ask annoying questions.

It was simply too bleak around here. Something had to give. Part of me wanted to throw open the stores for a regular bacchanalia. We and the neighbors could eat ourselves sick. At least we'd have some fun to take with us to our graves.

I found the last of our paper plates and plastic cups. I even came up with plastic forks and spoons and a crumpled packet of napkins. And I had a plastic tablecloth still in its package—purportedly disposable. Hard to fathom that we used to think nothing of creating so much garbage whenever we had a picnic or party.

On THAT FIFTY-DEGREE SUNDAY MORNING, we rose early and set to work. We loaded food, paper goods, and plasticware into wagons, along with balls, bats, gloves, Frisbees, ground blankets, Hank's guitar, jugs of water and sun tea. Pete filled an extra wagon with folding chairs.

Tasha had just finished throwing up and was lying on the living room couch with a damp rag on her forehead. "Y'all go on," I told the others. "I'll wait here with Tasha until she feels better, then we'll come down."

"Want me to wait with you, so I can push your wheelchair?" Eddie asked.

"No, I can push myself. Go on. Have fun!"

"Why does Tasha barf so much?" Mazie asked. "It's gross!"

"Mind your own business, Mazie, and go have a picnic."

"Picnic!" she squealed, and soon they were gone.

"Nana," Tasha said, rolling over to face me. "Is Uncle Pete ever gonna forgive me?"

"Sweetie, Uncle Pete has troubles of his own—bad things that happened to him that make him uptight. Try not to take him personally. He loves you. He's just cranky."

"Like Grandpa?" she said.

I laughed, surprised. "Yes, exactly like grumpy old Grandpa."

BEFORE LONG, WE JOINED THE REST OF OUR FAMILY at the neighborhood park two blocks east. We found them playing a rousing game of baseball. Tasha and I sat in the warm sun and watched the wild swings, the pop-up flies, the strikeouts, the diving catches and misses, the crazy escapes from being tagged. We hooted and hollered for everyone.

My beautiful family—having real fun for the first time in months. I'd almost forgotten what it was like to laugh so much, though it used to be our normal family thing. Even Hank acted nicer when the whole family got together.

Tasha took a turn batting with Milo as a pinch-runner. She hit a long fly-ball to centerfield, over Keno's head. Milo danced and hollered his way around the bases, walking backwards over home plate with his arms in the air.

We ate, the kids played soccer, and Tasha took a nap on a blanket. I sipped sun tea and laughed my head off. Pete played guitar and sang some country-ish songs, and the rest of us sang along when we knew the words.

Tasha woke up for the singing and asked her Uncle Pete for a guitar lesson. She learned two chords, then played them with an uneven strum while Alma sang a song in Spanish. Cesar and Mazie did somersaults and cartwheels, and Sonja coached them on technique. Milo played some kind of war game with Pedro and Chris that involved a lot of jumping off the jungle gym and running in circles, screaming.

Keno gave Alma a batting lesson, standing close behind her, his arms holding hers while they swung the bat together. I watched them, dreamily, then fell asleep in my chair.

Around dusk when the near-full moon was beginning to rise, we packed up reluctantly to go home. As we started to leave, Pete touched Sonja's arm.

"Would you like to go for a walk with me?" he asked.

"Oh, but I must take care of Cesar."

"I've got Cesar," said Eddie. He stooped in front of the boy. "Climb on my back, buddy." Cesar gleefully climbed on.

"Can I have a ride?" Mazie asked.

"Here, Mazie, ride on my back," Keno said, and Mazie hopped on with a yippee.

"Hey, I want a ride," Milo said.

"Milo, you're almost as big as Eddie and Keno," I said. "You wanted to be big, so here you are." He frowned for a moment, then grinned and flexed his muscles.

"So, a walk?" Pete asked Sonja.

"Yes, a walk," she said, smiling shyly.

Tasha and the Ibanez kids pulled the wagons home. Milo started pushing my wheelchair. I had an uneasy feeling and looked back to see several skinny kids watching us from the tree line. Uh-oh. I should have known better than to flaunt our good fortune.

I had some burritos wrapped in a tea towel in my lap. I sat the food on the picnic table and nodded toward those hungry kids. They started running toward us.

"Please push me fast, Milo. Let's catch up with the others."

WHEN WE GOT TO OUR HOUSE, CHAS WAS LOITERING IN OUR FRONT YARD.

"Tasha," he said, "you must be better now. You've been out all day."

"I'm a little better." She looked around nervously for me. "Nana, can I talk to him?"

"Only for a minute." I shooed the rest of the family into the house.

I hurried upstairs so I could listen to their conversation through the window, but it was slammed shut. Opening it would draw their attention. I stood, pondering the window and peeking down, until Chas led Tasha around the corner of the house. I rushed to the side window, but I couldn't see them from there. I heard voices, sounding heated but indistinct.

"What are you doing, Mom?" Eddie asked.

"Trying to hear Tasha and Chas, but I can't."

"Ooh, you're bad," he said, snickering. "I'll go out back and see if I can hear them." He dashed down the stairs and tiptoed out the back door.

After a minute or two, Tasha yelled, "You can't do that!"

"Yes, I can! It will be better, believe me. No rules like here. No old ladies listening to everything we say." His voice rose for that last statement. He wanted me to hear him.

"Don't do it, Chas," Tasha pleaded.

"I'm doing it, and you should come with me. They have cars."

Maddeningly, their voices dropped to a murmur. I was fixing to call Tasha in, when she ran inside and up the stairs to her room, leaving the front door wide open.

Eddie came in the back door, and he shut the front one on his way up to me.

"He wanted her to run away with him," Eddie whispered.

"My God!"

"Don't worry. She seemed to think about it for a minute, but then she said, 'No. No. No!' That shithead grabbed her arm and yanked her toward him really hard. Before I could react, she slapped him and ran inside."

"Bloody hell. Thank God she had the sense to refuse him." I imagine she'd had her fill of trouble from that boy. "Stupid kid. Where does he think he can run to?"

"Said he has friends with all the food you need, all the booze and pot. Even cars and gasoline."

"Where did they get all that?"

"They probably stole it, Mom."

EDDIE AND PETE STAYED WITH US for a total of eighteen days, during which they gave us a ton of help with gardens, outhouses, and repairs—and they put on a few pounds apiece. The many gallons of honey they harvested helped the whole neighborhood round out a bit. Now the neighbors were aware of the beehive, but that had turned out to be good. Eddie and Pete had needed scads of help harvesting the honey and extracting it from the combs.

"We left about half the honey in there," Pete told me.

"That's good. We'll need it later," I said. "You know, I've read that if you're going away for a while, you've got to tell your bees, or they'll swarm and leave the hive."

"Seriously?" Eddie said.

Pete looked at me skeptically. "Oh, Mom."

On the morning that Pete and Eddie departed, Milo and I went with Eddie to say goodbye to the bees, so Eddie could tell them that Milo and I would be looking out for them now. Pete didn't come with us, but he watched from the Pico backyard.

"Guys," I said to my stepsons as we returned to our yard, "don't go. This whole endeavor seems useless."

"Don't start, Mom," Pete said, shaking his head.

"We have to try," said Eddie.

"God damn it. We need you here!"

"Dad needs us more!" Pete barked.

"Jesus. Okay!"

Tasha and Mazie clung fiercely to Pete and Eddie when telling them goodbye. Pete managed to get a hug out of Sonja, along with a big smile. If we hadn't been watching, I'm sure he'd have gone for a kiss.

Milo and Keno tried to be stolid and manly with their handshakes and goodbyes, but they looked like they wanted to cry. I hugged my stepsons as hard as I could, and I made them promise to come back to us within two months, whether they found their father, sisters, and brother or not. I didn't allow myself to cry.

CHAPTER 42

One-hundred-and-twenty-one days since the world fell apart.

The absence of Eddie and Pete was palpable. My worry about what they might find in Waco banged around in my head like a shower of pinballs. I tried to put it out of my mind before my brain flashed a permanent "Tilt."

A few days after my sons departed, when Tasha's morning sickness seemed confined to the occasional early morning, I had Keno take Tasha to the South Austin clinic in the bicycle cart. Sonja left Cesar with Kathy Zizzo and rode a bike alongside my grandkids as adult moral support. I wanted to go with them so badly, but I couldn't fit in the cart with Tasha. I stood erect and stoic as I waved goodbye from my front yard.

Jack sneaked up on me while I was lost in thought. He put his arm around me and pulled me tight against him.

"Come on over to my place, Bea. I'll give you some tea and show you my hothouse."

I followed him to his backyard, amazed at the flowers still blooming in the hothouse despite his lack of care.

"You must have a magic touch," I said.

He peered into my eyes and stroked my face. "You used to think so."

I took a sharp breath. "Pretty corny, Jack."

"Yeah, but you like it, right?"

"Seems like I do."

"Bea." He studied my face. "I'm afraid Hank will come back, and I'll lose you before I get the chance to have you again."

"I'm afraid of that, too."

He kissed me, and I kissed him back. I started to pull away, but he said, "Don't." He waltzed me into his house and toward his bed. I followed his lead willingly, aching for him.

I won't lie. I made love to Jack Jeffers, and I wanted and needed every minute of it—every touch, every kiss, every thrust and spasm. Hank and I had never made love like that. I made greedy love to Jack, and he grabbed me and possessed me and I practically begged him to do it, in almost the same way we'd done all those years ago, as though he belonged inside me, as if we were home at last.

But I was plenty discombobulated afterward.

I returned home to find Milo and Mazie in a state of distress. They'd been hunting for me all over the neighborhood and were mad at me for not being found.

"Nana, we need you. You can't go off and not tell us where you're going!" Milo regarded me sternly. Good grief, I'd become the wayward child of my grandson.

"We need you to fire up the grill," Mazie said. "It's past lunchtime. We're hungry!" A tough disciplinarian, that Mazie.

"Sorry, kids," I said breathlessly. "Mr. Jeffers was teaching me about hothouses and how to grow things in them . . . stuff I need to know."

"Well, you shoulda told us," Mazie said.

"You're right. I should have. Let's start a fire and make some lunch."

I was tempted to tell my grandkids the truth, which would have been slightly insane of me. But I was sick of skirting the truth and omitting so many facts from the ones I loved. I chatted with the kids while we cooked and ate lunch, though all I could think about was how to sneak back to Jack and the warm feelings engulfing me.

LATE IN THE AFTERNOON, Keno came crashing through the front door, carrying Tasha in his arms.

"Nana, help! Come help!"

Sonja ran in behind Keno, removing Tasha's bike helmet, brushing hair from her face. "Bea, come fast, please!"

I shuddered all the way down the stairs to my granddaughter, who was bleeding from the seat of her pants and onto the arms of her frantic brother. Mazie screamed. Milo ran into the room and stood there, gaping.

"Lay her down on the floor!" I shouted. "Mazie get pillows. What happened?"

"That fucker Chas is what happened," Keno said, as he laid his sister gently on the floor. Mazie delivered a pile of couch pillows.

Chas! Did he find out Tasha was pregnant and slug her?

"How?" I said. "Boys, take Mazie and go outside or to the garage. I have to undress Tasha. Oh, sweetheart, what happened?"

"I think I'm okay," Tasha said, but she sounded weak. "Stupid Chas."

"We fell. The bike fell, and Tasha flew out onto her belly on the concrete." Keno backed across the room, gripping the arms of Mazie and Milo. "Chas was chasing us, trying to talk to Tasha, but she didn't want to talk to him. I shoulda stopped the bike and beat the shit out of him! I'm sorry, Tasha. I'm sorry, Nana!" Tears spurted down his cheeks.

"Keno, accidents happen. We know you didn't mean to fall. Go on outside."

"Yes, ma'am," Keno said, and he dragged his cousins with him out the back door.

Sonja had been running around gathering up water and washcloths, towels and basins, sheets and blankets. Now she returned, and we carefully removed Tasha's pants. Then we laid her on a blanket and put the pillows under her bottom, to elevate it and try to stop the blood.

"Does it hurt, Tasha?" I asked with a rasping wheeze.

"I have cramps. Bad cramps."

What an awful lot of blood—way more blood than should've been normal for a miscarriage. Sonja put towels between Tasha's legs, and they were quickly soaked. Whenever Tasha cringed with a cramp, blood actually gushed. We only had about five liters of blood inside us. Must have been a liter or two on Tasha and the floor. God knows how much was in the towels. There was no way to stop this. How could we stop this?

Sonja shot me worried looks and fussed over Tasha while I anxiously inspected Tasha's clothing and the soaked towels, searching for a tiny fetus. I found blood clots, but nothing that resembled a miniscule baby. Did that mean the fetus was still inside her? Was she going to keep bleeding until it came out?

"Sorry for the mess, Nana," Tasha said.

"Honey, you have nothing to be sorry for."

I threw a sheet over Tasha's body. "Keno, you kids come here! I need help!"

The three solemn kids rushed inside.

"Why's Tasha bleeding?" Mazie asked.

"She's hurt inside. Kids, run through the neighborhood and see if anyone knows how to stop bleeding. Tell them Tasha's bleeding bad, and we need help. Now! Go!"

They ran out the front door. Keno choked on a sob as he crossed the threshold.

Fuck me!

Why hadn't I learned how to stop a hemorrhage in all my plotting and scheming for an apocalypse? I couldn't catch my breath.

Within a minute or two, half the neighborhood was in our entryway, watching my beautiful granddaughter bleed through her sheet. I held her wrist and counted her pulse over and over until it was so thready that I couldn't count it on her wrist anymore and had to find the pulse in her neck.

Tasha smiled wistfully, trusting me when I was not worthy of her trust.

"Everyone except my family, please leave," I said.

They backed out the front door. Jack said, "I'll wait on the stoop," before he stepped outside. Sonja started to leave, too, but I asked her to take Milo and Mazie out back.

"Tasha, my beautiful love," I said, shakily gripping her hand as the back door slammed shut. "I don't know how to stop your bleeding, sweetheart."

"I feel so tired," she said with drooping eyelids, a clog in her throat. "Am I gonna die?" She looked at me so earnestly, so pleadingly, that I couldn't lie to her. She had a right to the truth, but I couldn't tell her.

I had a great debate with myself that took place in an instant. Tasha needed a chance to say her goodbyes, so I acted.

"Oh Tasha, your heart's slowing down, and I—"

Keno gasped. Tasha started shaking. "Don't let me die, Nana!"

"Honey, I would die myself to save you. I don't know how to save you. Please forgive me."

Tears gushed from Tasha's eyes. She swallowed hard. Her eyes darted between Keno and me as she took several quick breaths, then one very long one—a sigh of resignation I will never forget.

"Keno, tell me goodbye," she said, her voice quavering.

"I can't." Keno stood frozen and staring at his sister.

I tugged gently on Keno's arm and pulled him toward Tasha. "Honey, she wants you to."

He brushed tears and snot off his face with the back of his hand. He bent down to Tasha, kissing her pretty forehead. "I love you, sister," he said.

"It's okay to hug her, Keno."

He hugged her so tenderly that I almost couldn't watch. "I'm sorry," he said. Both their faces were flooded with tears.

"You didn't mean to fall, Keno. You were helping me. Don't you dare feel guilty about this. Promise me."

"But I screwed up. I turned too sharp, and—"

"Promise me, Keno! I mean it!"

"Okay, I promise!"

"I love you, Joaquin."

"I love you, too, Natasha."

"T-tell M-mom. Oh!" She panted for breath. "Tell Mom I love her."

"I will." He slowly stepped back, continuing to gaze into Tasha's eyes.

I grabbed my granddaughter, my gorgeous granddaughter Natasha Simms, and I hugged her for all I was worth.

"I'll come join you someday soon, my love. Maybe you'll find your mother or your grandfather there."

But Tasha was already fading away from us. She died with her big brown eyes open and peering straight through me, drained to the bone of blood.

Keno let out a piercing cry and crumpled to the floor.

I couldn't cry. I couldn't move. I couldn't breathe. I could not live another minute.

CHAPTER 43

Keno sat shaking on the floor with his head buried under his arms. Jack opened the front door a crack and peeked at Tasha. "Aw, no," he said.

I didn't look at him. I didn't do anything except watch over my beautiful girl and try to will the life back into her dark and empty eyes.

Jack bent down and held my arm. "I'm sorry, Bea."

I didn't respond. Such a stupid, obvious comment. Of course he was sorry. He didn't have to say so.

He rubbed my shoulder for a moment, then straightened up and followed the sound of Mazie's crying to the patio. I heard him murmuring with Sonja out there, but what did I care? Murmur away, you damn fools. Go ahead and waste your breath. It's worthless anyway.

Milo screamed "No!" from the backyard, then it sounded like someone was whacking the fence with a stick over and over and over again.

SOON, SONJA AND JACK RETURNED. Sonja sat Mazie in Keno's lap. "This little girl needs you, Joaquin." Keno swallowed Mazie in his long arms, and the two of them wept. After a while, he carried Mazie to the patio to rock her in the glider.

Sonja stooped down to me. "Bea, can I get you some tea?" I shook my head. She stood silently beside me with her hand on my shoulder. She may have been praying. At last, she said, "Should I prepare Natasha's body for burial?"

She had love and sadness in her eyes, but I hated her eyes because they were alive and Tasha's were not. I closed my own eyes so I wouldn't have to look at Sonja. I didn't say a word. I didn't know how.

Jack reached down and took my hand. "Bea, dear, you need to come away and let Sonja work."

I opened my eyes and said very quietly, "I am *not* going anywhere."

"Bea." He sighed and tried to hug me to him, but I was a ramrod, stiff and cold.

Sonja asked, "Do you mind if I ask Mrs. Zizzo and Mrs. Barnes to help me?"

"No."

The last light of day faded from the sky as Sonja left the house. Jack lit some candles. I held Tasha's hand and petted her forehead, shivering at the chill of it but not caring because I could still feel my granddaughter.

A loud pounding on the front door.

"Tasha! Tasha!" Chas screamed.

Jack opened the door and shoved Chas backward off the stoop.

"Hey! Let me see Tasha!" Chas yelled.

"If I were you, you punk bastard, I'd get as far away from here as I possibly could."

"Why can't I see her?"

"Because, you fucking idiot, she's dead!"

"She can't be!" Chas cried. I couldn't see his face, but he shut up, and Jack came back inside.

"Sorry, Bea," he said. I merely nodded.

I had to let go of Tasha's hand and stop stroking her forehead while the women removed her clothing and washed the blood off her firm breasts and slightly swollen tummy. I could not avert my eyes from the horror of it. Kathy turned Tasha on her side while Doris scoured blood off the tiled floor. Sonja disappeared and returned with a pretty dress of Tasha's, a dress she'd only recently brought here from her mother's house.

"Will this dress be alright?" Sonja asked.

"Yes, it's beautiful."

They carefully dressed my girl, and someone closed her eyes. I almost reached out to reopen them. I wanted to see her big brown eyes while they still existed.

Sonja held up a hairbrush and some clips. "Would you like to fix her hair, Bea?"

"I don't think I can."

"Don't you want to make one of your lovely French braids for her?"

"Will you help me?" I asked.

"Yes, Bea, I'll help."

The other two women stood by, sniffling, while my tremulous hands braided Tasha's hair and Sonja's steady hands smoothed my work. When I reached the end of the braid, Sonja tied it with a silky ribbon, but first she had to gently pry my hand loose from the thick chestnut hair of my girl.

I SAT WITH TASHA INTO THE NIGHT, a mindless mass of murderous pain, surrounded by a room full of candles. Sonja, Kathy, and Doris sat at the other end of the living room, hand-sewing sheets into some kind of burial shroud. It seemed right, but I couldn't pay attention to it.

The kids came in and out of the room—one by one, as pairs, all three together. They would cry or just sit and stare. Mazie climbed into my lap and stayed until my legs fell asleep from the weight of her, and still I held her.

Jack and Sonja each tried to convince me to take a few bites of the food Jack had cooked, but I couldn't. Silas brought some branches of a Christmas cactus still in bloom—delicate white flowers almost floating atop the soft, green branches. I kept thinking, what good are these beautiful flowers if Tasha can't see them?

Doris sat beside me and recited the 23rd Psalm. I looked at the ceiling while she spoke so I wouldn't have to see her living, breathing mouth.

Everyone tried to talk me into going to bed or for a walk, or getting some air on the patio, but I wouldn't budge. The adults and Keno conferred in a whisper as though they were worried about me, but they needed to be worried about themselves. Something was terribly wrong with them. They just kept moving and breathing and living when Tasha was dead.

Keno came over to me. "I'm sitting up with Tasha tonight. You should go to bed."

"No. You go to bed. I'll take care of this."

"Well, I'm sitting up anyway, so whatever."

"Keno, I said, 'Go to bed!'"

"No, Nana, I won't! You're not the only person who's sad around here. I want to honor my sister and watch over her, and you can't stop me!" His face was scarlet red. He had never defied me so vehemently before. His words shredded me.

"Okay," I muttered, and turned back to face Tasha in her angelic repose. The emotions storming through me ran the gamut of piercing loss, flaming rage, bottomless despair, and merciless self-recrimination, swirling in a stew of near-catatonic madness.

"Bea," Jack said from behind me, making me jump in my seat. "Keno is right. You need to collect yourself so you can comfort these kids."

"I said he could stay, Jack."

"Yes, but what about these other two? They need their grandmother."

"What good am I to them? I was so busy taking care of everyone else that I let my baby girl get pregnant and die. Then I had the chance to move my nurse friends over here, but I didn't, because I didn't think they could help enough to be worth feeding them. What kind of cold-hearted bitch am I, to do something like that? Then what happens next? Tasha bleeds to death before our eyes when the nurses might've saved her. I'm poison, Jack. My daughter will never forgive me. Hank will never forgive me. I should've been taking care of Tasha instead of fucking you!"

"Bea, shut up!"

Keno's mouth dropped open, and he flipped his pained, wet eyes from me to Jack and back again.

"I'm sorry you had to hear that, son," Jack said.

"Nana, get out of here!" Keno said through clenched teeth. "You're not gonna act this way around my sister!"

I glared at Keno. I glared at Jack, who was shaking his head. I couldn't look at the women in the corner, but I felt their eyes on me. I didn't care. I wanted to claw their eyes out. I wanted to rip my hair out by the roots. I turned to Keno and slapped him smack across the cheek. He stepped back, startled. Jack tried to grab me, and I unleashed a barrage of punches and slaps across his chest and stomach. I kicked him in the shins. I aimed higher, going for his balls. Keno clasped my arms and pulled me back from Jack. The two men hugged me from both sides and sat me down on the floor.

"Shit, Bea, you hurt me," Jack said.

"I hate you."

"No, you don't."

"Both of you shut up and get out of here!" Keno growled.

I looked up to see Mazie standing in the back doorway, bug-eyed.

"Come on, Bea. You heard the man. We need to get out of here." Jack tugged me to my feet, wrapped me in his arm, and ushered me out the back door. He sat me on a chair and stood next to me with his hand on my shoulder—to keep me from starting another fight, I guess.

"Nana, why are you fighting?" Mazie said. "We're not supposed to fight!"

"I'm sorry, Mazie." I pulled her into my lap. "I made a million mistakes today. I've been a very bad Nana."

"Did the devil make you do it? Daddy says sometimes the devil makes you do stuff."

"That must be what happened. Usually the devil can't fool me because I'm old and I'm mostly wise. But today, I wasn't wise." I didn't realize I was crying until Mazie wiped my tears away with her fingers.

Mazie snuggled into my bosom and cried with me. Jack patted me on the shoulder, tears in his eyes as well.

"Where's Milo?" I asked.

"Don't know," Jack said.

"Will you look for him?"

"Of course, Bea." He kissed the top of my head and went inside.

Jack returned with Milo a good while later. He'd found the boy down the street, breaking rocks into chunks with a hammer, and hurling chunks at the windows of empty houses.

Grief is a beast. Grief over a senselessly lost child can break your brain and kill you dead.

CHAPTER 44

We sat together in the living room all night. Even Jack and Sonja stayed. After a while, everyone except Keno and me fell asleep. When I was sure the others were sleeping, I went to sit by Keno and took his hand.

"I'm sorry, Keno. I lost my mind."

"Yeah, you did," he said, but he let me hug him. We were both numb at this point; neither of us cried, although I wanted to. We stared at Tasha together. We were quiet for a long time, until Keno whispered, "The doctor at the clinic said she couldn't get an abortion. No place to get one."

"I was afraid of that."

"Tasha was happy about it. She said she wanted to keep the baby anyway. She said she loved babies." Such agony in his voice.

"Oh, God." I doubled over with pain. It took me a while to straighten up. I had lost my first great-grandchild, too, and only now felt the weight of that loss.

Keno faced me, his eyes drilling into mine. "Did you really sleep with that old man?"

"Yes, but I'm sorry I told you in such a crude way."

"What about Grandpa?"

"I'll always care about your grandpa. He's not here though, and we don't know if he'll come back. I don't know why I did it. I guess I'm just lonely."

"Are you gonna keep seeing this guy?"

"Keno, you know his name. He's your friend."

"I *thought* he was my friend."

"Don't blame him. He was being sweet to me. I don't know if I'll see him again or not. It's hard to imagine doing anything right now."

"Yeah." Keno sighed. "I wish you wouldn't see him."

"I can't promise that, honey. I deserve a little love, don't I?"

My eldest grandson regarded me in a very peculiar way. Maybe he was seeing me more as a fellow adult than he ever had before. I reached over and tousled his hair.

"Don't think about it too much. Nobody wants to think about old people making love."

Keno smirked. "Yeah, it's gross."

"Yeah? Think how gross it is to be old."

He nodded and slid to the floor to continue his watch over his departed sister.

"CHILDREN," I SAID, shortly after the neighborhood roosters crowed at dawn. "It's time to get up and prepare for the day." This awful day when we would lay our Natasha to rest.

"Bea," Jack said as he rose to his feet, "I was thinking we could bury Tasha on a hill I know about. It's near the train tracks."

"It's not down where the poison is, is it? I won't bury her in poison."

"No, it's about a mile north, on the other side of William Cannon Drive. There's some nice trees there."

I stared off through the window at a leaden sky. "Think it will rain?"

"Don't know. It might."

I looked Jack squarely in the eyes. "How will I get to her grave? I need to be able to get there."

"I'll take you any time you want to go," he said.

"How would you take me? What if I want to go alone?"

"I'll push you in a wheelchair. If you want to be alone, I'll walk away for a while." He seemed sad to me, and he was genuinely offering help. But he was already making me dependent on him by trying to take Tasha so far away.

"I want her closer." I again stared through the window.

"Bea."

"I can't have her so far away from me, Jack."

"Honey, she's...."

"I know she's dead. Don't you think I know it? And don't call me honey."

"Yes, ma'am." He hesitated. Maybe he wanted me to look at him, but I wouldn't. Finally, he said, "I'll talk to some of the others and see what kind of place we can find."

"Thank you. And please come tell me about it before you start digging."

"Whatever you want. Only tryin' to help,"

"I know. I appreciate it."

BEFORE LONG, PEOPLE BEGAN TAPPING AT OUR DOOR and delivering hot food: scalloped potatoes, pecan turnovers made with honey, green beans stewed with onions, lentil soup, even a bit of fried chicken. Since we had no refrigeration, I assumed this meant we were expected to spend the day with a house full of awkward neighbors eating the food. I needed a place to hide.

Sonja left to pick up Cesar from the Zizzos and to take care of his needs. I couldn't tell Sonja how much I appreciated her right then. It would have set me to crying, and I knew I would have plenty of that before this day was over.

Without any prompting from me, Keno had already fed breakfast to Mazie and Milo. Now he led them upstairs to get cleaned up and dressed. Where Keno got these fatherly instincts, I didn't know. He didn't get them from his own father. Jimmy only visited his kids once or twice per year. And, although Jimmy had redeeming qualities—he paid most of his child support, for instance—he was uncomfortable around his kids, and they were equally uneasy around him.

Keno, however, had always been good with kids. He'd never picked on his sister like so many brothers do. He played with his younger cousins when they asked; he'd even babysat kids in his old neighborhood on occasion. Now, in our new world, Keno had grown into the role of family father, and, though I'd asked him to take that responsibility in my absence, I hadn't realized he'd come so far.

I couldn't dwell on these thoughts for long, or any other thoughts for that matter. My mind refused to focus. I took a chicken leg and went upstairs to wash up. I found a somber-looking pantsuit inside a dry cleaner's bag. I put the suit on, but it was much too big for me now, plus it looked so hideously dark and sad. Tasha liked beautiful things.

I dug through my closet until I found a black, hippie-style maxi-dress with colorful flowers—a dress I hadn't worn in thirty years. I'd only kept it to show hippie history to the grandkids. But I'd forgotten about it and had never shown it to Tasha. Well, I would show her today.

Jack knocked at my door, but I didn't answer it; I talked to him through it. He'd found a place for Tasha's grave—a tiny hillside, or more like an embankment, by the entrance to our subdivision.

"Lots of bluebonnets grow there," he said.

"Sounds perfect. Thank you." A perfect place to do a horrible thing.

I DRESSED AND PROPPED UP IN BED WITH A NOTEBOOK, leaning against the headboard to write an elegy for my granddaughter. The next thing I knew, someone was rapping at the door. As I opened my eyes, she slipped into my room. The sun glared on her face.

"Tasha?"

Sonja stepped from the sunlight, a catch in her breath.

"I'm sorry to wake you, Bea, but it's getting late. It's time for us to prepare for—"

"The funeral?"

"Yes. Everyone's waiting for you."

"Good Lord. How long did I sleep?"

"Many hours. It's after two p.m. I know you were very tired." Sonja's eyes shone with sympathy. I sat up in bed.

"Thank you, Sonja, for all you did for Tasha, and for all you do for my family. I've come to think of you as a daughter."

Sonja's eyes teared up. "Thank you," she said softly.

I stood and hugged her to me, but I wished I hadn't. All I could feel was that she wasn't Tasha. "I'll be down in a few minutes, honey."

As Sonja left the room, I heard murmuring voices through the opened door and was relieved when it closed. I straightened and smoothed my clothes. I brushed my hair and pulled it back into a severe knot, but I added a colorful comb for Tasha's sake. I found the notebook I'd taken to bed with me. I hadn't written a single word of eulogy.

I put on a black cardigan sweater. I draped my mother's black lace mantilla over my head and around my shoulders. I descended the stairs as the murmuring slowed to a stop

Keno and Jack stood up when they saw me on the stairs. I nodded at Jack and went to Keno. The house was filled with neighbors milling about the entire lower floor. From the corner of my eye I saw Tasha, encased in the shroud the women had sewn for her. I could hardly look, but I noticed they'd appliqued a pretty piece of embroidery over Tasha's chest. So sweet of them.

"Are we ready?" I asked. Mazie ran up and grabbed my hand, burrowing her face into my side. Milo shuffled up behind Mazie, his head down, his light hair hanging past his eyes, his Aviators in his hand.

"I cleaned up the bike cart for you, Nana," Keno said.

The bike cart? I hated that bike cart. It had killed my girl.

"Honey, thank you, but I think it would be better to walk. It would be more respectful, like an old-fashioned funeral." Or a new-fashioned one, I supposed.

"Sure." Keno seemed relieved. He probably hated that cart more than I did. "But can you walk that far?"

"As long as I can sit down when I get there."

"We took chairs over already," Jack said. I realized he was wearing a suit and tie. Keno and Milo also wore ties, and Mazie had on a dark velvet dress and patent-leather shoes. The kids had made themselves so beautiful, it choked me up. I couldn't look at my neighbors. I couldn't face them.

Sonja made her way to the front door, gripping Cesar by the hand. She wore a smart navy suit and sensible heels, her hair in a perfect French twist. Cesar was scrubbed pink in a little gray suit, his hair trimmed and gelled.

"You all look very nice," I told my family—my depleted but also extended family. "Best be going."

Outside, we were met by several others, including Silas and Doris and the Ibanez kids. Alma's eyes were swollen and red. She was Tasha's old friend and must have been devastated. I'd forgotten all about those Ibanez kids. The Carlisles from down Mint Lane were there, along with Sandra something-or-other and her family, plus Phil Hendrix. Even sour Mr. Bellows showed up in a starched shirt and tie.

I glanced back to see Kathy and Harvey Zizzo coming out of my house, along with two young couples and their children, followed by Gary and Lyla Matheson and their son Chas.

What? Someone let Chas into my house? Did Keno know about this? They must have just come in through the back door. My blood pressure spiked, and I wobbled a bit, but Keno, who was looking down the road and not at our house, caught me on one side. Milo caught me on the other.

"You okay, Bea?" Jack asked from behind me. He was pushing the empty wheelchair.

"I'm not okay, but I'm not going to faint. Not today."

Phil, Silas, and two young men whose names I kept forgetting went inside and came out carrying Tasha, wrapped in her shroud and lying on a plank.

CHAPTER 45

Frigid steel had replaced my bones. My heart was ice. I wasn't me; I was an automaton walking to the funeral of her granddaughter— her fifteen-year-old, pregnant, bled-to-death granddaughter. The only thoughts that crossed my mind were the agony Erin, Eddie, and Pete would feel about losing Tasha, and the recriminations that were bound to come at me from Jeri and Hank.

When we reached the site—a grassy kind of knoll, except the grass was fittingly dead for the winter—I wobbled again. A grave had been dug in the sod; a pile of dirt sat beside it. Rows of chairs were set up, and flowering plants in pots surrounded the scene. I can't do this, I thought, but I did it.

I climbed the knoll and sat in the front row with my grandkids around me, Sonja and Cesar on one end of the row, Jack on the other. I didn't look behind me, but I knew Chas was back there, and it hijacked my mind. My grief was too great to become coherent thought. All I felt was pain.

Doris sang an off-key hymn, "Oh Promise Me," I think. Jack said a few words that were heartfelt but brief. Silas played "Amazing Grace" on his guitar, and Alma sang it. She had an achingly pure voice, made more beautiful by its tremulousness and her tears.

Mr. Bellows led us in a poignant prayer, sounding sweet and sad, and not the least bit crabby. It was just as well that I hadn't written a eulogy. I wouldn't have been able to read it aloud.

We stood around the grave while men lowered Tasha into it with ropes. I thought my heart would burst. I could not leave Tasha in that hole in the ground. It would be dark down there. And cold. I couldn't let her be so cold.

People tossed dried wildflowers into the grave. Mazie cried so hard that I feared she'd pass out. Keno dropped a flower into the pit then sank to his knees and almost fell forward into the grave with his sister. Milo grabbed hold of Keno, Mazie latched onto his neck, and my three remaining grandchildren huddled on the ground, crying. I almost collapsed with them, but Jack scooted the wheelchair up behind me just in time.

We cried for an interminable length of time. I wanted to ululate, like grief-stricken women I'd seen on the news, but I didn't know how.

A wintry wind kicked up and at last broke our anguished reverie. People started shoveling dirt into the grave. I whipped my face around to see our neighbors watching us, including Chas and those three scary-looking interlopers who'd shown up when Darla's house exploded.

I stood and headed straight for the smug, entitled beast who had defiled my granddaughter. Jack ran to catch up with me.

"What are you doing?" He sounded alarmed and half-breathless. I ignored him.

I kept my eyes on Chas, who saw me coming and wiped his red eyes. He seemed alarmed, too. I stepped in front of him, toe-to-toe. He looked down at me with a puzzled snarl on his face.

"What do you think you're doing here, Chas? Have some respect and leave."

"Bea? What the hell?" Gary said. His wife, Lyla, frowned at Gary then looked away. She knew her son was an asshole.

"Chas knows what I'm talking about. Get the hell out of here now, Chas!" I stood on my tiptoes and leaned toward the boy.

Sonja stepped from behind me and slapped Chas, backhanded, across his face, cursing him in Spanish.

"Ow! Shit!" Chas backed away, blinking and rubbing his cheek. "Leave me alone, you bitches!"

I didn't see Keno coming until he was already there.

He charged full speed, head-first, straight into Chas's chest, knocking him flat to the ground, straddling his torso and pounding his smart-aleck face with blow after blow after blow. Jack clamped a wrestling hold on Milo to keep the boy from jumping into the fray. Mazie screamed, almost with delight. Snot and blood flew out of Chas's nose, and he bucked beneath Keno, trying to throw him off. But Keno rode that kid like a rodeo star and continued to rain jabs and uppercuts and haymakers on the killer of my granddaughter.

Phil and Silas jumped in to pull Keno back, but I could've sworn they were taking their time about it. And Keno wasn't making it easy. When burly Silas wrapped his arms around Keno from behind, then reared back to lift him off the ground, Keno kicked Chas in the mouth, surely breaking some teeth. Chas squealed in agony.

"Keno, what the hell?" Gary shouted. "Bea, what's going on?"

"Shut up, Gary!" said his wife.

"Lyla, what—"

"I said, 'shut up!'" Lyla glared at her husband, then turned crisply and walked down the slope toward home.

Our friends dragged us away from Chas and down to the street. Chas remained behind, writhing and moaning on the ground with a bloody face and his bewildered father staring down at him.

I was having an asthma attack and didn't realize it until Jack practically forced me into the wheelchair and started pushing me home. I hadn't brought my inhaler. I wanted to go back to check on Tasha. I wanted to put blankets and lanterns into her grave with her. I did not want to leave her alone. She would be scared.

When we were halfway home, Keno said, "I'm going back to sit with Tasha."

"You should wait until Chas is gone, honey."

"I wanna go, too," Milo said.

"Well, take some coats."

Jack pulled off his suit jacket and put it on Keno. I gave Milo my cardigan.

"I'll go with them, Bea," Silas said, "and make sure everything's alright." The three of them disappeared down the darkening street.

I turned the wheelchair around and watched them until I couldn't see them anymore, then I just kept sitting there.

"Should we go?" Jack finally said.

"Not yet. Let me get used to being this far from her first."

"I don't think you'll ever get used to it."

"I know, but still. . . ."

WHEN AT LAST WE REACHED HOME, our guests were leaving, thank heaven. I noticed that they'd put a big dent in the food though. Possibly they did that before the funeral, when I was sleeping. I just hoped my grandkids had eaten some fried chicken.

Sonja heated food for us, and I actually ate a solid meal. As she prepared to go home for the night, Milo and Keno came through the front door with Silas. They smelled of wood smoke.

"Whew. Got cold out there," Silas said. "We started a fire, but that wind was too cold."

"Come in and get warm while I get your food," said Sonja, God bless her.

Someone had lit a fire in the hearth, and I only then noticed it. Milo and Keno slouched down onto the loveseat near the fire, and after a few minutes they returned Jack's jacket and my sweater. They looked about as numb as I felt. Mazie had been cuddled against me for I don't know how long before I felt the warmth and pressure of her.

"Keno, let me see your hands, honey," I said. He held up his red and swollen mitts. "Wiggle your fingers for me. You didn't break any bones, did you?"

He wiggled his fingers and said, "No."

"He broke Chas's nose," Milo said.

"How do you know?"

"'Cause we saw him, and he said so. He talked funny, too."

"Well, good," I said, and Milo laughed. Keno looked empty-eyed.

Sonja brought damp rags. She wiped Keno's hands with some of them and wrapped others around his palms, leaving the tips of his fingers free. "Elevate your hands," she said, placing his hands atop his head. He kept them there obediently until Sonja brought dinner.

"Does anyone know who those three men were, standing behind the chairs at the funeral?" I asked. The boys barely glanced toward me and shook their heads.

"Those bikers?" Jack said. "I thought y'all knew them."

"I saw them when the Beldings' house blew up. Thought they were relatives of some neighbor, or maybe they lived nearby and came to check out the explosion. Then one of them nodded to Chas, and he nodded back, like they knew each other."

"That's worrisome. I don't remember 'em from back then."

"Well, I do. Don't know why they came to Tasha's funeral though. Seems creepy."

"They were ugly," Mazie said.

"Ugly? Honey, they can't help how they look."

"Well, they scared me."

"Some folks have morbid fascinations," Jack said.

"That's what I mean. Creepy." I don't know why I kept talking—to distract myself from grief, I suppose. "Silas, thank you for the music." He nodded as he chewed. "That Alma has a beautiful voice. Don't you think so, boys?" I wanted to see Keno's reaction, but he and Milo went right on eating, bleary-eyed.

I gave up on talking. It didn't help the sadness one bit.

The boys and Silas finished eating, and Silas departed with Sonja and Cesar close behind.

"Kids, we should get some rest. We've had a horrible day." Mazie was already asleep. Keno stood up wearily, picked Mazie up, and carried her up the stairs. Milo followed behind him, scuffing his heels on the stairs as he went.

"I love you," I said, but they didn't respond. Too tired and sad. "Put your hands on a pillow to sleep, Keno. Keep them higher than your heart as much as you can."

Suddenly, I was alone with Jack, flickering shadows from the firelight moving across his face. This had not been part of my plan. He sat down beside me and searched my eyes.

"Bea, I—"

"Shhh,"

"But—"

"Don't."

He swallowed. "Okay?"

I sat quietly, listening to the boys murmuring in the upstairs bathroom, then going to the bedroom that had been assigned to the absent Ibanez boys, and closing the door. I guess those other kids were staying with the Barneses or with Sonja. I didn't know, and I didn't really care.

When we hadn't heard footsteps or squeaking bed springs for a couple of minutes, Jack stirred as if rising to go. I grabbed that hunky man with his crooked mustache and sparkling blue eyes, and I kissed him until I couldn't breathe. I kissed him so hard that it bruised my lips. I kept kissing him until he pretty much forced me off him.

"Now, go home," I said and looked away.

He ran his hand along my cheek, he stood up, and he left my house.

The Matheson family left our neighborhood within a week. Chas's mouth and nose were still swollen, his face still covered with cuts and bruises, when I saw him mount a bicycle loaded with bags and follow his parents down the street.

They couldn't get gone fast enough for me.

CHAPTER 46

Five months since this series of catastrophes began. The rest of our family wasn't ever coming home to us, were they?

Over the lonely remainder of the winter, I thought spring would never arrive. But it showed up in early March, which was normal for Austin. Spring didn't seem beautiful, though, in the way I had hoped. Nothing felt beautiful to me without Tasha in the world. I tried not to dwell on it, but I couldn't stop myself.

Honestly, I didn't know how much longer I could keep doing this—this carrying on and pressing forward, this raising of ragged, sun-parched children in such a dangerous world, this herding of neighbors with their problems and complaints. Most of all, I didn't know how to hold out hope as a beacon for my grandchildren when I'd all but lost hope myself.

Spring brought me out of the house and forced me back to organizing the neighborhood, especially the farming. Our winter crops hadn't fared well in the unusually cold winter we'd had. The root crops at the Mint held out longest, since the hired gardener had mulched them heavily before the EMP. We needed to put much more organic matter into all our garden soils.

It was time to plant greens and lettuces, and past time to start tomato and pepper seedlings indoors. We hadn't ended up canning a thing from our winter crops. We'd lost the fall batches of tomatoes, peppers, and squash when we had a hard freeze in February. Fortunately, we'd harvested winter squash and stashed it in the root cellar. That squash and last season's cabbage, onions, and sweet potatoes were the only vegetables we had to eat until we could grow new ones. If we were lucky, we'd get broccoli and greens before the other veggies ran out.

Then, not only had we lost Tasha, we'd also lost the Mathesons. Although Chas was an ass, he was a strong one, and he'd done a lot of work building gardens. It must have been his mother who got him to work, because his dad was a clueless wimp in regard to his son. Gary was an engineering-type guy. He'd designed and overseen the construction of our outhouses and rain collection systems.

Losing that family was hard on our group, but it did clear the air around here. There didn't seem to be much drama going on in the neighborhood. Everyone was too emotionally exhausted to be dramatic—that was my take on it. But give them enough time, and they would surely come up with something.

I didn't see much of Jack. I certainly didn't go to his house. I think I freaked him out with my breath-stealing kiss. He checked in with us now and then, and I caught him more than once regarding me with longing. He seemed to be giving me time and space to heal.

I didn't expect to heal, though. I was too old to get over something so horribly raw and traumatic. I just hoped to gain enough distance from it that I didn't wake up every morning wanting to puke.

Mazie had started climbing into bed with me in the middle of every night shortly after Tasha died. I finally told Mazie to go to bed in my room in the first place. It comforted us both to sleep in the same bed.

In an effort to give Mazie solace, I let her listen to her *Frozen* record on the phonograph until the batteries went dead, and I had no replacements.

I saw those same three sinister-looking men from the funeral and from Darla's explosion twice more. They drove slowly through the neighborhood in an old muscle car—a ruby red GTO from the early 70's, with that unique cross-hatched grille. Neighbors stopped to watch them. The first time, I don't think the men saw me, but the second time they looked right at me and squeaked their tires, then sped away, chased by a pack of mangy dogs and mangier kids.

Suddenly, I realized that I'd seen these men on the night of the train wreck—unloading the ice chest at the Beldings' house. At the time I'd thought the ice chest was full of beer, but maybe it contained metham-phetamines, or it was used to carry the meth away.

They must've come to Darla's explosion because they'd been watching the Beldings' house. Maybe they still had drugs stored there, or maybe they'd planned to break in and steal them. Surely the drugs burned up in the fire, or I hoped they had.

But why did they come to the funeral? And what were they doing here now? Whatever their reason, it couldn't be good.

I explained all this to Jack, and he put the patrollers on high alert.

I WENT TO TASHA'S GRAVE EVERY DAY, no matter the weather. I rolled myself down there in my wheelchair, then walked up the embankment and sat on an old chair Jack had left there for me. Usually Mazie came along, and we talked about how much we missed Tasha. Sometimes I asked Mazie to be quiet. I told her I wanted to listen to God, but I really wanted to grieve in silence. Keno and Milo never came with us, but Keno often went on his own. I don't know if Milo went or not.

I wasn't sure what was going on with Milo. The only time he seemed the least bit pleased was when he and Keno went to shoot guns at Jack's range. Milo brooded a lot, stayed to himself most of the time, and never smiled anymore. The rest of us were gloomy, too, but we cried openly, we comforted one another, and sometimes we laughed at silly things Tasha had said or done in her short life. We were "processing" our grief, as they say.

Yet Milo never cried, never talked about his departed cousin, and never laughed. His moods seemed darker by the day. I tried to get him to tell me his feelings, but he refused.

ONE AFTERNOON WHEN SONJA HAD GONE HOME EARLY, Milo started mocking Mazie, holding her Barbie doll out of her reach and making her jump for it.

"Give it to me, Milo!" Mazie demanded.

"Don't feel like it," he said.

"Please." Mazie turned up her charms, flashing him a grin.

"Make me!"

"Tasha, make Milo give it to me!" Mazie hollered, then she gasped when she realized what she'd said, and she let out a squealing cry.

Milo burst out laughing, wickedly laughing. "You yelled for Tasha, stupid, and she's dead!"

"Don't say 'dead'!" Mazie screamed, covering her ears and crying hysterically.

"Milo! For God's sake! What a nasty way to tease your sister." I hopped up from my seat and reached toward Milo. "Give me the doll!"

He sneered and wrenched the doll's head off, then hurled the head and body across the room, where they slammed against the wall and fell behind the couch.

"Milo, what's wrong with you? Go to your room!"

"No! I won't!" He yanked open the back door to rush out, only to run straight into Keno.

"Stop him, Keno."

"I hate you, Milo!" Mazie proclaimed.

Keno grabbed Milo by the arm and tugged the boy into the house.

"What's going on, Milo?" Keno examined the squirming boy, gripping him tighter.

"He's being mean to Mazie and disobeying me. I told him to go to his room."

"He broke my doll!" Mazie wailed.

Although Milo had more height than he'd ever had, Keno was still a head taller and still had a grip on Milo's arm. Milo tried to jerk away, but Keno latched on with both hands and twisted the younger boy around into a headlock.

"Better apologize to Mazie and go to your room," Keno said.

"Leave me alone, asshole!" Milo commenced kicking backward at Keno's shins and feet.

"Stop it, you little jerk!" Keno pushed his weight into Milo, spun him around, and wrestled him to the ground, until Keno knelt astride Milo's thighs, pinning his arms to the ground.

"Milo, what's gotten into you?" I said.

"Nothing!"

"Something. What is wrong?"

"Mazie yelled for Tasha." Milo cackled. "Stupid Mazie yelled for stupid, dead Tasha."

"What?" Keno's eyes hardened.

"I got mixed up," Mazie cried. "I didn't mean to."

Keno ignored Mazie and glared at Milo, pinned beneath him on the floor. Milo stared back, his eyes bulging. Keno closed his eyes and took slow, deep breaths.

"Fucking shit!" Keno roared, then he dropped to his side on the floor. "Fucking, fucking shit!" He curled into a ball, shaking with sobs.

Milo raised up on his elbows, flabbergasted. He didn't say a word. He scrambled to his feet and ran upstairs to his room.

"I can't get my doll from behind this thing." Mazie tugged on the heavy couch, which didn't budge an inch.

With Keno curled on the floor crying, and me not knowing what to do for him, I used a broom to sweep Mazie's broken doll from under the couch. She snapped its head back in place, good as new. I sat down and tried to calm my rat-a-tatting heart.

"That boy will be the death of me." I sighed heavily and leaned back in the chair to close my eyes.

"He'll grow out of it," Mazie said. "That's what Daddy says when Mommy gets mad at Milo for being bad." She deepened her voice to imitate her father, "Jeri, the boy will grow out of it.'"

"Your daddy's pretty smart." I just hoped to hell her daddy was right.

"Milo's acting out his pain like the rest of us," Keno muttered, sitting up on the tile and rubbing his eyes, breathing stuttering breaths. "I can't stand this fucking shit." He rose and headed back outside. When did he get so wise?

Mazie climbed into my lap. She was getting too big for it but somehow squirmed around to fit.

"Mazie, what happened to your princess skirt?"

"I put it away," she said. "It was Tasha's. It makes me sad."

"Then it's good you put it away. You can keep it to remember Tasha by."

"Yeah," she sighed and snuggled closer.

"Honey, don't feel bad about calling for Tasha. It's a normal thing to do. I almost call for her dozens of times every day."

"You do?"

"Sometimes I forget for a second that she's gone."

"Me, too," Mazie said. "I wish she wasn't gone."

"So do I, honey.... So do I."

I'M SURE MILO'S THIRTEEN-YEAR-OLD HORMONES were raging and making him slightly insane, but that tirade of his shook me up. Usually I don't really pray, but I prayed to God that Milo's insanity would be temporary.

Within an hour, Milo tiptoed down the stairs. I was still sitting with my eyes closed, not exactly sleeping, but trying to rest in the midst of our sorrow.

"Nana?" he said, a contrite tone to his changing voice. I opened my eyes to see a sheepish boy with a hank of dirty hair dangling over his downcast face.

"Yes?"

"Can I come out now?"

"I don't know. What made you act so crazy and mean like that? Here we are, hurting and missing Tasha. And your sweet little sister, who you are very lucky to have—Keno doesn't have his little sister, you know—Mazie calls for Tasha in a moment of confusion, and you go berserk."

I sat forward and took Milo's limp hand, squeezing it hard. "Look at me."

He skittered his eyes in my direction and gulped.

"Why did you do that? Do you miss Tasha and it makes you act crazy?"

"I guess." He wouldn't focus on me.

"Don't you know whether or not you miss her?"

"I do, but it's just—" He smeared tears off his cheeks. "I don't wanna miss her, so I try not to."

"Oh, Milo." I pulled him to me for a hug. "You have to go ahead and let yourself feel it. You have to cry like the rest of us do. Because if you don't let your grief out, you'll bottle it up, and that's what makes you act crazy."

I surveyed Milo's puzzled face. I couldn't tell what he was thinking.

"Do you understand me, kiddo?"

"I don't know," he said.

"Are you angry?"

He nodded.

"I understand. I'm so angry I could scream all day and night, for weeks on end."

"Yeah."

"Hammering things is good. Go build something and hammer the hell out of it."

Milo grinned crookedly. "Okay."

I gave him a half-playful swat on his behind and sent him outside.

NEAR DUSK, WHILE I MADE DINNER ON THE GRILL, Milo sat in the grass in a cloud of gloom. Keno came home from gardening and sat down beside Milo.

"Hey," Keno said.

"Hey," Milo muttered without looking up. The two of them just sat there, picking at blades of dead grass. Soon, they lay on their backs and gazed at the sky. If they ever said more than "hey" to one another, I didn't hear it.

Mazie knew better than to chatter at Milo in her usual way. She brought her Barbie and sat beside the boys, playing with the doll while the boys ignored her. After a while, she went inside and came back with a book, which she handed to Milo.

"Read *Winnie the Pooh* to me," she said. To my surprise, Milo read to Mazie until dark, when I called them for supper.

Every time I called my grandkids, I expected four kids to respond, but I only got three and a stab of pain.

THAT NIGHT NEAR BEDTIME, I hollered upstairs for the kids to come down. The three of them reached the bottom of the stairs and saw me, sitting on the couch and holding out the stethoscope.

"Come here," I said.

"What are you doing?" Keno asked, indignation in his tone.

"What do you mean? I need to check your lungs. You know that."

"What?" said Mazie.

"That's crazy," Milo said, laughing.

But Keno's face grew stern. "Nana, you just checked us."

"What? No, I didn't. Get over here."

"Yes, you did. You checked us half an hour ago."

"That's right." Mazie gaped at me worriedly.

"You did, Nana. You really did," Milo said.

I glared at my grandkids while I flipped through memory files in my brain. The kids regarded me solemnly.

"I don't remember checking you," I muttered.

"Well, you did," Keno said. The other two nodded, but still I couldn't remember it.

"You guys are just saying that to get out of it. You shouldn't tease me that way."

"No, we're not!" Mazie said. "You said I sounded right as rain. Remember?"

"You asked me where I got this scratch." Milo yanked up his T-shirt to show me a red welt on his rib cage that I'd never seen.

"Where did you get it?" I mumbled, my brain throbbing.

"On that rosebush by the Mint." He scrunched his eyes. "I told you."

I dropped my face into my hands and sat there with an aching mind until Keno said, "Nana?"

"Sorry. Go on to bed."

The kids slinked away, staring back at me. I plowed through my brain for hours and never did remember checking those kids.

CHAPTER 47

Since Keno needed to keep occupied, he started teaching math and science in the evenings to the kids in our co-op group, and he took over the neighborhood gardening as a type of straw-boss, prioritizing the workload and that sort of thing.

One day I was inspecting our home garden, making notes for Keno on what needed to be done. Jack opened my gate and strode up in front of me, inches away. I started to step back, but he reached out to caress my cheek. He leaned in and puckered up for a kiss.

"Whoa!" I put my hand on his chest to stop his forward motion. "Don't."

"Why not?"

"People are watching." I glanced around quickly but didn't find a soul to support my excuse.

"So what? Everyone knows about us anyway. It's not like it's a secret."

"What, exactly, do they know about us, Jack? That we slept together a few months ago?"

"Well, I hope it happens more often than that."

"Is that what you want? Sex?"

"No." He leaned backward. "I mean, yes, I want sex, but I want it with you and only you. I thought you knew me better than that."

"What am I supposed to know? I can't read your mind."

"Well, that I love you."

"Love me?" I raised my voice. "That's a huge statement. What makes you think you love me?"

"I don't think it. I know it. I've been in love before, Bea. I know what it feels like." He crinkled his wrinkly old eyes while scanning my face. "Don't you love me?"

"Jack Jeffers, do not come here and ask me questions I can't answer. Can't you see that I'm busy? Don't you have work to do?"

To my chagrin, Jack laughed. "You didn't say 'no,'" he said.

"Oh, go home!" I spun away from him, stomped past Sonja as she came out to the grill, and went in the house.

Sonja waited a minute, then followed me inside. She'd become the emotional rock of our household during our time of grief. She seemed to know the right tone to take with each of us—when to be cheerful, when to be solemn, when to console us or leave us alone.

"Are you alright, Bea?" she asked.

"That old man is driving me crazy. Everybody wants something from me. They just demand more and more and more. Can't they see I have nothing left to give? I feel so damned empty."

"Don't you think love can fill you back up?" Sonja took my hand.

"Love," I muttered.

"Do you not love Mr. Jeffers?"

"I don't know. I guess I might, if I had any love left in me."

"Maybe you should let him give love to you, and soon you will have love to give." Sonja—such a deep well of wisdom and heart.

I sat down on the edge of the couch. "I just feel like everyone—except you, Sonja— everyone else is always after me for something. Time, advice, attention, food. I can't take it anymore."

"It's very hard when people demand things from you that you don't feel you can give."

"Especially men," I said. "Why do they pressure us to make decisions?"

"My husband did this to me, about something I should not have been pressured about."

"Oh?" I sat still, hoping she would finally feel comfortable enough to confide in me.

"Cesar the elder wanted another child," Sonja said. "I wanted one, too, but I wanted to wait because I wanted to work. But I obeyed my husband, and I tried for a while to make another baby. Yet, nothing happened. And Cesar kept pushing me for not getting pregnant fast enough. I was very hurt and angry."

"Excuse me, but that is just wrong."

She nodded sadly. "I did a bad thing." She paused, reluctant to say more.

"I bet it wasn't so bad."

"It was deceitful." Sonja winced, blurting out the story in a rapid stream. "I took birth-control pills without telling my husband. I did this for a year or more, but then he caught me, so I stopped. But I didn't get my period. Cesar was watching me closely, asking about my period every day. When it didn't come, he was elated and bought pregnancy tests and vitamins.

"I took a test but got a negative. I thought I took it too early, so I waited a week and got another negative. Then, I went to my doctor, and she gave me hormone shots to start my period. Cesar was furious with me. He wasn't rational at all. He packed his bags and left me, said he was going to Mexico. I thought he would be back when he calmed down, but he'd already been gone five weeks when the EMP happened."

I sat quietly, taking it all in. If Cesar II was that controlling, Sonja was probably better off without him. "Don't you think he should have forgiven you for that by now?"

"Yes! Yes, I do." Tears pooled in her eyes. "But because of the EMP, I cannot know his feelings. It makes me feel crazy."

"Aw, honey, come here," I pulled her down beside me on the couch, enfolding her in my arms while she shuddered and sniffled. At last, I asked her, "Are you still going to try to go find him in Mexico? It's warmer now."

Sonja sat forward, wiping her face with her palms. "I can't leave you now. You need me."

"It's true that we need you, but someone else could help us while you're gone. I mean, I'd miss you terribly, and I'd be worried sick for you, but I want you to be happy." Then I wondered something. "You and me are okay, aren't we?"

She sucked in a breath. "I think it was kind and motherly of you to keep me from going to Mexico. I was not in my right mind. You kept me safe, and got me healthier."

"But I shouldn't have done it."

"It's true, you shouldn't have. But I'm glad that you did."

"Sonja, you're too kind to me. You're some kind of saint."

"I need the love you give me, Bea. I did not get it from my husband. And there is no one else to help you like I do."

"It's true that no one else would be as much help or be such a great cook." I smiled. "And we couldn't possibly love anyone else as much as we love you. I'm closer to you than I've ever been with my daughters."

Sonja smiled, too. "Thank you." She kissed me on the cheek as she stood up. "I will just have to find other ways to be happy." She headed toward the kitchen.

When she was almost there, she turned back.

"Bea, at least Mr. Jeffers is only asking you for love. Nothing else, am I right?"

I sighed. "You're right, but love is a very tall order."

"Yes, it is," she said, and she went back to work.

A COUPLE OF DAYS LATER, SONJA ASKED ME IF PETE HAD EVER BEEN MARRIED.

"No, he hasn't. I don't know why."

I'd given up long ago trying to make sense of my kids' love-lives. Pete had always had a steady stream of lovers, but it had been ages since I'd seen him show real romantic interest in anyone, until Sonja.

CHAPTER 48

L ate April, six and a half months since the solar pulse.
Eddie and Pete still hadn't returned from their search for the rest of the family. They'd promised to be home in two months, but it had been thirteen weeks. I wished I could've talked them out of going. That damnable town, Waco, Texas—Wacko as I liked to call it—was a big, stinking sinkhole, sucking my family members away from me.

There were still far too many gunshots at night, and last week our patrollers had been forced to kill another man. He'd stolen water from the Carlisles, and when the patrollers tried to get it back, the guy took shots at them. The intruders were getting bolder.

The trips to the water well were growing more fraught with too many men watching them drive down the street. Any minute someone could find our folks at the well, and God knows what horrid things would happen.

We had another bout of allergic illness, this time from live oak pollen. Thick green pollen powder and strings of spent tree flowers covered everything—roofs, sidewalks, dead cars, plants in the garden that we had to put our faces near to do our work. Cesar went back to struggling for air.

Then we got two solid days of hard rain, and the air was rinsed clean of pollen. Green rivulets of rainwater washed down from our rooftops and spattered into puddles covered with neon green pollen scum. The air was breathable again, and cleaner than it had been in decades. The rain barrels were full of pollen water. I wasn't sure if it was okay to drink as it was, but we could filter it.

But Cesar got better much more slowly this time. These allergy bouts were wearing him down. He worried me, he really did. I loaned Sonja my medical books and told her she could use whatever medications I had on hand for the quiet little boy. It may have helped some; I don't know.

The crops loved the rain and were bounteous. We'd been eating lettuce, broccoli, and kale for a couple of weeks, and soon we should have more tomatoes and peppers than we'd be able to eat fresh. I read up on canning, and organized volunteers to mount a canning operation for the weeks ahead.

But I couldn't escape a feeling of futility, a foreboding that our hard work would end up being useless in the face of unknowable threats that almost certainly awaited us.

"NANA," Keno said one day from the blue. "You should've let me bring your nurse friends to our neighborhood to live."

"You're right. I should have listened to you. I'm sorry."

"Tell that to Tasha," he said.

Christ, that hurt like hell. I could think of only one way to atone, and it was feeble compared to the cost of my callous decision.

We moved the wood and kerosene cookstoves into the garage of the empty house next door to mine. Keno, Phil, and Silas cut holes in the side wall of that garage and ran vent pipes from the stoves. The men installed tables, counters, and chopping blocks. They hauled canning supplies from the Mint and set up shelves for the jars. Sonja and Kathy brought in huge pots, pressure cookers, and a big supply of sharpened knives and cleavers. We had a little celebration in our spanking new canning kitchen with glasses of wine for all.

I conferred with Keno and Sonja, and the next day they left at dawn with Silas and Phil—Keno riding his bike with the cart, Sonja riding Tasha's bike, and Silas and Phil pushing empty wheelbarrows and carrying guns. It took two days, but they moved June and Charlotte into the house next door and put them in charge of canning.

My friends were bubbling over with thanks for me, but I could hardly bear to be near them on account of my guilt. These women had once been my closest friends, though I hadn't spent much time with them in recent years. They annoyed me, like church ladies—overly proper and full of gossip. I had no time for it.

"We're so sorry about Tasha, Bea," June chirruped with her most winning smile of compassion.

"Thank you," I said, uncomfortable with the sympathy and the subject matter.

"You know, honey, God doesn't give us burdens we can't carry," Charlotte weighed in, stroking my arm. "There are lessons to learn from this. There's a reason for everything that happens."

"Bullshit!" I glared back and forth between the two old women. "God doesn't give us burdens we can't carry? Are you fucking serious?" I had no time for empty platitudes either.

"Calm down, Bea," June said. "We know you're upset—"

"Don't you dare patronize me, June. Don't you dare! You think God wanted a beautiful teenager to be without her mother, to get pregnant and die? What kind of grand divine plan is that?"

"It's normal to be angry with God when things don't go our way," Charlotte said.

"Yeah? Whose way is this? Who designed a world where God's children destroy their own home, their own planet, and have to work like dogs—only to die of starvation and thirst and malnutrition and horrible accidents? Because whoever designed that world is an evil son-of-a-bitch!"

"Bea, you don't mean that!" June said.

"The hell I don't!" I glowered at June and Charlotte, spun around, and headed home. They were wary of me afterward and didn't talk to me much, which was fine with me.

Everything happens for a reason? Like the Holocaust, or child rape? Such unthinking tripe.

God may have taken away our ability to further destroy the planet, but all this tragedy and heartache was our own doing. Unless God was a sadist, which was a distinct possibility. Regardless, there was absolutely no evidence of a divine plan that gave everything a logical and positive reason.

In fact, the opposite seemed more likely to me—random chaos, which on rare occasions was tamed by love, our one and only saving grace.

I STUDIED UP ON HOW TO GROW GRAINS. The rice was gone, and we only had enough wheat flour to last another year if we were lucky and careful. We needed a plan to grow more. Rice would take entirely too much water, so we'd have to live without it. Maybe, maybe, we could grow wheat in the fall, although we'd need a bigger patch of land to grow enough for all of us. I looked into alternative grains, like oats and barley and quinoa. I had seed, but I didn't know a thing about how to grow any of them.

Corn we could do, and I had lots of seed corn—the kind of corn we could make into cornmeal, grits, and masa. Corn could handle the Texas heat, too, as long as it had *some* water. Yet it also needed more space—as in acreage. But how could we till whole acres, and how could we protect a crop that wasn't close to home?

At the next neighborhood meeting, we decided to plow up our front yards for corn fields, and to use the park to plant wheat and other grains. At least for now, we still had rototillers and gasoline to run them. Silas planted his whole backyard in lentils, and Jack planted his with pinto beans. Phil was trying black beans along the road median on Dittmar.

Melba Carlisle's brother, his wife, and teenage son came to live with them. Some folks grumbled, but I welcomed the help. To me, we'd replaced the Matheson family with nicer people. Mr. Bellows' grown son walked up from Corpus Christi to join us as well.

Spring brought the Zizzos a new crop of bunny rabbits, which, unsurprisingly, were adorable and fluffy. I begged Kathy not to let Mazie see the bunnies or we'd never be able to eat another rabbit at our house.

ONE BRIGHT JUNE DAY in the middle of this bustling activity, Mazie let out a scream that damned near stopped my heart. I hurried to open the back door just as Mazie reached the patio, still screeching.

"The ugly men! They're over by the Mint!"

"What ugly men? Where are they?" I couldn't see anyone. Mazie dragged me to the side fence in time to see the ruby red GTO peel out from in front of the Mint. Inside the car were the same three creepy men as before, but now there was a fourth man.

As they turned the corner to speed away, the fourth man swung his head around to grin at me, devilishly, toothlessly. Chas Matheson. Shit! He'd shown them where we stored the food.

"Jack!" I screamed. "Jack! Silas! Phil! Come quick!"

WITH GREAT URGENCY and a good deal of hand-wringing, we beefed up our security at the Mint beginning that very afternoon. We stationed at least two armed guards there around the clock, day in and day out. Since we only had about twelve fully grown men who weren't old or in ill health, we had to expand our guard force. Jack and Mr. Bellows joined as the group's most elderly members; Keno and Alma joined as its youngest. Kathy and Doris also signed on to work as guards on shifts when their husbands could watch their children.

Doris was elated to have the Ibanez kids living with her now. She called them, "my kids."

The secret well down past Manchaca was drying up. The questers had an increasingly hard time filling water jugs, and we didn't have gasoline to spare for Sam's truck anyway. We hadn't had much rain for the duration of the spring, not since the rain that cleared the air of oak pollen. It was now late June, and it rarely rained here in July or August. We would have to open the cistern soon for our water supply. I kept this to myself, though. I still wanted people to be extremely careful with the water they had.

But I was secretly excited about the ten thousand gallons of cistern water—a life-saving treasure trove in a world such as ours.

CHAPTER 49

I'd had one of those mini heart attacks a few years back, an ischemic event where my heart was deprived of oxygen and got damaged. Hank had always planned to keep his job until he turned seventy, but when I had my heart event, he retired right away. At first, I thought it was sweet of him—uncharacteristically and unsustainably sweet, as it turned out. It took him mere weeks to get so cranky that I wanted to scream.

He harangued me daily about my so-called "heart-damaging lifestyle." What heart-damaging lifestyle? I ate well. I didn't smoke. I exercised. Yes, I was fat, but so was he, and I wasn't *that* fat.

But according to Hank, I was the author of my own diseased fate. And though he never quite said it, he regularly implied that my illness was due to some sort of moral failing of mine. Since I didn't have the fortitude to stay healthy for eternity, it was up to Hank to keep me in line. Never mind that heart disease ran in my family. By Hank's way of thinking, my family members had their own moral failings, and they'd passed this weakness on to me. I can't describe how maddening this was—to be treated like a reprobate for getting old and ill.

At first, I tried to persuade Hank that he was looking at this all wrong. We had several loud arguments about it. After that, I tuned him out and closed my heart to him once and for all. Oh, I'd been in denial about it until recently, and I'd kept trying, out of habit, to love him. But deep in my heart, hidden even from myself, I knew we were done.

Now I realized that the internal dialogue I continually ran through my head was full of the same sorts of reprimands I got from Hank. No wonder I felt responsible for everything and everyone. Hank had trained me well.

ONE AFTERNOON, WHEN MY GRANDKIDS, Cesar, and Sonja were out harvesting green beans, I went looking for Jack. I didn't see him on the streets, and it wasn't his turn for Mint guard duty, so I knocked nervously on his front door.

"Bea! I wondered if you'd ever come see me again." Jack ushered me inside, yapping about his plans to expand his chicken coop.

"Want a warm beer?" he said, grinning.

"No thanks." I looked out his glass doors to his backyard, which used to be beautifully landscaped with flowers, and now was filled with rows of pinto beans and poles for them to climb.

"What can I do for you?" he asked.

"Jack?" I picked at a splotch of dried food on the hem on my shirt.

"Bea?" He chuckled.

I gazed into his kind and gentle eyes. "Do you think it's my fault that I'm sick, you know, with my heart?"

"Of course not. Why would I think it's your fault?"

"Hank thinks it's my fault, that it's due to some sort of character flaw."

"I see." Jack frowned. "Seems like that old man of yours has something permanently stuck up his ass."

I laughed. "I know, right? And what pisses me off most is that he's still scolding me in my head, even though I haven't seen him in nine months."

"That must be infuriating."

"It is. I've had all of Hank I can take. I'm done with him, Jack. I really am."

Jack put a hand on each of my shoulders, running his blue eyes over every square inch of my face.

"Are you saying what I think you're saying?"

"I'm saying, Jack Jeffers, that I have been in love with you for years. I tried not to be, because I was married, but I never quit."

"Really?"

"Really. You are a warm and caring man, nothing the least bit like Hank Crenshaw, and, if you'll allow me to, I have a big backlog of love I'd like to give you."

"You mean that?" He searched my eyes. "I never quit loving you either." He turned his face away for a moment. Then he looked back and read my eyes more deeply than they'd ever been read—my near-sighted eyes, which were filling with tears.

"Bea, you won't change your mind? What if Hank comes back? It hurt me bad when you cut me off before. I don't know if I could live through it again."

"Jack, I'm so sorry. Hank has hurt us both quite enough. I won't let him do it anymore. I love you, and I won't hurt you again. I'm all yours, if you want me."

"God, Bea. You know I do." He hugged me to him perfectly—strongly, protectively, tenderly. "Can I have you now?" he whispered in my ear as he snuggled his whiskery face into my neck.

"Yes, Jack, you can have me always."

I VISITED JACK EVERY DAY after lunch, when it was acceptable in our community to take a break from the heat. I didn't try to hide my visits from the kids. In fact, I told them I was in love with Mr. Jeffers and was giving myself a divorce from their grandfather.

"How can you get divorced?" Mazie said. "Grandpa's not even here!"

"I snapped my fingers three times and said, 'I'm divorced. I'm divorced. I'm divorced.'"

"Don't you have to go to court?" Milo asked.

"Not anymore, honey. There's no court to go to."

Milo and Mazie looked aghast, while Keno shook his head.

"I'm sorry if you don't like this. But I deserve to be happy, and I haven't been happy with your grandfather for years."

"Well, why not?" Milo threw his hands in the air.

"You said it yourself, kiddo. He can be mean, and he was meanest of all to me. He stayed mad at me all the time."

"Is that true?" Mazie asked.

"It's true," Keno said, bowling me over. "My mom said so."

"She did?" I was shocked.

"Yep." Keno curled his mouth into an embarrassed smirk.

"Well, why didn't Erin say something to me?"

"She said she tried to, but you didn't listen."

"Maybe she did. I don't remember. But I know I didn't want to face it for years."

"Not easy to face, I guess," Keno said so maturely that it blew my mind. Then he sneezed into his hand and wiped it on his jeans.

Teenagers.

CHAPTER 50

What was Murphy's Law again? If something can go wrong, it will? I was on the back patio shelling peas and trying to keep Mazie on task to help me. Sonja was starting beans on the grill, and Cesar was rocking in the glider, reading and wheezing. I stopped shelling peas for a moment to fuss with the wind-up radio so I could listen to Rick the Stick. I hoped to get clues about why Eddie and Pete hadn't returned.

"Some of my neighbors walked to Waco last week to check on family, and the National Guard turned them away. Don't know what's up with that.

"Anyone ever hear this song, Sinner Man? I've been thinking a lot about the coming of the Lord lately, praying for it to happen before we get more miserable. Got me to thinkin' about this song."

A beat of silence was followed by a haunting tune:

"Oh, sinner man, where you gonna run to. . . .
You gonna run to the rocks, but the rocks will be meltin'. . . .
You gonna run to the sea, but the sea will be boilin'. . . .
You gonna run to the Lord, beggin' him to hide you—"

The song suddenly changed tempo. No, wait, that was a car engine—a loud one. I looked up as the ruby GTO peeled around a corner and onto the street behind us, skidding and squealing toward the front of the Mint. Sonja gasped. The kids and I jumped to our feet.

The GTO braked hard and slid out of sight, but it was idling out front of the Mint, probably in its driveway. Within seconds, an early 1960s Chevy truck roared around the same corner and screeched its brakes, also stopping on the frontside of the Mint.

"Keno!" I called to my grandson, who was on Mint guard duty. He leapt up from its back porch, rifle in hand.

"Stay back, Keno!" I yelled, then the motors died. Car and truck doors opened and slammed. Phil hollered, "Halt!" from the Mint front yard.

"No, you halt, Hendrix!" shouted a voice that had to be Chas, followed by gunshots. Phil!

Sonja flew into action, shoving me, Mazie, and Cesar into the Pico house, ordering the kids to run upstairs and hide under different beds. But I was already back outside, crying, "Where's Milo? Milo!" while my eyes stayed fixed on Keno, who raised his rifle as he slipped toward the Mint's back-left corner.

People ran toward the Mint from around the neighborhood. Silas and Alma sprinted down the side street; Bobby Carlisle and his brother-in-law cut through backyards a few doors down; Jack and Mr. Bellows jogged down the sidewalk. All these madly scurrying people were armed.

"Milo? Milo!" I screamed again and ran back and forth across my yard, searching the sides of my house for my youngest grandson. I took my eyes off Keno for only seconds. I shot my gaze back to him just as Chas zipped up behind Keno and jammed the barrel of an AR-15 into the meat of my grandson's neck.

"Drop those weapons, people!" Chas shouted.

Keno dropped his gun and threw up his hands. Jack crouched behind my cedar fence and kept his rifle, but the others, especially Alma and Silas, were too close to Chas and the Mint to have any hope of hiding. They let their rifles fall to the ground, and I stopped breathing.

Everything went silent. Then we heard the Mint's garage door open, followed quickly by the opening of the house's back door. There stood the three men who'd spied on our disasters, along with four unfamiliar teen boys.

"Came to open the grocery store, Miss Bea," called the leader with the skull earring.

"Get out of here!" I stomped toward them. "How will we feed these children?"

"Think I give a shit? Y'all best stay out of the way." He ducked back inside, taking with him all but one leather-clad man, who swung his rifle to aim it first at Silas and Alma, then at me, then at Bobby Carlisle in the backyard next to the Mint. Keno continued to stand with his arms raised, his head tilted forward, while I barely breathed. Banging erupted inside the Mint garage.

Sonja came out of the Pico house and stepped swiftly to my side. The man aimed his rifle right at her. She disregarded him. "I can't find Milo," she said. "Come inside!"

"I can't!"

"Come inside, Bea. We'll watch from the back door."

"How can—"

"Damn it, Bea. Don't be dense. You must!"

I backed toward my patio door. The armed man switched his aim to Silas and Alma. I kept my eyes riveted on Keno, but I didn't step inside until I heard Sonja behind me, chambering a round in a rifle.

"Bea." Sonja spoke with the barest movement of her lips, handing me a pistol. "I'm going to crawl through the yard next door and try to get an angle to shoot Chas without hitting Keno."

"Do you know how to use that rifle?"

"I've used them before. Cesar and Mazie are hiding upstairs."

With her usual agility and quick steps, Sonja slipped into the garage and out of my sight. My garage door opened with a minimum of creaks.

I stood vigil in my doorway with my eyes glued to Keno, my ears tuned to the yard next door. I didn't hear a peep out of Sonja. I couldn't see the front of Keno's face, only his left profile. I kept my right hand inside the house, gripping the pistol.

Next door to me, June stepped out to her deck. Before she could blow Sonja's cover, I hollered, "Get back inside, June. Be quiet!"

"What—?"

"Guns, June! Go!"

She hopped inside and slammed the door.

We had to save Keno. I hoped it wasn't too late to save Phil. And the food—my God, the food. We would starve to death. And where was Milo?

The disarmed neighbors stayed stonily silent. Even the dogs knew better than to yelp. The only noise came from inside the Mint: the slamming of cabinets and doors; the scraping of heavy items along the floor—barrels of food, most likely—and the clangor of the truck being loaded with weighty objects out front of the Mint.

"Hey, Simms!" Chas shouted at Keno, though the two were only one step apart. "Did you fuck that piece Alma yet?"

"Shut up," Keno muttered.

"Not man enough, eh Simms?" Chas cackled. "Guess I better take her with me."

"Leave her alone!" Keno yelled.

"Easy, Keno. He ain't nothin'!" Alma shouted.

"I'm too much man for you, bitch!" Chas's rifle arm started to shake. "Don't argue with him, kids!"

Flicking my eyes to Alma and Silas, then back to Keno and Chas, I saw a quick shadowy movement through the upstairs blinds at the Mint. Now those men were upstairs? Christ, the guns and seeds were up there.

But just above where Keno stood with Chas's rifle at his neck—the edge of those upstairs blinds pulled back only inches and revealed a thick shock of light hair. Milo!

I tried not to look, to keep others from noticing him, but my eyes kept jumping between Keno and Milo so fast I felt dizzy.

The window where Milo stood jerked open. "Keno! Get down!"

Chas swung his rifle toward Milo. Keno hit the dirt. Milo fired a burst of shots into Chas's face, blowing his brains everywhere as he flew backward through the air to hit the ground with a thud.

The guard at the Mint back door darted into the house. Hide, Milo, hide!

The neighbors snatched up their guns and raced toward the Mint's frontside. Keno, rifle in hand, ran in through its back door—to protect Milo, I hoped. Jack stepped from behind the fence and trotted quickly to the corner of Mint Lane. Sonja popped up from the yard next door and scaled the corner of the fence, landing in the Mint backyard and scrambling to its front.

"Mazie! Cesar! Stay hidden!" I bellowed, and I rushed after Milo and Keno. As I ran—as much as I could run—the Chevy truck and GTO started up. The Mint front door slammed hard.

As I neared the Mint patio, gunfire burst from the street, followed by the din of automatic weapons in a firefight. Bullets pinged and splatted into the street side of the Mint.

"Stop!" I screeched, uselessly. The gunfire only got louder, and I kept running. Then, the guns did stop, but only for a beat. As I rushed into the Mint dining room—insanely stupid of me—another burst of gunfire came from above me. First one rifle, then another. God in Heaven, was someone upstairs shooting my boys?

But instantly, tires squealed and metal crunched deafeningly, continuing to crunch for an everlasting moment. Then came an atrociously loud slam, and exclamations from above me of boys crying, "Woohoo!" "Got 'em!"

"Keno! Milo! Are you okay?"

"Yes! We got 'em!" Milo hollered.

"Are you guys alone up there?"

"Yes!" Keno shouted.

I raced out the Mint front door to see the red GTO on its back a block down the street, its rear tires still spinning, though its front end was halfway through a limestone retaining wall. A wrecked sedan sat between me and the GTO. From scraps of metal on the ground and dents and tire marks on the sedan, it looked like the GTO had hit the sedan at an odd angle, raking higher and higher along its side, causing the GTO to flip.

The man with the skull earring, bleeding from his head, worked his way out of the GTO while we watched. Jack and Phil—alive!—marched up to the man, and Phil shot him in the head.

No sign of the Chevy pickup. It was gone, with God knows how much of our food and a truckload of men and boys who would surely be out for revenge.

CHAPTER 51

Phil had been shot clean through the muscle tissue in his upper left arm. He'd played dead, so they didn't actually kill him. Silas had his right temple grazed, but no one else was hurt. Sonja took the injured men and Kathy to the Pico house to bandage Silas and cauterize Phil's wound. I told them where to find whiskey in my pantry for the pain. Thank God no one had a bullet inside them. Getting it out might have been beyond our means.

Keno, Milo, Jack, and several others heaved and shoved at the GTO until they had it right-side up, flattened roof and all. A guy with a crowbar pried open the trunk, and from it they extracted several bags of beans or grains.

Mr. Bellows was prying at the driver-side door when he jumped back, pointing under the GTO and yelling, "Fuel leak!"

"Get back! Way back!" Jack shouted. Everyone took off running.

Within instants, the car caught fire, then quickly exploded with a shower of charred ruby metal and a huge ball of orange flame.

We all cowered and watched it, utterly stunned.

When the fire died back a bit, Keno and others carried the nearly headless Chas Matheson and tossed him atop the burning car. They flung the other dead man up there, too.

Milo hopped around in some sort of frenzy, grinning maniacally, screaming, "Wahoo!" and "Yeehaw!" and other craziness.

"Milo, calm down!" I hollered. "Killing a man is nothing to be jubilant about."

"Milo saved my life, Nana," Keno said.

"And I killed Chas! He killed Tasha!"

"I know." I grabbed Keno and hugged him. "Thank God you're okay." Milo came up, and I grabbed him, too. "Thank you, Milo, for being brave and saving Keno. I couldn't bear to lose another one of you." We hugged and cried until we ran out of energy for it.

Soon we joined Jack, Harvey Zizzo, Mr. Bellows, and several others in the veritable wasteland of the Mint garage.

"God," I muttered, surveying the devastation. "What all did they take?"

"You got the energy for this, Bea?" Jack said. "You've had an awful shock. Don't you need to rest?"

"How can I rest? Look at this place! It'll take all night to figure out what's missing and damaged."

Jack wrapped me in a firm hug, his voice cracking. "I'm so glad you're not hurt." He kissed me hard on the lips. I kissed him back with so much passion it hurt me.

"Ahem," said Mr. Bellows, wearing his trademark scowl but with a hint of humor in his eyes.

"Thank God everyone's alright." I stepped back from Jack but gripped his hand.

"Come on, Bea," Jack said. "I'll take you home to rest. This cleanup can wait."

"I'll lock up," said Mr. Bellows. "Me and some of these fellas will guard the Mint tonight. We can meet back here after breakfast."

"Thank you," I said, suddenly overcome with weakness and fatigue. I leaned heavily on Jack and wheezed for breath all the way into my house.

On the stairs as I headed to bed, Jack asked, "Aren't these stairs awful hard on you, Bea? Don't you need to sleep on the ground floor?"

I gaped at Jack in disbelief. No one had ever mentioned how hard these stairs were on me, not even Hank the control-freak. I fought back tears.

"There's no place to sleep on the ground floor."

"You can sleep at my house, darlin', if you want to."

"Maybe I will someday." I slid my hand over Jack's cheek as I sat down on my bed.

Jack grinned and clutched my arm. He gave me a long and tender kiss. I wanted to keep kissing him, but we heard kids coming up the stairs.

"We'll continue this later?" he said.

"It's a date," I replied.

As Jack departed, Mazie and Cesar brought me a bowl of wash water. Milo came in, chattering and bouncing around, still buzzing with adrenaline. I was too full of emotion, too exhausted to sort out my feelings on what had taken place. Chas was dead. All I could feel about that tragic turn was enormous relief.

Soon Sonja brought me some beans—slightly burned but not bad. She and the kids sat with me, sharing details about the siege of the Mint and decompressing until I started nodding off.

THE INVENTORY OF OUR LOSSES at the Mint was bleak, but I suppose it could have been worse. The looters had taken several five-gallon cans of peanut butter and vegetable oil. They'd absconded with the last canned goods, and most of the powdered milk and eggs. Some sacks of beans and a couple barrels each of flour and oatmeal were also gone.

Almost as bad as the thievery was the damage they'd wrought with their damnable bullets. A few remaining cans of cooking oil had bullet holes, with the oil leaked out to the level of the lowest holes. Some barrels of dry food were bullet-riddled, too—at least they didn't leak like the oil—and two cans of gasoline were missing. Bottles of wine were broken across the floor. A wagon and a wheelbarrow were full of holes, and several tools were shot to shreds. The garage door and part of the house front were dotted with bullet holes.

But the bottled water was mostly okay. A few five-gallon jugs were either gone or bullet-riven and empty, but about twenty jugs were intact. Of the dozens of empties, which I'd been saving for cistern water, a few were hole-filled, but most were alright. And we still had the root cellar packed with home-grown veggies and other canned and dried edibles.

We'd gone from a year's supply of food to a few months' worth. The loss was so devastating that my brain shut down trying to fathom it.

Not for the first time, I was forced to seriously consider whether we would survive this disaster or not.

A DAY OR SO AFTER THE RAID, Jack told me that the lock on the Mint's weapon closet had been busted to hell—by Milo, I presumed.

"How'd you end up upstairs when those men came?" I asked Milo when I found him in the backyard.

"I was helping Keno guard the Mint."

"You know you weren't supposed to be there."

"Good thing I was," he said.

"Yes.... Yes, a good thing. So how did you bust open that lock on the weapons closet without being heard?"

"I don't know," he mumbled.

"Milo, tell me the truth."

He kept his head down and remained silent. I gently removed his sunglasses to search his blue eyes.

"Were you fiddling with the guns before the men came?"

He sighed and continued to stare at the dead lawn beneath his feet.

"I see. And how long have you been going up there to mess with the guns?"

"Umm...."

"Milo, tell me."

"Since Uncle Eddie and Uncle Pete taught me how to shoot."

"Good grief. Have you been firing those weapons?"

"No! But when they left, they took their guns, and I needed to practice. So, I practiced aiming." His plan must have worked, because his aim had been pretty well perfect.

"And were those guns loaded?" I asked him.

"Maybe," he muttered.

"Did you load them?"

"I don't know."

I picked up his chin to make him look at me. "Milo, I'm very proud of you for saving Keno. But you're forbidden from touching guns without supervision from Keno or an adult except in emergencies."

"Nana! That's not fair!"

"Yes, it is, and I'm not negotiating about it."

"When my uncles come back, can I shoot with them?"

Would his uncles be coming back? It didn't seem like it.

"As long as it's okay with them. But I'm worried about you. Nothing makes you happy except guns. That's not good."

"Guess there's not much to be happy about."

I sighed and hugged Milo to me. "I understand, honey, but you have to try.... Why don't you play sports with those Ibanez boys? They're almost your age."

"I don't think they like me," he said.

"Why? Were you mean to them?"

"Not mean, just...you know."

"Not friendly?"

"Yeah."

"I bet you can win them back over. Why don't you invite them to play soccer or Monopoly? That could be a start."

"Can I? Today?"

"Yes, today." I handed his Aviators back to him.

Milo stuck the sunglasses on, crookedly, and started to run away, but then he stopped. "I'm happier now," he said.

"Really? How come?"

"Because, when Tasha died, I couldn't do anything. But now I did something." My skinny, thirteen-year-old grandson squared his shoulders, adjusted his sunglasses, and gave me a very adult grin. Then he sped away toward the Barnes' house where the Ibanez boys lived.

I was seriously conflicted about Milo—worried sick about the effects of the violence on him but also elated to see him feel empowered again. It was horrifying to me that it took such nasty violence to empower him.

Had our lives really become a clichéd version of a post-apocalyptic movie—marauding thieves raping and pillaging, and the meek taking up arms to defend themselves, thereby corrupting their souls?

All we needed to make the motif complete were heinous hordes of zombies, vampires, and pod people. And possibly some UFOs.

After we set provisions aside for communal canning and baking, we divvied up the remaining food at the Mint and gave each household its share. The stock looked awfully paltry once it was divided. It couldn't last more than six months, if that.

The loss of peanut butter and powdered milk and eggs for the kids and the nursing or pregnant women overwhelmed me. We still had lots of beans and grains in various forms, but those could be pretty indigestible if they were the only food one had to eat.

Yet the biggest loss, to my mind, was the vegetable oil. We had less than a half-gallon per person left. What would happen to us with no fat in our diets? It was bound to cause some sort of malnutrition.

We could get fat from animals, but the bony rabbits and scrawny chickens around here wouldn't provide much fat per serving, plus we only got to eat meat once or twice a month. We had more fresh eggs now. Surely, they contained a bit of fat.

I'd always been stressed about cooking oil, but now I became obsessed with it. I spent days digging through books. Finally, I found instructions about pressing peanut and sunflower oils. I got the crew to start planting sunflowers. They would grow fast and could be put almost anywhere as long as they had sun. We could plant peanuts next spring.

On top of our food losses from thievery and bullets, something was terribly wrong with our tomatoes. They had a blight or fungus. From photos I found in gardening books, the tomato diseases seemed impossible to distinguish. We tried different remedies—spraying water mixed with baking soda and dish soap, painstakingly removing blighted leaves—while the tomato plants continued to blotch and wither, and the few tomatoes we harvested were full of black splotches. We needed more biodiversity to protect us from a disease like this, which might affect one variety of tomatoes but spare others. I had heirloom varieties of tomato seed we could try.

Some of the field corn growing tall in our front yards had worms. The nose-pieces on my glasses snapped off, and I had to replace them with duct tape. We ran out of batteries for flashlights and were down to the last batteries for clocks. The Geiger counter showed a new uptick in gamma radiation, which made me crazy. At least we had spare batteries for that instrument.

I was running short on blood pressure meds. I thought sure I had more, but I couldn't find them. I took half-doses and checked my blood pressure every few days as it inched steadily higher.

A pack of mongrel dogs snuck into our backyard in broad daylight and broke into our chicken coop—I couldn't figure out how—killing a chicken before Sonja shot two dogs and the others raced away. We ate those gristly dogs. We had to. Mazie refused to eat them, and who could blame her?

We gave the remaining dry dog food to the Zizzos for their rabbits, so the neighborhood dogs had to fend for themselves. Some of them wandered away and never returned. Someone probably ate them.

The heat was simply unbearable, passing one hundred degrees daily beginning in late May, and never falling below eighty—even at night—for weeks. The little grass we had left baked to a crisp and turned to dust. I wondered if the world would eventually cool down without industrial and auto pollution, but I recalled reading that we'd already doomed ourselves to hotter and hotter climes because of the many-year time lag between the creation of atmospheric carbon and the resultant heating of the planet.

Jack and I focused our time on growing and protecting food. Jack's presence comforted me, and it tempered my worry over what calamity would next befall us, how bad the environment was going to get, and what the hell had happened to Eddie and Pete. My dread about the fickle nature of the sun underlaid everything, a droning anxiety that never left me.

Most of the veggies we grew got canned by Charlotte and June in the canning kitchen next door. Other neighbors helped when they could—I sometimes chopped veggies for them. We now had a few hundred Mason jars filled with okra, cucumber pickles, squash, peppers, peas, green beans, and eggplant.

But the canning operation did in our stashes of water from the rain barrels. The five-gallon jugs were nearly empty, and the neighbors were freaking out.

GARY MATHESON WANDERED into the neighborhood one afternoon and called to me from my fence. Man, did he look lost and old.

"Bea, I'm sorry about everything that happened," he said when I stood up to face him from several feet away.

"That's nice. But if you're asking me to forgive you, I can't."

"I didn't know he would turn out like he did. He was so good when he was little. I tried to teach him right and wrong. But he was headstrong—"

"I get it, Gary. But I can't forgive him, and I can't forgive you. If you need forgiveness, talk to your Maker."

Bad as it was, I was done with trying to be good. It had got me exactly nowhere. I knew it wasn't rational to blame only Chas and his wimp of a father for Tasha's death, but I blamed them anyway.

Gary nodded and rubbed at his eyes, sighing loudly. Finally, he said, "I just wanted to tell you that."

"In case you're wanting me to ask you back into the neighborhood, I won't. I couldn't look at you every day."

He whipped his face around, revealing a version of Chas's defiant sneer. "You can't stop me from living in my house."

"True, but I'm not going to feed you."

He glared at me, rage and despair warring in the twitching muscles of his face.

"Okay. Too much to hope for, I guess." He started shuffling slowly away.

But I was struck by a pang of conscience.

"Gary? Didn't you get any of the food Chas's friends stole from us?"

"Only a couple of meals. They made me beg, and I couldn't do it anymore." I guess even Gary had his pride.

"Send Lyla to help in the gardens, and Jack will give her food when she comes."

"Thank you, Bea. Thank you!" He stifled a sob.

"I'm buying your silence about the Mint, Gary. Now get out of here."

"What? Okay. I'm going." He loped off, shaking his head.

CHAPTER 52

S o ironic how, by drenching us in extreme light, the sun had taken us into darkness. I'd always thought that light and dark maintained a balance—the yin and the yang—but here the dark was winning and taunting me by throwing its tentacles over everything. My candles wouldn't light the corners of a room or the subtleties of a face, and they wouldn't hold out forever. Worse, the dark was overshadowing the light in my heart.

Those of us who remained were the privileged few in our post-catastrophe world. We had each other to cling to. We could only pray that the sun would refrain from further eruptions that could plunge us into the deepest darkness of all.

On this August day, I was exhausted. My hands were so shaky that I could barely read my own handwriting. My eyesight had kept deteriorating so that reading in poor light was rough.

Yet, there was so much to attend to for our survival. On today's agenda, for instance: Sonja and Mazie were baking bread next door, but they kept running in and out of this house to get things. Cesar was wheezing in the living room, building things with dominoes, while I kept an eye on him. Milo and Keno were at Jack's, harvesting pinto beans, then they planned to start enlarging his chicken coop. I wanted to read up on how to make cornmeal and masa for tortillas. Maybe tomorrow Sonja and I could give cornmeal a try.

Man, my head hurt—a lot. Nothing new about that though.

I was making lists of things to discuss at this evening's neighborhood meeting. We needed to dry and store those pinto beans and plant more. If we were lucky, we could grow another crop before the first frost. It was almost time to plant wheat and other grains in the park. Fall was the best time to start them in Texas. And there was the ongoing corn harvest—the picking, shucking, drying, canning, the saving of seed.

Time to plant more fall veggies, too.

Construction of composting toilets and rain collection systems had stalled for the time being. Everyone was too busy growing and preserving food.

Ouch! A piercing pain shot through my skull, and my hands would not shop shaking. Damn it!

I TOOK A BREAK and drank some water, closed my eyes for a minute. I was probably dehydrated in this stifling heat.

I wanted to get the farming business over with at the beginning of tonight's meeting. Once I told them all about the cistern, everyone would be too thrilled to think about farming. They'd want to see the pump and taste the water. So exciting.

The neighbors had been upset about the scarcity of water for weeks. Maybe it was cruel of me, but I didn't want to mention the cistern until the other water was almost gone, as it was now. I hoped people weren't going to be pissed at me for keeping the cistern a secret. I was only trying to make the water last longer, but they might not see it that way.

Yesterday I hinted to Keno, Jack, and Sonja that I had a big surprise for tonight's meeting. They badgered me to tell them what it was, but I was adamant that it wouldn't be a surprise if I told them. There were so few opportunities around here to celebrate, and I—

"Christ!" That pain in my head is killing me & my heart—

What's wrong Cesar says

but

I can't—

PRESENT DAY

CHAPTER 53

A squawking bird snaps me out of my daydream here on the patio. The sun is hanging low in the west, casting long shadows across the yard.

"She didn't eat much today," some young woman tells Keno.

"She needs to go to bed," he says.

Did anyone ask me if I wanted to go to bed? I almost never want to go to bed. And don't I have a name?

They say I had some kind of episode—a stroke, I think, but I don't know. I can't remember what happened after I blacked out and, I guess, for a long time after. I do know that people treat me funny now. They discuss me in front of my face as if I'm not here.

I can't talk much anymore, so I tell our story to myself over and over to remind myself who I am. Nowadays my brain lets me think pretty straight, but certain situations confuse me and some of my memories are lost.

Sometimes they sit me on the patio and forget about me. I know they're busy, so I mostly don't mind. They bring me food with no salt in it, then they wonder why I don't eat much. Why would I want to eat food with no salt? Hello! I'm still alive over here! What I will eat is spoons full of honey, but no more than one at a time.

A beautiful young Hispanic woman who is not Sonja takes care of me when I need it, when she and Mazie aren't busy gardening, cooking, and cleaning. Once in a while she sings me songs like "Amazing Grace," and we cry.

Now that I'm better, Jack takes me to his house each evening after supper. Whatever happened to me doesn't keep me from wanting Jack. I want him more than ever, but....

The first night that Jack took me home, he made me comfy in his bed then climbed in beside me. I reached for him, eager to make love.

"Whoa," he said, searching my eyes, his face full of emotion. "Are you sure?"

"It's okay," I said and tugged him to me.

He squinted his eyes and studied me. He gave me some gentle kisses. I felt his tension melting. He even stroked my breasts. But then, he pulled back and sat on his knees in the bed, looking down at me.

"I can't do this, Bea. You're too fragile. I'm afraid I'll hurt you." Such a tortured expression on that lovely man's face. My heart broke for him. I patted his pillow, and he laid his head on it, having trouble meeting my gaze.

"It's okay," I said, and I stroked his head, his strong shoulders and arms, while he wept against me. I meant that it was okay if we didn't make love. I think he understood. No matter how much I ache for full sexual union with Jack, I won't put him through that pain again.

Many nights we just sit in his house and hold each other. So nice. . . . Often I'm the one who ends up crying, because it's too nice to believe.

CERTAIN DAYS, I remember things that happened right after my episode: thrashing and crying at full volume in my bed, the kids crying around me. I wanted to stop writhing and wailing for their sake, but I couldn't stop. I had things I needed to tell them, stuff I needed to do, but I couldn't speak or do anything except thrash and cry, my insides exploding with fear and rage.

Then I remember Jack, sweet Jack, lying beside me, wrapping his arms around me and hugging me with an uncanny strength. He kept my arms to my sides within his embrace. He laid his leg on top of my kicking feet. He held me in place, absorbing wave after wave of my anguish and speaking into my ear. I'm not sure what he said, but the warmth of his love calmed me down after what could have been hours.

I soon gave up, hoping to die. I recall long, empty hours of oppressive heat and mental paralysis, with no feeling except a tortured mind and a heart full of loss. Over and over, I heard Tasha's sigh of resignation, her plea to me, "Don't let me die!"

Then Mazie, darling little Mazie. She crawled into bed beside me and petted my hands and face. She told me stories—or they seemed to be stories, but I don't really know what she said. I think she did this for days on end. I woke in darkness many times to find her sleeping beside me. I saw Jack asleep on my loveseat more than once, dangling his long legs over the seat's arm.

When Mazie was awake, she talked to me nonstop, until at some point she got a nonverbal response from me. Then she became extra resolute, asking me questions she expected me to answer with one blink for "yes," two blinks for "no."

I indulged her for a while, blinking once for yes when she asked if I was seventy years old, blinking twice for no when she asked if the oceans were red, and so on. She asked if I was going to get better. I froze in panic, then closed my teary eyes and rolled away.

"Nana! You can't give up! You have to get better!"

I moaned and began to tremble.

Mazie climbed over me and put her pink face in front of my eyes.

"Nana, you promised you'd never forget me. That's what you said. But if you don't get better, you'll forget me. I know you will."

For the first time since the stroke that I was aware of, my hands and arms complied with my wishes and pulled Mazie to me.

"Nana, you're hugging me. Are you getting better now?"

"Yes," I croaked aloud.

The girl kissed me repeatedly, then scampered down the stairs, hollering, "Nana's better! She talked! Nana talked!"

Soon everyone was in my room, begging me to perform more talking tricks like a trained seal—only I didn't get treats for succeeding, just encouraging words.

I kissed each of my grandkids plus Sonja and Cesar that night. I spoke a handful of words.

Then they were all gone except Jack. I kissed him until my mouth and tongue remembered all I'd ever known about kissing.

"I love you, Bea," Jack said, stroking my forehead.

"Yes," I said, blinking once.

He kissed me again, and I think I fell asleep kissing him.

Within days they had me taking small steps around my bedroom as a few words returned to my spoken vocabulary and the fog slowly cleared from my mind. One day, Jack and Keno carried me down the stairs, sitting on their locked arms.

"You've lost so much weight, Bea," Jack said, worriedly.

"We will fatten you up," Sonja said from the bottom of the stairs where Milo, Mazie, and Cesar also waited.

I smiled at them all. I never went upstairs again.

SOME LATER DAY, I SAW SONJA AND A MAN—her husband I guess—leaving with Cesar in the bicycle cart that I'm happy to be rid of. I don't recollect why they went, I only remember Sonja holding me and quivering.

I saw Keno kissing the new woman in the old laundry room. He reached his hand under her shirt. He makes moon-eyes at her whenever she talks. It's clear that he loves her, and she seems like she loves him, too, but I don't know her so well.

"When did Sonja's husband come back?" I ask.

"He didn't," Keno says. "We told you that." He has no patience left for me.

"Who was that man?" I say. "Where did they go?"

"It was Uncle Pete, Nana. Uncle Pete. They went to Mexico to get medicine for Cesar. To get him away from the pollen. He was real sick."

"Well, where's, uh, uh…?"

"I'm here, Mom," Eddie says. "Right here where I've been for weeks."

"That's nice. Where's that other man and those girls?"

"We never found Dad and Erin and Jeri and Wayne. Remember?"

"Well, no, I don't remember," I say, as I'd apparently said before.

THEY BRING ME GLASSES OF CLOUDY WATER, and I make them last for two or three days. They admonish me to drink more, but it's my fault we have so little water. That's one thing I know for sure.

I keep thinking I could help with the water problem, but I don't recall how. I keep wishing the others knew my secrets, but I can't think which ones or why.

I should have shot that boy Chas before he had a chance to make Tasha pregnant and kill her. Before his friends stole our food. I should have killed him myself before Milo had to do it. It makes me sick that I left that horrid chore to a child.

Another thing I know is that the Geiger counter is showing higher levels of radiation. I sometimes watch it ticking for hours, or it seems like hours. But I can get lost inside a minute these days.

"Look!" I say to whoever's around when the radiation level seems high.

"Uh-huh," or "I see," my family members say, and never much more than that.

I'M GLAD THEY LEAVE ME ON THE PATIO, because the house is like an oven inside. It's hellishly hot out here, too, but there are breezes—hot breezes, but still. . . .

I like to watch birds and cats, though I can't remember the names of the different kinds. I watch sunflowers seems like everywhere, waving in the wind.

My favorite things to watch are the giant white birds with black tips on their wings, flying high above the pond. Those birds almost died off, I do remember that. And now they are back again. I don't know if humans will survive, but maybe the Earth and life will endure with or without us.

I try not to look at the sun. I hate that horrid, hot thing.

Once I tried to show the family things that I'd learned about making vegetable oil and cornmeal, about treating diseases on the tomatoes and corn, but I couldn't follow the books, and I never came up with enough spoken words to make myself understood.

"I'll read the books, Mom," Eddie said when I slapped the arm of my wheelchair.

ANOTHER DAY—I think it was another day—I tried to tell them to check the Mint storage shed for bleach to treat the water they were getting from God knows where. We hadn't had rain since before my episode, unless it rained during the weeks I lost. I'm so glad I'm not that lost anymore.

"Get the thing and go to the ... the thing," I told Keno.

"What thing? I don't know what you mean."

I tried to draw pictures, but my hands shook too much. My right hand was too weak to keep a grip on the pen. I let out a squeal of frustration.

"I'm sorry." Keno looked stressed. "I don't understand."

"Nana," said Mazie, "I'll help you. What thing is the first thing?"

I pointed toward the kitchen wall, where keys dangled from hooks.

"This thing?" Mazie asked, showing me a pad that you hold a pot with.

"No."

"These things?" She waved two kitchen tools in the air.

"No."

With great patience and good cheer, Mazie showed me about a dozen items until she grabbed a ring of car keys off a hook.

"These keys?" she said.

"Yes, but no."

"Yes, but no? What does that mean, Nana?" Milo said, joining in the mystery game.

I pointed toward keys hanging on the wall.

"Other keys?"

"Yes!" I nodded.

Mazie and Milo yanked key rings off their hooks and laid them on the table. I picked through the keys and chose two. I wasn't sure which one was correct, but I poked at the two keys and held up one finger.

"What do the keys go to, Nana?" Mazie asked.

I pointed to the backyard.

"The Mint!" exclaimed Milo.

"No," I said.

The kids scanned out the window.

"A car?" Milo asked.

"No."

"Our storage shed!" Mazie said.

"Yes, but no."

They looked at me, at each other, then out the back door.

"The Mint storage shed!" they cried. They snatched up the keys and took off.

Soon they were digging in the Mint shed, calling out, "There's gasoline!" "And fertilizer!" "Here's some chicken feed." "What's this? Bleach!"

"Yes!" I screamed to the kids in the yard behind mine. Keno and Eddie arrived at the shed, slapping high fives with Mazie and Milo and hooting about the bleach.

"Yay, Nana!" Mazie hollered, and raced back to smother me in kisses while I cried.

"Oh, don't cry," she cooed. "We got bleach now, so don't cry."

CHAPTER 54

Today I'm sitting in Hank's rocker on the patio, my wheelchair parked beside me and my glass of cloudy water on the table near my hand. I'm listening to beautiful bird calls and the whir of a machine in the neighborhood. I'm daydreaming about making love to Jack, feeling his lean muscles and the beat of his heart.

The dog next door starts barking. Why? He's about the only dog we have left.

A group of strangers pass by the side fence, staring at my house. They don't seem to notice me, and am I ever glad. But where are the patrollers? I wait until the strangers are out of sight, then I holler, "Kids!" but no one responds.

Moments later, people start shouting inside the house. Did they see the intruders? Are they fighting with them? My heart is hammering. I want to run or hide, but I can't. The loud talking goes on forever.

The back door bursts open, and Mazie flies out to throw her arms around my neck.

"Nana! They're back! Oh, they're back!"

"Who?" I say, anxiously patting her lifeless hair.

"Mama! Daddy! Aunt Erin and Grandpa!"

"What?" My heart sends an electric shock through my body.

The door opens again. Keno, Eddie, and Milo appear, grinning wildly and crying. They move aside, and out step four skeletal, filthy people, the strangers who passed by. I don't know these people. Why are they here?

I'm shaking with fear. "Mom!" "Mama!" two skinny women cry and proceed to choke me with hugs until I screech.

"Better give her some air," says my caretaker as she runs up. "She needs air."

The women draw back fast and examine me sadly, their dirty faces covered in tears. "Oh, Mama," one of them says and strokes my face. She has dark hair.

"Mom, what's wrong? What happened to Mom?" The yellow-haired one looks at the others accusingly.

"We don't know," Eddie says. "We think she had a stroke."

"You think? Didn't you find her a doctor?"

"We don't have a way to get her to a doctor, Aunt Jeri," Keno says.

"How could you let this happen?" the blonde woman says.

"We didn't *let* it happen. What are you talking about?" Keno says.

"Mom, we're kids!" Milo says.

"Yeah, we're kids!" Mazie shouts, frowning at the woman.

"Leave them alone, Jeri," the brunette says. "The kids look healthy. They did great."

"I guess you had it hard, didn't you, kids?" says the blonde.

A tall man wraps his arms around Mazie and Milo and begins to cry. They cry with him, and Mazie keeps saying, "Daddy. Oh, Daddy."

"Wayne went home with Pam," the blonde says. "He'll come down here soon. They wouldn't let us leave Waco. They kept us all in an auditorium and wouldn't let us leave."

"Who wouldn't let you leave?" Eddie asks.

"The National Guard," says Mazie's daddy. "Said it was martial law."

"That's what we found when Pete and I went looking for you," Eddie says. "They got hold of us, too, only they kept us in a warehouse, but after a couple of months we escaped."

"Wow," the blonde says. "Don't they have martial law here?"

"No," Eddie says. "In Waco, local assholes are throwing their weight around."

"Yeah, well," says Mazie's daddy, "I guess they got tired of feeding us, because they let us go last week."

Keno steps over to my caretaker. He stands behind her, snuggles his chin into her shoulder, and wraps his arms around her to stroke her belly. She leans into him and sighs.

"Mom," he says. "This is Alma. She's my wife."

His wife?

"Your wife?!" the new people shout.

"Keno, you're too young to be married!" the brunette says, aghast.

"I'm eighteen, Mom. And we're already married. So...."

Good for you, Keno, I think.

"But Keno," the woman says, tearing up. "How could you get married? Who married you?" She turns to look at me. "Mom, did you know about this?"

I nod my head yes, even though I didn't know, just to give Keno some backup. Keno gapes at me, but he has a smile in his eyes.

"We married ourselves, Mom," he says.

"Well, it's not legal! What about the law?" the blonde says.

"What law?" says Eddie.

Keno walks slowly away from his wife—Alma, so that's her name? He goes to his dark-haired mother and hugs her. But no one is welcoming Alma to the family. How very rude of them.

An old man stands behind the others, shuffling his feet and staring at me with bloodshot eyes.

"Bea," he says dryly, as if something is stuck in his throat. He steps up and stoops before me, taking my hand. "I was afraid you would have a stroke. Looks like I was right. I know I drove you crazy, being protective of you, but you never were any good at taking care of yourself. I'm so glad to be home."

Home? He thinks this is his home?

"Maybe you know," I say. "No one knows, but maybe you know."

The old man's brushing tears off his face, blowing his nose into a filthy rag. "Maybe I know what?" he says.

"What happened to the frogs? We used to have frogs."

"Frogs?" He stands up and frowns. The tears stop running down his face. "I haven't seen you in more than a year, and all you can say is, 'what happened to the frogs?'"

I guess I've hurt his feelings, but if he's so easily upset, I don't want him to live *here*.

"Dad," Eddie says, "she doesn't understand."

The hell I don't! This old man is butting into my life and expecting things of me without so much as a how-do-you-do. Insulting me about taking care of myself. Who does he think he is?

"Keno," the brunette says. "Where's Tasha? Gosh, you've grown so much. I bet she's grown a bunch, too. Where is she?"

Everyone stops moving, almost stops breathing. My grandkids, Eddie, and my caretaker—Alma—drop their heads to face the patio.

"What?" the woman says. "What's wrong?" She sounds panicked. Keno takes her hand. "Sit down, Mom."

"Sit down? Why?" She darts her eyes around, then stares indignantly at Keno. "Keno, tell me why!"

Keno looks at his mother, then looks hard at me and swallows.

"She's dead," I say.

"Mom," Eddie breathes. "That was harsh."

"She's dead? Is Tasha dead?!" the woman howls, glaring at us with lost eyes.

"Yes, Mom," Keno says, crying. "She, uh, she got pregnant and—"

"Pregnant!" The blonde shoots daggers at me with her eyes.

"She had a miscarriage, and she bled to death," Keno whispers. He latches on to his wife while his mother whirls away and sits down hard on the patio floor.

Then everyone is crying and wailing and moving around, yelling things at one another, scurrying away and returning. I am lost here. I don't know who's doing what, except Eddie holds my hand a while.

"Oh, God, I can't breathe," the dark-haired woman says. "Tasha! Oh my God!"

"Mom, how did she get pregnant?!" the blonde woman shouts.

Well, the usual way, of course.

"Tasha didn't listen to Nana. She snuck off and got pregnant," Keno mutters.

"Don't yell at Nana!" Mazie says, covering her ears.

People disappear, and I'm left on the patio with a screaming heart and only Keno and Alma, who start making dinner. I want so bad to comfort Tasha's mother, but she seems to be gone. My emotions exhaust me. Maybe I fall asleep, but I don't even know.

The next thing, Hank's yelling at me again, looming over me, giving me heart palpitations. The sun's falling toward the horizon.

I see Jack outside my fence, watching me unhappily with questions posed on his lips. I shake my head at him. He continues to watch. Other neighbors gather beside him. The woman with oily hair blows me a kiss.

"Bea!" Hank says. "How could this happen? You just let these kids run willy-nilly and do whatever they wanted?"

I am hating this old man more by the minute. I suppose he blames me for the EMP, too, and for the environment going to hell, and for the fact that we don't have enough food to feed his sorry ass. I don't have words to tell him how offended I am. I have thoughts, but I can't make my mouth pronounce them.

All these demanding people who have the nerve to come here and stare at me with their blame and judgment and accusations. These people who weren't here to help because they just had to go to a goddamned football game? Aren't they supposed to be my family? Why are they treating me this way?

"Bea," Hank says, "you should come inside and go to bed."

To bed? Whatever for? He just got here, and he's already bossing me around.

"No!" I say.

The young Mexican woman—what's her name again?—she steps to my side and crosses her arms, staring at the others in a show of support for me. Keno regards her proudly with a sad sort of love in his eyes.

"Nana kept us alive!" Milo spits out, yanking off his crooked sunglasses. He stands next to the young woman and crosses his arms, too.

"She had lots of food and water," Mazie says. "She taught us how to sew and cook and grow gardens." She stands between Keno's wife and Milo, her fists on her hips.

Keno says, "It's not Nana's fault. She saved us, and the whole neighborhood, too."

"She saved the neighborhood? Bea did?" Hank says with a skeptical laugh. "She gave away food I paid for—food she should have kept for this family. Bea, come inside! This is too much for you. It's too hot out here."

So now he's going to punish me for giving away food he thinks he bought?

"It's hot inside, too, Dad. Hotter, really," Eddie says. "And she didn't give away your food."

I look at Hank, who is scowling at me. My daughter Jeri refuses to return my gaze. I look at Eddie and my four grandkids, whose eyes are full of love for me and grief for all the rest.

I look at Jack, who's watching me alertly, lovingly. I look back at Hank, who's turning redder and redder with anger.

I'd always known I would have to confront Hank if he ever came home, but now I have no words. Still, there's no time like the present, before Hank gives me another stroke.

"Jack?" I holler. "Jack?"

"Yes, Bea?"

"Jack who?" says Hank. "Jack Jeffers?"

"Jack, come take me home. Now, Jack. Take me home now!"

"Home?!" Hank shouts. The others make startled noises.

"Coming, Bea," Jack says.

I turn away from the rest of them. My heart swells with warmth as Jack comes through the gate, and his eyes meet mine.

CHAPTER 55

I'm like a broken record, the way I repeat our story to myself nonstop. My brain works better than it did right after the stroke, but too many things still escape me. The sun and the darkness haunt me. I have no control over anything.

Jack is my shelter and my saving grace.

Night after night, we just sit in his house and hold each other. It's so nice. . . . I end up crying sometimes. I find it hard to believe that I deserve Jack and his love. I blame myself for so much that's gone wrong.

When I'm upset, Jack tells me that I have saved my family and all these neighbors—that they, that he, would not be alive without me. I try to believe him. . . . I try.

But, goddammit! I knew something important about the water, and I can't shake it loose from my mind.

There's an old man who scowls at me when he spots me outside. There are two women who see me and look away. They all live in the house behind mine now. I feel like I once knew them, but I'm not sure they ever knew me.

All my life, I tried to control things, although now, I can't remember why.

ACKNOWLEDGEMENTS

An author can craft a novel, but it takes a village or two to produce a good book. I give all credit to whatever is good about this novel to the myriad folks who've helped me from its inception through the polished and published product. All errors are my own.

First and foremost, I thank my stellar critique partners, Laura Creedle and Aden Polydoros, who've pored over countless drafts of this novel. Without their valuable insights and tireless tolerance of my quirks and hard-headedness, much drama would have been left on the table, the through-line would have been lost, and all kinds of bad choices would remain in the book. Best CPs ever, and awesome award-winning authors in their own right. Lucky me!

Next, I must thank the great people at SFK Press for hosting their 2018 novel contest and choosing this book as the winner. SFK is small but mighty in its mission to showcase Southern literary voices of the new millennium. The team should be commended for their mission alone, but their execution of it is professional and dynamic, making them a force to reckon with.

Special thanks at SFK go to: Pinckney Benedict, contest judge, development editor, and writer/teacher extraordinaire, for his belief in the novel, his lovely quote to describe it, his great suggestions, and his boundless patience and kindness regarding my questions and emails; Steve McCondichie, Co-Founder of SFK, who made my year plus the many writing years leading up to it by calling to tell me I had won the contest, and for saying, "You have found your literary tribe" (so true, and an indescribable relief); Grant Gerald Miller and A.M. O'Malley for their extremely helpful style edit; Cade Leebron for her thorough sensitivity read and copy-edit; and, April Ford, Associate Publisher, for the interior design and layout, and for coordinating hundreds of details including the book's many edits, always in a cheerful and supportive way despite her harrying workload. Thanks also to: Gisele Firmino and Nicole Byrne, Marketing Assistants; Emery Duffey, Social Media Coordinator; Alison McCondichie, Audiobook Producer; Olivia Croom, Book Cover Designer; Eleanor Burden, Proofreader; and all the others who helped behind the scenes.

Editors are unsung heroes and deserve my everlasting gratitude. An early draft of the novel was edited by David H. Morgan, who took me to school on plot, drama, and craft. Cate Hogan did an amazing job of development-editing. Her attention to detail, characters, and the consistency of tone and voice were invaluable. R.R. Campbell gave me a thoughtful edit of the book's opening, improving it a good deal.

I started this novel in NaNoWriMo 2013 and wrote more of it in their 2014 event. Thanks to them for getting me going and pumping me up. I workshopped this book like crazy at Scribophile online, in their Candied Sea Urchins group and in a full beta read. Thanks to these folks for catching embarrassing errors and for pressing me to improve the characters and pace.

This novel was a finalist in the Twitter contest Nightmare on Query Street in 2015 and 2017. It also made the finals in the PitProm contest in 2017. Many thanks to my mentors from those contests: Tracy Townsend, Brett Armstrong, and Peggy Rothschild, all amazing authors and extremely helpful to me. Special thanks to contest host Michelle Hauck for her belief in the book. And I have a great bunch of Twitter followers and a network of friends I can always count on for help and encouragement. I never could have made it without each and every one of you.

Then I thank the readers of both early and late drafts, a few of whom read it more than once, some of them long-standing friends, others new friends from Twitter: Rosemary Coronella, Aaron Longnion, Julie

Benedict, Carla Halpern, Rosario Alcala, George Randall Leake III, Branwen O'Shea-Refai, Mary Holm, Katie Zhao, Jenny Dewes, Mary Shotwell, Joni Gentry Riley, Phyllis Thomson, Kat Turner, Pauline Mattiaccio, and Brooke, who never gave me her last name. Special reader thanks to Michelle Reardon who went above and beyond in her last-minute full edit, and Flor Salcedo, who critiqued the book twice (and quickly) and brought dinner for my family to celebrate the SFK contest win.

I studied fiction in the UCLA Writers Program, and my teachers there were exceptionally good: Roberta Morris, Caroline Leavitt, and Dennis Foley, all great novelists who helped me immensely.

I was inspired to write this story after listening to Mike Malloy's podcasts while huge fires were burning all over Texas and I stared out my window at the dead lawn and parched trees. Blogger Bruce Enberg, aka Prairie2, who's forever exhorting us to stock up on canned goods, told a story about what could happen as the result of a solar pulse. I interviewed Bruce for more detail and confirmed his views with another scientist on Quora, Malcolm Sargent. I added a speculative element to their scientific facts, but a solar pulse can certainly fry our poorly maintained grid, and the nuclear consequences of that could be beyond devastating.

Many thanks to Bruce and Malcolm; any scientific errors are mine alone.

Big thanks to John Foxworth of Pearl Street Photography for kindly enduring my camera-related peccadilloes, and Jo Bertram and Shirley Berwick for putting me together and keeping me there for the photo shoot. Thanks also to Winnie Brooke for helping me explore cover ideas.

I started writing stories when I was five years old and have wanted to be a writer ever since, though I didn't get a chance to seriously work at it until my kids were grown. Great teachers who encouraged me to write, fed me wonderful books to read, and deserve special thanks are Penny Ellis and Gary Watson.

All enduring gratitude goes to my big loving family for putting up with me and cheering me on: Les Jr., Denise, Candace, Steve, Teresa, Dustin, Dylan, Shiryn, Jennifer, Bob, Michael, Ryan, David, Shelly, Leigh, Amy, Shirley, and Robin; my sons and stepsons Aaron, Jared, Ron, Jeremy, and Matt, daughter-in-law Nikki; and my grandchildren, Sophia and Miles. Sophia has a gift for story, and Miles is gracious when I accidentally call him Milo, a kid character in the book who is near Miles's age.

Enormous appreciation goes to my parents, Leslie and Patricia Smith, who didn't live to see my books published but who encouraged me to be smart when smart women were not cool, forever on my side, and always believing in me so strongly that I can feel them doing it even now.

My fabulous and indulgent husband, Doug Goebel, had a bad day that gave me the idea for Hank the Crank, but in truth Doug is more like Jack Jeffers, a very good and extremely helpful man. Douglas Wayne, you are my muse, my heart, and my reason to live.

All my thanks to you readers and reviewers as well. I hope you find the novel satisfying.

Better stock up on those canned goods, although it is my fervent hope that you will never need them.

ABOUT THE AUTHOR

Brenda Marie Smith studied fiction in the UCLA Writers Program. Born and raised in Oklahoma City, she was part of the back-to-the-land movement, living off the grid in the Ozark Mountains, and then joining the Farm—an off-grid, vegan hippie community, based in Tennessee— where her sons were delivered by midwives.

In Austin, Brenda managed student housing co-ops near the University of Texas for fifteen years. *If Darkness Takes Us* is her second novel. Her first, *Something Radiates*, is a paranormal thriller.

Brenda and her husband own and reside in a grid-connected, solar-powered home in South Austin. They have five grown sons, two grandkids, and a self-assured kitty cat.

SHARE YOUR THOUGHTS

Help make *If Darkness Takes Us* a bestselling novel by leaving an honest review on Goodreads, on your personal author website or blog, and anywhere else readers go for recommendations. It's our priority at SFK Press to publish books for readers to enjoy, and our authors appreciate and value your feedback.

OUR SOUTHERN FRIED GUARANTEE

If you wouldn't enthusiastically recommend one of our books with a 4- or 5-star rating to a friend, then the next story is on us. We believe that much in the stories we're telling. Simply email us at pr@sfkmultimedia.com.

ALSO BY SFK PRESS

CPSIA information can be obtained
at www.ICGtesting.com
Printed in the USA
LVHW031710280120
645065LV00004B/872